# A Wartime Summer

Inspired by the Malory Towers and St. Clare's novels of Enid Blyton, Rosie Meddon spent much of her childhood either with her nose in a book or writing stories and plays, enlisting the neighbours' children to perform them to anyone who would watch.

Professional life, though, was to take her into a world of structure and rules, where creativity was frowned upon. It wasn't until she was finally able to leave rigid thinking behind that she returned to writing, her research into her ancestry and a growing fascination for rural life in the nineteenth century inspiring and shaping her early stories.

She now resides with her husband in North Devon – the setting for the Woodicombe House Saga – where she enjoys the area's natural history, exploring the dramatic scenery, and keeping busy on her allotment.

# Also by Rosie Meddon

## The Woodicombe House Sagas

*The Housekeeper's Daughter*
*A Wife's War*
*The Soldier's Return*

## On the Home Front

*Her Patriotic Duty*
*Her Heart's Choice*
*Ties That Bind*

## The Sisters' War

*A Wartime Summer*

# ROSIE MEDDON

# A *W*artime Summer

CANELO

First published in the United Kingdom in 2022 by

Canelo
Unit 9, 5th Floor
Cargo Works, 1-2 Hatfields
London SE1 9PG
United Kingdom

A CIP catalogue record for this book is available from the British Library.

Print ISBN 978 1 80032 661 3
Ebook ISBN 978 1 80032 660 6

Cover design by Rose Cooper

Cover images © Shutterstock and © Arcangel

Look for more great books at www.canelo.co

Printed and bound in Great Britain by Clays Ltd, Elcograf S.p.A.

I

*Exeter, England*

*May 1942*

# I. Stirrings

# Chapter 1

'Huh. So much for coming back to save our belongings. Look at it all. There's nothing left. Those Jerry bastards have destroyed the lot.'

Staring in disbelief, May Warren fought back tears. Pearl was right. While the three of them had been cowering in that horrid little air raid shelter, up here the Luftwaffe had been flattening everything in sight. She'd guessed the damage would be bad, of course she had. After the best part of four hours spent clinging together in terror, none of them had been expecting to come up this morning and find everything just as they'd left it. But even as they'd sat, listening helplessly to bomb after bomb whistling its way down to Earth, every new explosion rattling their ribs, she'd consoled herself with the thought that even had the blasts blown out the windows and damaged the roof, they would still be able to rescue their belongings. At the very least, she'd pictured them salvaging the essentials such as clothes and shoes and ration books. Last year, when Plymouth had been blitzed, the newspapers had printed photographs of people carrying furniture from their bomb-damaged homes and stacking it in the street. *Poor things*, she remembered thinking as she'd peered with morbid curiosity at their possessions. But it was plain now that those were the households who'd got off lightly, the newspapers choosing not to print pictures of families whose homes had been completely razed, whose owners had been left with nothing but the clothes they stood up in. Despair of that sort was *bad for the nation's morale.*

Swiping at the tears now spilling down her cheeks, she glanced about. It wasn't just Albert Terrace that had caught it: the whole of Chandlery Street had been levelled – the old sail lofts, the coal yard, even the dairy. In fact, with the first proper rays of daylight now breaking through the haze of brick dust and ash, it was clear that this entire side of the city had been flattened, the only building seeming to have escaped being the cathedral, its twin towers rising like ghostly apparitions through the murk. Had the Germans deliberately avoided bombing it, she wondered, or had it been saved by a more divine power? After all, just across the green from it, the once grand façade of the Sovereign Hotel, where she had worked as a cleaner, was nothing more than a charred silhouette.

A few feet away, May's sister, Clemmie, stood sobbing. 'What are we… going… to do? Everything's… gone. All of it.'

'Yeah,' Pearl piped up. Having pulled from the debris what appeared to be a fire poker, she was stabbing angrily at the rubble. 'Ain't so much as a matchstick to be saved from this lot.'

Pearl was right about that. The pile of blackened timbers suggested their home had been set on fire by an incendiary, its subsequent collapse likely down to a direct hit from a high explosive – or 'HE', as everyone had come to know them.

Desperate to be rid of the taste of smoke in her mouth, May forced a swallow. How was she supposed to look after Clemmie and Pearl now? What did she even say to them? To a passer-by, Albert Terrace had been just another old building, but to the three of them, and to the dozen or so other families living either side, it had been home, and the sight of it all smashed and broken made her want to rail at the unfairness and the cruelty. Look at it: a few feet in front of her was a brass finial from someone's bedstead; a little further over, the iron door from their kitchen range. And by her feet, wet from the firemen's hoses and muddied from their boots, a scrap of gaily patterned cloth that might once have hung as curtains at someone's window or lain as a bedspread over their slumbers.

With a sharp sniff, she wiped a hand across her cheeks. It was all very well men like Churchill telling them they mustn't lose hope, that no matter the hardships they must stay strong, but how the devil were they supposed to do that now? She would do her best, of course she would. As the eldest, she would take charge as she always had. But stay strong? After this? Huh. She defied even Winnie himself to do that.

'I don't suppose...' Beside her, Clemmie's voice was still choked by sobs. '...we're in... the wrong... place. Only...'

May shook her head; of all the useful things she could do now, giving her sisters false hope wasn't one of them. 'No,' she said, her voice scratchy from the dust in her throat. 'We're in the right place. I know it.'

In truth, what did it matter? This smouldering heap of rubble here, or that one over there, the upshot was the same: their home was gone. And yes, it might only have been two rooms on the ground floor of a building that ought more properly to have been condemned years ago, but it had been their shelter against the world, in it

7

all the things that were dear to them: the few remaining pieces of their mother's furniture; the last of her china; the tiny box with the inlaid lid that had contained locks of their hair from when they were babies. But now it was all gone. And for what? What had the three of *them* ever done to the Germans? As if making them homeless wasn't enough, Hitler had snatched away her livelihood as well, and Clemmie's at the bakery too, from what she could see through the smoke. In fact, given how few buildings were still standing, there wasn't much hope for Pearl's either. So thoroughly had the enemy done their job that the three of them were now destitute: without work, they would have no money; without money, they couldn't pay rent. Rent? Huh. Where on earth would they find to rent now? With everywhere flattened, where would they even start to look?

'You know…' At the edge of the debris, Pearl's prodding had taken on a desultory air. 'There is *one* good thing…'

Struck by her sister's tone, May turned to see a smirk on her lips. 'Really? Not sure how you fathom that.'

'Well, you got to think we've seen the last of Charlie.'

Dear God, yes. Mr Warren. When the siren had started up, he'd been slumped in one of his drunken stupors over the kitchen table, none of them daring to rouse him on their way past, which had to mean—

'You think he were definitely still in there, then?' Clemmie's tone, as she asked, suggested she daren't believe it. 'You don't think he could have got himself out *before* the bombs started falling? He couldn't have… he couldn't have woken up after we'd left and took himself off to shelter someplace else?'

May shook her head. Charlie Warren's latest bout of inebriation had left him, as it always did, so deeply comatose that if the air raid siren hadn't roused him, nothing would have. And the chance that he had survived what looked to have been a direct hit by an HE defied belief. No, Charlie Warren was gone. His reign of terror was over.

'Think about it,' she said, casting a glance to where Pearl – the only one of them to have Charlie Warren as her real father – was now clambering over the ruins. 'When we crept out, he was snoring fit to wake old Mrs Tuckett on the top floor. So, no, I reckon that skinful he had yesterday was his last… and that when he came stumbling in, cursing and lashing out as usual, it was for the final ever time.'

'Yeah,' Pearl looked back at them to agree. 'There's no way he could have got out. He's gone. Dead and buried. And I for one shan't mourn his passing.'

'But Pearl—'

'Face it, Clemmie.' Continuing to poke about in the rubble, Pearl was unrepentant. 'That foul-mouthed bastard might have been my father but he were rotten through and through. And yes, I know you're not supposed to speak ill of the dead, but you're also not supposed to tell lies, either. So, let's none of us pretend we'll miss him. *You* might have been the one to feel the back of his hand most often but weren't none of us spared his wrath. It was me he swore at for fighting off the drunks he brought home. It was me he told not to be so prissy every time I complained about one of them putting a hand up my skirt or trying to reach inside my blouse. And if I can't forgive him that, why would I mourn him? And you, May – don't tell me you weren't brassed off with him constantly helping himself to the coins from your purse...'

*So what if I took some of your money, you sour-faced bint. This is my house. You don't like it, you can leave. But try taking my girl Pearl with you and it'll be the last thing you ever do. Don't say I haven't warned you.*

'Trust me,' May said shortly, the memory of Charlie Warren's bloated features making her itch with rage, 'many's the time I could gladly have taken the carving knife to that man—'

'...or that you, Clemmie, weren't browned off with him sending you out with your own money to fetch his booze or his fags.'

'I daren't never disobey him.'

'See, that's what I mean. So, no, I shan't lose sleep over him being dead, and nor should either of you.'

'It's true,' May said, watching Clemmie mop at her eyes with her handkerchief. 'He don't deserve to be neither mourned nor remembered.' For the misery he'd brought upon their mother alone, that vile excuse of a man deserved to be entirely forgotten, his passing from this world going completely unmarked.

Still sobbing, Clemmie made to reply. 'Even... so...'

'Look,' May said. She did wish Clemmie wouldn't get so upset over things that weren't worth her tears. Fragile as a china doll, Mum always said. She even looked it, with her pale wispy hair and their father's blue eyes. 'You've had a shock. You're tired. We all are.'

'Besides,' Pearl added, rising to her feet and gesturing about her, 'we've more important things than the demise of Charlie Warren to worry about. I mean, what the hell do we do now? Where do we even go?'

Before their discussion had turned to the fate of her stepfather, May had been wondering the same thing.

'Well,' she said, deciding there was only one thing they *could* do. 'When we came up out of the shelter, that warden told us we were to go up the church and wait. So, I suppose we go there and see what the arrangements are — see if a rest centre's been set up like that day Marsh Barton was bombed, and then go and find it. I don't see as we have a choice. I mean, look about you. High Street's flattened. Fore Street's burned out. Even Bedford Circus is gone. There's nowhere left.'

Feeling a fleck of ash landing on her cheek, she moved to wipe it away, only to then curse as it fell onto her lapel. She doubted her poor jacket, already peppered with smuts, would ever be the same again. And it was her second-best one, too; one of the few garments she'd owned that brightened her lacklustre complexion and set off her plain brown hair. And now it was ruined. She could weep at the unfairness of that alone.

Heaving a resigned sigh, she looked back up to see Pearl tugging something from the rubble. Glinting in the light, it appeared to be a tiny mirror — the sort that might hang in a birdcage. With Mrs Duncan in number seven having kept budgerigars, she supposed it had been one of hers.

'So,' Pearl said as she picked her way back towards them, 'that's what we're going to do, is it? Go up the church?'

Reasoning that their most pressing task ought to be ensuring they at least had somewhere to sleep, May nodded. 'It is. We'll go and see what's what… and we'll do it now, early, before we're left to traipse here, there and everywhere in search of any old place that'll have us.'

'Which makes me proper glad then,' Pearl said, her lips curling into a grin, 'that on the way down the shelter last night I thought to grab this.' When she held aloft her vanity case as though she had just won it at a fair, May shook her head in dismay; Pearl and her bloomin' make-up. 'Because at least I shan't be without my curlers or my toothbrush. Nor lipstick and mascara.'

'Yes, because let's face it,' May said, glass crunching under her shoes as she turned her back on the remains of Albert Terrace, 'looking your best really ought to be your biggest concern when you've just lost your livelihood, your home, and everything that was in it.'

# Chapter 2

It was now, May realised, ten days since those German bombs had brought her world – *their* world – crashing down about them. And still there was no sign of them being found anywhere to live. Night after night, they traipsed back to the rest centre to lie on those hard and narrow little camp beds, drifting in and out of sleep as they kept one ear alert for the sound of the air raid siren. And it seemed they would be there for a good while longer yet; when it came to being found a home, the young and the unmarried were at the very bottom of the list.

'Don't you have *any* family?' the worn-out woman from the city corporation had asked when they'd gone to the emergency centre to enquire whether there was any news.

'Have you thought about joining up?' another suggested on a separate occasion, her voice lowered to a conspiratorial whisper. 'Only, the WRNS have such a natty uniform, don't they? And one hears naval officers are terribly dashing.'

Ignoring that Pearl was too young to enlist anyway, none of them felt in the least inclined towards a life at His Majesty's service – even if it did seem the obvious answer to their predicament.

One encouraging development – to May's mind at least – was that this last week, Clemmie had taken to volunteering with the WVS.

'I'm doing it to feel useful,' she had said. 'To feel as though, amid all this awfulness and despair, I'm being of some help.'

Her sister's announcement had come as no surprise; of the three of them, Clemmie always had been the one to put other people first. And although so far she'd only been helping for a few mornings, it was clearly doing her good. Not only was she now carrying herself with more purpose, but she also had some of the colour back in her cheeks.

Pearl, on the other hand, was still at a loose end, although not for want of trying. In the last couple of days, she'd been to every cinema still open – as well as to the couple of theatres to have escaped serious damage – explaining that she'd worked as an usherette at the Plaza, sadly gutted in the raids by a fireball, and that if they were looking for staff, not only did she know the ropes, but she was popular with customers too. Pearl through and through, that was – bags of *get-up-and-go*. If she, May, had even half Pearl's talents, then she too would be putting herself about. But describing herself as hard-working was never going to endear her to anyone. Nor would it help her stand out from the crowd. And that was where Pearl had another advantage: with her willowy limbs, hazel eyes and auburn hair, she certainly made an impression.

No, in times like these, every woman in need of a job – especially those whose abilities, like her own, were rather run-of-the-mill – described herself as hard-working. And that, she supposed, was why the offer that *had* cropped up felt like one she shouldn't turn down. Had she been qualified to do anything other than domestic work, and were she not convinced that Clemmie and Pearl would find their feet without her, she wouldn't even be entertaining it.

Continuing to stare at the remains of Albert Terrace, she heaved a sigh. Her old life might no longer exist but the decision to leave it behind was proving harder than she'd expected. Not that there was anything left *to* leave: the important things, she kept telling herself – things like memories of her mother and father – weren't bound to bricks and mortar; those, she kept in her heart.

Thoughts of her parents filling her eyes with tears, she sniffed. In the last day or two, showers of rain had dampened down the dust and helped to clear the air. If only it had done the same for her thoughts! If only she didn't feel so guilty about what she was considering doing.

Staring ahead, she raised a wry smile. Perhaps by coming back to Albert Terrace she had been hoping for a sign, something to tell her whether she should stay in Exeter and try to make the best of it, or say goodbye to her past and start over somewhere new.

It wasn't just a sense of responsibility to her sisters holding her back, though. Homeless and jobless, she felt adrift, displaced, questioning who she even was. Life in Albert Terrace might have been one long struggle, but it was those very battles that had given her purpose. Through sheer doggedness, she had seen to it that the three of them had kept their heads above water. And yes, the place had been a dump, the whole building rife with rats and rotten with rising damp. Shortly after the end of the last war – the Great War, *The War To End All Wars* as the generation before her had rather optimistically called it – she'd been born there, the first child of Frederick and Maude Huxford. Indeed, the entire twenty-one years of her life had unfolded in those two rooms, the smaller one at the front facing directly onto Chandlery Street, the larger one at the rear looking straight onto the back of Wolcott's Laundry. Her earliest memory of the place was one of sitting on a rug, playing with her doll, and watching with fascination as the undertakers had carried away the lifeless form of her gentle but broken father. Just four years old, she would have been. Sixteen years later, she had nursed her mother through *her* last days, before watching her succumb too, albeit to an altogether different malady. But now, in those few seconds it had taken a bomb to drop to Earth, the Luftwaffe had seen to it that memories were all she had left. No wonder she felt uneasy at the prospect of leaving it all behind.

The other thing she was unexpectedly struggling to accept was that Charlie Warren really was dead. *Charlie Warren*. She never had fathomed what her gentle mum had seen in that man – what slippery deceit on his part had fooled her into believing he would make a sound husband and reliable stepfather. She must have seen *something* in him, although whatever it was must quickly have evaporated because, the moment the lazy so-and-so had landed Mum with another mouth to feed in the shape of their half-sister, Pearl, he'd upped and left without so much as a word. *Shell shock* was how the poor woman had excused his behaviour – and her bruises. But *two* soldier husbands, *both* afflicted by it? As May had more than once overheard concerned neighbours ask one another, *how unlucky could the poor soul be?*

Yes, that day all those years ago when Charlie Warren had walked out on them had come as a relief, and none of them had seen hide nor hair of him again until a couple of months back, when, having apparently learned of Maude's death, he'd shown up on their doorstep. He hadn't changed. He'd still had that same beer-soaked breath, still put on those same weaselly smiles. He hadn't even tried to hide why he'd come back. How he'd seriously thought Mum would still have had anything of value – that there would have been anything for him to claim as his by right and snatch up to pawn or sell – she simply couldn't fathom. For the best part of fifteen years, their poor mother had held down three jobs just to keep up with paying the rent for those two run-down rooms, everything of value long since sold to put food on the table. Well, let her mother's misfortune at the hands of Charlie Warren serve as a warning: never would she allow herself – nor Clemmie or Pearl, for that matter – to be taken in a by a brute, even if he did come promising the earth.

Returning her attention to her own quandary, she let out a sigh. Was it sacrilegious, when so many homes had been destroyed, and so many more left without gas or electricity or water, and when there were no buses or taxis to get anywhere, to wonder whether the Luftwaffe had done them a favour? They *had* flattened a slum, after all. And they *had* finished off that monster Charlie Warren. Perhaps they'd even done three favours if you counted this chance she'd been given to start over somewhere new.

Pausing to reflect, she sighed. If only she could banish the feeling that by putting her own needs above those of her sisters – above Clemmie's, in particular – she was being selfish. That day she'd responded to the advertisement in the local newspaper, she hadn't expected to even receive a reply, let alone be offered the job, the letter's arrival plunging her into a state of perpetual to-ing and fro-ing over what to do. Ordinarily, before even contemplating something so precarious, she would have hoped to feel more certain; she would have hoped to know that, in grasping the chance to haul herself up out of the gutter and take her life in a different direction, she wouldn't end up regretting it. On this occasion, all she felt was completely at sea.

From the ruins of her old home, she cast her eyes to the heavens. *Come on, Mum,* she pleaded. *What do I do? If you're up there looking down, send me a sign. You always said that when one door closes, another one opens. So, tell me, do I take this chance and leave, or do I stay?*

Her thoughts interrupted by the sound of scrunching, she spun about. Picking his way across the rubble towards her was an elderly ARP warden.

'Oy, miss.'

Doing her best to look contrite, she braced for a telling-off. 'Yes?'

'You shouldn't be here. You know that.'

*You shouldn't be here.* The sign she'd been hoping for? Probably as close as she was going to get…

# II. Bud Burst

# Chapter 3

'Are you *sure* about this? Only, you don't have to go. You know that, don't you?'

With the three of them having spent their entire lives looking out for one another, May knew it was only natural that Clemmie should be concerned – which was why she owed it to her to be truthful.

'If I'm honest, no, I'm not in the least sure.'

'Then don't go,' Clemmie urged. 'Stay here and we'll keep looking for work together.'

It was now Monday morning and, as she shifted the weight of her canvas shopping bag from one hand to the other, May heaved a weary sigh. They'd been over this a dozen times. No, she *wasn't* sure she was doing the right thing, but neither was she going to be talked out of it. How could she turn down the offer of a job when it was the only vacancy she'd seen that she'd stood any chance of getting? And yes, Pearl had been right to say it was odd to be offered it without so much as an interview. But, in her situation, she couldn't afford to look a gift horse in the mouth; she needed a home, a wage, and some hope. They all did. It was just that they were all now at ages where what each of them wanted was not only different but also to be secured by different means. From the moment Clemmie had been old enough to understand they didn't have a father, the only things she'd wanted when she grew up were a husband and a family – and that was fair enough. As for Pearl, well, what *she* wanted seemed to grow more fanciful every time you asked her: to sing with a big band; to act on the stage; to *be famous*. And who knew? Perhaps, one day, she would be. She certainly didn't want for confidence.

'We can *look* all we like,' she answered Clemmie carefully, 'but looking don't mean we'll *find* anything… least of all together.'

'We never did get round to trying the parachute factory,' Clemmie pointed out. 'They're *always* after girls.'

Not so long ago that would have been true. But Clemmie was overlooking one vital fact.

'They might have been once, but they won't be now – not with the High Street bombed out. Now they'll be inundated with shopgirls, all as desperate for work as we are. No, tell the Labour Exchange that's the sort of work we're looking for and as likely as not they'll send us straight to a munitions factory somewhere. And then we'd probably end up separated anyway. You remember Ethel Carter from school?' With a frown, Clemmie nodded. 'She got sent some place in Gloucestershire that makes torpedoes, and her sister's Lord-knows-where in the Black Country making parts for aeroplanes. Mrs Carter said it's months since she's seen either of them.'

'But *you* were the one who said you were done with cleaning for a living.' This latest observation came from Pearl, who for the last five minutes had been checking her wristwatch as though she had somewhere to be. 'Now, suddenly, you're happy to go an' be a housekeeper? And in some far-flung place none of us has ever heard of?'

'I *did* say I was done with cleaning,' May replied. 'I'll own to that. And believe me, if I could be doing anything else, I would be. If Hitler hadn't bombed us out, I wouldn't even be considering going off like this. You know that. But here we are. Besides, this isn't cleaning, it's housekeeping. It's different.'

'Hm.'

To be fair, Pearl's scepticism wasn't unfounded. But with jobs so hard to come by, May sensed that if she didn't grasp this opportunity, she would probably live to regret it. She *had* become tired of cleaning – constantly vacuuming corridors, polishing mirrors, repeatedly wiping the finger-prints from door-pushes and lift buttons. She'd also had quite enough of slipping out of sight the moment a guest appeared: heaven forbid some fancy holidaymaker should have her day spoiled by the sight of a cleaner wielding a duster. Until now, though, every time she'd thought about finding different work, she'd been left wrestling with the prospect of having to leave home to do so, of having to move to another part of the city – or even out of it altogether. But then Charlie Warren had shown up again and her decision had been made for her, all thoughts of leaving Albert Terrace struck from her mind; Clemmie could never have stood up to that evil sod by herself. Even Pearl, his own daughter, had struggled. Now, with him – and everything else that had shaped their daily lives – gone, choice was a luxury she didn't have. Moreover, the job she'd been offered came with lodgings – something that in their current situation was to be grabbed with both hands. So, no, ready or not, she had to do this. The time had come to be brave.

That said, leaving Clemmie and Pearl was going to be the hardest thing she'd ever done. Even now, about to get on the bus, she was in two minds – could feel tears not far below the surface. But what she had to remember was that, sooner or later, Clemmie would find a husband and settle to raising a family. And, one way or another, Pearl would land on her feet, too; her sheer bloody-mindedness would see to that.

'Anyway,' she said, glancing between her sisters' faces and trying to ignore the lump in her throat, 'since the driver looks to be getting ready to leave, I'd best say goodbye. The fellow's letter said to be there this morning – miss this bus and I shan't be there until mid-afternoon.' Giving Clemmie the briefest of hugs, and then squeezing Pearl's shoulder, she went on, 'Watch what you're up to, the pair of you. And first chance I get, I'll write and tell you all about it.'

At the kerb, the engine of the single-decker bus rattled into life.

'Any more for Crediton?' the driver called through the open door.

'Well, just *you* be careful, too,' Clemmie said as May climbed the steps and paid her fare.

'Yeah, and be proper careful with them Yanks,' Pearl yelled after her.

Yes, May reflected as she slid into an empty seat towards the back of the bus and tucked her bag at her feet, she wasn't sure about this at all. But, if it turned out she'd made a mistake, she could always come back. Granted, she'd have to register for war work again and then simply accept wherever they sent her – she was only exempt now because she was going to take up employment on a farm. But with a bit of luck, it wouldn't come to that. With a bit of luck, keeping house for a farmer would work out just fine – despite the surprising and somewhat indecent haste with which the whole thing seemed to have come about.

She'd never been out of Exeter before. And the thing surprising May most about the view from the window of the bus as it trundled up the Exe Valley was the lushness of the countryside. After the devastation in the city, where her eyes had quickly grown accustomed to blackened ruins, mounds of rubble, and air that even on a breezy day remained stubbornly fawn with dust, the gently rolling hills and palette of soft hues here was a sight for sore eyes.

Rather less restful was the *otherness* of everything, the foreignness of it all. Compared to Exeter, the horizon was so distant, the space so vast that, even from the safety of the bus, she felt small and exposed. And then there were the dwellings; with them dotted so far apart along the roadside, she had to wonder how anyone would hear their neighbour calling for help if they had need of it. And the sky: there was *so much* sky!

After a while, her thoughts in turmoil, she stopped looking out of the window and took instead to staring into her lap. What on earth had possessed her to think she could do this? How had she thought she could leave Exeter – flattened or not – to go and live on a farm? What did *she* know of farms? For all she knew of the countryside, she might as well be heading to the other side of the world.

But when she was eventually set down at the edge of a village green, and stood watching the bus pull away, she realised she had no choice but to get on with it. To that end, and with a heavy sigh, she glanced about. Behind her was a surprisingly ostentatious and rather severe-looking church of brown stone, on the opposite side of the road a terrace of cottages, some with shopfronts, among them a post office. At either end of the row was a public house. To her right, the Bell was a half-timbered building with tiny leaded lights for windows. By contrast, the Duke's Head was a dun-coloured stucco affair with an imposing porch, above which were painted the words *Free House* and, in smaller letters beneath, *Rooms & Hot Meals*. But as far as she could see, the only sign of life anywhere was a family of sparrows squabbling in the dust just yards from her feet.

Her earlier doubt hardening into panic, she reached into her pocket and pulled out the letter offering her the job as housekeeper at a place called Fair Maids Farm. *Mrs M. Huxford*, the envelope was addressed.

'You're calling yourself *Huxford*?' Clemmie had reproached her upon seeing it.

'I'm not *calling* myself anything,' May had risen stoutly to her own defence. 'I'm simply using my own name – the name our father gave to our mother.'

'But our names were changed to Warren.'

'Not properly, they weren't,' she had corrected her sister. 'Mr Warren just insisted we use his. Reckon he didn't want Mum reminded of Dad. I've been meaning for years to change it back. And now I have.'

'But—'

'You're welcome to stay as Warren if you want.'

'Well, I—'

'And before you say anything,' she recalled rushing to add, 'no, I didn't write in my letter that I was *Mrs*. That's a mistake on *his* part.'

Squinting again now at the unsteady hand, she reread the little missive she'd received at the end of last week.

*Dear Mrs Huxford,*

*Regarding your letter to be housekeeper. Please start Monday morning.*

*Yours Sincerely,*

*George Beer Esquire.*

The first time she'd read it, she'd quite liked the fact that it was to the point. If George Beer was a man of few words, that would suit her just fine. People who liked the sound of their own voice were wont to grow tiresome. But looking at it again now, she had to wonder whether, rather than succinct, the tone of the letter wasn't a trifle terse.

Too late to worry about that now, she stuffed the letter back into her pocket and took another look around. With no clue how to find this Fair Maids Farm, nor how long it would take her to walk there, she supposed she could do worse than go and ask in the post office. With that in mind, her handbag over her shoulder, her shopping bag in her hand, and more used to busy city streets, she checked in both directions for traffic and crossed the road. *Please*, she willed, *let it not be miles and miles to this place. Not in these shoes.* The fellow who'd sold her the smart brown leather lace-ups from a barrow near the bombed-out market hadn't been wrong to describe them as sturdy, but they were also as stiff as hell and in need of a good deal more breaking in before they would be anything approaching comfortable.

In front of the post office, she paused for a moment to compose herself. Then she turned the door handle, ducked beneath the low frame and stepped inside. While the tinkling of the bell finished announcing her arrival, she cast quickly along the shelves: oddments of stationery;

a rack of knitting patterns; jars for sweets sold by the ounce – empty, of course. And in the air hung the sort of mustiness that came from rain-soaked floors and damp cardboard.

Eventually, through a doorway behind the counter came a woman with tightly curled hair and a shapeless grey cardigan. From the way she paused to take in May's appearance, it was clear she didn't serve many strangers. 'Morning. How can I help you?'

Despite the directness of the woman's scrutiny, May reminded herself to smile and sound friendly; having only just arrived, she had no idea who might one day turn out to be an ally.

'Good morning,' she replied. 'I'm sorry to trouble you but is this Pippinswell?'

'Round here we call it *Pinswell*, love. But yes, this is it.'

'Oh. Forgive me. I didn't know.' *Pinswell. She must remember that.* 'Anyway, I was wondering if you could give me directions for how to get at Fair Maids Farm. Only, I'm due to start work there.'

The woman's eyes widened. 'George Beer's place? You sure about that, dear?'

'Um… well, yes. The letter says George Beer Esquire of Fair Maids Farm. I'm the new housekeeper.'

'Well, well. Wonders will never cease. Just come off the bus, have you?'

Her unease deepening, May nodded. 'From Exeter, yes.'

At the mention of Exeter, the woman's expression softened. 'Bombed out, were you, love?'

Again, May nodded. 'Lost everything.'

'Poor mite. What's your name?'

'May Huxford.'

28

'Well, May Huxford, I'm Nan Parker and my husband's Arnie. Come out the front with me and I'll show you where you've to go.'

Softening her hunched shoulders, May smiled gratefully. 'Very kind of you.'

Once out on the pavement, having raised an eyebrow at May's shoes, Nan Parker pointed to the left of the green. 'Over there, that's Church Lane. Follow it down under the railway bridge, then keep on to the crossroads where you'll want to turn right. About a mile or so after that, you'll see a broken-down gate into some orchards. That'll be Fair Maids Farm.'

Having repeated Nan Parker's directions, May smiled warmly. 'Thank you.'

'Happen we'll see you about the village… once you're settled.'

May nodded. 'Happen you will.'

'Well, good luck then.'

'Yes. Thank you. Goodbye.'

What, May wondered as she crossed back over the road, did Nan Parker mean by *wonders will never cease*? And why wish her luck? Her trepidation having built to the point where she was beginning to feel light-headed, she was in two minds now whether to even bother trailing all the way out to this place at all. Why put herself to a lot of trouble if she was only going to turn round and come back again? Why not just wait here for the next bus back to Exeter?

Weighed down by indecision, she looked across the green to where Church Lane passed a row of thatched cottages. No, she mustn't let herself be put off by what might have been nothing more than a figure of speech. Without this position she was homeless and jobless. Besides, she'd come all this way – not to mention upset

Clemmie in the process. So, no, she would ignore her doubts, find this George Beer and his Fair Maids Farm, and then knuckle down and get on with it. After all, she was only going there to do housework. So how bad could it possibly be?

# Chapter 4

'Coo-ee. Hullo?' When her enquiry drew no response, May gave a disappointed sigh. Even allowing for the time she'd spent loosening and retying her laces in a bid to stop her shoes chafing her heels, the traipse over potholed lanes to Fair Maids Farm had taken longer than she'd expected from Nan Parker's directions. Adding to her discomfort had been the fact that the warmth from the sun combined with the shelter of the dense hedgerows had quickly made her feel hot and sticky and left her gasping for something to drink. Worse still, now that she'd finally arrived there didn't seem to be anyone about. Clearly, she *could* venture beyond the building's little porch in search of someone, but since she wasn't even sure she was in the correct place it didn't seem right. Instead, she confined herself to peering along the passage that led away behind it and tried again to attract attention. 'Hullo? Anybody there?'

When there was still no answer, she glanced about. *Was* she in the right place? The sign hanging from the broken-down gate had said Fair Maids Farm plain enough. And as Nan Parker had described, this forlorn little building did stand in the middle of an orchard. But, plodding along that last stretch of lane, this wasn't the building to which she'd thought she'd been heading, her attention having been drawn to a larger dwelling set at the foot of a lush green slope. Picked out sharp and white in the sunshine, and looking to all her mind like a farmhouse, she'd assumed it was where she was going, her spirits lifting at the welcoming sight of it. Once she'd left the lane and started through the gate, though, the track had taken her in a different direction, to this peculiar little cottage of dark stone nestled so close to the ground that it hadn't even appeared from between the trees until she was almost on top of it. The eventual sight of it had made her heart sink. The setting itself didn't disappoint – the surrounding countryside was quite captivating – but the farmhouse, if this was indeed it, was nothing like the picture she'd had in her mind.

There still being no sign of anyone, she stepped back to more closely study its appearance. Comprising two mismatched halves, it was unlike anything she'd seen before, and put her more in mind of a barn than a house. To her left, the higher section had tiny windows under a slate roof; to her right, the lower half, entirely without apertures, sat squashed beneath ragged grey thatch. Where the two met, the slates swept down low over the porch. Compared to the fine building on the hillside, this one felt ramshackle and down-at-heel. Was it possible she'd followed the wrong track and ended up here by mistake? To establish that required that she find someone to ask. But if the tightening in her gut was anything to go by, she had a feeling she already knew how they would answer.

Needing to be sure nonetheless, she reached to unlatch the lower half of the door, took a single step inside and set down her bag. Then she refolded her mac, placed it carefully on top and looked about. No more than fifteen feet long, the stone passageway terminated at a second stable door, the bottom section of it held wide by a cast-iron boot scraper. Beyond was a cobbled yard and a tumbledown shed. Could this funny little place *really* be a farmhouse? And if so, was this all there was to it?

Despite a pleasingly cool draught flapping at her dress, growing unease was making her feel clammy. Even just inside the passage, the summery green scent from the orchards had given way to the aroma of damp earth combined with a sickly sweetness that reminded her of fermenting fruit. Noticing an opening in the cob wall to her right, she went towards it and peered in. Beyond it, the rough stone floor contained a recessed channel leading to a small square opening in the far wall. In that same elevation were three tiny windows, all at different and seemingly random heights from the ground. From the troughs around the walls and the fittings on the posts, and from what she knew of the old sheds at the dairy just round the corner from Albert Terrace, she guessed this had once been a shelter for animals. Given its proximity to the rest of the house, it seemed fortunate it was no longer in use.

Turning back in to the passage, she spotted a doorway on the left. Hoping to come across someone, she went towards it and found herself looking into a square parlour with an opening in the far wall to another room beyond. Apart from a fireplace, it was home to just two armchairs and a long-case clock. From a lifetime spent too close to the window, the scarlet fabric of the left-hand chair was badly faded, the front seams of the seat squabs so worn that tufts of horsehair were poking through. On the arm of the second chair lay a grey woollen rug that, even from a distance, she could see was lacy with moth holes. And on the stone window ledge stood a Cornishware jug, scattered about it on the sill crispy strands of what must once have been a posy of flowers. Casting her eyes to the low ceiling, she noted a bare light bulb, thick with cobwebs. At least – small mercy – the place had electricity.

Sighing with dismay, she stood and listened. Apart from the distant rattling of a door in the breeze, the place was silent. Where was everyone? With some trepidation, she continued along the passage and stepped out into the yard.

'Can I help 'ee, maid?'

Startled, she turned to see a short wiry man staring at her. His greying hair put him at upwards of fifty; his face and neck were outdoors brown, his thin lips pursed about the stem of a pipe, the glossy bowl of which he cupped in his right hand. Taking in the frayed cuffs of his collarless shirt and the stains down the front of his faded overalls, her spirits sank further. *Please don't let* this *be George Beer!*

'Forgive me,' she said, and then paused to clear her throat. 'But is this Fair Maids Farm?'

Done with looking her up and down, the man's attention came to rest on her shoes. Following his eyes to her feet, she noticed with dismay that the creases across their once-shiny chestnut-brown leather were ingrained with dust. And she knew without looking that both her heels were blistered.

'You Mrs Huxford?'

She looked back up. 'I am.'

'Better come in then.'

Clinging fervently to the hope it wasn't the case, she asked, 'Are you Mr Beer?'

'I am.'

Her spirits plummeting further still, she trailed after him. How frequently, she wondered, did the buses run back to Exeter? Surely there would be at least one service this afternoon. But what if there wasn't? Or what if, by the time she had walked all the way back to the village, she had missed it? Growing hot with panic, she spotted her bag where she had left it in the passage, and dithered over what to do. Eventually, she picked it up; before she did anything hasty, she should at least establish the lie of the land.

She carried her bag through to the parlour and steeled herself. 'Does anyone else live here?'

'Jus' me.'

She gripped the handles of her bag tightly. Did she really want to be alone out here with this peculiar little man? She might have assumed the mantle of Mrs Huxford, but if folk thought the two of them were alone here together they would tattle nonetheless. And she could do without having her character picked over by people who didn't know her from Adam. More importantly, was this man to be trusted? He certainly seemed odd. Then there was the matter of the house: not only was it marooned in the middle of nowhere, but it looked even more run-down than Albert Terrace – than Albert Terrace *had been*. If Clemmie could see it she would be appalled and beg her to have nothing to do with it. But then Clemmie's face had crumpled with the pain of just watching her get on the bus.

Still clinging to her bag, she let out a sigh. That she'd upset her sister was something she regretted deeply anyway, but that she'd upset her for this dirty little hovel made the betrayal seem even worse – so much worse that she feared she might cry.

In truth, part of her felt duped – as though she'd been got there under false pretences. The wiser part of her, though, saw the situation differently: that the place wasn't what she'd been expecting – or, more accurately, hoping for – was no one's fault but her own for not questioning what she was coming to; for not even thinking to ask; for jumping at the first job that had come along.

'Just you,' she belatedly acknowledged Mr Beer's statement.

'And two land girls, in the lean-to... if you count them.'

Count them? Was there any reason why she shouldn't?

She set her bag on the floor. The presence of two other women did put things in a marginally more favourable light.

Ahead of her, George Beer went through to the adjoining room. 'This here's the kitchen,' she heard him say. Wincing as her shoes rubbed her heels, she scurried to join him. 'Through there's the scullery,' he went on, gesturing vaguely. 'Then the lav. Then the lean-to. Above here's two bedrooms. Your'n be the near one. Not the far one. Don't no one use the far one.'

'The near one. Right...'

'I comes up for me dinner at twelve, me supper at six. The other two mostly take their dinner off out with them.'

'And where are they now?' May asked. 'The two land girls?' Before she headed back to the village, she should at least meet them – at least judge this peculiar set-up on all the facts. If nothing else, it would put her in a stronger position to explain to Clemmie and Pearl why she had decided not to stay. *The farmer was a real odd sort, the land girls no better. Unsavoury, the lot of them.*

Offering up a tobacco-stained forefinger and thumb, George Beer slid the stem of his pipe from his mouth; where it had been resting on his lips there remained a dent. 'Couldn't say.'

*Couldn't say?* What sort of farmer didn't know where his workers were?

'So...'

'Never wanted them in the first place.'

Under the weight of her despair, May exhaled heavily. Her best course of action was surely to give the place a once-over – at the very least inspect the sleeping arrangements – and then get the measure of these two land girls. That way, no one could accuse her of being hasty. After that, her conscience placated, she could go with her instinct and retrace her steps to the village in the hope of there being an afternoon bus back to civilisation. Returning to Exeter would mean having to eat humble pie when she got there, she knew that, but it wouldn't be the first time she'd had to admit to misjudging a situation. For certain Pearl would have a field day with the news. *I told you so!* But she could handle that. Dearest Clemmie, on the other hand, would most likely sob with relief, suffocate her in a hug, and suggest they go straight to the parachute factory. To be honest, there were worse ways to earn a living, this Fair Maids Farm place among them. So, yes, that's what she would do; the sooner she set off back to the village, the sooner she would be on her way home: least said, soonest mended.

Feeling calmer for having reached a decision, she turned about. 'Mr Beer? Mr Beer, are you... there?'

But while she had been considering what to do, Mr Beer had disappeared. Presumably he had assumed she would just get on with it and had gone back to his work. So, now what? It would be bad form to just disappear; she should at least find him and explain that she'd made a mistake and wouldn't be staying. *Good manners cost nothing*, her mother had forever chided the three of them.

Having stepped out into the yard, though, the flaw in her plan quickly became apparent: she could only explain herself to Mr Beer if she could find him, and that supposed she had a clue where to start. The yard alone looked to have upwards of a dozen outbuildings.

With that, she heard a clatter and, judging it to have come from a corrugated iron shed away to the right, she limped towards it, her blasted shoes continuing to rub at her heels, and ducked in through the door.

'Lord, you didn't half frighten me.' Disturbed from rooting about among a pile of rusty implements was a young girl with freckled cheeks. Despite the fact that she was wearing the unform of the Women's Land Army, she wasn't what May had been expecting. For a start, she was tiny: barely five feet tall and with the frame of a twelve-year-old.

'Yes, sorry,' May apologised. 'But I wonder if you can tell me where I'll find Mr Beer.'

Pausing to poke a strand of pale hair behind her ear, the girl shrugged. 'Couldn't rightly say. We don't see that much of him.'

Recalling that George Beer had said much the same of them, May frowned. 'No?'

'If he speaks to us at all, he just tells us what's to be done and leaves us to it.'

May continued to frown. 'Seems an odd way of carrying on.'

'Seems that way to me, too. But who am I to say? I'm just a land girl. I'm Bonnie, by the way. Bonnie Hawkins.'

'Pleased to meet you, Bonnie. I'm May Huxford.' In the company of someone so young, it seemed deceitful to call herself Mrs. It did, though, feel like the perfect opportunity to find out more about the place – if only to reassure herself that she was right to leave.

'What's he like to work for, then, Mr Beer? Quick to anger, is he?' Miss Shorland – her supervisor at the hotel – had been possessed of such an almightily short fuse that her employer's temperament was something May had vowed to establish in advance this time around.

'Mostly not. Though he don't hide how he's not much taken with neither me nor Nessa.'

'Nessa?'

'There's two of us – me an' Nessa. Nessa got two whole months training at a college up near Bristol. I got two weeks in a classroom and then got sent here because they said there was urgent need.'

Something about Bonnie's gentle manner reminded May of Clemmie. She softened her approach. 'So, this is your first farm then.'

'Uh-huh.'

'And do you like it – the work?'

'I like the hens. And the cow. I've took to milking all right. But I don't like clearing out ditches, nor am I much good with the tractor. Nessa says any damn fool – pardon my language – can drive it, but I'm more than happy to leave that to her. Lumbering great thing.' After pausing to regard May doubtfully, the girl went on, 'You come about the housekeeper's job?'

'I have, yes.' It wasn't a lie: she had come about it. No need for the poor girl to know she'd decided to have nothing to do with it. On the other hand, having gained the girl's confidence, something was drawing her to keep going, to edge her questions away from farming and back to matters domestic. After all, if a slip of a thing like this could stick it out in such a godforsaken place…

'And what about where you sleep?'

'The lean-to?'

39

May nodded. 'If that's where you sleep.'

'Bit damp. And fearful cold in winter, even with the stove. Mum sent me an extra blanket. That helped. And Gran knitted me some bedsocks. Real thick and warm, they are.'

'And what about food? How do you go on about that?'

'In the pantry, there's a barrel of oats. We soak them overnight for porridge and have it with damson jam. The baker comes twice a week with loaves – we get extra rations, see – and we get given sheep's cheese from Higher Cleave. We use that to make ourselves a sort of ploughman's for dinner... though Nessa says I should call it lunch. I didn't like the cheese at first – it's sort of sour and sharp – but I'm used to it now. And Mrs Beer gives us jars of pickles.'

'Mrs Beer?'

*There was a* Mrs *Beer?* How had Farmer Beer not mentioned that?

'There's two of 'em,' Bonnie continued in the same tone. 'There's the other Mr Beer's wife – you know, with the sheep over at Higher Cleave – and then there's his mother.'

'Ah, I see.' So, there was another Mr Beer, presumably at the white farmhouse she'd seen on the way in. Trust her to get landed with the poor relation!

'I think Mrs Beer feels sorry for us,' Bonnie continued in the same vein as previously. 'Whenever she sees us, she gives us something to bring back. Anyway, then we do our best for supper. The butcher's van comes on Wednesday and Saturday. And the fishmonger comes Friday. The van from the grocer's – Newcombe's, in the village, that is – calls twice a week but don't come all the way up here. He stops in the lane and if we want anything, we have to go down the track to him.'

'You have to get all the food?' To May, the arrangement smacked of neglect on the part of Mr Beer. But then there *could* be more to this than met the eye.

'Only since Alma went.'

'Alma?'

'The housekeeper before.'

That there had been someone here before her came as a surprise. 'And when did she leave – this Alma?'

Raising her gaze towards the rafters, and then looking back down to count on her fingers, Bonnie paused to work it out. 'Some time in February, I'd say. Yes, that'd be it because when the snow came, she said it was the final straw. Couldn't stand it no more. The cold, I mean. She had terrible chilblains. We all did. She got them on her toes and her heels. I got them on my fingers and ears. She got us some pink stuff from the chemist to stop them itching.'

'So, Alma left,' May said. She knew to her cost that chilblains were evil.

'Got herself work in Ex'ter. Walked out on the Friday, just like that. Mr Beer wasn't half cross *that* day, I can tell you.'

'And there's been no one here since.'

Bonnie shook her head. 'No one. Though to be fair, not for want of trying on Mr Beer's part. Put a card in the post office, he did. Even placed a notice in the local paper. Didn't fetch a single reply.'

Prickling with humiliation, May shifted her weight. Now it made sense. Having failed to attract any replies, Mr Beer had been obliged to widen his search, which was how *she'd* come to get the job no questions asked –

because no one else had applied. How foolish did she feel now?

'So, Alma cooked your meals?'

Finally, Bonnie smiled. 'Alma did everything. She was nice. Like a big sister. See, I only got brothers.'

With a light sigh, May shook her head. No wonder the poor girl looked in need of a decent meal. By the sound of it, she'd been existing on little more than thin air for the last three months. 'Have you been here long?'

'Me and Nessa both came on the same day in January.'

'And your family, are they nearby?'

Bonnie lowered her head. 'No. They're… they're…'

Thinking the poor soul was about to cry, May moved to put an arm across her shoulders; she could feel the girl's bones through her thin Aertex shirt. 'It's all right,' she said softly. Choose her words poorly and the floodgates would open, same as happened with Clemmie. 'Bit homesick?'

Sniffing loudly, Bonnie nodded. 'Mum and Dad and Gran are back near Weymouth. They didn't want me to be a land girl – didn't want me to do *anything* that meant leaving home. But both me brothers had gone in the navy and when I saw the pair of them looking so smart in their uniforms, and how proud of them Gran was, I wanted to do something too, you know, to help the war.'

'Course you did,' May said, hoping she'd found an encouraging tone.

'But Dad was livid. Said daughters didn't leave home, that we weren't that sort of family – that the Hawkinses stuck together. Said it was my place to stay and help Mum with Gran. Said it was bad enough both boys going off, when they could have gone on the buses where he could have kept an eye on them.'

No wonder they'd wanted to get away, May found herself thinking. With young men being called up left, right and centre, Bonnie's father sounded twenty years behind the times. 'But you stuck to your guns,' she said, removing her arm from Bonnie's shoulder.

Fishing about in the pocket of her dungarees, Bonnie pulled out a man's checked handkerchief and proceeded to blow her nose. 'I did. But the Land Army woman told me I'd get proper training. Like Nessa got. But now I'm here, I'm next to useless. And I miss Mum. And Gran. Dad, too.'

May gave the girl a kindly smile. 'Course you do.'

'I didn't never expect being a land girl to be easy. War's hard on everyone, I know that. But nor did I ever expect it to be such a struggle. Nor for me to feel so… well, though there's two of us, I do get terrible lonely.'

'I suppose you would do,' May acknowledged, her thoughts all over the place.

'When we started our training, they told us the country hadn't got enough food and that by growing more, we would be helping out. So, whenever I feel a bit gloomy, I try and remind myself it's worth it. The hardship, I mean.'

'Mm.'

'But if *you* were here,' Bonnie went on, 'maybe it would be a bit easier…'

Clearly, the poor thing was desperately unhappy. And yet, she was still here. *She* hadn't bolted at the first sign of discomfort; she was sticking it out because, no matter the privations and the lack of training, she wanted to do her bit. By contrast, what could she, May, claim to have done for the greater good? The recognition that to date she had done nothing made her pause and reflect. *Should* she stay? If she did, there could be no half measures. She couldn't do as this Alma had done and, deciding she'd had enough, just up sticks and leave. Either she took this on, got the place cleaned up and put meals on the table, or else she left, now, without getting up anyone's hopes. To try it for a few weeks and then throw in the towel would be grossly unfair of her. On the other hand, haste, as her mother always used to say, was the enemy of good judgement. So, what was it to be?

Feeling her earlier intentions deserting her, she gave a weary sigh. She supposed she *could* stay. It wasn't as though she had other jobs to consider. Her choice was straight-forward enough: stay here and make the best of it or go back to Exeter – where there still wouldn't be a home for them, and where she would have to take whatever war work she was given. Life back there wouldn't be like it had been, either: the city had been ravaged; the people she'd known scattered to the four corners; Clemmie and Pearl with their own plans and ideas. With hindsight, they were probably right to accuse her of being hasty. Moreover, she was already missing them. But Bonnie, here, missed her family too. And if it was Clemmie stuck out here like this, wouldn't she, May, hope that someone would stop and take care of *her*?

Beginning to come together in her mind was the notion that, with a little effort, she could make the place more homely for all of them: for Mr Beer; for Bonnie; for herself. Even for this other girl, Nessa. But she *had* to be sure. She had to choose between admitting defeat and going home, or else seizing the opportunity to grasp the sort of independence and freedom over her labours she'd previously only been able to dream of. But – and this was a big 'but' – as she'd already come to acknowledge, if she was going to stay, she had to keep at it come what may, stick with it through thick and thin.

'For God's sake, Bonnie, how long can it possibly take you to find a—' As May turned sharply in the direction of this new voice, in through the door strode the second land girl, as unlikely in her own way as Bonnie. Wide-hipped in her sturdy corduroy breeches, her bottle-green jersey straining over her chest, she wore her hat tipped back on her head, her mass of dark hair perfectly framing the strong features of her face. But it was her plump scarlet lips that held May's attention the longest and brought to her mind the word *siren*.

'Good Lord. Who are you?'

Seeing instantly why Mr Beer had taken a dislike to the woman, May straightened herself up and extended a hand. 'I'm Mrs Huxford.' Since the woman didn't seem backwards in coming forwards, it struck her that with this one, it might be prudent to show that she wasn't to be underestimated. 'And you are?'

With a light but at the same time condescending smile, the woman shook May's hand. 'Nessa Croft.' Looking May up and down, she added, 'George never mentioned another land girl.'

Instant dislike concealed behind a false smile, May held herself stiffly. 'That's because I'm not a land girl. I'm the new housekeeper.'

'Explains the unsuitable shoes. Although he still didn't mention you.'

'I don't suppose he had time,' May replied, her tone this time rather sharper than she would have liked, the words *because it's none of your business* fortuitously remaining stuck to her tongue. Already, she could see she was going to have the devil's own job being civil to this Nessa woman.

'Anyway,' she continued, looking back at Bonnie with a rather more sincere smile, 'since you've got work to do, and I've got things to see to myself, I shan't keep you no further.'

As she went back across the yard in the direction of the house, May regretted letting the woman rankle her. But it was all right. There would be plenty of time to take her down a peg or two. In the short term, her concern would be better saved for poor Bonnie.

Ducking under the door into the passage, she laughed. It would seem, then, that she'd made her decision. This peculiar little place was to become her home. *I'm the new housekeeper.* She'd said so herself.

# Chapter 5

May gave a weary sigh. What *on earth* had she let herself in for? Despite having determined not to act in haste, she hadn't even stuck to her plan to give the place a proper once-over. Instead, through some misplaced sense of duty to a young girl she didn't even know – and through a desire to show that stuck-up Nessa who was who – she had committed herself to staying on here, and to all the heartache that no doubt came with it.

Looking about the dreary little parlour, she could see now why Nan Parker had wished her luck: the place was filthy, its owner not much better. Even cleaned up, a hovel like this could never be homely. Albert Terrace had been spartan, but this place… As though to reassure herself on the point, she glanced about: on the rough plastered wall separating the parlour from the passage was a hearth in which lay the ashes from a previous fire and what appeared to be a dead starling; from the smoke-stained chimney breast hung a badly de-silvered mirror in a dust-covered frame; on the flagstone floor lay a threadbare rug exhibiting the same charred burn marks as one of the armchairs. All told, the room was miserable and mean enough to make her question what the devil she was doing there.

On the other hand, by hastily announcing that she was the new housekeeper, she had at least taken responsibility for the direction of her life from hereon in. Returning home to look for work – home, huh! – would never provide her with anywhere close to the level of freedom she sensed she would have here. Back in Exeter, she would almost certainly be forced to settle for war work in a factory, where she could only ever hope to pass the time until she caught the eye of one of her fellow workers, eventually heading up the aisle with him, resentment and disappointment only ever a couple of cross words away. In that light, this place did seem the lesser of two evils: taking on dirt and squalor, she could justify; passing up a chance of relative freedom, not so much.

Feeling tears welling, she gave a cross shake of her head and told herself not to be feeble. If she'd got upset every time something in her life had been unfair, she would never have stopped crying. Given all she'd been through lately, a degree of uncertainty was only to be expected; far-reaching change brought on misgivings in even the strongest of women. But that didn't excuse tears. No: if she was going to see this through, she would have to summon some of the backbone and the resolve for which Clemmie and Pearl had always admired her.

Fishing about in her pocket for her handkerchief, she dabbed at her eyes and blew her nose. Then, with a determined sniff, she cast her gaze around the room. Rather than feel sorry for herself, she should make a closer inspection of the place and see what was to be done.

The kitchen, she noted, was similar to the parlour: same size; same uneven flagstone floor; same low and badly yellowed ceiling. On the outer wall was a stone fireplace, in it a range, older and larger than the one she'd been used to in Albert Terrace. Steeling herself for what she might find, she grasped the fragment of towel hanging from a hook on the surround, opened the front and peered in – it was alight, but only just. Taking the poker, she prodded the embers and watched as they roused themselves to a reluctant glow. On the floor nearby stood an empty coal scuttle; clearly, the last person to use it hadn't bothered to fill it up again.

Despairing at people's laziness, she closed the range and got to her feet. In the recess alongside the hearth stood a dresser. Running her eyes over the collection of pottery bowls and plates, she noted among them the odd piece of porcelain. Intrigued, and wondering what else the dresser might conceal, she pulled at the handle of one of the drawers. When it wouldn't budge, she tugged harder, tutting when it still wouldn't give. She tried one of the doors instead, and opened it to find an assortment of kitchen paraphernalia that included a jelly mould, a Maslin pan, several large tin trays, and a couple of pottery serving dishes. In the topmost of the last lay a dead moth.

Ducking under the lintel, she stepped down into the scullery – in reality, little more than a passageway with a sink set into a wooden drainer. On the wall above it was a plate rack, beyond it a copper with a wooden laundry dolly propped against it. Peering through the door to the yard, she noted the brick shelter that housed the lavatory. Hands on hips, she gave a dismayed shake of her head. The description that kept coming to mind was *rudimentary*. Growing up, it had been a word that always made her giggle, leaving a lasting impression on her by virtue of containing the sound *rude*. Sadly, these days, it rarely even drew a smile.

Continuing to look about, she sighed. Albert Terrace had been basic but at least, in its own way, it had been homely, whereas this place was just… just what? Dirt and dilapidation aside, there *was* something about it –

something calling to her to get stuck in and knock it into shape. But was a short-term challenge, no matter how vast, good enough reason to stay? Once she'd got everything shipshape and up together, what then? Stuck out here, how did a person get by? How did they get that they needed – anything from shoes to soap to sewing thread – let alone make friends?

Her thoughts interrupted by the sound of boots coming across the yard, she craned round the doorframe to check who it was. Seeing Bonnie approaching, she sent her a smile. 'Everything all right, love?'

The girl's manner was coy. 'Just came to check... you hadn't left.'

'No. I've not left.' *Though you can't possibly know how close I've been.*

Bonnie's demeanour softened. 'Good. Then I'll go and get on.'

'You do that.'

'Oh, and I thought you might want this.' Fishing about in her pocket, the girl pulled out a thin roll of lint. 'Only, I seen your heels.'

Struck by the girl's kindness, May smiled. 'Thank you. That's very thoughtful.'

'Had the same problem with these bloomin' boots when I first got them. You can give me back later what you don't need.'

'Thank you. I'll make sure an' do that.'

With Bonnie heading away, May stood fingering the lint. If the feeling building in her chest was to be trusted, then perhaps she *should* just get stuck in. If nothing else, occupying her mind with the mundane usually helped her put larger concerns into perspective. And if she was going to start anywhere, common sense said the room in greatest need of her attention was the kitchen which, by the look of it, was going to call for hot water – and plenty of it. That being the case, she would see to her heels and then get some pans heating on the range.

Having delved about in her bag for her housecoat, tugged it over the top of her dress and buttoned the front, she seized the scuttle, headed out into the yard and looked about for the coal shed. Once located, she shovelled as much coke as she could carry, then lugged the filthy thing back into the kitchen, stoked up the range and put two pans of water to boil. In the scullery, rooting about for anything that might be of use, she found a scrubbing brush with just enough bristles to be serviceable, a soft broom, a box of soda crystals and a feather duster. Unable to do much until the water heated up, she threw open the window, pegged back the door, and set to work poking the broom into the corners of the ceilings and sweeping it down the walls to dislodge the cobwebs. Then, having chipped away sufficient soda to dissolve in a bucket of hot water, she proceeded to clean every ledge and scrub every surface. That done, she directed her attention to the kitchen table. Stood hard against the wall beneath the window, it was a sturdy elm affair, its surface badly pockmarked and ringed with stains. Arranged about it were three chairs. Presumably, she thought, as she set about giving the table a good scour, the fourth chair was here somewhere. Nobody owned just three.

Having previously spotted in the dresser a blue-checked oilcloth, she wiped it clean and set it aside to put on the table. At the window, she took down the single curtain, hung it from the washing line that stretched from the back door to the outhouse, and gave it a good thrashing with the carpet beater she'd found hanging on the back of the door. Then she put the curtain in the scullery to launder when she did a wash. Returning to the kitchen, she removed from the dresser every serviceable plate, bowl and mug, gave them a thorough scrub, and left them to drain. She scoured cutlery – *silver plate* cutlery, she noted with interest – and unclogged the spout of the teapot with a meat skewer. Coming across an ancient but half-full bottle of Izal, she disinfected the meat safe. After that, drawn to check the time, she took down the wooden clock from beside the door, wiped it clean, gave it a wind and set the hour to match her wristwatch. Recalling that in the corner of the parlour she'd seen a grandmother clock, and ignoring the urge to thoroughly dust it first, she opened the front, adjusted the hands to show the correct hour, and cranked the weights. It thanked her with a weighty *tock*.

Having been on her feet since first light, what she craved more than anything by then was a sit-down. But she knew that if she gave in she wouldn't want to get up again, and so, heading back into the parlour, she braced herself for what she might find and climbed the curving stone steps to inspect where she would be sleeping.

The room into which she emerged was stuffy and warm, and of the same dimensions as the one beneath it. Her weight, as she crossed the floorboards, caused them to creak and sigh, the gaps between them allowing her to see straight down into the parlour below.

Through the tiny window in the eaves, a band of sunlight was falling across a single bedstead, at the foot of which stood a washstand and a chest of drawers. In the corner nearest the stairs was a door. *Your'n be the near one. Not the far one. Don't no one use the far one.* Mr Beer's statement notwithstanding, she reached for the handle, but wasn't in the least surprised when it wouldn't turn. Curious to know what, in a place like this, could warrant locking away, she bent to peer through the keyhole. Unable to see anything other than a blank patch of wall, she shrugged and turned back to examine her sleeping quarters more closely.

Reaching to the bed, she pressed her fingers into the mattress; surprisingly well stuffed but pleasingly soft, the condition of the ticking suggested it was reasonably new, the bolster likewise. She supposed she had Alma to thank for that. *Alma did everything. She was nice. Like a big sister.* Poor Bonnie: not only did she miss her family, but she seemed to miss the paragon of virtue that had been Alma, too.

Noting how the general level of neglect downstairs was replicated up here, May ran a fingertip along the top of the chest and stared without surprise at the deep trail it left behind. Idly, she pulled open the top drawer and was greeted by a waft of camphor. At the washstand, she ran a finger round the rim of the basin – in keeping with its matching ewer it was white enamel, plain but functional. Under the bed, she spotted the matching chamber pot. There could be no denying that life here was going to be basic – a disappointing realisation given how she'd hoped that by taking this position she would be bettering herself. On the other hand, the more she saw of it, the more she realised it was barely any worse than Albert Terrace, in some respects better: out here, miles from anywhere, at least it was quiet, which ought to mean that her sleep wouldn't be broken in the middle of the night by arguing neighbours and wailing infants. Likewise, the smells of the countryside had to be less stomach-turning than those from the tannery or, if the wind was both strong enough and from the wrong direction, from the gasworks. Another bonus was that when she was about her chores, there would be no Head of Housekeeping to keep popping up every couple of minutes and check she wasn't slacking.

Yes, she thought as she stood staring out through the tiny window, her eyes drawn to the evenly spaced rows of apple trees, perhaps the place might not be *entirely* bad after all…

–

'Funny smell.'

Arriving in the kitchen at a little after six o'clock that evening, George Beer came to a halt and sniffed the air, his dirtiness a sight that made May determine to start as she meant to go on; as Miss Shorland had been forever reminding the chambermaids and cleaners at the Sovereign Hotel, you only had one chance to make a first impression.

'Mr Beer,' she replied to his observation, her tone straightforward, 'before you question my attempt to conjure you up a supper out of thin air, please be good enough to go back through there and knock the worst of that mud off your boots.' Noticing Nessa about to follow him in, she went on, 'You too, missy. The kitchen is where I cook your meals, and food and muck don't mix. So, from now on, there's to be no mud beyond the scullery. And *on* the matter of dirt, don't none of you come in here with filthy hands, either. Wash them through there first.'

George Beer teetered uncertainly, his expression that of a man unable to work out what was going on.

Over his shoulder, Nessa raised a single eyebrow. 'Yes, ma'am.'

Behind the pair of them, Bonnie simply grinned.

'From now on, six o'clock means just that. If you're not here, the rest of us start without you, and yours goes cold. And in answer to your question about that *funny smell*, Mr Beer,' May resumed when George eventually returned to sit at the table, 'since all I could find were some taters, two cans of bully beef and a half-dozen tomatoes that looked like they'd given up the will to live, if you're feeling generous you can call it corned beef hash.'

The look that came across George Beer's face was one of even deeper confusion. 'But on Mondays I haves stew.'

'And in future,' May continued, carrying to the table four pottery bowls she'd put to warm in the range, 'if there's something to stew, I'll make you one.' Her sense of satisfaction tinged with concern at the directness of her tone, she sat heavily on the remaining chair. Direct or not, if she was going to do this, she wasn't going to be pushed around. The wage she was being paid was nowhere near enough for that.

Pulling the ladle from where she'd stuffed it into the pocket on the front of her floral apron, she proceeded to dole a decent portion of the hash into the bowl she then handed to Mr Beer, similar quantities into those for the two girls, and the remaining smaller amount into her own. But when no one raised any cutlery or made to start eating, she worried that the directness of her manner had left them all afraid to. Then a different thought occurred. 'Do we say grace?' she asked, looking about the table for confirmation. 'Or are none of us so minded?'

It was Bonnie who replied. 'We don't say it. But we could always start…'

Alongside her, Mr Beer shifted uneasily in his seat.

'No, that's fine.' Presumably, she thought, not wanting to upset the order of things *too* much on her first night, he'd taken her on to make their lives easier, not more fraught. Scant point rubbing them completely up the wrong way. 'Just so long as I know where I stand. So, come on then, tuck in while it's still hot.'

Given the paucity of ingredients, the hash was surprisingly good, such that, within minutes, May found herself looking around the table at three empty bowls.

'Try not to fall out with this one,' Nessa warned Mr Beer. Looking across at him, she leaned back in her chair and pulled her sweater from the waistband of her breeches. 'Try not to make her flee, like you did with the others.'

*Others?*

Determining that Nessa was simply trying to unsettle her, May paid no heed. Better to foster a friendship with the girl, no matter how grudging, than get off on the wrong foot. Besides, Nessa showed the sort of worldliness that Bonnie lacked. And who knew when that sort of insight might prove useful – when she might be able to wheedle out of her answers to the hundreds of questions already washing about in her head?

'Thank you for supper,' Bonnie said as they were all getting to their feet. 'Nicest thing I've had in ages. Would you like me to stop an' lend you a hand with the clearing up?'

May made her smile a warm one. 'Kind of you to offer but no, that's *my* job. You've done your work for the day, so you go and put your feet up… or whatever it is you do.'

'You know, I have to admit,' Nessa observed, straightening the front of her jersey and regarding May as though unsure what to make of her, 'I admire your spunk –

coming in and showing him who's in charge. Hats off to you in that regard.'

'Only doing what he's employing me to,' May replied. Side by side, at least she was a match for the woman's height, if not her build.

'I'm curious, where did you keep house previously?'

From Nessa's tone, May suspected a trap. 'In Exeter, at the Sovereign Hotel.'

The girl shrugged. 'I'm not familiar with it. Why did you leave?'

'The Germans flattened it.'

'Mm. Was it big, this Sovereign Hotel?'

'Largest in Exeter. Fifty-two rooms and the King's Suite.' The girl's questions might sound polite but May knew when she was being sounded out.

'If that's true,' Nessa went on, 'then what on earth are you doing *here*? A bit of a comedown, isn't it?'

In a bid to remain calm, May drew a breath. 'If you'd read the papers or heard the news lately, you'd know why I'm here. The city's in ruins. There's no work to be had anywhere.'

'Did you live in?'

'No,' she replied levelly. 'I lived nearby. But that was bombed too.'

'I see.'

Not so much as a word of commiseration nor murmur of sympathy, May noted. But then girls like Nessa didn't concern themselves with the plight of others. 'By the way,' she said, turning pointedly away. 'Where do he sleep, Mr Beer?'

'Wherever the mood takes him,' Nessa replied, also turning to leave. 'A bit like the cat.'

'In the barn, mostly,' Bonnie more helpfully whispered as Nessa brushed past her. 'Or, that week back in the winter when it was real icy,' she went on, gesturing to the parlour, 'in one of the chairs through there.'

Watching Bonnie follow Nessa out, May stood shaking her head. If Nessa wanted to be unwelcoming and cold, so be it. As for Mr Beer, well, if the man chose to be uncomfortable, that was down to him: his house, his prerogative. But now, for her part, she was going to fetch the sheets she'd found in a drawer – and had the foresight to hang on the line to air – and make up her bed. Then, once she'd cleared up down here, and had a quick flannel wash, she was going to climb onto that nice mattress and hope to sleep like a log. After all, if she was going to get this place – and its occupants – up together, she was going to need all the strength and stamina she could muster: if this afternoon was anything to go by, every single ounce of it.

*III. Blossom*

## Chapter 6

Five days. As she marvelled at the peacefulness of another dawn and inhaled the sweet morning air, May realised that five days was all it had taken for Mr Beer and the girls to fall into line with her routines; for order to suffocate chaos and for living cleanly and tidily to seem like the only sensible way of carrying on. Not that she could afford to feel smug just yet. There was still much she had to fathom about the place, Mr Beer topmost on her list. After all, what sort of man shunned a comfortable bed for a draughty and mouse-infested barn? Given his old bones, it seemed a proper daft way of carrying on. Still, as she kept reminding herself, it was none of her business. She was the housekeeper, not his mother.

Yes, all in all, it was going quite well. She was even growing used to the lack of hurly burly, coming to recognise instead the more muted sounds of the countryside: the sheep on the hillside kept up a constant bleating; the wind whispered through the meadow grasses and rustled the leaves on the trees; and the birds, well, she'd never heard birdsong like it. Catching the dawn chorus for the first time had been nothing short of a revelation.

Continuing to inhale deeply, she lengthened her gaze to the horizon and listened. She supposed someone like Mr Beer could tell which song came from which bird, whereas to her it sounded like two dozen six-year-olds at playtime: a joyous outpouring of shrieks, warbles and trills. And all of it at full throat.

With a light and contented sigh, she wondered what time it was; but rather than fret about being late to start work, she felt light and at ease. With the sun still low in the sky, she could stand a while longer and appreciate the miracle of another new dawn.

In the last day or two, the apple blossom had opened, the specks of magenta that had been peeping from emerald shrouds bursting into a profusion of blushing pinks and snowy whites, the aroma drifting towards her this morning soft and sweet and fresh. And the bees! To make such a deafening hum there must be thousands of them. According to Bonnie, Granny Beer over at Higher Cleave tended a couple of hives, from which she bottled the most fragrant honey, some of it still on the comb. Having never before tasted honey, May imagined it to be sticky and sweet and satisfying, and hoped one day to try some. It would be something to write and tell Clemmie about.

Dearest Clemmie. She did miss her. Ironically, her sister would like it here – not at first, perhaps, but of the two of them Clemmie always had been more easily moved by beauty or joy, or by sadness and pain. She wondered what her sister would be doing right now. Hopefully, at this hour she was comfortable and safe and still asleep. On Monday morning, when they'd been stood together waiting for the bus to depart, her sister had mentioned the possibility of going to lodge with one of the other WVS volunteers. For her sister's sake, she hoped it had come about; knowing Clemmie was all right would ease her guilt. Perhaps, later, she would drop her a line. If she could get on top of her chores this morning, this afternoon she could jot down her news and walk into the village for some stamps. After all, she *had* promised to let her know how she was settling in.

With another light sigh, she went indoors to direct her thoughts to breakfast. Always first to appear in the kitchen each morning was Bonnie, her complexion fresh, her hair brushed and plaited, her stomach growling for a bowl of porridge – on top of which she liked a dollop of damson jam.

By contrast, when Nessa arrived she looked ready for a night out: her hair pinned into a roll; her eyes picked out with lines of black that flicked upwards at the outer edges; her lashes painted and curled. And the colour of her lips would be a match for the breast of the robin that bobbed about in the yard, one eye out for the cat.

This morning, when Nessa proceeded to pull out a chair and sit down, May had to quell a smirk. Who in their right mind put on make-up to work in a field?

'Toast, either of you?' she asked, struggling not to laugh.

'Please,' both girls replied.

To May, that they were eating more in the mornings was a good sign. Bringing the toast to the table, she said, 'Newcombe's van had some bloater paste. If you like, I can make you up a round of sandwiches to go with your cheese an' pickles.'

But while Nessa nodded, Bonnie shook her head. 'Not for me, thanks. Not real keen on bloater.'

'Dripping, then?'

'Only if it won't leave you short.'

'Don't worry, I'll leave some for Mr Beer.'

Bonnie sent her a grateful grin. 'Then yes please.'

Their sandwiches made and the Thermos filled with tea, May wrapped the fare in a tea towel, tied the corners, and handed it to Bonnie. 'You must be almost done with that turnip field by now.'

The expression that flickered across Bonnie's face was unmistakeably one of guilt. 'Could have been done with it Wednesday,' she whispered, nodding towards Nessa's departing back. 'But apparently, there's no point finishing a job early if it means being given something else to do.'

'Is that right?' That Nessa should think only to take advantage rattled May; slackers were one of her pet hates.

'But we'll be done by tonight. Thanks for seeing to our dinn— I mean lunch.'

Watching Bonnie trail behind Nessa across the yard, May smiled. Odd pair, those two, but they seemed to get along right enough. And that, she thought, was all it really needed. The three of them didn't have to be best friends: as long as the work got done, they just had to make the best of the situation and rub along together as well as they could.

–

'Are you sure about this, love? Sure you want to share it?'

'Course I do. Why wouldn't I?'

'Only, it's real generous of you. Isn't it, Nessa?'

It was now Saturday evening and, having overheard at supper that Nessa was going to wash her hair, May had suggested that while she sat waiting for it to dry, the girls join her in the parlour. Her aim had been to get to know the two of them better, the fact that her invitation had taken Nessa by surprise merely a bonus. While she knew deriving pleasure from wrong-footing the girl was mean-spirited, it served to highlight the fact that when it came to the house she, May, was the one in charge.

'You realise that by bringing us in here, you run the risk of upsetting George,' Nessa had remarked, her expression suggesting she suspected a trap. 'Apart from when we're taking our meals, it isn't something he permits.'

'A chance I'll take,' May had replied, turning her attention to Bonnie to ask, 'You washing yours?'

For different reasons, Bonnie had also seemed wary. 'Don't normally do it until tomorrow. But I suppose it couldn't harm.' It was then the girl had suggested they have some of the cocoa her mother had sent her. 'Mum's got it into her head chocolate's going on the ration,' she had explained. 'So, when she saw tins of cocoa, she snapped them up.'

'All the more reason to be sure you want to share it,' May had pointed out.

'Seems only fair, what with you inviting us in.'

Despite the evening being nowhere chilly enough to warrant it, for the benefit of the two girls drying their hair, May had lit a fire, in front of which the three of them were now enjoying their cocoa.

Noticing the pair of needles and the skein of blue wool in the top of Bonnie's bag, she asked, 'What are you knitting?'

'Jumper. Though with the time it's taking me, I'm beginning to think I should have chosen a colour more suited to winter. I can't seem to get the hang of the pattern down the front. Keep having to unpick it and start over.'

'And what is it you're darning?' she went on to enquire, thinking the bright red colour of the silky garment in the girl's lap an unlikely choice for someone of Bonnie's timid disposition.

'Nessa's blouse,' Bonnie said without looking up. 'She's split the seam under the arm.'

From where she was perched on the windowsill, cutting her nails, May felt her fingers curl more tightly about her scissors. 'Why aren't you doing your own darning, Nessa?'

Examining her chin in a small hand mirror, Nessa shrugged. 'Bonnie will make a far better job of it than I ever could. But don't worry, it's not slave labour. In return, I'm going to pluck her eyebrows for her.'

She had to hand it to Nessa – she was sharp, almost too sharp. The thing she had come to dislike about her most, though, was the way she referred to Mr Beer as 'George'. By any measure it was disrespectful but, in Nessa's clipped tones, and since she clearly knew better, it reeked of insolence. What had she yet to find out about the girl, May wondered? Why had Bonnie intimated on several occasions that Mr Beer didn't much like Nessa? What had happened to set the two at odds? Perhaps, in due course, Bonnie could be persuaded to tell.

'And I really should like them done,' Bonnie piped up, prompting May to look across at her eyebrows. The same pale colour as her hair, they were barely discernible. 'Nessa's are lovely.'

'See,' Nessa said, inspecting the reflection of her own arched brows. 'I'm not taking advantage.'

*Just see to it that you don't*, was the warning May held off giving. Yes, Nessa was a sly one all right; the fact that she called herself Nessa Croft when her ration book had her down as Vanessa Hutchison-Croft suggested she wasn't being entirely genuine. Still, May thought, trying to lower her shoulders from where, in her frustration, they had become hunched up around her ears, that was why she

66

had invited the two of them in – to find out more about what went on around here, as well as hopefully fostering some trust.

To that end, she said, 'So, tell me, Mr Beer ever been married?'

'Why?' Nessa immediately asked, her tone dry. 'Taken a fancy to him?'

'We think he's widowed,' Bonnie rather more usefully replied. 'He's never said, it's just an idea I got from old Granny Beer – you know, over at Higher Cleave.'

It would certainly explain a thing or two, May reflected, picturing the locked bedroom door and the man's curious habits. 'And do he only grow apples – aside from the vegetables, I mean?'

Again, it was Bonnie who answered. 'The apples are for cider. He presses it himself. That's why there's all that stuff in the old barn – you know, the one round the back with the hulking great press and all them barrels.'

It was then May realised she had yet to venture beyond the immediate yard.

'Credit where it's due,' Nessa chipped in, 'his cider is good stuff. Strong, but not rough. Some of it he sells by the barrel to public houses, but most of it goes into hogshead for dealers. Oh, and some he keeps for himself.'

'But lately he grows vegetables, too,' May observed.

'Only because he has to,' Bonnie explained. 'To help the war.'

'And only then under threat of action from the War Ags.'

'War Ags?' It wasn't a term with which May was familiar.

'The War Agricultural Executive Committees.'

'Part of the Ministry of Agriculture and Fisheries,' Nessa expanded. 'To make sure the nation has enough food, every county has War Ags to plan and control what's grown – how much of it, when, and so on.' When May frowned, Nessa went on, 'Look, say we don't have enough wheat. The government will determine how much extra we need, then divide that amount between the counties where it can be grown. The counties then divide it between the districts, and the districts between their farms.'

To May, it seemed a clever way to get the job done. 'I see.'

'The idea is that by giving control to people with first-hand knowledge of local difficulties such as terrain or water supply, the farmers get help and advice from people who understand their individual circumstances. War Ags can recommend a farmer be given fertilisers that are right for his land, or pest control or even equipment. It's how George has a tractor – when he only had orchards, he didn't need one, but ploughing up meadows meant he did.'

To May, this was all enlightening stuff. 'I see.'

'Of course, there's a downside, too. Knowing so much about individual farms gives the War Ags power. And since the countryside is rife with centuries-old grudges, some farmers object to having their peers telling them what to do. Hence the resentment.'

'I can understand that.' May knew what it was like to have someone constantly watching over even the simplest of tasks, tasks there was no earthly way to do any differently. To her mind, farming had to be much the same: there could only be one way to grow an apple or a turnip.

'Mr Beer don't like 'em at all,' Bonnie chipped in. 'Makes no secret of it. *Ruddy meddling busybodies*, he calls them.'

'Which isn't surprising when you realise that if a farmer doesn't comply with War Ag instructions, they can recommend he be removed from his land and someone new put in.'

'Really? They can do that?' To May, wartime or not, it seemed draconian.

'They can and they do.'

Then no wonder Mr Beer never looked happy. 'And it's these War Ags telling him to grow vegetables.'

'That's right. They came last year to survey here and Higher Cleave. That's when they told George to plough up a couple of the meadows and sow vegetables. They told him he could have fertilisers to improve the soil and help meet yields but, according to him, the amount they sent was nowhere near enough. You see, what most people don't understand is that meadows generally have poor fertility, and that's before considering the question of irrigation and drainage. Very few farmers can just plough up some grass, sow some seeds and get a decent crop. When it comes to having good soil, it *is* possible to just be lucky, but more usually it needs years and years of hard work, which no one in their right mind would put into a meadow they don't use.'

'So, he's a bit hard done by, then,' May observed, surprised by the extent of Nessa's knowledge on the matter, especially since it seemed unlikely she hailed from farming folk.

'In some ways, he is. But no worse than a lot of other people. Besides, isn't everyone hard done by in wartime? Would the three of us be here if we had a choice?'

'True,' May agreed, reminded of her own circumstances.

'There you go, look.' Raising the sleeve of Nessa's blouse, Bonnie tugged at the darn to test that it would hold. 'That should do you.'

Taking the garment from her, Nessa nodded. 'I'll do your eyebrows tomorrow, in better light. It's too dark in here now.'

'All right. Thanks.'

One by one, May thought as she got into bed that night, she was unlocking some of the place's many puzzles. Moreover, while Bonnie might be shy, and Nessa Croft might play her cards close to her chest, she was starting to feel as though she was slowly winning them over. Keep it up, and it wouldn't be long before not only did she have the place running to her liking, but she had it running harmoniously, too.

–

Blast. As cross as she was dismayed, May stared down at her sheet of notepaper: a blob of ink from the nib of her pen had dropped onto the last line of her writing! Until that had happened, she'd only made one small mistake. But now look at it. Curse her stupid pen for leaking right at the very end like that!

Disinclined to go to the bother of rewriting the entire letter – after all, who was to say it wouldn't happen again? – and knowing that as long as it was news, Clemmie would overlook the smudge, May settled instead for reading aloud what she had written.

> *Dearest Clemmie,*
>    *I hope you are well.*

Pausing to glance over her shoulder and check that she was still alone, she cleared her throat and continued.

*I have now been here just over a week and I suppose you could say I am as settled as can be expected. After the ruins of Exeter, this place do truly feel like another world. Not long after I got here, the apple trees all burst into blossom at once. It is quite the sight. And there is so much space and so much quiet that my first few days I felt a proper fish out of water. But already I am grown used to it.*

*So far away from everything, there are very few signs of the war. Other than grumble about rationing, folk seem to carry on much as they always have done. We have rabbit and pigeon to eat, and I'm told sometimes lamb from the farm next door, though I have not had the fortune to have any of that yet. There is also plenty of cheese from there, too, if you don't mind it being made from ewes' milk.*

*From what I can gather, there have been no air raids here, though apparently, when we had those first ones in Exeter back in April, a single bomb fell near the cattle market and around that same time, a Jerry plane came down in a farmer's field.*

*On the farm are land girls called Bonnie and Nessa. Two more different souls you would struggle to find. The farmer, who is called Mr Beer, is the most private and secretive man I ever met. He has no time at all for the land girls. But I think that is because they are here to grow vegetables and he has no interest in doing that. Seems to me his apple trees are his whole world. He's a funny feller all right. Anyway, now that I have the place a bit more up together, the work is not too bad and leaves me some time to myself.*

*Well, I hope this letter reaches you without too much delay and I am sorry I did not get around to writing until now. I did sorely mean to, but you will know how it is. Are you still ~~volent~~ volunteering with the WVS? Do you see much of Pearl? Please let me know soonest where you are staying and how you are going along.*

*With warmest love,*

*Your sister May*

Satisfied with what she had written, May let out a sigh. It was strange to think of Clemmie and Pearl still being in Exeter – even more strange not to know what they were doing. Had they found somewhere to live? Had they found work? Did they miss her? It was unlikely Pearl did, but for certain Clemmie would. Strangely, while she missed both – albeit in different ways – the ache for her old life was already beginning to fade, only surfacing when she stopped to wonder whether the two of them were all right. When she was busy the hours flew, and she barely gave either of them a thought. She supposed it came from being in new surroundings, where the three of them had never been together.

Folding the sheet of notepaper in half and slipping it into the envelope upon which she had already written Clemmie's name and the address of the WVS centre, she put it to one side. Later, once the weekly wash had dried on the line and she had fetched it in, she would walk into the village and buy some stamps.

The thought of the post office made her smile; Nan Parker would probably be surprised to see her – would no doubt have been expecting that, the moment she'd got here, she would have thrown up her hands in horror and gone straight back to Exeter. To be fair, she almost had. Even so, the woman should know better than to judge a person by their shoes. And while a pair of fancy brown lace-ups with two-inch heels clearly hadn't been the wisest choice for country lanes and farmyards, they didn't mean she was flighty. Had she known what lay in store for her, she would have picked a pair of flat brogues instead. But, as Nan Parker would come to realise, and as she suspected Nessa was already beginning to, there was more to May Huxford than met the eye, certainly more than her unfortunate choice of footwear might lead them to believe!

# Chapter 7

At the time, the idea had seemed a sensible one.

'Borrow the bike,' Bonnie had blithely suggested when May explained she was going into the village.

Immediately, she had dismissed the idea as foolhardy. But eventually – despite knowing that the only time she'd ever ridden a bicycle was when, at the age of about eight, Tommy Willcocks had helped her to wobble up and down the back alley on one he'd found in the canal – she had relented. The prospect of cutting down the time it would take her to get there and back was a considerable part of the draw, especially after the morning she'd had. What she'd hadn't been prepared for, though, was just how boneshaking an experience it would turn out to be, nor quite how much effort would be required even to simply pedal the thing along on the level. Once or twice, she had almost toppled off. On another occasion, having failed to avoid a particularly deep rut, she'd veered onto the verge, only narrowly avoiding ending up in the ditch. Grateful to have somehow made it to the village in one piece, the return journey was something upon which she decided not to dwell.

'So, love,' Nan Parker greeted her. If she was surprised to see her, she didn't show it. 'How are you finding things at Fair Maids Farm?'

'Oh, much as I expected,' May replied evenly. 'Gradually getting it up together.'

'Good for you, dear. Just the weather for a bit of a belated spring-clean.'

'That's right.' The less she said, May thought, the less likely she was to give anything away.

'So, what can I do for you today?'

Her stamps purchased, and her letter dropped into the postbox, May returned to the dreaded bicycle, the prospect of having to ride it home making her wish she'd never gone along with Bonnie's suggestion in the first place. Still, she supposed as she steered it across the road towards Church Lane, when she reached the stretch that was particularly badly rutted she could always get off and wheel it. Though it might make for slow progress, it seemed preferable to falling off.

Walking with a bicycle, though, turned out to be just as wearying as actually riding the thing, a fact she discovered when the increasing effort required to keep the thing going along saw her wobbling to a halt, climbing off, and trying to work out what was wrong. It was then she'd noticed that the front tyre had gone flat. Since it hadn't been that way when she'd set off, she supposed it had a puncture. Blast the thing. Now what was she going to do?

Exhaling a sigh of despair, she stared down at the wheel. On the frame was one of those hand-pump things but, even had she known how to use it, where was the point getting all hot and bothered if, just a few hundred yards on, the tyre was just going to go flat all over again?

Tired, hot and exasperated, she let out a growl and pushed the wretched thing into the hedge. It could stay there. She would walk home. If either of the girls wanted to use it, Nessa would have to come for it with the tractor. But as she turned away, two things brought her to a stop: firstly, her conscience wouldn't let her just abandon it; secondly, Nessa would have a field day. *You don't know how to pump up a bicycle tyre?*

And so, having wrestled the infernal contraption back out of the hedge, she was now plodding along, her left shin smarting from where she'd twice caught it with the pedal, the back of her hand burning from where she'd brushed against a stinging nettle. Still, she reasoned, looking up after a while to notice that she was barely halfway back, it could be worse: at least it wasn't threatening rain.

Some distance further on, she heard the sound of an engine and turned to see a cloud of dust being thrown up by a little tractor. As it drew closer and she wheeled the bicycle up onto the grass to be out of its way, she saw that riding in the trailer, ears cocked, nose in the air, was a black and white dog.

When he'd drawn almost level with her, the driver slowed the machine to a stop and, leaving the engine idling, jumped down. Snatching his tweed cap from his head as though by way of afterthought, he came towards her.

'Everything all right there, miss?'

Taking in his features, she felt her eyes widen. Not only was he a good three decades younger than she'd been expecting, but he looked like a more youthful version of George; the line from his nose to his chin was identical. Clearly, with his dark eyes and wavy hair, he had to be the son of the other Mr Beer and, by that token, George's nephew – not that George had ever mentioned having one. But then he'd never mentioned the other Mr Beer, either.

'Puncture,' she said, flushing and gesturing to the front of the bicycle.

Moving to look, the man stooped to examine her front wheel. 'It's flat all right.'

Really? Hadn't *she* just told *him* that? 'It is indeed.'

'You must be Mrs Huxford.'

More consternation: he knew who she was. 'May… Huxford. Yes.'

'Fair Maids' new housekeeper.'

'Yes.'

'Well then, Mrs Huxford—'

'Please,' she said. Allowing someone so close to her own age to address her as 'Mrs' made her squirm. 'You should call me May.'

Seeing his lips twitch, she blushed. Clearly, she had overstepped.

'Well then, May. Let's put this ancient heap in the back and I'll give you a lift home. As long as you don't mind riding in the trailer.'

For the luxury of a ride home, she would happily bear the humiliation of arriving in the yard like a bale of hay.

'Only if it's no trouble.'

'Wouldn't offer if 'twas,' he said, moving to grasp the handlebars of her bicycle. 'Here, keep hold of your bag.'

Snatching her handbag from the basket on the front, May waited until he had lifted the bike from the ground and then followed him along the side of the tractor. Painted grey, it bore the name *Ferguson* in fancy script above the radiator.

'I'm Dan, by the way,' he said, quickly wiping his hand down the side of his overalls before extending it towards her.

'May,' she said, reaching to shake it and then blushing wildly. What an idiot! 'Sorry. I've already said.'

Her bike laid flat on the trailer, and with May perching as instructed on a little wooden bench at the front, Dan climbed back into the driver's seat, sent her a grin and pulled away. 'Tell you what,' he shouted a moment later, 'if we go back to *our* yard, I could see to your tyre for you.'

Although she would prefer to go straight home, May nodded. Despite having been on the point of abandoning the thing, it did make sense to get it fixed; Bonnie and Nessa relied on it to get into the village and having it out of action would be an inconvenience for them.

'Thank you,' she called towards him. 'If you're sure.'

The entrance to Higher Cleave Farm was several hundred yards further along the lane from the track leading to Fair Maids, and May's first thought as they drove through it was that it was altogether tidier, the gate closing smartly, the name plaque on the brick pillar neat and legible. The approach had fewer potholes too. In fact, as Dan drew the tractor to a halt in the yard behind the house and she looked around, the general air was one of organisation and purpose. There was still a good deal of mud – the place *was* a working sheep farm – but the sense she got was one of industry, even of moderate prosperity. This part of the Beer family clearly knew what they were doing.

In a workshop at the far corner of the yard, Dan found a wooden stool, which, after giving it a quick wipe with a cloth, he set down for her to sit on. 'Shouldn't take too long,' he said brightly.

'I'm just real grateful to you for your effort.'

Within moments, Dan had levered the tyre from the wheel and was inspecting the inner tube. 'Can't see a tear. So, once I find the hole, I should be able to patch it.'

Feeling uncomfortable to be just sitting there while he did all the work, May glanced around. The dog who'd been sat in the trailer was now stretched out just inside the door, eyes closed but one ear twitching.

'What's your dog's name?' she asked.

'That's Flash,' Dan said without looking up. Hearing its name, the dog raised its head. 'On account of the white stripe through her face. Border collie. Reliable with sheep.'

'She's pretty.'

Dan paused before continuing. 'Word is you're from Ex'ter. Bombed out, they say.'

If she had a shilling for everyone who already knew that…

'Yes.'

'Right, well, here's your problem. Hole so small I can barely see it. I'll have that patched in no time.'

'You're very kind.'

His attention back on the tyre, Dan shrugged. 'Always help if you can. Out here, you never know when you might be stuck yourself.'

'That's how I try to be, too.'

'Best way.'

Watching him at work, she wondered whether to risk asking him what had happened to create a rift between the two parts of the family – for something clearly had. Why else did the two Mr Beers have nothing to do with one another? If she was careful and kept her questions broad, he might fill her in on some family history. On the other hand, he was already doing her a sizeable favour, and so the last thing she wanted was to risk coming across as nosy.

Eventually, growing uncomfortable with the continuing silence, she said, 'It's a very long time since I've ridden a bike.'

'Yeah?'

'In Exeter, we walked everywhere.' Dear God, now she was just prattling.

'Well, you know what they say.'

She studied his expression. Since he was fitting the tyre back onto the rim, it seemed to be one of concentration. 'Um...'

'You never forget how to ride one.'

She laughed. 'Oh. Yes. Although, after this afternoon, I'm not sure I believe that.'

'Well, there you go,' he said, righting the bicycle and propping it against the bench. 'All done. But you'll have to wheel it back. And then leave it overnight for the glue to dry.'

'Yes. Of course. I will. Well, thank you for all your effort,' she said, gesturing towards the bike. 'I'm indebted.'

'Think nothing of it.' He grinned broadly. 'Well, off you go. But just remember, give the glue a chance to dry or you'll be accusing me of shoddy workmanship.'

'Hardly,' she murmured, taking the handlebars from him and wheeling the ancient machine out into the yard.

Several minutes later, steering it through the dilapidated gate into Fair Maids Farm, May glanced back to the white farmhouse nestled on the hillside. How different could two farms possibly be? Here, everything felt rundown and neglected, whereas just a couple of fields away the impression was one of purpose. One day, she would have to find out what had happened to set the two farms on such different courses – would have to establish over what the two men had fallen out, and who had been at fault. If nothing else, it might help her to understand Mr Beer and his curious ways. But for now, she had more important matters with which to concern herself, supper being topmost among them.

Propping the bike against the wall, she looked up to see Bonnie and Nessa returning from the fields.

'You didn't fall off then,' Bonnie called towards her.

'Cheeky madam. No, I did not. Though, to be honest, there were one or two close shaves. Bloomin' potholes.'

'You got to be careful.'

'Hm. By the way,' she said casually, brushing at a mark on the hem of her jacket; thankfully, it didn't look to be grease, 'no one told me we've got a good-looking neighbour.'

'You met Dan?'

The sharpness of Nessa's tone made May turn in surprise to regard her. 'Unless we've more than one.'

'Where was he?'

Why the sudden interest, May wondered? 'Along the lane,' she replied, her tone deliberately airy. 'We had quite the chat.' She was only doing it for devilment. Had Nessa not shown such a curious interest, she would have said no more. 'Very helpful, he was. Jolly convenient having *him* as a neighbour.'

'You do know he's George's nephew, don't you?'

To May, it felt as though Nessa was sending her a warning. Well, she would take no notice. 'Hard to miss *that* likeness.'

'He is very nice,' Bonnie said. 'Always chirpy and friendly.'

'So I noticed.'

Bonnie was right; Dan did seem friendly. He was certainly too nice for Nessa – if that was her game. Perhaps she should keep an eye on her, just in case. No sense letting the girl lark about and cause an upset, especially since, if everyone at Higher Cleave was as neighbourly as Dan, it might be a good idea to become acquainted. After all, they did live just across the fields. And as Dan himself had remarked, out here, you never knew when you might find yourself needing help…

Bloomin' drawer. Now what was the matter with it? It always had been a struggle to close, but today it seemed even more reluctant than usual.

It was after supper that same evening and, minded to go for a stroll before retiring for the night, May had gone to fetch a cardigan. But now, having found the garment in question, she had to work out what was wrong with this drawer.

Kneeling in front of it, she tugged it open and then heaved it all the way out. She switched on her torch and bent low to direct the paltry beam of light into the gap. No wonder it wouldn't close; there was something stopping it. Scrabbling lower, she reached in and felt about. Her fingers landed on what felt like a book, about the size of her mother's book of prayer.

Sitting back on her haunches, she turned it over and ran a hand across the jacket. A pocket-sized volume, the cover bore a gaily coloured illustration of a buttercup, its title reading *A Guide to the Wildflowers of Devon*. It was clearly old, the smell from its pages reminding her of school, and of being allowed to choose something to read: warm pepper, damp earth, tangy resin, aromas that, when smelled together, hinted at thrilling adventures in mystical lands.

Opening the cover, she noticed that on the flyleaf someone had written the initials *JB*. When she'd first pulled it out from behind the drawer, she'd supposed it had belonged to Alma. But *JB* suggested someone with the surname Beer. John? Joseph? Jane? Idly, she flicked through the pages, a drawing entitled *Purple Campion* catching her eye; she'd seen that plant growing down by the gate. She turned the page. *Wild Carrot*. Just this afternoon, trailing along with that bloomin' bicycle, she'd been head-high in that same white froth. Fascinated, she continued to scan the illustrations: Bird's-Foot Trefoil; Meadow Cranesbill; Yellow Rattle. Such intriguing names.

With that, she had an idea. What if she learned to put names to the flowers she saw? With this book to guide her, she could see how many of them she could find; it could become a sort of challenge, and bring purpose to her strolls. In fact, since she'd been about to go out anyway, she would take it with her now.

The drawer replaced, she pulled on her cardigan, tucked a handkerchief into her sleeve, picked up the book and went downstairs. From the yard, she headed through the wicket and into the orchard. Earlier, she'd thought she might try to find the stream but, now that she was later setting off, she wouldn't go too far; before long it would be dusk, and she had no idea what hazards might trip her up.

Having decided not to stray too far from the house, her attention was caught by the same patch of white blooms she'd seen a week or so back. In the bright sunlight, their whiteness had dazzled like sheets rinsed in bluing; this evening, despite being in deep shadow, they appeared to glow as though reflecting moonlight. Surely such a bold and simple flower ought to be easy to identify?

She flicked through the pages, drawing to a halt at an illustration entitled *Ox-Eye Daisy. Daisies*. Of course – like the saying *fresh as a daisy*, and like the tiny ones in the grass on Cathedral Green, the ones that closed every night and opened again every morning.

Although pleased to have identified something, she was also a mite disappointed. A daisy? Surely she could do better than that.

Following the path worn into the grass, she found her eye drawn to where, beyond the lower edge of the orchard, a swathe of creamy yellow was rippling in the breeze. As she drew closer, she saw it comprised hundreds of tiny nodding heads. In her excitement to identify them, she knelt in the grass and leafed through the pages. Golly, this book had a lot of yellow flowers! One by one, she scanned the pictures: too big; wrong shape; nothing like it. Oh, but wait, here they were. *Clusters of tiny egg-yolk-coloured bells held on upright stems.* She glanced to the top of the page. Cowslip. They were called cowslips. She'd named another one. Who would have thought putting names to flowers would feel so satisfying?

Getting to her feet, she brushed at the hem of her dress. What a little gem this book was turning out to be. How fortunate to have found it. Yes, she knew it wasn't hers but, since there was no one in the house with the initials JB, she couldn't imagine anyone objecting to her using it. From now on, she would bring it every time she came out for a walk; she would make it her mission to know the names of as many plants as she could.

Turning back in the direction of the yard, she smiled. Had someone told her, back on the day she'd arrived here, that she would so quickly come to feel at home in this funny little place, she would have eyed them with mistrust. Without question, there would still be ups and downs; there were bound to be days when she would question her sanity. Mr Beer was a peculiar soul; Nessa displayed rather a lot of what her mother would have called 'side'; the farmhouse itself was little more than a crumbling hovel, not to mention miles from anywhere. But, if she was prepared to keep an open mind and continue putting herself out, she was beginning to think that life at Fair Maids Farm could turn out to be rather more rewarding than she had first imagined...

*IV. Petal Fall*

## Chapter 8

Rubbing the sleep from her eyes, May bent to look out through her bedroom window. It was another glorious dawn, the meadows draped in the sheerest of misty veils, a light dew glinting on the grass. So captivating was the scene that she felt moved to go out and be a part of it – to bathe in the pale light and inhale the cool fresh air. Moreover, since the apple blossom would soon be finished, she felt bound to enjoy the spectacle of it while she still could. A couple of days ago she'd noticed the first petals starting to fall but, while it was enchanting to see it fluttering to the grass like confetti at a wedding, it was also a confounded nuisance, sticking to the soles of shoes and being tramped into the house.

Watching now, as a shower of pink and white drifted to the ground, she sighed. When she'd remarked to Mr Beer that it was a shame to see such pretty flowers coming to an end, he'd laughed. Without petal fall, he'd said, there would be no apples. It was the natural way of things: bees pollinated the flowers so the blossom could beget fruit. Inevitable or not, she still thought it sad that such a breathtaking sight should be so fleeting.

Fastening the buttons of her blouse, she went downstairs and let herself out through the scullery. At the little wicket gate, she raised the latch and went into the orchard.

Through the trees, alive with the hum of nectar gathering, she spotted Mr Beer and craned to see what he was doing. With the palm of one hand pressed flat against a particularly stout trunk, he appeared to be gazing up into the crown. And although she couldn't be sure, as he stood, pipe in hand, it appeared that his lips were moving. Intrigued, she lifted the hem of her dress, stole through the dewy grass, and secreted herself behind one of the trees closer to. People who talked to things were usually held to be mad but, while Mr Beer was certainly odd, he'd still seemed a way off losing his marbles. She wouldn't mind hearing what he was saying, even so.

In a way, she felt sorry for him; his feelings for his land and his trees clearly ran deep, learning that he'd been told to plough up meadows making her indignant on his behalf. After a lifetime spent growing apples and making cider, he was now being forced to grow something in which he had no interest whatsoever and for which, according to Nessa, his land wasn't well suited. In addition, he had these War Ag fellows breathing down his neck, waiting to pounce if he didn't measure up. And to help him with all of it, he had but two land girls, who might as well have come from the moon for all he could probably relate to them – and they to him. It was a shame he didn't have a family. Even just one son to learn the ropes would surely have eased his burden.

On the other hand, his plight wasn't unique; he wasn't the only one being ordered to grow new and unfamiliar crops. From what Nessa had said, whether they liked it or not, farmers everywhere were having to change their ways. And since, out in the wider world, working men were being drafted to fight the enemy, it seemed only right that farmers pitched in and shouldered some of the nation's difficulties, too. Besides, if ordinary folk could find space to raise vegetables around an Andersen shelter in their back garden, they could hardly be difficult to grow, could they? It wasn't as though he'd been instructed to dig up his orchards; it was only empty meadows he'd been told to plough and plant. Looked at like that, she did have to wonder why he was being so stubborn.

Watching him withdraw his hand from the trunk and return his pipe to his mouth, she felt a twinge of guilt. Since matters beyond the farmhouse were none of her business, who was she to question his way of carrying on? She shouldn't be spying on him, either, even if he did have some peculiar habits. If he spotted her, he'd be mortified – as would she.

Cheeks burning, she dropped her gaze. It was time she got back indoors anyway. The girls would be up soon, and she did like to have things shipshape before they came in for their breakfast. As Bonnie so often remarked of their need to rise with the lark six mornings out of every seven, there really was no rest for the wicked. So, whatever Mr Beer was up to, she would leave him to it and direct her energy to her own tasks. It wasn't as though there weren't plenty of them!

–

The sigh May heaved was one of exhaustion. She hadn't stopped for a moment all day. But now, with the supper things cleared and her chores for the day done, she could finally sit down. On the other hand… Going to peer out at the small square of sky visible through the kitchen window, she changed her mind. Just as restful would be to take her wildflower book and go for a stroll – perhaps venture a little farther afield this time; apart from her couple of brief forays into the orchard, she'd seen very little of the wider farm. So, yes, that's what she would do.

Having pulled on her cardigan and collected her book, she set off between the outbuildings and, finding herself after a while on a path trodden into the lush grass, decided to follow it. A short distance on, the grasses gave way to an area of cultivated ground, home to long rows of tiny seedlings. Those nearest-to had rounded silvery-green leaves that put her in mind of cabbages. Taking in the patterns made by the evenly spaced rows, her eyes came to rest upon a pair of stocky wood pigeons, who every now and again broke off from sauntering up and down to peck at the leaves. Incensed, she waved her arms and ran at them. With considerable reluctance, they took flight, the clap-clap-clap of their wings seeming in protest as they lumbered up from the ground.

Pausing to look about, she noted that the field appeared well-tended, with few signs of weeds; only as she peered between the young plants did she notice that the soil was pale and parched. In places it was even cracking. But then there hadn't been much rain of late – certainly none of note.

By contrast to the first plot, the one she came upon next was overrun with weeds. Among them she recognised the same white bell flowers that grew up – that *used* to grow up – the chestnut fence separating the school playground from Chandlery Street, except that here they scrabbled low over the ground, only rising upwards to strangle the occasional thistle or dandelion.

Continuing further still, she saw what she supposed to be the detested turnips, their leaves resembling those of the bunches of radishes she used to buy from Sidley's barrow. She loved a hot and fiery radish in a sandwich, but neither Clemmie nor Pearl could stand them.

Thoughts of her sisters bringing a pang of homesickness, she lifted her gaze just in time to catch movement; among the greenery was something small and grey-brown in colour. Was it… rabbits? Yes! And they were eating the turnip tops.

Raising her arms above her head, she made a shooing noise and ran towards them. Ahead of her, a dozen or more white bobtails zigzagged into the distance. Sadly, driving them off was probably futile; they would doubtless come straight back the moment she left, the pickings too easy and too rich to resist.

Drawing a long breath of the evening air, she turned her gaze towards Higher Cleave. It seemed peculiar that both farms should be in the hands of the same family and yet, as far as she knew, no one ever went between them; peculiar that Bonnie and Nessa should know the occupants, but that Mr Beer never spoke of them – not that he ever uttered more than a dozen words about anything. Were it not for the meals she put in front of him, she doubted he would trouble the inside of the house at all.

Distracted now from her original purpose, she decided to turn back. She had a feeling that, were it not for Bonnie and Nessa, this place would have fallen apart some time ago. Even *with* their help it seemed to be going to the dogs. But why? Where was Mr Beer's pride? Didn't he want to do his bit? Some men would give their right arm for a place like this, for the chance to support themselves and not have to worry so much about getting vegetables and fruit to eat, let alone milk and eggs. In fact, when it came to certain foods, it was easy to forget there was a war on at all. Perhaps that was the problem: perhaps George Beer didn't know how lucky he was.

Returning over a different path to the one she'd come by, May found herself on the far side of the outbuildings. Taking in a cob-walled barn with a thatched roof, she supposed it was the one where Bonnie had said Mr Beer pressed the apples into cider. Seeing the door hanging open, she went towards it, the smell as she approached pungent and ripe.

With a quick check over her shoulder first, she climbed the couple of stone steps and peered into the near darkness beyond. To her right was all manner of paraphernalia: a wooden ramp; something that appeared to be a chute; a metal hopper with a large wheel and what looked to be mincing blades in the bottom. On the floor was strewn pale straw, along the left-hand wall barrels ranging in size from those that would stand on the bar of a public house to others that could easily accommodate a full-grown man. But most striking, and dwarfing all else, was what she assumed to be the press itself. A couple of feet up from the ground, its hefty wooden platform was seven or eight feet across, at its front edge a spout, up through its centre a massive iron pole with a screw thread, at the top of which was a substantial wooden plinth. Presumably, she thought, eyeing the device with interest, the fruit was put on the bottom platform and pressed by lowering the one above, the apple juice running out through the spout into a receptacle placed for the purpose. And from there, she supposed it went into the barrels to ferment.

The fumes alone making her light-headed, she stepped back outside and, looking around, decided to find her way back through the orchard. But as she rounded the end of the barn, she saw Mr Beer fiddling with something hanging from one of the trees, at his feet a rectangular gallon tin with a screw lid. Making no attempt to disguise her approach, she continued towards him, greeting her nose as she drew nearer the aroma of something sour and sharp. Vinegar, perhaps?

Having heard her coming, George stepped back from the tree and removed his pipe. As he did so, she noticed that suspended by a string from one of the branches was a tin can with circles cut from the sides.

'Traps,' he said when he saw her looking. Replacing his pipe in his mouth, he went on, 'Codling moths.'

Momentarily thrown by the fact that he'd been first to speak, she said, 'Is it vinegar inside?'

'Cider vinegar and a bit o' sugar. The smell attracts them.'

'Oh.' She supposed the trap acted in the same way as a jam jar to a wasp: the creature went in and then, unable to get out again, drowned.

'Got to keep the dead ones emptied out and the vinegar topped up else the smell goes off.'

'And then they wouldn't be lured in.'

'Hatch about now, late May, the moths do. Tiny little buggers. Moment the flower's been pollinated, they show up an' lay their eggs. Then the caterpillars bore into the new fruit and stay there, gorging on the insides until they're minded to come out. Lose your entire apple crop to 'em, you can.'

'But these traps stop that happening.'

'Provided you keep watch.'

There was so much she wanted to ask this man and yet she couldn't picture there ever being the right moment. Already, after what was for him a lengthy discourse, he had withdrawn and their conversation was seemingly at an end.

Feeling the breeze getting up, her eyes fell upon the nearest branch and what was left of the blossom. The sight of such dainty petals browning at the edges brought a pang of wistfulness. But with it came something else: a sense of urgency; a call to act – although to act how, she had no idea. All she knew for certain was that she felt drawn to do something. Despite having been there no time at all, she had come to feel a sense of protectiveness towards this peculiar little place and its odd and insular owner, not to mention a powerful desire to prevent things slipping from his control. Even to her untrained eye, it was clear that Bonnie and Nessa could be put to better use – Bonnie for her eagerness and Nessa for what she suspected to be a decent understanding of what had to be done. But what the place was crying out for most, she realised, was someone to take charge – for Mr Beer to see what could be gained by all of them working together.

While she couldn't be the only one of them to have seen as much, didn't the fact that she had behove her to act? After all, if what Nessa said about the power of these War Ags was true, and through his inaction and unwillingness to change Mr Beer lost the farm, then all four of them would be out on their ears. And for so many reasons, that would be a terrible crime – a crime she couldn't simply stand by and allow to happen.

# Chapter 9

'Excuse me, Mrs Beer?'

It was now Monday morning and, startled from where she had been at the copper, boiling the sheets she'd just stripped from the beds in the lean-to, May turned to find two men peering in through the door.

'Mrs Huxford,' she corrected them, her senses immediately on alert; anyone who knew Fair Maids Farm would also know there *was* no Mrs Beer. Noting their flat caps and tweed jackets, and how they wore their corduroy trousers tucked into wellingtons, she immediately marked them down as farmers. 'And you would be?'

'I'm Mr Robinson and this is Mr Stone. We're from the Devonshire County War Agricultural Executive Committee.'

May stiffened. *War Agricultural Executive Committee?* Wasn't that the dreaded War Ags? Reaching to dry her hands on a strip of towel, she tried to conceal her panic by giving a light laugh. 'Well, there's a mouthful an' no mistake.'

'Yes,' the second man, Stone, continued unmoved. 'And we've come to follow up with Mr Beer about the potatoes.'

May frowned. 'Potatoes?'

'The crop he was instructed to plant, and that should be in the ground by now.'

'*For* which,' the second man continued, 'if he's done as instructed, we should be able to find a requisition.'

'But there isn't one.'

*Requisition?* What the devil was one of those when it was at home?

'And we've given him the best part of two months to comply.'

Although she was perspiring from the heat of the fire under the copper, May shivered. 'Don't know nothing about that,' she said, wondering whether to go and find Mr Beer or whether, if she said he was out, these two might go away. 'I've only been here a few weeks.' If there was going to be any awkwardness, fetching Nessa might be of more use. Or would it? If it came down to it, could she be relied upon to take the right side?

'Then perhaps you could take us straight to Mr Beer.'

Glancing over her shoulder to the copper, May had no idea what to do for the best: did she get involved or did she stay out of it?

'Well,' she said, giving them a deliberately uncertain look, 'I'm right in the middle of a boil wash… which, as any housewife will tell you, can't be left unattended…'

'Then we'll find Mr Beer for ourselves,' the man called Robinson said. 'And we're sorry to have troubled you.'

'No matter, I'm sure.' With the two visitors starting across the yard, May wiped at the beads of perspiration on her forehead and tried to think. Instinct told her this wasn't going to end well; Mr Beer might have been told to plant potatoes, but she was certain he had done nothing of the sort. At the very least, she would have heard the girls talking about them.

Well, whatever she chose to do next, before setting off to warn him, she ought first to lift the sheets from the copper and put them in the sink. But how to track him down without being seen by those two busybodies? And even if she succeeded in finding him before they did, what was she expecting him to do? If he hadn't complied with an order to plant potatoes, what could he do about that now?

Staring at the sink full of steaming sheets, she eventually came down in favour of finding Nessa. If Nessa knew where to find Mr Beer, she could warn him.

But Nessa, by the time May tracked her down to the cabbage field, was already in the company of the War Ags men, and was leaning on a hoe, gesturing broadly.

Thwarted, May turned back; no sense getting in the middle of it now. Despite her concerns about what might happen, it wasn't her job to shield Mr Beer from the scrutiny of the Ministry of Agriculture and Fisheries. In fact, having to face the consequences of ignoring official instructions might be just the fillip he needed – might persuade him to knuckle down and get on with it.

Back in the scullery, having threaded the rinsed sheets through the mangle, she went out to peg them on the washing line in the orchard. Since first light, the sky this morning had had a different look to it, leading her to sense that a change was in the offing. After weeks of fair weather and just the one night of rain, the clouds today were more ragged, their edges dun-grey, the wind funnelling them up the valley coming from the coast rather than from the drier easterly direction. The hot parched spell was about to break, she'd put money on it. She'd also put money on the likelihood that where these two War Ag fellows were concerned, trouble was brewing. And no matter how many times she tried to persuade herself it had nothing to do with her, she had a feeling that if she wanted to hang on to this job, she might have to get involved nonetheless.

Back indoors a while later, she tried to distract herself by preparing supper. In line with Mr Beer's preferences, today it was to be stew, although since there wasn't much to go in it, she had better knock up some suet dumplings for the top.

'Ah, Mrs… uh, Mrs…'

'Huxford,' she said shortly, turning back from the pantry to see one of the two War Ags men peering from the scullery into the kitchen – Stone, was it? 'And don't you even *think* about coming in here in those boots.'

Reddening all the way up his neck and then as far as his forehead, the man backed out. 'Begging your pardon.'

Following him through, May ran her floury hands under the tap and then dried them on the corner of her apron. Stepping out into the yard, she tried to conceal how badly she was suddenly trembling. From the expression on Stone's face, she thought he looked distinctly displeased. 'What can I do for you?'

'We have been unable to locate Mr Beer.'

'Don't surprise me. It's a big old place. He could be anywhere.'

'But we did find your… his… two girls from the Women's Land Army,' Robinson continued.

Deliberately, May made to start back inside. 'Right-o. Well, good day to you then.'

'No, Mrs… er, Huxford,' Stone picked up. 'I'm afraid we can't leave without seeing him.'

Turning back, May shrugged. 'No?'

'We have to present him with our findings. With our report.'

'Happen you'll want to leave it with me, then,' she said, the directness of her tone at odds with how she felt inside. 'And I'll see to it he gets it.'

The men exchanged uneasy looks. 'We can't really do that.'

'Seems you've something of a dilemma, then,' May observed. When her statement met with puzzlement, she went on, 'Since either you can wait out here until Mr Beer shows up – which could be nightfall for all I know of his movements – or you can take me at my word when I say I'll be sure he gets it.'

Again, the two men looked at one another. 'With a report like this one, we're supposed to go through it with the owner. Check there's no doubt in his mind as to what needs doing. You see, Mrs Huxford, Fair Maids Farm is falling well short on just about every measure. It's certainly the weakest in this district—'

'Despite the numerous recommendations we made last time—'

'And the time before that.'

'And the requirements in such a situation are clear. There can only be one more inspection without improvement before—'

'Then you'd better clean off your boots and go round there into the parlour,' May said shortly. 'And explain to me, clear and proper, what it is you think needs doing.'

—

'You *knew* they were here, didn't you?'

'Knew who were here?'

When, some long time after midday, George finally came in for his dinner, and then had the audacity to shrug, May saw red.

'Those two from the War Ags. You knew they were coming. Most likely even saw them arrive. How else did you know to disappear?'

To her surprise, George didn't flinch. 'Don't know what you mean. I've been hereabouts all morning.'

'Don't give me that. I wasn't born yesterday. If you're going to lie, at least take the trouble to be convincing about it.' Inside, she couldn't believe how direct she was being; after all, the man did pay her wages. But it was *because* he paid her wages that she couldn't afford to just let the matter go. If he wanted to play fast and loose with his own livelihood, that was down to him. But she wasn't about to let him do the same with hers. She needed this work – not to mention the roof over her head. Bloomin' man – she had come to enjoy living here. She liked taking charge of her days. She even liked the peace and quiet. And that had to be why she felt roused to protect the place.

Shamefacedly, George met her stare. 'So, what did they have to say, then?'

Bringing her hands to her hips, May tutted. 'Oh, for goodness' sake, sit down and I'll fetch over your dinner. Trust me, what they wrote ain't hardly the sort of thing you want to hear on an empty stomach.' Setting his plate in front of him, she stepped back. 'Eat that and I'll tell you once you're done.'

Forced to watch him slowly chewing each mouthful made her despair of him even more. When he'd finally scraped his plate, she snatched it away, deposited it in the scullery sink and returned with the sheaf of papers left with her by Messrs Robinson and Stone.

'Bad, were it?' George enquired as she sat down opposite him. 'Only those two always have had it in for me—'

'Bad?' Remembering her vow to hold a calm and civilised discussion with the man, she lowered her tone. 'I'll have you know I got the world's worst dressing-down for something that's not even the first thing to do with me. Tore into me, they did. As though *I* have any say in the matter! So, yes, *bad* would certainly be one word for it.'

Across the table, George's expression took a turn for the remorseful. 'What do it say?'

'Well, since we're both busy people – or both *should* be after this – how about I skip the niceties and get straight to the parts he underlined?'

With an air of defeat, George nodded. 'Aye. Go on then.'

Section by section, May read aloud the observations written against each of the headings on the report. They certainly didn't beat about the bush.

'*Condition of Arable Land: poor.*'

'Now that ain't fair—'

'Mr Beer,' she said, her patience already thin, 'I'm of a mind this'll go a lot quicker if you just listen. Even to my untaught eye, there ain't nothing here a reasonable man could take issue with.'

'But…'

'Now, where was I? Oh, yes. *Infestation*, after which, in brackets, it says, *by animals*, they've marked down as *widespread. Infestation by weeds: severe.*' She continued down the page. The remarks were all similarly damning. 'To be honest,' she stopped halfway through the second sheet to remark, 'just about the only things they've put down as *fair*, as opposed to *bad* or *poor*, are the state of the farm tracks and the availability of water, against which they wrote "stream".'

His lips pressed together, George glowered. 'Aye. But that ruddy stream can be as much a blight as a blessing. Come wintertime, it backs right the way up to—'

'I don't doubt it,' May cut in, unable to see the point to discussing one of the few areas where there was no issue. 'Of greater import, surely, are the matters they claim to have marked down last time round as well, and the time before that—'

'Such as?'

'Well, by all accounts, your seeds are always late going in the ground. So late, in fact, that the turnips and the cabbages and the kale you've got over there now were meant for growing *last* year—'

'And how was I supposed to see to that on my own? Eh? No good just sending me three sacks of seed and telling me to apply for fertiliser. Seed and fertiliser don't prepare the ground. Nor do they sow themselves. Nor keep themselves weeded and watered.'

Though he might in all reason have a point, she was in no mind to get bogged down in a discussion about what might or might not have been a problem *last* year. 'Perhaps not. But I imagine that's the very reason they've sent you two land girls—'

'*Land girls.*'

'—although even they can only do what you instruct them to. *Inexcusable*, was what they called your lack of sowing.'

'Like I said just now, those two have got it in for me... telling me to plough up meadows and turn them over to vegetables when any fool can see that's a hiding to nothing... and then to have the audacity to tell me which meadow and when… and how much of a harvest I should expect from each of them. All the fertiliser in the county won't get a silk purse out of a sow's ear. But do they care? Do they hell. And as for that colonel fellow they answer to, riding around on that fancy horse of his, ordering folk about. I don't see him ploughing up no meadows.'

'Yes, well,' May said, shaking her head in despair. 'As you might imagine, your own reluctance in that regard didn't go unnoticed, it saying here that you have apparently *still failed to plough up the total agreed acreage of meadows for bringing under cultivation*.' When she looked across at him this time, he simply stared ahead. 'Which, in times of war, they said, is indeef— indefensible. Or some such word. They also lectured me – at some great length, I might add – upon the overgrown state of the ditches, which apparently leads to bogginess of otherwise useable land, and which they said was so simple to remedy that your failure to do so could only be put down to *incompetence*. Oh, and they also said,' she went on without allowing him to reply, 'and I'll read this to you as it's wrote here, *there is a complete absence of any and all direction or supervision of the two land girls, which can only be attributed to ineptitude of the highest order on the part of the owner*.'

''Neptitude, is it?' George replied hotly. 'What would either of those two know of land girls? Eh? I'll tell you. Nothing, that's what. Neither of them ever had two *girls* foisted on them. Girls. I ask you. What ruddy good are schoolgirls? No, I'll tell you now, with no doubt in my mind whatsoever, that neither Robinson nor Stone ever had to contend with such a brazen hussy as that Nessa.'

'Brazen or not,' May said, in part offended, in equal part stifling the urge to laugh, 'the upshot of all this is that I'm to tell you, in no uncertain terms, that, solely out of respect for your late father, they're going to give you one final chance.'

'Huh. And what if I ignore them? What then?'

'If I were you, and I wanted to hang on to this place,' May began, suddenly feeling drained, 'I'd knuckle under and do as they say. Because, if you don't, then if, in eight weeks' time, they come back to find... what was it? Oh, yes, look, here,' she said, stabbing at the document with her forefinger, '*insufficient evidence of remedial action*, they will have no choice but to *submit a recommendation to the Devonshire War Agricultural Executive Committee that George Beer Esquire, of the aforesaid Fair Maids Farm, be replaced by person or persons more capable of bringing the required acreage into full and continuing productivity.*'

His face turning scarlet, George slammed his fist on the table. 'Just... let them... try.'

'I doubt they'll have to try very hard,' May remarked, albeit more carefully this time. Having never, until now, seen Mr Beer raise his voice, she suddenly felt on less certain ground. For all she knew, not far below the surface he had the same sort of temper as Charlie Warren— as Charlie Warren *had had*. 'From what I understand,' she said softly, 'such a thing would be well within their power.'

'Power? Woman, this is *my* land. And I will not be treated like a tenant on it – not by those two nor by anyone else for that matter. Just because *they* were tenants – because that's all those two were, you know, tenants on dairy farms. No brains in that. Couldn't even manage to scrape a proper living at it, either.'

'Mr Beer,' May resumed, still with some caution, 'please, listen to me. This is serious. When they said to me that your position here hangs by a thread, they meant it. *Grave and urgent*, was how they described it.'

'Grave and urgent my ar—'

'But *you* can change that. You can make all this go away—'

'They'll go away all right. If they come back here, trying to take my land, they'll get both barrels of my shotgun. That's what they'll get.'

'George! For God's sake!' To her surprise, it didn't seem to be the volume of her voice that silenced him as much as her unexpected use of his Christian name. 'Don't you want to keep this place? Isn't all of this worth saving? If you just do what they're asking, which is simply to grow some food for people in this time of war, then all this trouble… and all these threats… will go away. Talk of guns will help no one. On the contrary. So, please, help me to understand. What's the problem with just growing some vegetables?'

'Ain't so much a problem with the vegetables,' George said sharply, 'it's the being told what to do with my own land. That's the problem. And being told by old codgers without the least idea of what I do here, to boot.'

Watching as he rose stiffly to his feet and left the room, May exhaled a mixture of fatigue and disbelief. While she could understand how being told what to grow would rankle any farmer, surely it was obvious to him that eventually he would have to give in.

Closing her eyes against the pounding in her head, she pressed her thumbs into her temples in the hope of bringing some relief. Perhaps, left alone to reflect, the man would come to his senses. Unfortunately, though, given the way he'd just stormed off, it seemed highly unlikely.

# Chapter 10

Leaning the ancient bicycle against the wall of the post office and feeling how the sinews in her calves and thighs were quivering, May stopped to pull a handkerchief from her pocket and discreetly mop at her brow. That her face was probably scarlet from her exertions couldn't be helped. All she had to do was get her stamps, drop her letter into the postbox, and make her way home. Yes, she *had* vowed never to ride the blasted contraption again but, even the feeble speed she pedalled along at made it quicker than walking both ways. And this afternoon, time was of the essence: when she got back, together with Bonnie and Nessa, she was going to try to reason with Mr Beer. They'd agreed they had no other choice. And this time, she wasn't going to let him simply shrug and walk away. This time, she wasn't going to give up until they'd made him see sense.

Glancing through the window, she noted with a sigh that already inside the post office were three women: two of them, standing together by the display of greetings cards, appeared to be deep in discussion, the third in the process of being attended to at the counter. Rueing her state of dishevelment, May nevertheless turned the door handle and stepped inside. When the tinkling of the bell on the door drew all four faces in her direction, she acknowledged them with a polite nod and went to queue at the counter. Given the effort it had taken her to get there, and since she would always need stamps, she might as well buy half a dozen. Better still would be to buy a book of them and be done with. But that would set her back half a crown and she knew without even having to open her purse that she didn't have enough money.

When the woman at the counter re-joined the two stood talking, and May's turn came to be served, Nan Parker greeted her with a friendly smile. 'Afternoon, Mrs Huxford. Still going along all right, are you?'

Behind her, the conversation ceased. Imagining three pairs of ears pricking up, May nodded. 'Very well, thank you for asking. And are you keeping well yourself?' Although not especially interested, May had a feeling it was from the post office – and from Nan Parker in partic- ular – that news and gossip spread about the village. And while she had no intention of giving away anything that could make her the subject of the latter, being privy to an occasional snippet of the former could be of no harm.

Behind her, the murmur of discussion started up again.

'Can't complain, thank you, all things considered. What can I do for you? Stamps, is it?'

Her business transacted, May thanked Nan Parker and, securing her purse and her book of stamps safely in her handbag, found herself listening to what had now become a three-way conversation among the other women.

'By the way, you haven't forgotten I shan't be able to make it on Thursday, have you?'

'Faith. I had so. Tell me again – where is it you're going to?'

'Land club. Peggy Smale have had to go up her mother's. So I shall be on me own to work out the labour.'

'Who's after help this time?'

'Old Maurice up Elm Tree Farm. Got a field o' kale seedlings what needs thinnin'. Youngster's job, that is. Calls for nimble fingers and small feet, so I'm minded to send the scout group up there. If no one else asks for help, the others can have a weekend off.'

Her interest piqued, May dithered: would it be too forward to ask what they were talking about? Probably. But if she were to introduce herself first, she might ease her way in.

'Forgive me,' she said, turning on a smile she hoped was bright and yet at the same time humble, 'but I'm May Huxford. I've just started as the housekeeper for Mr Beer at Fair Maids Farm. I hope you'll forgive me intruding on your conversation, but I don't know anyone here yet. So, when I heard you talking about farming, I thought it a chance to make your acquaintance.'

In turn, and with a friendly enough smile, each woman shook May's hand and introduced herself. The one doing most of the conversing went by the name of Joyce Haldon.

'Only the other day Nan was saying how George Beer had a new housekeeper.' Just as May had suspected, this was indeed the point from which news found its way around the village. And, no doubt, was either embellished or inflated according to the generosity of the person delivering it.

May smiled. 'That would be me.'

'Bombed out of Ex'ter, wasn't you?'

'That's right.'

'Poor love. How're you finding it all the way out at Fair Maids then?'

'Oh, you know,' May replied, her tone heavy with humility. 'Takes a while to get things running how you like them, doesn't it?'

Joyce Haldon nodded sagely. 'For certain not everyone has the same standards.'

'Forgive me again,' May hastened on, the conversation appearing to have stalled, 'but I couldn't help hearing you mention labour for a farm...'

'That's right, love. Between us, me an' Mrs Smale run the land club.'

'Land club. I don't think I've come across one of those before...'

As though unable to resist, Joyce Haldon launched into an explanation, from which May learned that land clubs were bands of volunteers who, in their free time at weekends, helped any local farm in need of extra workers.

'We have schoolboys and girls,' Joyce explained, 'a retired solicitor, a teacher, a Scoutmaster, a doctor's secretary... all sorts, really.'

In May's spine, a tingling sensation accompanied the dawning of an idea. 'What sort of work do they take on?'

'Oh, you know, anything that relies on a bit of enthusiasm and hard work rather than skill. Jobs like weeding – we get asked a lot for help with that – planting, clearing undergrowth. You know the sort of thing.'

She did indeed. Get hold of a team of workers for a couple of days – or even just one – to get to grips with weeding and the like and, from thereon in, perhaps Bonnie and Nessa would keep on top of it by themselves. 'So...'

'Way it works, see, is that the farmer telephones and tells us what sort of job needs doing, and how many pairs of hands he thinks could get it done. *We* see how many of our volunteers fit the bill and put together a gang and a leader. The gang works for up to five hours, with a half-hour break in the middle. They brings their own food but it's usual for the farmer's wife to lay on tea.'

'Seems fair,' May said, struggling to conceal growing excitement. 'And do it cost anything – the help? You know, wages or whatnot?'

'In some districts,' Joyce replied, 'the farmer pays an equivalent amount, and once the committee has covered the volunteers' expenses, they donate what's left to the Red Cross Agricultural Workers' Fund. But out here, well, we like to keep it simple. If the farm is close by, the gang can walk or cycle there at no cost to themselves anyway. If it's further out, we tell the farmer to send a tractor and trailer to fetch them and then bring them back again when they're done.'

'The people who do the work don't mind not getting paid?'

Joyce Haldon smiled. 'There's a war on, love. We all do our bit, don't we? Besides, if they didn't enjoy it – get a sense of satisfaction from it – they wouldn't keep volunteering, would they? If it got too much, they'd wouldn't come no more.'

Free help? To May, it seemed too good to be true. 'And can any farm ask?'

'Any farm with a job to be done and no one to do it.'

'So…' Dare she ask? Dare she summon the courage? Dare she risk Mr Beer's wrath – because for certain he wouldn't be pleased. '…would you be able to help Fair Maids?'

'Depends on what needs doing.'

It was only then May realised that the two other women had taken themselves off outside, the way they kept stealing glances through the window suggesting they'd done so to talk about her. Well, let them. Within her grasp might be a chance to help Fair Maids.

'Would I have to tell you right now? Only...'

Joyce Haldon angled her head in thought. 'If I send Elm Tree Farm the scout troop, then I could probably round you up a gang of a dozen or so who can turn their hands to most things.'

A dozen? What luck!

'It's just that I'd have to work out where best to use them. There's quite a bit needs getting up together.'

'Look,' Joyce said. 'Friday mornings, me an' a couple of ladies do a spot of cleaning in the church. Send word to me there and I'll do my best to get folk to suit. How do that sound?'

Still struggling to believe her good fortune, May beamed with delight. 'It sounds perfect. I'll do that. Friday. Thank you.'

'My pleasure, love. See you Friday.'

'Yes. Thank you. I'll be there.'

Goodness, May thought as she stepped out onto the pavement. This might just work! All she had to do was to decide, before Friday, which of the jobs on the War Ags' report would go furthest to keeping Messrs Robinson and Stone off Mr Beer's back. Oh, and fathom how on earth she was going to explain to him what she'd done...

–

When it came to explaining to Mr Beer about the land club, Nessa and Bonnie wanted nothing to do with it.

'More than happy to have the help,' Nessa admitted when May told them what she was proposing. 'Happy to keep an eye on them, direct them. But trust me, I have rather more sense than to sit here while you tell George.'

'Me too,' Bonnie agreed. 'Ask me to do a thing and I won't complain. I'll work till I'm fit to drop if it gets the job done. But I shall see to it I'm far away when you tell Mr Beer about this land club.'

'What *I* don't understand,' Nessa went on, 'is why you're getting involved at all. I mean, what does it matter to you what the place does or doesn't grow? You're just the char.'

With no desire to court an argument, May gritted her teeth. 'Housekeeper or otherwise, I have no desire to see Mr Beer out on his ear, certainly not for want of something so simple as a day's extra labour – *free* labour, at that. Think about it – if someone else is put in to run this place, they might not take such a casual attitude to the hired help. For certain they could make all our lives a lot less pleasant.'

Nessa shrugged. 'If I don't like them, I don't have to stay. There's always plenty of farms needing land girls.'

Yes, May thought, but there weren't plenty of farms needing housekeepers.

'Actually,' Bonnie chipped in, saving May the need to work out how to say so without coming across as desperate. 'We *can't* just up and leave. Only the district rep can move us to another farm.'

'Well, I for one don't intend being here when she tells George what she's doing.'

'To be honest,' May confessed, 'it's occurring to me now not to tell him at all – to just set the volunteers to work and see whether he even notices.' To her mind, it might even cause *less* of an upset, experience having taught her it was often better to ask forgiveness after the event than to seek permission beforehand. Of course, that did assume the volunteers' work came up to the mark, and that they didn't do any damage in the completing of it. It also carried the risk that, when Mr Beer found out she'd gone behind his back, he would never trust her again.

Sure enough, though, the moment supper was finished, Nessa and Bonnie slipped away, leaving May to break the news by herself.

'Mr Beer,' she said, hoping he wouldn't notice how badly she was suddenly shaking. 'I've something to tell you...'

'You better not be leaving.'

For a man who was concerned she might be about to up sticks, he looked decidedly untroubled, his expression as flat and as lifeless as ever.

'No, no,' she hastened to reassure him. In truth, he might just have made her task easier; if he feared she might leave, then what she'd actually done might come as a relief – might seem the lesser of two evils. 'No,' she proceeded carefully, 'but I've arranged for some folk – some volunteers, that is – to come and lend a hand.'

'Volunteers? To do what, 'xactly?'

Having got into her stride, May met his look. 'Well, strikes me they would be good put to weeding... or thinning... or even planting. I was hoping you would know what—'

'Farmers, are they, then? Know their way about, do they?'

May checked her despair. He knew very well they wouldn't be farmers; he was just trying to undermine her faith.

'Not farmers, no, but they're eager and willing and watched over by a gang leader, who sees to it they do as instructed. And since this is something they do most weekends, they're not altogether without skill. I'm told most every farm in Pippinswell has had their help at some point. There's no shame in it. It's not charity.'

'Maybe it idn't. But pound to a penny they'll cause more trouble than they're worth. You see if I'm not wrong.'

So far, he hadn't said anything she hadn't been expecting. More importantly, he hadn't told her she couldn't do it. 'With respect, Mr Beer,' she picked up again, 'I disagree. This could be a real boon. For certain we'd be foolish not to at least give it a try. It won't cost you a penny—'

'Hadn't ruddy better.'

'But it *will* help get things up together. And if we can do that then perhaps Bonnie and Nessa—'

'Those two? Waste of time, the pair of 'em.'

Under the table, May uncurled her fists. *Stay calm*, she urged herself.

'So you keep telling me. But I don't see you coming up with any better ideas. This business with the War Ags isn't going to go away, you know. One way or another, they'll get their way. And it won't matter to them how they get it, either. With or without you, they'll get the vegetables they want, and they'll get them grown here on Fair Maids, too. So, unless you have a plan of your own for getting out of this fix – and by which I mean one that doesn't involve a shotgun – then I'm going to go ahead and tell them to come. If we're lucky, we'll get about a dozen and—'

'What I'd like to know,' George said, his voice held low as he met her look, 'is who put you up to this? That Nessa, were it? Idle madam. Because I doubt it was that other one. Wouldn't say boo to a goose, that little one.'

Her patience wearing thin, May raised herself up. If he was going to forbid her to do it, why didn't he just come out and say so? Why not just show some spine and tell her? But oh, no, he couldn't even do that. And he couldn't do it because he knew she was on to something; he knew her plan stood a chance of working, of hauling them one small step in the right direction. Well, she wouldn't be cowed. But she would be careful.

'Mr Beer, you don't have to like the idea, and I'm not asking for thanks. To be honest, I don't even care whether, once they're done, you bother to go and see—'

'What *do* you want then? Why meddle? Since I doubt you could even find the 'andle end of a spade, why not just stick to your cleaning?'

Meddle? Was that what he thought she was doing? Holding herself rigidly, all care not to raise her voice deserted her. 'I don't doubt you're right. I've never so much as held a spade in my life. But doesn't that prove my point? Doesn't that go to show it doesn't need a farmer to see what's wrong here? If I – me, *a cleaner* – can see it, then surely you can too. In fact, I happen to know you see it perfectly well. So, do I have your permission to bring these people on to the farm or not? A simple yes or no is all I ask. After that, you can wash your hands of it.'

Scraping back his chair, George got to his feet. 'Do whatever you want woman. You're the one with it all worked out. Have your bloody *volunteers*. In fact, since you reckon you can see what needs doing here, have the lot of it – have those two bloody land girls, as well. See for yourself what I'm up against.'

When he stared down at her, she held his look. He'd probably only said that because she'd backed him into a corner, but she'd take it. And she'd show him she could make a go of it, too.

'Very well. But if you're going to let me get on with it, then let me get on with it.'

'And you stay clear of my orchards.'

'Gladly.' Golly, she was livid.

'Right then.'

'Right then.'

On his way to the door, George paused. 'No wonder there ain't no Mr Huxford no more. Doubtless *he* couldn't take your meddling ways either.'

*Mr* Huxford? Now what was he on about? Then the penny dropped: he thought she was here because her husband had walked out on her. Well, she wouldn't even dignify such wrong-headedness with a reply.

Waiting until she imagined him to be well away from the door, she peered out to check where he was headed, unsurprised to see him tramping in the direction of his precious orchards. Drained, she sank back against the wall and drew a long breath. Hopefully, now, her heart would stop pounding quite so fiercely. This might not be the first time she'd been driven to despair by an unreasonable man, but it *was* the first time she'd dared to challenge one, certainly to raise her voice to him.

As it happened, by refusing to back down, by sticking to her guns, she'd got what she wanted – either that, or she'd simply landed herself in the deepest trouble imaginable. Maybe she'd even done both; only time would tell. Either way, all that mattered for now was that Mr Beer had given her licence to bring in the land club. That she also now had responsibility for Bonnie and Nessa was icing on the top.

The deeper ramifications of what she'd done hitting home, she flushed hot. Not content with taking on the burden of satisfying the demands of the War Ags, she'd also upset the man who paid her wages and allowed her to live under his roof. Madness, really, but there it was. What was done, was done. All she could do now was get on with it; at least from here on, she would succeed or fail by her own endeavours. But golly, did she suddenly have an almighty task ahead of her — not to mention an awful lot to learn.

*V. Fruit Set*

# Chapter 11

Hanging her apron on the scullery door, May sighed with relief. She was done for the day: the supper things were washed up; the kitchen had been tidied and the pail of peelings put out for Bonnie to give to the chickens. She was finished. Granted, she still had to decide how to use the land club volunteers but, since it was such a lovely evening again, she was tempted to forget about that for a while, fetch her flower book and go for a stroll. Perhaps, outdoors, with her head free from household concerns, she might even come up with an answer.

In some ways, she wouldn't mind some company, and it occurred to her to ask Bonnie to join her. But she couldn't really do that without extending the same invitation to Nessa. And Nessa didn't always bring out the best in her. In fact, much of the time the girl rankled her; she did it deliberately, of course. *You're just the char.* No, invite Nessa and she would have to leave her book behind; Nessa would have no time for flowers. In fact, she would probably mock. So, she would go alone. That way she could keep her own pace and stop as often as she wanted.

Flower book in hand, she shunned the path that would take her through the orchard – with George having told her to stay clear of it, she feared he meant *completely* clear of it – and strolled instead in the direction of the fields. Out of sight of the lean-to, she stood for a moment to draw a long breath. How balmy the air was tonight; in Albert Terrace, a summer's evening would have meant an even more pungent smell from the sewage works, and the frayed tempers of mothers with infants too hot and grouchy to sleep. By contrast, a warm evening here was heavenly.

Lowering her eyes from the pastel shades of the sky, she spotted in the grass a cluster of pink flowers. Drawing closer and noticing a fragrance, she bent to examine them. In the soft light, they looked like fairy-sized bowls. She determined to learn their name; she opened her book and flicked through the pages. Who knew there were so many plants with the same purplish-pink flowers! She hesitated once or twice over pictures that almost matched and kept going. Just as she was beginning to think the plant in front of her was missing from her book, she spotted it: Musk Mallow. *Flowers up to 2" across, rose-pink with deeper pink veins. Borne June to August. Leaves mid-green, broad and hairy. In a warm confined situation, flowers give off a musky smell.* Musky, yes! The description was a perfect match. Buoyed by her success, she rose to her feet and looked around. What else might she— Oh. That looked like Dan coming across the field. Determining from the directness of his approach that he was coming to see her, she snapped shut her book and thrust it behind her back.

'Hello,' he called as he drew near.

She returned his greeting. 'Hello.'

'Out for a stroll?'

Watching as he came all the way up to the fence, she nodded. 'Yes.'

'Nice evenin' for it.'

'Yes.'

'That tyre holding up?'

She smiled. 'It is, thank you. You did a good job.'

'Had a fair bit of practice over the years.'

As she continued to smile, she was struck by a thought: Dan would be a good person to ask about the War Ags and the land club. After her disagreement with George, and her hasty decision to assume responsibility for growing the vegetables, she'd been left with a head full of questions and only Nessa she might reasonably quiz.

'Can I ask you something?' No sense prevaricating.

'Never harms to ask. I might even answer you.'

Despite knowing he was teasing her, she couldn't help ducking her head. 'It's about the War Ags.'

'Dad said you had a visit.' In her surprise, she looked straight back up; since it seemed unlikely George would have broadcast the news, she wondered how his brother could have found out. 'Word travels fast round here.'

'As I'm finding.'

'Sorry. What did you want to know?'

'Well, can they really remove a farmer from his land?'

Thrusting his hands into his pockets, Dan nodded. 'They can. Though they'd only ever do so as a last resort.'

'I see.' So, their warnings hadn't been idle ones; Mr Beer really could find someone else brought in to work his land. And she really could be homeless.

'Is that what they've threatened?'

Slowly, May nodded. 'They threatened it, yes. Though, to be honest, they blustered about a lot of things.'

'Tricky old business, dealing with the War Ags. Half the district committee is made up of locals with old grudges. Many's the farmer who resents them. You know about the reports they send back, I suppose.'

'I do.' There was no need to tell him quite how dire the one about Fair Maids had been; no need to humiliate Mr Beer in front of family.

'On the other hand, there are benefits to be had, too. Approach them right and you can get moved up the list for equipment and supplies. To be honest, George is a fool not to play along.'

'I don't doubt it,' she said. 'But it's going to take a better person than me to get him to see it.'

'Hm. Anyway,' Dan said, reaching to rest a hand on the top of the nearest fence post. 'Anything else I can help you with?'

'Actually, yes,' she said. 'I was wondering whether you know much about Mrs Haldon and her land club?'

'Some. What I hear from other farms is that they're a hard-working lot. Something of a lifeline for farmers who've had their hands go off to join up, especially given they'd no need to. Why do you want to know?'

'This Saturday they're coming to Fair Maids. I thought they could help the land girls with the weeding... or something.'

'They *could*,' Dan said, angling his head as though about to disagree. 'But putting a dozen labourers to weeding's only of any benefit if you're intending to plant straight afterwards, or else have the means to keep it tended. Otherwise, it's a waste of time. If it were me under threat from the War Ags, I'd put their labour to something of greater use.'

To her surprise, May saw his point: there was more to this than getting a band of eager locals to pull out some dandelions. 'Yes,' she said. 'I see that. So, what would *you* get them to do?'

Directing his gaze to the horizon, Dan thought for a moment. 'What crops has George been told to grow this year? Only, it's getting late now for a lot of things.'

'I'm not sure. He's already got turnips, cabbages and kale.'

'Potatoes, then. I bet they told him to put in potatoes.'

'Yes,' she said, remembering the fact. 'They did. This year he was supposed to grow beetroot and potatoes.'

'Well, you've still time to get a field of maincrops in. So, if it were me, I'd get your volunteers to plant that long strip beside the stream. That way, if we don't get much rain, it'll be less effort for you to keep them watered. Yeah. Get Nessa to plough it up, then get your land club to scrape some trenches, throw some manure in the bottom, stick in the taters, and cover them over. No need to chit maincrops—'

'Chit?'

'Leave them to sprout before putting them in the ground. In fact, with maincrops, chitting works against you – you're growing them to store, so you want them in the ground as long as possible. Anyway, do that and by the time your two War Ags come back, you'll have a field of green shoots to show them.'

'Really?' To May it seemed hard to believe. 'It's that straightforward?'

'God's honest.'

'Heavens.'

'Look,' Dan went on, 'far be it from me to interfere but tomorrow morning I've got to go to Cooper's merchants for worming tablets. So, how about I bring you back whatever seed potatoes they've got left? I doubt they'll have enough, and you'll have to take pot luck on the variety, but it'd be a start. Ten tubers per ten-foot run is what the War Ags will be expecting. In truth, you could do with a ton of the things. But show them you can make a start, and then George can ask them for help getting some more.'

Hm. The problem was, she knew something Dan didn't. Having washed his hands of the responsibility, George would no more ask the War Ags for their help than he would plant the things himself. But it was helpful to know, nonetheless.

'What about paying for these seed things?' As spanners in the works went, the matter of affording them was an almighty one. 'Only, I don't have—'

'George has an account at Cooper's. Everyone round here does. I'll charge it to that. But it'll be down to you to tell him, so he knows to settle it.'

'Yes. Of course. Cooper's, you say.'

'Uh-huh.'

'Well, thank you,' she said, her head brimming. 'Once again, I'm in your debt.'

'Happy to help. I'll see you when I've been to Cooper's.'

'You will.'

On her way back to the farmhouse, May struggled to believe her luck. With Dan having come to her rescue a second time, it meant that on Friday she could go along to the church and tell Joyce Haldon what help to send.

Continuing towards the yard, she realised something: until she'd walked through the gate and up the track that first day, she'd only ever thought of farms as quaint places with happy cows and rosy-cheeked milkmaids. How quickly the scales had fallen from her eyes! Now she understood that no matter how pretty the fields and the orchards, a farm was no place for sentiment. Even under favourable conditions, livelihoods had to be carved from the earth, and Mother Nature continually battled just to survive. Moreover, with this war requiring that people be fed from the country's own fields, there was no room for old men who talked to trees. Still, with the fortuitous stroke of luck that had led her to discover the land club, and through talking to Dan, she might just have found a way to save not only Mr Beer's skin, but her own home and livelihood too.

# Chapter 12

'So, there's a dozen in the gang. Their leader's called Mr Deacon and they'll be here at half past nine—'

'Yes, you said.'

'Now, you won't let them forget to put the manure in first.'

'We won't.'

'And you've had a look for yourself to check it's well rotted.'

'It's just fine.'

'And you'll get the sacks containing the seed potatoes over there beforehand.'

'We will.'

'And you know exactly where they're to be planted.'

'For heaven's sake, May,' Nessa erupted, her tone one of exasperation. 'I *should* do. I spent all ruddy afternoon yesterday ploughing it.'

Not wanting the day to get off on the wrong foot, May sent Nessa a rueful smile. 'Yes. Sorry,' she said. 'I know you did. It's just that since I'm the one who's committed us to this whole… this whole land club and potato business, I'm a bit… well, I suppose you could say I'm a bit nervy.'

*A bit nervy* was an understatement. Despite spending all yesterday evening poring over the Ministry of Agriculture and Fisheries' pamphlet about planting potatoes, and despite Nessa claiming that her training had included a crash course on growing the blessed things, since Dan had arrived with a trailer filled with sacks of tubers May had been unable to think about anything else. She hadn't slept, she hadn't fancied breakfast, and she felt more nervous now than the day she'd got on the bus to come here in the first place. Ridiculous, really, but there it was.

'Trust me,' Nessa said, 'it will be fine. If what that organiser woman said was true, it won't be the first time this lot have planted a field of potatoes.'

'No,' May agreed. 'Course not.'

'So, might I suggest you stop fretting and get on with something else.'

'Yes. I'll do that.'

'There's a summer fayre at the church hall this afternoon,' Bonnie piped up. 'It's in aid of the WVS refugee fund. You could go along to that. Two o'clock, the sign said.'

May thought for a moment. 'Happen that's not a bad idea.' If she did decide to go, then this time she would leave the bike at home and walk. After all, what were the chances of Dan coming to her rescue for a third time in such quick succession?

–

'Mrs Huxford. How nice to see you.' When May didn't immediately reply, the woman greeting her went on, 'Kathleen Adams. We met last week in the post office.'

'Oh, yes, of course. Mrs Adams. Nice to see you too.'

It was later that afternoon and, having finished her chores and furnished the land club with several gallons of tea, May had taken Bonnie's advice and gone to the fayre. If nothing else, being away from the farm removed the chance for her to keep checking on progress with the planting.

'Mrs Haldon said you've got the land club out there today.'

May held her smile. 'That's right. They're helping the girls with maincrop potatoes.' She liked using the word 'maincrop'. It made her sound as though she knew what she was talking about.

'Tell me,' Mrs Adams lowered her voice to ask, 'is it true what they say about land girls?'

May frowned. 'Is what true?'

'Well, that they're all…' Kathleen Adams cast over her shoulder. '…*man-mad*. Out for a good time. All hat and no knickers. *Always in the barn*. You know, keep them away from your husband. Only, many's the time I've heard say so.'

'I think,' May replied, uncertain whether to be amused or incensed, 'somebody is having you on. Obviously, I can't speak for every one of them, but my two are hard-working girls from decent families, and no trouble whatsoever.'

'Yes. Of course they are.'

'Now, though it's lovely to see you again, I mustn't tarry. I've not long to spare and I want to have a good old look around.'

*That told her*, May reflected as she smiled sweetly and then headed smartly to the nearest stall, where she then proceeded to take rather too much interest in the array of what appeared to be last year's unsold bottled fruit pie fillings.

'Those are all sixpence, dear,' the elderly woman behind the trestle looked up to inform her.

Deciding to move on, May spotted a stall piled with books. She wouldn't mind something to read. Nothing scary. Nor racy. Running her finger along a row of well-worn spines, she laughed at herself. Racy? At the WVS fayre? She doubted there was any danger of that.

With nothing among the assortment of well-thumbed fiction capturing her imagination, she skirted the cake display and found herself in front of a table laden with boxes of clothing. Drawn to a pretty fabric in the top of the one labelled 'Dresses,' she lifted it out to find a summery frock, the fabric cut on the bias, the sleeves short and puffed. She held it to her body. The style might be from before the war, but it looked barely worn. The fabric had a good weight to it, the hem deep enough to let down by an inch or so if it hung too short on her – especially since she would be wearing it with bare legs.

'That soft green colour really suits you,' the young woman behind the stall remarked. '*I* couldn't pull it off, but *you* could. That little creamy sprig on it is so fresh, isn't it? Why not slip behind the curtain here and try it on?'

May hesitated. 'How much is it?'

The girl pointed to a cardboard sign. 'They're all the same, which makes that one something of a bargain, don't you think?'

It was certainly tempting. But where would *she* get to wear such a flimsy frock? On the other hand, it was clearly good quality. She squinted at the embroidered label stitched at the back of the neck. *Clarice Modes.* Hadn't she seen those in the window of that posh little shop near the cathedral?

'No, it's all right,' she said, less than keen to try to undress behind a curtain. The garment was good enough quality that she could probably let it out or take it in if it wasn't quite right. 'I'll take it.'

The girl smiled. 'Good choice. I would have bought it myself had it been a different colour.'

Her money handed over, May glanced at her wrist-watch; she'd been out long enough. By the time she got back, the land club should be finished and gone, and she was itching to know whether they'd been able to do the whole job. They'd certainly got off to a flyer of a start.

She needn't have worried. When she eventually arrived back, hot and thirsty, it was to find Nessa and Bonnie sat in the shade of the barn clutching mugs of tea. They looked as exhausted as she herself felt.

'Hope you don't mind,' Bonnie said, making to get to her feet. 'But we was gasping.'

'Course I don't mind,' May replied. 'How did it go? Get it all done, did they?'

'Yep. The gang leader did a proper job of getting them organised and they barely stopped.'

'All credit to them,' Nessa acknowledged. 'They didn't slack.'

'Want a piece of cake with that?' May asked, gesturing towards the mug in Bonnie's hand.

The girl started to grin. 'Sorry. We've already had it. We were starving.'

'No matter. So, it went well, then.'

'I'd tell you to go and see for yourself,' Nessa said, stretching her arms above her head. 'But there's nothing to see. Just neatly raked soil and markers at the end of each row.'

'And what about Mr Beer?' May enquired.

'Haven't set eyes on him all day.'

No, *they* might not have seen *him*, May thought as she turned to go indoors, but he would have been there somewhere, watching, ready at the drop of a hat to criticise or to complain. Well, let him try. For no effort on his part, he had now a crop of potatoes on the way. And, with a bit of luck, the War Ags off his back – not for ever, of course, but hopefully for a good while yet.

–

It was another beautiful evening: from just above the westerly horizon, the sun was casting lengthy purple shadows; the waist-high grasses were buzzing with insects; the warm air was heady with the scent of a dozen different plants. Some distance from the yard, book in hand, May was following the path towards the stream and taking it all in, a sense of calm about her shoulders. She'd come this way not only to see for herself the result of the day's labours but also in the hope of identifying at least two or three new wildflowers on the way.

Arriving at the potato field, she realised with a mixture of satisfaction and disappointment that Nessa was right: there was absolutely nothing to see, the only evidence of activity being the complete lack of weeds and the pleasing uniformity of the earth. Strange, she reflected, how the sight of nothing should make her feel such a sense of achievement!

From there, she headed into the trees, intent this evening on finding the stream. Although she didn't know what she'd been expecting, when the trickling of water drew her to the edge of a damp bank, what she saw came as a let-down: just a few inches of spring-clear water chuckling its way over the red–brown rocks, eddying around the occasional stump, or pooling lazily among the roots of trees. Well, while it wasn't in the least picturesque, at least she'd found it.

The slope appearing too treacherous to risk going any lower, and in any event having achieved what she set out to, she scrambled back to the top of the bank and stood to take in the view. From the hillside away to her left sheep were calling, the high-pitched bleats from the lambs acknowledged by grunts of reassurance from the ewes.

'I *thought* it was you.'

With a start, she spun about. 'Oh!' Coming around the edge of the potato field was Dan.

'Sorry,' he said, reading her surprise. 'Thought you'd hear me coming.'

Recovering her composure, she forced a swallow. 'You're light of foot. That or I was miles away.'

'You did look lost to your thoughts.'

'I was just… taking it all in.' She had been about to explain that she was going to try to learn the names of some flowers, but stopped for fear of looking silly.

'See you got the taters in then.'

'Well, not *me*,' she hastened to point out. 'I just saw to it they got proper organised. Left to me, they would probably all have been in the ground upside down.'

'Wouldn't have been a disaster. Nature has a way of sorting it out.'

'No, the land club did really well,' she said. 'Got it all done. Wouldn't have come about without *you*, though.'

'Nah. You were the one with the idea to start with. Anyway,' he went on, 'since it looks like you came out for a bit o' peace and quiet, I'll leave you be.'

When she saw him nod towards her book, she shook her head. 'Oh, no, it's all right.' Angling the front cover for him to see, she went on, 'I'm trying to learn the names of some wildflowers.'

'Yeah? How's it going?'

She grinned. 'Slowly. So far I've learned ox-eye daisy, cowslip and…' The name of the pink one momentarily deserting her, she fought to recall it. '…something… mallow?'

'Musk mallow.'

'That's it. Had an unusual smell.'

'Your book tell you folk eat them?'

May frowned. 'Eat the flowers?'

'Flowers, seeds, the whole thing. Mostly, the leaves are chopped up to go in salad. But Gran picks them to dry.' When he saw her continuing to frown, he went on, 'She makes potions and remedies and the like. Got her own little room up in the attic. I used to call it Granny's coven. Makes all sorts up there. Tonics for women, mainly. Learned it all from her grandmother.'

'Ah.' She'd heard about country women who could use plants to cure ills.

'Learned any other names?'

'Not yet, but I thought I'd try for two a day.'

'Don't suppose your book tells you the names we call them by here?'

'You have different names for them?' Suddenly, her book seemed less useful.

'We don't have a different name for everything. I mean, mallow is still mallow. But the ox-eyes we call horse daisies. Forget-me-nots we call mouse's ear. Oh, and cowslips we call milk maidens.'

Unsure whether he was having her on – the names he'd reeled off sounded so quaint he could easily be making them up – she studied his expression. But since she hardly knew him, it told her nothing. 'Truthfully?'

'Truthfully. Here, come and look at this.' When he beckoned her over, she followed him back across the grass. 'See if this one's in your book.'

Uncertainly, she squatted down beside him. Between thumb and finger, he grasped a narrow stem, at the top of which was a soft lilac-blue flower with ragged petals around a paler centre.

Growing warm under his scrutiny, she turned the pages of her book. 'This one?' she asked, pointing to a page with an illustration that looked similar.

'Close. Same family.'

She turned the page. 'This one?'

'That's it. Now, there it says field scabious.' She was glad he'd pronounced it; she would have made a real dog's dinner of a tricky name like that.

'But you call it…?'

'Most folk round here would know it as bachelor's buttons. But Gran calls it lady's cushion.'

'Any particular reason?'

Pressing his lips together, he shrugged. 'For certain, though I couldn't tell you what. I know she makes a tincture of it. Seen it on her shelf often enough. Though whether it's to take for a sore throat or to put on a blister, I couldn't tell you.'

'Your gran sounds a useful person to have in the house.'

'If you don't mind having evil-tasting liquids thrust down your throat, and being told *don't mewl, it'll make you better. Or don't you want rid of the pain?*'

Getting to her feet, May smiled. 'Say its name again?'

'Field scabious. Bachelor's buttons.'

She repeated it. 'Field scabious.'

'And for your second one, how about…' He cast about the grasses. 'Here. This one. Got this in your book?'

She stooped to more closely inspect the plant he was indicating. Thin white petals with a balloon-like green bulge directly behind them. 'Funny-looking thing,' she said, starting to flick through her book. It wasn't hard to match to the drawing. 'Bladder campion. Happen because of the shape.'

Straightening himself up, Dan laughed. 'You're getting the hang of it.'

'What's it used for?'

'You'd have to ask Gran. But for certain she'll have some or other place for it.'

'Says here it's common.' She looked about. 'There do seem to be a lot of it. It also says it's a favourite food of froghoppers, which settle upon it and then wrap themselves in something called cuckoo spit.'

'Foamy stuff up the stems.'

'There's my two plants then,' she said, wondering how best to now take her leave of him.

'Yeah. Here's me, saying I won't disturb you, and then I go and do just that.'

She smiled lightly. 'No, it was helpful. Thank you.'

'Next time I see you, I'll be expecting you to remember their names. No sense learning and then forgetting.'

'None at all,' she agreed and then watched as, thrusting his hands into his pockets, he strode away through the grasses and didn't look back.

How fortunate to have him as a neighbour. How fortunate he'd been so quick to come to the rescue with those seed potatoes. In fact, May thought, snatching a quick look at his departing back, without him her first attempt at taking responsibility for the vegetables would have got off to a very sorry start indeed.

# Chapter 13

What on earth was the matter with her? Why was she crying? If the sight of Clemmie's handwriting could bring on tears, what on earth was she going to be like when she read what her sister had written?

Holding herself stiffly, May slid her finger under the flap of the envelope the postman had just brought her and pulled from inside the sheet of notepaper. Then, having paused for a moment to make sure she wasn't about to cry again, she started to read.

> *My Dearest sister May,*
>
> *Thank you for your letter. I am pleased to know you are settling in all right. Sometimes I try to picture what you are doing there but not knowing anything about farms, all I see is cows and mud. Since you didn't say nothing about cows, maybe you don't have any.*

So far, so good; still dry-eyed, she could read on.

> *As you will see from my address, I now have lodgings. A lady at the WVS offered me a room in her house for as long as I need to get on my feet. Her name is Miss Dorothy Evercott, and she is a spinster of about forty years old. There*

*is another girl called Gwen who stays here too. She is a little older than me and jokes that we are Miss Evercott's rescued strays. The house is nice. It has an indoors bathroom and I have my own tiny bedroom. Gwen and I try to repay Miss Evercott's kindness by doing most of the housework.*

*At the WVS we are kept busy. Many hundreds of people still do not have anywhere to live and still need food and clothes. Although it is very sad to see these people and their hardships, I am always glad when I can help, no matter how small the thing I do for them.*

*I still have not been able to find proper work. I look every day for jobs but with nearly all the shops gone, there is nothing. Some streets like High Street and Queen Street have now been cleared of rubble and each morning, some of the old shops set up barrows or stalls in the road to sell a few things but it is all a very sorry sight.*

*Well, as I must get some sleep, I will end here. Glad you are well.*

*With love from your sister, Clemmie*

*P.S. Pearl is well. She has a job but I will give her your address so she can write and tell you all about it for herself.*

Refolding the sheet of paper and tucking it back into the envelope, May sighed. What a relief to know that Clemmie was no longer in the shelter; that Pearl would fare all right had never unduly concerned her. Abandoning Clemmie to fend for herself, on the other hand, had been much more of a worry; Clemmie didn't have Pearl's front.

Still, as it happened, she seemed to be all right. Given her circumstances, she even sounded quite bright. And Pearl, well, by the sound of it she was fine, too. Who knew, maybe the disaster of losing their home would turn out to be the making of them – of all three of them – just as she'd been left to hope at the time.

–

'Do you know how to dance?'

Caught off guard by Nessa's question, May decided to check she hadn't misheard. 'Do I know how to dance?' Crossing the kitchen with a plate of toast, she set it down on the table. 'Depends what sort of dance you had in mind, I suppose.'

'Well,' Nessa said, helping herself to a slice, 'I was thinking of the foxtrot or the quickstep. But there's usually one or two waltzes to keep the oldies happy.'

Since the waltz was the only dance May had ever been taught how to do, and since she had no idea what had prompted Nessa to ask, she felt wary of replying. As it was, she'd only learned it at school, in a single lesson during which she had found herself being squeezed to breathlessness by Bobby Jones – at least, she had until the music teacher spotted what was happening and rescued her from his ardent clutches.

'Why d'you want to know?'

'There's a dance on Saturday. And before you say anything, it's in the church hall, so it's quite respectable.'

'A dance.' Now she genuinely feared where this was leading.

'Ordinarily, it's just a once-a-month do for the locals. But, since there's a RAF unit up the road now—'

'There is?'

'There is,' Bonnie chimed in. 'Bonham Hall has been turned into a training centre. Word is it's hush-hush.'

Returning from the pantry with the butter dish, May put it on the table. 'If it's hush-hush, how come you two know about it?'

'Dan told us.'

'Just to be clear,' Nessa corrected Bonnie's statement, scraping her knife across the top of the block of margarine as she did so, 'he *didn't* say it was hush-hush.'

'He didn't, no,' Bonnie conceded. 'But it could be.'

'I think you'll find it's about as likely to be hush-hush,' Nessa said wearily, 'as it is that May's a German spy.'

'Anyway,' Bonnie went on, 'since there might be a few more… *young folk* there this time round—'

'Men,' Nessa interrupted. 'Since there might be some men there this time. You can say the word *men*, Bonn. May won't be shocked.'

'—we thought we'd go.'

'So, do you want to come with us?'

'Saturday, you say?' The only reason May asked was to give herself a moment to come up with a reason to decline.

'It's all proper and decent,' Bonnie took pains to point out.

'I'll think about it.'

'In other words,' Nessa said, now spreading her toast with gooseberry jam, 'no.'

'Oh, *don't* say *no*.'

'I didn't *say* no,' May replied, wishing now that she had. 'I said I'll think about it. And I will.'

'Well, it's entirely up to you,' Nessa remarked before crunching into her slice of toast.

'But *we're* going anyway.'

'Good for you.' As it happened, Nessa was right: she hadn't the slightest intention of going. Why court the ignominy of standing around, waiting to be asked to dance while both Nessa and Bonnie were rarely off the floor? Worse than that, why face having to repeatedly turn down some toothless old farmer? No, thank you very much; she could do without that torment. There was no need to put herself through that sort of agony just to please these two; it wasn't as though they needed a chaperone – or a wallflower to dampen their enjoyment. 'So, what are your jobs for today then?' she asked in a bid to distract the pair of them.

'Well, we *should* be earthing up the potatoes and spraying them against blight with Bordeaux mixture,' Nessa replied. 'But since they were so late going in, they're not through yet.'

'So instead, we thought we might clear that spare piece of ground up behind the sheds,' Bonnie added. 'Have our own little veg patch to take us through the winter. Put in some of those carrot seeds we found. Spinach, the same. And the thinnings from anything else we get.'

Careful not to show surprise at this unexpected burst of purpose, May nodded. Draw attention to it and she might kill it off before it even got going; they could be funny like that, these two. 'Good idea. Find anything else in the shed you could put in?'

But Bonnie could be just as sly. 'If you promise to think proper about coming with us to the dance, we'll have another look.'

Despairing of the pair of them, May shook her head. 'Fair enough,' she replied, careful to avoid using the word 'promise'. 'You sow us some vegetables and I'll give proper thought to this dance of yours.'

She'd have to keep an eye this newly emboldened Bonnie, May reflected as she watched the two girls get up from the table and go out through the scullery. She'd certainly gained in confidence these last weeks – talking about men and trying to cajole her into going to a dance. Cheeky miss. What on earth did she, May, want with going to a dance?

–

'Wow. Look at you. Aren't you the dark horse?'

'Oh, my word, May, you look lovely.'

It was Saturday evening and, against every ounce of her better judgement dressed and ready to go to the dance, May blushed. 'Stop it, the pair of you. You're just not used to seeing me out of a housecoat.' For once, though, she felt pleased with the way she looked. She especially liked how the skirt of her new dress swished about her legs to make her feel ladylike.

'Glad I loaned you my curlers now, aren't you?' Nessa said, glancing up from where she was ferreting about in a little quilted purse.

'I suppose,' May conceded, aiming for nonchalance but, hearing the tone of her response, fearing she'd over-done it. Having spent the entire day resisting Nessa's suggestion that she *do something with her hair*, at the last minute she had relented and allowed her to dab it with setting solution and then roll it around some curlers. The effect, once her normally straight and weighty hair had been pinned to frame her face, was nothing short of extraordinary.

'You just need,' Nessa said, still fishing about, 'some colour on your lips.'

Bonnie was quick to agree. 'Yes! That's what's missing – a bit of colour.'

Seeing Nessa brandishing a lipstick, May backed away. 'Oh, no, I don't think—'

But Nessa already had hold of her arm. 'You know your problem? You *think* too much. Now, for Pete's sake stand still and lower your bottom lip.' Seeing no point in prolonging the agony, May obeyed, the feel of Nessa pressing on her lips with the stub from a slender gilt tube immediately causing her regret. 'Good. Now, do this.'

Reluctantly, May complied, the act of pressing her lips together reminding her what sticky stuff lipstick was; she'd only ever worn it a couple of times, each of those at the suggestion of someone else – well, of Pearl – who had insisted it would do wonders for her appearance. Pearl with her hair done up and a bit of make-up on was forever being mistaken for the eldest of them. Hardly surprising – the girl had learned early on what could be won by flaunting her womanliness. And that wasn't something she'd got from their mother, either.

'Now,' Bonnie said with a grin, 'we'll be able to tell who she's been kissing!'

'I could order you to stay at home, you know.' Kissing indeed. Getting involved with some village lad was the last thing she needed.

To hide that she was blushing anyway, she turned sharply about, the sight of her reflection in the mirror over the mantle making her swallow down a gasp: gone was her usual scrubbed appearance, in its place someone who could have been Pearl – an unsettling realisation, to say the least.

'Right, then. Next on the list is dancing.'

Still unnerved by her likeness to Pearl, May turned back to find Nessa regarding her. 'What?'

'Do you, or do you not, know the steps to the foxtrot?'

'It's all right if you don't,' Bonnie quickly reassured her. '*I* didn't know – Dad would never let me go dancing – but since Nessa showed me, I can take a reasonable turn at it.'

'Look, come here,' Nessa directed. 'If you can do the waltz, you can foxtrot. It's quite… safe and sedate.' Evidently seeing May's hesitation, she went on, 'Seriously, what's the point of going to a dance if when we get there you're not going to take a turn around the floor?'

What indeed. It was the matter that had been bothering her most since she'd agreed to go. *Agreed to go?* Huh. Since she had been coerced, more like.

'Nessa's right,' Bonnie said. 'It's easy.'

'Come on. I'll be the man.'

With a shake of her head and a long sigh, May relented. 'Very well. What do I do?'

'Think of it as a smooth walk around the room in the same direction as everyone else.'

'All right.' A smooth walk didn't sound so bad.

'You'll probably want to count in your head to start with. But once you get under way, timing your steps to the music will just seem obvious.'

'Can't see how.'

'Just don't move your lips when you count,' Bonnie chipped in.

Regretting it more with each second she stood there, May exhaled heavily. 'Count but don't move my lips.'

'Your partner will take your right hand in his left, like this. He'll bring his other hand quite high onto your back, here. Once he's done that, you rest your left hand on either his arm or his shoulder. Depends how tall he is. There. You see. Once he's taken hold, you don't have much choice anyway. He leads, you follow.'

'He leads, I follow.'

'Like life,' Bonnie said, her remark bringing from Nessa a derisory snort.

'Now, you're going to be going backwards. So, starting with your feet together, your weight slightly on your left, take a small ordinary sort of walking step back with your right foot… that's it… and a slightly longer step back with your left. Yes. And see how I've come with you?'

Feeling utterly foolish and extraordinarily hot, May nodded. 'Suppose.'

'Now, your right foot is going to step slightly more quickly across to your right.'

'Across to my right,' May repeated. How the devil had she got herself into this?

'And then your left will slide across to join it.'

'Left… across to join it.'

'See,' Nessa said. 'Simple.'

'That's it?' Surely, there had to be more to it than that?

'Pretty much. Just repeat the same pattern and let the man guide you around the floor. If he starts to turn, follow – without standing on his feet – and then resume the pattern of steps we just did.'

'Right…' *Turn. Follow. Resume.* It sounded like a recipe for a disaster.

'Tell you what,' Nessa said, glancing about, 'since there's no room in here, let's go out into the yard.'

When Nessa dropped her hold, May remained where she was. 'To do what?'

'To put more than two steps together.'

'In the yard.' Had Nessa taken leave of her senses?

'It's all right,' Bonnie was quick to point out. 'A couple of months back, she taught *me* out there. There's no one to watch… if that's what you're worried about.'

With a slow and resigned shake of her head, May sighed. 'Very well. Come on then. Might as well make sure I've got it, I suppose.'

With Nessa adopting the sort of firmness May supposed a male partner would, she was astonished to find that it was true: where the man led, she had no choice but to follow. She was also surprised by how quickly she mastered the repeating set of steps. She even understood about them being taken *slow, slow, quick, quick*.

'Well,' Nessa said after a while, 'you seem to have taken to that easily enough.'

'But what if the dance isn't a foxtrot?' As concerns went, to May, it didn't seem an unreasonable one. 'What if it's one of those fast new tunes – that what's-it-called music?'

'Swing, I imagine you mean. Such fun! So lively. But you needn't fear that,' Nessa replied. 'Not tonight. Somewhere as behind the times as this place won't even have heard of it. No, when Bonnie and I went last time, pretty much every dance was either a foxtrot or a waltz. It was all very… sedate. If we were going to a club up in town, then yes, the dances would be far more modern. But tonight, in the unlikely event you don't know the dance, just sit it out.'

Not only was that the most reassuring thing Nessa had said all evening, but it was also the most sensible. 'Good advice.'

'Right then, ladies,' Nessa said, starting back indoors, 'it's just gone seven. Shame we have to walk but it can't be helped. At least we won't be there too early.'

Watching Nessa go in through the scullery door, May found herself observing the way her hips swayed. Did she *make* them do that? Was it something she practised? Or was that just the way things moved when you were blessed with curves like those? Her black skirt was certainly a close fit – one sudden movement and that kick-pleat wouldn't be the only split in it. And that red silk blouse wasn't exactly loose over her chest, either. Still, May thought, feeling slightly more charitable after the trouble Nessa had taken to show her how to foxtrot, while she wouldn't want to draw quite so much attention herself – it was one thing to know your mind and not allow yourself to be trodden on, but quite another to deliberately set out to be the cynosure of all eyes – she wouldn't mind a dose of the girl's confidence.

Moments later, as ready to leave as she felt she would ever be, and with her mac over her arm and the strap of her handbag over her shoulder, May stepped through the door and pulled it shut behind her. Reaching to check it had latched, she spotted movement at the edge of the orchard: Mr Beer, it had to be. Yes, there he was, his expression hardening to distaste as his eyes roved Nessa's shapeliness. Skipping dismissively over Bonnie – the latter demure but colourful in a spotted blue shirt-dress – his eyes landed on her own form and lingered a moment longer than felt decent, before his whole demeanour seemed to take on an air of disappointment. What did *he* have to be disappointed about, she wondered, or even to disapprove of for that matter? Compared to Nessa, she looked positively matronly, showing neither an undue amount of cleavage nor an indecent amount of leg. Besides, what did *her* appearance have to do with *him* anyway? George Beer wasn't her husband, nor was he her father. In fact, he had no reason to even be regarding her. But then, as she had quickly come to find out, he was peculiar through and through. She would just have to hope there weren't too many like him at this dance tonight because, as determined as she could sometimes be, she never had been very good at turning people down…

# Chapter 14

The church hall appeared to be in complete darkness. With blackout shutters at the windows, and the doors to the front porch firmly closed, a passer-by could be forgiven for thinking the place was empty. But, once inside, May was surprised by the number of people already there. Where she had been expecting a mere half-dozen couples to be waltzing to something sedate, the musicians on the little stage were playing an upbeat song to which as many as twenty couples were trotting around the floor.

Her thruppence entry fee handed to the elderly gent inside the porch – for which she received a cloakroom ticket for her mac and a second ticket for either a lemonade or a ginger beer – she followed Nessa and Bonnie into the main hall.

'Look,' Bonnie said, pointing across to the left, 'there's some chairs. Should we go and claim them?'

May nodded. 'Wouldn't mind resting my feet a minute.' Declining an invitation to dance would surely be easier if she was already seated; standing at the edge of the dance floor, she might look as though she was angling to be asked. That was more Nessa's domain.

'Bit of a rough old walk,' Bonnie agreed, heading towards the vacant chairs.

The weight off her feet, May let out a little sigh, and then chuckled at the sight of Nessa looking at her wristwatch. 'Somewhere else to be?'

'If only. No, just trying to gauge how long before it will fill up.'

'Will it, then? Fill up, I mean?'

'It did last time,' Bonnie said.

'Really?' Given that Pippinswell was in the middle of nowhere, it seemed hard to believe.

Gradually, though, people started to drift in, crane to see who was already there, greet friends and, in the case of the older folk, look around for somewhere to sit. By contrast, some of the younger couples didn't even wait for the start of the next song to slip among the dancers, take up hold, and join the whirl.

Tapping her foot to the music, May studied the band. A quintet, they looked and sounded to be more than a few friends who sang and played together for fun. The pianist, sporting a trilby, was clearly the eldest, then there was a drummer, a trombonist, and a chap with a saxophone. Of all of them, the singer was probably the youngest – slicked-back hair, natty tie, and a surprisingly good voice. All told, for a church hall they sounded surprisingly accomplished.

Alerted by a brightening of Bonnie's expression, May turned to see the cause. Bowling through the door, and immediately on the lookout for dance partners, were a dozen young men in air force blue. Instinctively, she ducked her head. It wasn't that she had anything against dancing. Nor was she altogether against the company and attention of a young man. But what she *was* desperate to avoid was getting drawn into anything more than just that. After all, this was probably how things had started for her mother: a young man in uniform caught her eye, promised her the world, came back from the war a changed man and, well, before she knew it, she was a widow with two young daughters and, in the absence of anyone to provide for them, three jobs to wear her down. Yes, a dance – assuming anyone asked her – was fair enough. But *just* a dance. She wasn't there to meet a husband.

And Nessa had been right about it filling up. Before long the floor was crowded with couples, not just youngsters, either, but men and women old enough to be their parents and, occasionally, their grandparents. Watching them, May sighed. Day-to-day life here was so different. With so many families connected to farming, the community still had menfolk at home, whereas in Exeter they were generally all long gone. Apart from shopkeepers, she'd quite got out of the habit of talking to men.

As the evening wore on, however, she did accept a couple of invitations to dance.

'May I?' a young RAF chap approached her to ask.

'I'm not very good,' she said, getting to her feet nevertheless.

'I'll take a chance. I'm Reg, by the way.'

'May.'

To her mortification, once on the floor she couldn't remember a thing Nessa had shown her. Was it her right foot or her left that went back first? Her only saving grace was that with the dance floor so crowded, there was no space for her partner to do much other than lead her in a steady progression around it. Even so, before long she had kicked the poor chap's ankle, after which she completely lost all sense of where she was supposed to be putting her feet. And the moment she became aware of how sticky her hands had become, things only grew worse. But her partner was nothing if not gallant, smiling every time they caught one another's eye and delivering her in gentlemanly fashion back to the edge of the floor when the music ended. To her relief, he then quickly disappeared, and she never saw him again.

Moments later, Bonnie came to stand alongside her. 'Golly, I'm hot.' In a bid to relieve her discomfort, she flapped the collar of her dress.

Noticing that she did seem rather flushed, May said, 'Fancy a lemonade to cool down?' Of Nessa, she noted, there was no sign.

'I've already used my ticket.'

'Come on, my treat.'

'Then yes please!'

After that, May deliberately avoided straying too close to the dance floor. Content to stand and watch the fun, each time a new song began she made herself appear busy: she stood on tiptoe as though searching for someone; she threaded her way around the room as though on her way somewhere; she busied herself searching in her pocket, ostensibly for something she had lost.

And it worked. She was left alone. Until a voice to her left said, 'You look worn out.'

Surprised that she'd recognised it, she turned to see Dan and, with a rueful shake of her head, raised her own voice to reply. 'Is it that obvious?'

He gestured to a couple of empty chairs. 'Shall we?'

'Good idea.'

'Quite lively tonight.' He indicated the dance floor. 'The boys in blue are from that new training centre up at Bonham Hall.'

'So I gather.'

When the music came to an end and the applause had died down, Dan continued at a more normal volume. 'They're certainly putting a twinkle in the eyes of some of the local girls. And not just the young ones, either.'

May grinned. 'The maids and matrons of Pippinswell have never seen anything so well turned out?'

'Notch up from us farm boys, that's for sure.'

'Oh, I don't know,' May replied, 'before someone put them in that uniform, they probably weren't anything special.'

'Happen not.'

She grinned. 'But you could do without the competition.'

'Me? Nah. Not bothered. Don't get me wrong, I like the ladies. I'm just not…'

'Not looking to be tied down.'

'Not yet.'

On the point of saying *me neither*, she changed her mind. 'Good for you.'

'Had a chance to look over those pamphlets I gave you?'

Their conversation back in more comfortable territory, May nodded. 'I did look at them, yes. The way they set it all out makes growing things look real easy.'

'For the most part, it is. You can do worse than follow them. Your Nessa knows what she's about, too. Don't let her fool you into thinking otherwise.'

When, at the mention of Nessa, May cast a glance over the dancers, it was to see her straining red blouse in the eager clutches of one of the airmen. 'Don't worry,' she said evenly. 'I've got the measure of our Miss Croft.'

When the next song started, Dan shifted his weight. 'If I told you I can manage a half-decent waltz, would you risk this dance with me?'

She looked up to see that the dancers had thinned somewhat. 'All right,' she said. 'Though I think yours is the bigger risk. I'm terrible rusty.'

As it transpired, she was glad she had ignored her instinct to decline him. In Dan's somewhat forthright hold, she didn't fear forgetting where her feet were supposed to be; as Nessa had pointed out, a good partner made it seem obvious.

'You know, I didn't expect to see you here,' he said as they moved gently around the floor.

'To be honest, neither did I. Nessa talked me into it. Although, to be fair, Bonnie was just as insistent.'

'Doesn't surprise me in the least,' Dan said. 'About Nessa, I mean. She's certainly not backwards in coming forwards.'

Digesting his words, May didn't reply. Had Nessa been pursuing him? She would have thought someone from a background like hers would have her sights set rather higher – not that there was anything wrong with Dan, far from it. It was just that Nessa didn't seem the sort to settle for life on a farm. But perhaps her thoughts hadn't been on the long term. These days, girls seemed far less concerned about their reputation, especially those no longer under the watchful eyes of their parents; many of them just seemed to want nothing more than to have some fun. And who could blame them? She wouldn't mind a bit herself if it weren't for the ease with which it could all go so horribly wrong.

'To be fair,' she said, 'just recent, she's turned a bit of a corner. Since we've started to get things on more of an even keel, she's been quite… useful. Put her back into the work a bit more.'

'I seen that,' Dan replied.

On the stage, the band were bringing the number to a close.

'Thank you,' she said. 'I even managed to avoid stepping on your toes.'

'You did.'

'Well, then—'

'Would you like a lift home?'

'I—'

'And in case you're worried, I do mean just a lift home. When you're up as early as I am, you know better than to stay on too long at these things.'

'Then yes, please,' she said. 'That would be kind.'

'I assume the other two will find their way back without you.'

May shrugged. 'Not my place to mollycoddle them.' Besides, she thought, they looked to be getting on well with those two airmen and were unlikely to welcome her spoiling their fun. 'How they get home is down to them.'

'Fair enough.'

'But I should just go and tell them I'm leaving.'

A few minutes later, riding along in Dan's little green Austin pickup, May was grateful to have been spared the tramp home. How she would have managed it with the way her feet were throbbing, she had no idea. She could see why, after a night on the tiles, some men succumbed to the lure of falling asleep under a hedge.

'So, you settled in here now then?' Dan asked as he changed down through the gears to make a right turn.

'I do seem to be.' Staring out into the dimpsy, she felt her fingers curling around the edge of the seat and hoped

Dan could see far enough ahead to avoid going into a ditch. Presumably he could go along at this speed because he knew the lane and its potholes so well, rather than because he was trusting to luck. While there might still be some patches of brightness in the sky, down between these hedgerows everything had already become a fuzzy grey. 'I do think about my sisters a lot. But from their letters it would seem they're getting along all right.'

'Not about to bolt, then?'

She looked across at him. Even in the poor light, his profile and his dark colouring made him look unnervingly like George.

'Bolt?'

'Do a runner? Like the ones before.'

'Don't know anything about them,' she said, recalling only what Bonnie had told her about Alma. 'No, though I might be town born and bred, and at times feel like a fish out of water, keeping house is much the same wherever you do it. That said, out here, it does at least come with fresh air and a bit of peace. Oh, and from what I've seen of it so far, fewer shortages… especially when it comes to food. And no air raids either.'

'Having never lived anywhere else, I sometimes think I don't appreciate that.'

'Well,' she said, realising they were approaching the gate to Fair Maids, 'no need for you to trail all the way up the track. I can walk the rest of the way.'

His tone didn't change. 'I said I'd give you a lift home and I will. I doubt you've even got a torch.'

In the darkness, May blushed. He was right; Nessa was the one with the torch. 'Actually, no, I haven't.'

In any event, by now they were drawing up to the farmhouse.

'Stay there, I'll let you out. That door sticks.'

While grateful more than anything to be home, as May watched Dan get out and come round to assist her she felt a tinge of something she couldn't put her finger on. The closest she could get to it was regret. But regret about what? Surely she wasn't rueing that Dan was being so gentlemanly, was she?

'Well, thanks again,' she said, trying not to sound overly formal.

'No trouble. Can you see to get in?'

With a smile into the darkness, she started across the grass. 'Just fine, thanks. It's not locked.'

'All right then. Good night.'

Once inside, without switching on the light, May felt her way along the passage and through the parlour, from where, tracing one hand up the wall to steady herself, she edged her way up the stairs. Arriving in her bedroom, she switched on the light and then hurried to press the square of blackout against the window. What an odd night it had been! Thank goodness tomorrow was Sunday; for once, she might allow her tired old feet a little lie-in. If Nessa and Bonnie were late getting back tonight, they were unlikely to be up at the crack of dawn.

Unbuttoning her dress, and then remembering just in time that she was wearing lipstick, she quickly wiped her mouth with the corner of her damp flannel. Then, having removed her clothes and tugged her nightdress over her head, she folded back the corner of the eiderdown and got into bed, grateful for the way her body sank into the mattress. Her thoughts wandered back to Dan. What a nice fellow he was. Far too good for that hussy Nessa. Hoity-toity madams like her just took what they wanted for as long as they felt like it and then, when they got fed up, cast the poor fellow off cold. Not that she need fear for Dan on that front; clearly, he knew all about girls like Nessa Croft.

And no, to return to his question from earlier, she wasn't about to bolt. Funny little old place though this was, and for all the trials and tribulations it seemed to bring her, it really had come to feel like home.

*VI. June Drop*

# Chapter 15

'So, what's on your list of jobs to do today, then?'

It was a bright June morning at the start of a new week and, to May's relief, the vegetable-growing seemed to be coming along nicely. Knowing so little of what was required, she had deliberately made her involvement gradual, taking care to encourage and nudge the girls rather than just order them about. As a result, her fear that Nessa would prove difficult – or even refuse outright to work with her – had been unfounded. In fact, the woman seemed almost relieved that someone – anyone – was finally showing an interest.

'Water the kale,' Nessa answered her enquiry. 'And there's always plenty of hoeing and weeding.'

'Also,' Bonnie chipped in, 'we found some left-over seed for Savoy cabbages and thought we'd put some in our little vegetable garden, you know, to give us some greens through next winter.'

'Good idea.'

'The packet says they're not to be sown *by individuals for private consumption* but there's only a small amount...'

'And once they're in the ground, who's to say where they came from?' May said with a wink. 'It's not as though we haven't already got a whole field of cabbages for the War Ags anyway.'

'That's what we thought.'

'Unfortunately,' Nessa said, 'there's also the beetroot to thin. It's a mind-numbing and back-breaking job but we can't keep putting it off.'

'So, you'll be busy then,' May observed.

'More than busy,' Bonnie replied before succumbing to a wide yawn.

'And yet,' May said, turning towards her, 'here you are, still stood about indoors…'

'Beggin' your forgiveness, master,' Nessa responded with a tug of her forelock and a put-on country accent. 'Come on, Miss Bonnie, we've had our gruel, and though we still be starvin' and rickety, Mas' has ordered us out into the fields.'

When May replied, it was with a deliberately broadened accent of her own and a despairing shake of her head. 'Be off with you, curs. Or I'll tan 'ees backsides.'

Eventually, with the house to herself, May started on her own jobs for the day. Last night, although she hadn't felt like it, she had forced herself to ready everything for the weekly laundry. She had filled the wash copper with water, separated the garments into colours and whites, and put the latter to soak with a dose of bluing. The girls' socks, which were always ingrained with dirt, and Mr Beer's shirts and overalls, which were perpetually stained from where he continually wiped his hands down the front, were in the dolly tub with water and soap flakes.

At first light, grateful for the head start, she had brought a shovel of hot coals from the kitchen to start the fire beneath the copper so that now, with it billowing steam, she was ready to go.

Plunging her hands into the sink, she pulled out the whites and put them on the drainer. Then, with the mangle wheeled into position over the washtub, she ran each garment through it and then dropped them into the copper, the steam subsiding as she did so. Bending low, she checked the fire and added a few more lumps of coke.

Content that the water would come back up to the boil, she turned her attention to the soiled items soaking in the tub, grabbing the dolly stick to give them a thorough agitating. At least here, she thought, as she grew steadily hotter and hotter, she had the luxury of a scullery and a copper all to herself; in Albert Terrace, laundry day had meant a trip to the wash house on the corner – but only once she'd finished her shift at the Sovereign. And if she went to fill the copper and found it greasy inside, it was because *she'd* skimped on cleaning it last time round, rather than because the woman who'd used it before her hadn't bothered. Moreover, here, the washing line was out in the open – where the clothes and bedsheets got a good blow – rather than strung across a backyard like at Albert Terrace, where more often than not it hung limply until she brought it back in, covered in smuts from the chimneys of Wolcott's Laundry. The irony of the situation never had ceased to make her cross.

Yes, if she had to do the washing every Monday, doing it here could only be made easier by having a laundry maid. In the steam-filled scullery, she chuckled. Have a laundry maid? Her? Only in her dreams!

Eventually, with everything washed, rinsed, mangled and pegged to the line, she cleaned the inside of the copper with soft soap. Finally, having raked out and disposed of the ashes from underneath, she ripped off her headscarf and went outside to cool down before she had to start making supper. Ordinarily, Monday was stew day, but the rabbits George had brought for Sunday dinner, while tasty enough, had been too small to produce leftovers. Remembering the fact, she went indoors to the pantry, where she stared into the vegetable basket: the remaining half of yesterday's cabbage; a dozen carrots that were already going rubbery; a small onion – the latter, as rare as hen's teeth. On the shelf above was a can of peas and another containing the sort of horrible slippery tomatoes she abhorred. The tin in question had been staring at her since the day she'd arrived. She supposed she would eventually find a palatable way to use them; by all accounts, they were full of goodness.

Glancing to the clock and noting the time, she wondered how Nessa and Bonnie were getting on. It was around about now that they usually stopped to eat. As it was such a warm day, she might make a fresh flask of tea and take it out to them.

Carrying the Thermos – and the end of a loaf dabbed with dripping for her own lunch – she spotted the girls sprawled in the dappled shade of an ash tree, Bonnie blowing the seeds from a dandelion clock.

'Coo-ee,' she called ahead.

Looking up, Nessa called back. 'What's the matter?'

May continued towards them. 'Nothing. Why?'

'It's just that you don't usually trek all the way over here without reason.'

'Not ordinarily, no,' May agreed. 'I just thought you might welcome a fresh Thermos of tea.'

'Thanks.'

The tea poured into three receptacles, May scanned the field. 'How are you getting on?'

It was Bonnie who replied. 'Not too bad. We've thinned half the beets.'

'Other half this afternoon?'

'Yep.'

Eventually, draining the dregs of her tea and securing the cup back on the top of the Thermos, May got to her feet. In doing so, something about the seedlings in the adjacent patch caught her eye. Going towards them, she bent low. 'What's going on with these cabbages, then?' To her eye, it looked as though the leaves had been torn from the stems. It also appeared as though the whole area had been trampled.

'We think it's deer to blame,' Bonnie called across.

'Deer?'

'Though probably just a single animal,' Nessa added, propping her head on her elbow to look at her. 'Otherwise, the whole field would have been eaten.'

'We think something probably startled it away. Fox, maybe.'

Uncertain what to make of the discovery, May frowned. 'So, deer eat cabbage?'

'They'll eat almost anything,' Nessa said. 'Although, unless they're starving, they usually avoid plants with spikes or thorns, or hairy leaves. Oh, and they're not fond of onions.'

'So... will these plants still grow?' When she looked across, Nessa was shaking her head.

'Unlikely. Had they munched just a few leaves from fully grown plants, the damage might not be a disaster. But those left without even a single leaf will die.'

Die? They'd gone to all this effort just to have the plants seen off by animals?

'So... what do we do about it?'

'We *could* tell Mr Beer—'

'Which as we all know,' Nessa responded drily to Bonnie's observation, 'will be a complete waste of breath.'

Nessa had a point. If Mr Beer hadn't wanted to grow vegetables to start with, then why would he be bothered that they were all being eaten? It wasn't even his labours that were going to waste. 'But if he *was* concerned, what do you think he would say we should do?'

'The most sensible solution,' Nessa said, 'would be to put up wire fencing – tall enough that the deer couldn't jump over it.'

Was Nessa having her on? 'Deer can *jump*?'

'They'd clear Bonnie's height without difficulty.'

Unable to picture Mr Beer going to the cost and bother of fencing when he wouldn't even shell out for seeds unless forced to, May sighed. 'Is there nothing else to be done?'

'There are things that can be used to put the deer off. But they don't always work.'

'Such as?'

'Putting out things that give off a smell. I remember reading that you can plant garlic around the edges of your other crops. But clearly, that wouldn't work on an area as big as this.'

'No,' May said, her tone despairing.

'Same goes for a hedge,' Bonnie added. 'When I was little, Grandad always grew hawthorn to stop deer from coming through from the copse.'

'What about the beet? Will they eat *them*, too?'

'Once they've finished off the cabbage, they're bound to at least try them.'

'Dear Lord,' May said, her despair deepening. 'So, what do we do?'

From beneath the tree, both girls shrugged.

'You could *try* asking George,' Nessa ventured. 'Coming from you rather than us two, he might take greater interest.'

Wandering back to the farmhouse a while later, May felt as though all the pleasure from a morning well spent had been sucked from her day. Talking to Mr Beer would be pointless. Ask him how to prevent moths from infesting his apples and he would describe a dozen different remedies. But ask him about vegetables and he would probably just shrug. On the other hand, who else was she going to ask? Those two War Ags? She'd rather not. Someone from the land club? They were just volunteer labourers.

It was then that she had an idea. She could ask Dan. Even if he didn't know off the top of his head, he was bound to know someone who would. She glanced to Higher Cleave farmhouse. Yes, but she couldn't just stroll over there and ask. For a start, it would look as though she was always on the scrounge. In truth, she was. But if she kept an eye out for him, she could make her approach seem merely casual.

Struck by another idea, she swivelled about and made her way back to Bonnie and Nessa. Beneath the tree, they were stretching their arms above their heads and staring out over the rows of beetroot.

'Smells,' she said, puffing from the warmth as she drew near.

'What does?' Nessa turned to ask.

'You said deer can be put off by smells.'

'Supposedly.'

'So, what about Jeyes Fluid? Would that work? It stinks to high heaven, and there's that great big can of it in the outhouse. What if we were to mix it with water and put it around the edge of the cabbage field? I know for certain cats can't abide the stuff.'

The way Nessa raised an eyebrow suggested she was impressed. 'That might work.'

'Even if the smell only lasts a couple of days, it would give us time to come up with something better.'

'It's worth a try. When we've finished the beetroot, we'll make up a solution.'

'All right then. And come suppertime, we'll talk to Mr Beer.'

–

'What the devil do you expect?'

George Beer's expression, when May raised the subject with him that evening, was nothing short of triumphant.

'Well, we were rather hoping—'

'Time and again I've said how these damn fool ideas are a waste of time. Lost count of the occasions I pointed out to them ruddy War Ag know-it-alls what tripe it all is. But do they listen? Course not. *It's to be done by order of the Executive Committee*, says they – they as haven't a single farming brain between them. Jumped up little tenant farmers, that's all they were. Ruddy war was the best thing ever to happen to either of 'em. Power in the hands of duffers, that's what it is. Wouldn't know a lump of clay from a flint, a shovel from a pitchfork. No, you want the deer to stop eating your blasted vegetables? Try picking *their* brains. See what *they've* got to say. Because I'll tell you this for nothing. I'd no more save *their* hides than I'd poke out my own eyes with a burnt stick.'

George's tirade seemingly blown out, May contained a sigh. Nessa was right: she might as well have saved her breath, not to mention spared her pride. Waiting until George had risen stiffly from the table and tramped from the room, she cast a look to Nessa and Bonnie. The expression on the face of the latter was one of shock.

Nessa, though, was unmoved. 'Well,' she said, 'while I could say *I told you so*, I won't.'

'No, fair do's,' May acknowledged. 'I'm not too big to admit you were right. But at least whatever we do now, he can't complain we've gone behind his back.'

'But what *are* we going to do?' Bonnie enquired. By looking as though she might cry, the poor girl's face reminded May of Clemmie.

'Leave it with me,' she said, reaching to stack their bowls. 'With any luck, the Jeyes will have given us a day or two to work something out.'

'As long as we don't get a thunderstorm to wash it all away.'

'That,' she said, shooting Bonnie a grin, 'is something I can do nothing about. Now, go and put your feet up, the pair of you, and let me have a think.'

In truth, she didn't need to think, she just needed to hope. Twenty minutes later, her face washed, her hair brushed, her apron on the kitchen peg and her field guide to wildflowers under her arm, May crossed the yard and headed towards the stream. Choosing a route that would make her clearly visible from across the fields, she paused now and again to stoop and examine anything that caught her eye. Eventually, after fifteen minutes spent plodding along with her head angled towards the ground, the realisation that she had arrived at the potato field made her stop and stare across it. To her astonishment, poking through the soil were dozens of tiny green leaf tips – tips that appeared too evenly spaced to be weeds. Good grief, it had worked; it had only gone and worked! The potatoes were growing. They were going to have a crop of spuds! Well, assuming marauding wildlife didn't take a fancy to them as well. Oh, dear God – what if the same fate befell the potato crop as had struck the cabbages? What then? She *had* to talk to Dan: if she didn't see him this evening, then tomorrow, she would have to summon her courage and go over there, even if it did mean making herself seem a nuisance. There was too much at stake not to.

'Surprising how quick they come through, ain't it?'

She swivelled about. 'Dan!'

Caught off guard by her enthusiasm, Dan reeled back-wards. 'Forgive me,' he ventured uncertainly, 'seems I've disturbed you. Again. So—'

'No. No,' she said with a shake of her head for emphasis. 'No. Far from it. I came out to look for flowers but in truth I seem to have become distracted by a worry.'

'Yeah? Well, you know what they say about worries.'

With no idea what he was talking about, she stared back at him. 'And that is?'

'A worry shared is a worry halved.'

'Ah,' she said. 'I think perhaps that's a *problem* shared is a *problem* halved.'

'Problems and worries not one and the same where you come from, then?'

She gave a light laugh. 'With the way they're prone to gnawing away at you, I suppose they are, yes.'

'Well, since I've got two ears for listening with, how about halving whatever's eating away at *you* tonight?'

'As it happens,' she said, 'this particular problem is right up your street.'

'Yeah? Come on, then. Out with it.'

'It's a problem with the cabbages.' Turning away from him, she gestured towards the lower field.

'Aye?'

'And deer.'

'Ah.'

'Least, we think it's deer.'

'Care to show me?'

Thank goodness he'd asked. While being underhand didn't sit comfortably with her – especially when he was such an approachable fellow – she couldn't bear to have him think her always after something.

At the cabbage field, he bent down to examine the seedlings.

'Nessa says they're done for,' she said when he stood up again.

''Fraid so. And you're right. It's deer. See these marks?'

She followed the line of his finger. 'What of them?'

'Two toe shapes together like this, a bit like an upside-down heart, that's deer. They'll take anything with a soft green top.'

'Oh. So...'

'You've put down Jeyes?'

Suddenly, she was left to hope the idea wasn't as ridiculous as it now sounded. 'Nessa said they don't like strong smells.'

'She's right. They don't.'

'It's all I could come up with.'

'May Huxford, we'll make a farmer of you yet.'

She blushed hotly. And then, mortified to have done so, blushed even harder. 'Mm.'

'Seriously. It was a good idea. But there are cheaper things that will work just as well.'

Ever so slightly, she relaxed. 'Thank heavens for that. Because I couldn't bear it if just as we were getting some-where, all our effort was in vain.'

Turning towards her, he grinned. 'For a farmer, it's the daily struggle. Anyway,' he went on, 'if this was just a small patch of land, say, a garden, you'd plant herbs around the edge – anything with a whiff to it. Mint, chives, rosemary, sage. Lavender. But if it was me, out here I'd use eggs.'

'Eggs?' Was he having her on?

'Old ones will do fine. Mix up a dozen in a gallon of water. Then spray it round the edge of your crop. A gallon ought to be enough to do round an acre field. As the eggs rot, they give off a smell the deer don't like.'

'Nor will Nessa and Bonnie,' May observed.

'Believe it or not,' Dan said, 'out in the open air, our noses don't smell it.'

'Truthfully?'

'Truthfully.'

'The other thing you're going to have to watch out for is rabbits. The ones George brings you for the pot all come from round here somewhere, you know. And overnight, a family of 'em will devour a whole field.'

Rabbits. Yes. She remembered having seen some a while back. 'The eggs won't keep *them* away, too?'

''Fraid not. Different vermin need different deterrents. For rabbits, folk use animal blood—'

'Animal blood?' It didn't bear thinking about.

'—or ammonia. Or, since you've most likely got a pantry full of the stuff, rags soaked in cider vinegar.'

'That, we do have a–plenty, yes.'

'Downside is you got to keep the rags fresh. Once they dry out, or it rains, you got to redo them.'

'Right.' *More work.*

'If it were me, and I could get hold of Epsom salts, I'd use those. You dissolve them in water and spray the leaves of the plants. It's a big job to do so many in one go, will take up a lot of time, I know that. But not only will it keep the rabbits from eating them, it will also give the plants a dose of magnesium, which does them good.'

'I see.'

'Want me to try and get you a sack on George's account?'

'You'd do that?'

'I go to Cooper's pretty much every week. Instructions for diluting will be on the label.'

With that, she had an idea. 'Happen I could get the land club back to help – you know, get it done quick this first time?'

'I could bring you over a couple of spray pumps if you like.'

'You could?' Golly, he was a saviour!

'Course.'

'Then yes please.'

'I'll bring them over with the Epsom. Though in the meantime, you might want to have a go with the vinegar.'

'Oh, I will. Definitely. We'll get onto it first thing.'

'Right, then. Well, best leave you to your… walk.'

'Oh, right, yes,' she said. 'But thank you. Thank you ever so much.'

'Happy to help.'

Watching as Dan started around the edge of the field, May felt her head might burst from everything she had to tell Nessa and Bonnie: a dozen eggs in a gallon of water against deer; Epsom salts against the rabbits – vinegar-soaked rags in the meantime; help from the land club to do it. Oh, and how nice and how helpful Dan had been again. Although no, perhaps *that* little bit of information was something better kept to herself...

## Chapter 16

'Almost too lovely not to be outside this evening.'

It was a couple of days after May's meeting with Dan and, despite her fear that a storm would come and wash away the deterrents they had painstakingly set up, the weather remained warm and fine, the mornings sparkly with dew, the continuing double summertime meaning that the rosy glow from the setting sun didn't give way to proper darkness until gone eleven o'clock. Unfortunately, in the warmth of her little dormer bedroom, May often found herself awake long after that.

'It is truly lovely,' she replied to Bonnie's observation as the three of them were stood in the yard.

'You know it's nights like these,' Nessa said, 'that I miss being able to have a proper bath.'

'A bath?' In her surprise, May turned to regard her.

'I quite crave one. An illegally deep one. None of this measly five-inch business but a proper immersion in cool water. Nothing to beat it on a warm night.'

'Wouldn't know,' May said. 'Where I grew up, unless you went down the public baths, like I seem to remember Dad doing – but which Mum would never let *us* do on account of what she called the *dirty sorts* that went there – the best I ever got was a couple of inches of lukewarm water in a tin bath on the kitchen floor. And only then after Mum had used it.'

'Same here,' Bonnie said. 'Though where I grew up, there weren't no public baths. But we did have the river. And on a night like this, me an' my brothers thought it was heaven.'

'Then perhaps...'

'What?' Alerted by a slyness to Nessa's tone, May turned to see her glancing to Bonnie. Now what were they up to?

'We can go down the river *here*.'

Picturing the stream and the steep bank knitted with tree roots, May frowned. 'That little trickle of water?'

Now it was Nessa's turn to frown. 'What?'

'Far side of the potato field.'

'Good Lord, no,' Nessa replied with a laugh. 'The spring for that rises in the sheep pasture. There could be all manner of nasties in there. No, I'm talking about the river.'

'Other side of the orchard,' Bonnie explained. 'Water's clear as can be.'

'There's a river?'

Nessa nodded. 'It marks the boundary between George's land and that of Bonham Hall. About two miles or so further down, it joins the River Creedy.'

'Goodness.' How, she wondered, had she missed that there was a river? She supposed because she'd never explored the far side of the orchard. After her spat with Mr Beer, she'd kept well away.

'Why don't we take a walk down there?' Bonnie said.

'Better still,' Nessa picked up, 'why don't we go and have a bathe?'

'A bathe.' To May's mind, it was a poor idea for so many reasons.

'Freshen up.'

'Cool down.'

'Enjoy the evening.'

'I don't mind a walk to see the thing,' May said, lost as to how to get out of such a hare-brained idea, 'but I'm not sure I fancy bathing in it.'

'Oh, go on with you,' Nessa said dismissively. 'I've done it half a dozen times. Maybe more. There's never anyone about, if that's your concern.'

'Apart from several dozen RAF lads,' May reminded her. 'The ones you said are training at Bonham Hall.'

'It's only the *land* that adjoins the river,' Nessa said, already turning away, 'the hall itself is a good couple of miles further over. No one from there would trek that far. They're more likely to spend all their free time in the village pub.'

'Well, I still say—'

'Then fetch a towel and just come for a paddle,' Nessa called from inside the lean-to. 'Bonn, you'll come for a dip, won't you?'

Casting a doubtful glance at May, Bonnie hesitated.

'Don't look at *me*. You're old enough to make up your own mind.'

'Hold on, then,' Bonnie called towards the open door of the lean-to. 'I'll get out of these overalls and pull on my shorts. Easier to put back on after.'

As Bonnie disappeared inside, May gave a despairing shake of her head; turn down too many invitations and she risked becoming a wet blanket. Against her better judgement, she nevertheless went up to her room, snatched up her towel and, seeing it on the chest of drawers, the scarf she used to keep her hair clean. Then, rueing her lack of willpower, she went back outside to wait with Nessa for Bonnie to reappear.

'What you got there?' she asked.

From where she had been concealing it among the folds of her long flowery dress, Nessa produced a stone jar with a stopper in the top. 'Something to drink. Plunged into the water while we're bathing, it will cool down a treat.'

Before she was even aware she was doing it, May gave a disapproving sigh. 'Weren't you the one who told me that's strong stuff?'

'It's not that strong. Not really. At least, *I* don't think it is.'

'Well, I'll say this now. Get Bonnie tipsy, and you'll be the one carrying her home.'

'And what about if *you* get tipsy?' Nessa asked with a grin. 'I can't carry both of you.'

'*I* shan't get tipsy,' May replied flatly. 'Can't afford the headache.' She saw no reason to mention that, after seeing what drink did to Charlie Warren – in particular the suffering it caused her mother – she had vowed never to let a drop pass her lips. Business like that was private.

Moments later, the three of them emerged on the far side of the orchard and May found herself standing still to listen. Far from falling silent, the countryside at dusk was alive with sound: crickets rasping in the long grasses; birds singing in defence of their patch of woodland; cattle lowing in the distant pasture. And then there was the air itself, heady with the scent of so many blooms. If only she knew which flowers were responsible; she *must* get back to coming out with her book – and not simply carry it about as an excuse for being out there in the first place. Living among these natural riches, she really should know what they were.

Several yards ahead of her, Nessa called over her shoulder. 'Here we are.'

Bonnie also turned back. 'There. See? Nice, isn't it?' On her face was a look of genuine delight.

Arriving alongside them, May looked around. They were at the top of a grassy slope, at the lower edge of which the river had widened to form a natural pool, the far bank rising more steeply to a copse, where the silvery-grey leaves of a line of towering willows shaded the bank. Bonnie had been right to say the water was clean. Even from that height, she could see through it to the riverbed. It was certainly nicer than she had been expecting.

'Is it deep?' she asked, unable to gauge the distance to the bottom.

'Up to my waist in the centre,' Nessa said as she started to edge sideways down the grassy slope. 'Shallower by the bank.' When she reached the bottom, she indicated further along. 'You see that gravel?' May nodded. 'That's where it's at its shallowest and easiest to get out.'

'Just be careful,' Bonnie cautioned, tracking Nessa's path down the slope. 'This shiny grass is slippery.'

For a moment, May wondered whether she might be better staying where she was. There was space up here to sit comfortably. But, down by the water's edge, Nessa was already pulling her dress over her head, and Bonnie was stepping out of her shorts. Moreover, the water did look inviting. And as Nessa had promised, there was no one about. And she was awfully sticky. In fact, what was stopping her? Why not go in?

Edging sideways as she had seen the other two do, she reached with her free hand to clutch at the grasses and steady her descent.

While she was still barely halfway down there was a weighty splash, followed by an exclamation of surprise.

'Whoa!'

'Is it *really* cold?' Bonnie called to Nessa.

'Only… where my skin… was so hot!'

The splash that followed might have been smaller but the shrieks that accompanied it contained just as much alarm.

'Oh. Oh! OH!'

Reaching the bottom of the bank, May put her towel on the grass. Having decided she was going in, the only question now was whether she did as those two had just done and jump, or chose the safer route via the gravel. Warily, she glanced along the bank.

'Don't even think about it!' Nessa yelled towards her. 'Trust me, try coming in gradually and you'll never succeed.'

'It's true.' Bonnie grinned up at her, her bony white shoulders bobbing about above the surface of the water. 'You got to do it in one go.'

Unbuttoning her dress, May sighed. If ever there was a time she needed her head examined, it had to be this very minute. On the other hand, here she was, living with the sort of freedom that barely four weeks back would have been unimaginable: from being weighed by cares and woes in the aftermath of the raids, she had found a modicum of stability; from starting every day in Albert Terrace with a frown, she now got out of bed with a smile. So, why not embrace it further? Why not, for once just—

*Whoosh!*

Ye Gods! As the shockingly cold water smacked against her flesh, May gasped for air. But as her astonishment began to subside, she realised that although it was cold, it wasn't freezing. As Nessa had said, it was the hottest parts of her body – her forearms and her back – that felt it most. In fact, as she let her arms float out from her sides, she wished she could do it again, just to experience the sensation of thousands of tiny needles pricking her skin. It was the most enlivening thing she could ever recall doing. Not to mention the most reckless, and completely at odds with her sensible nature. Had Clemmie been watching, she would have been horrified. Pearl, on the other hand, would have whooped and cheered and stripped off to join her.

'Glad you were persuaded?' Nessa asked from where she was running a hand back and forth across the surface of the water.

With a grin, May nodded. 'Not too stubborn to admit I am, yes.'

'She'll be down here every night now,' Bonnie remarked.

May's response was accompanied by a vigorous shake of her head. 'I wouldn't go *that* far. There's not many days, even in a Devon summer, when it would be warm enough for that.'

'Do you know,' Nessa began. Together, Bonnie and May turned to regard her. 'In Scandinavia, they go into the water even in the depths of winter? They go out, break a hole in the ice, and then plunge in.'

'They never do!'

'I'm telling you, Bonnie, it's true. They maintain it's good for longevity.'

'Long what?' May asked, noticing that, already, the lower halves of her legs were beginning to grow numb.

'Enables them to live a long life.'

'If the shock doesn't take them first.'

'Before the war,' Nessa picked up again, 'My sister had a pen pal in Sweden. That's how I know about it.'

'Well, one thing's for certain, *I* shan't be breaking any ice. Good for you or not.'

'Me neither,' Bonnie agreed. 'Bad enough how cold it got in the lean-to last winter, without jumping into freezing water.'

'And on which note,' May said, a shiver unexpectedly running the length of her body, 'I think I'm done.'

Some while later, reclined on the bank, her clothes clinging to her still-damp skin, May let out a sigh. Coupled with the after-effects of the cold water, the last little bit of warmth from the sinking sun was making her feel… feel what, exactly? Not only had her body relaxed but in her mind she felt a sense of contentedness. Of well-being. Perhaps even of *euphoria*. Wasn't that a word she'd heard used somewhere? Nessa would know, not that she would ever show herself up by asking her. Whatever its name, she felt both invigorated and peaceful.

Further along the bank, her underwear still in a pile on the grass but her dress back on, Nessa got up and scrambled down to the water's edge. 'Who's for some of this?' Hauling the cider jar from the river, she held it up and grinned. 'Feels nicely chilled.'

Remaining determined to abstain, May shook her head. 'Not for me, thanks.'

'Not even sure I like it,' Bonnie answered.

Flopping down onto the grass alongside them, Nessa looked incredulous. 'You've never tried cider? I thought it was the drink of country girls the land over.'

'No, I've tried it,' Bonnie said and raised herself to sit upright. 'But that were out of a bottle my brother had. And it were really… sour.'

'This won't be. This is good stuff. Rounded. Mellow.'

May scoffed. 'Rounded? What do that even mean?'

'It's a term used when tasting wine.'

'If you say so.'

'Here,' Nessa said, tugging at the stopper until it left the neck of the jar with a fat *whoomp*. Offering it to Bonnie, she went on, 'Take just the merest sip. See what you think. Just don't tip it up too much or it will gush out all over you.'

Should she stop her, May wondered as she regarded Bonnie's doubtful expression? As she'd said to the girl before, she wasn't her mother; she wasn't even her sister. But wouldn't she want someone to stop Clemmie doing something daft? She would. But that was Clemmie. Bonnie was different.

Accepting the jar, Bonnie nodded her understanding. 'Just a sip.' Raising the rim to her lips, she carefully tilted the vessel, the moment the liquid met her tongue evident from the sudden narrowing of her eyes.

'Don't say what you think just yet,' Nessa urged as Bonnie lowered the jar. 'Your taste buds need a moment to take it in.'

*Take it in?* The girl did talk some twaddle.

'I didn't get much anyway,' Bonnie insisted. 'If I'm to get a proper idea, I'm going to need a bit more.' Despite the caution with which she tilted the jar on her lips, the force with which she swallowed suggested to May that, by accident or otherwise, she'd had rather more than just another sip. 'It's very apple-y.'

Taking the cider back from her, Nessa laughed. 'You don't say!'

'But like fallers smell when you gather them up from the grass. You know, that ripe smell they get.'

187

'That's the fermentation,' Nessa said, offering the jar in May's direction. 'Want some?'

'No thank you.'

'Go on. You don't have to drink so much you can't walk. Just try it to see how it tastes. I've seen you looking at the blossom on the trees, so why not discover what it ends up as? George Beer might be one of the most peculiar men to walk God's earth, but he knows how to make good cider.'

Nessa had a point: if she, May, was going to live in a cider orchard, shouldn't she at least know how the stuff tasted? 'Go on, then.'

The jar, when she took it, was heavier than she'd been expecting, the cider, when she held it to her lips, rushing without warning to fill her mouth. When it then went on to warm the length of her throat, she realised that Bonnie was right; the overwhelming sensation was that of very ripe apples – apples that had gone past red to a very pale yellow before dropping over a garden wall to sit on the pavement and wait for a passing schoolchild to swipe them up. As she recalled, though, the excitement of the find usually outweighed the enjoyment of the eating, the fruit having by then become woolly and dry. Nevertheless, the taste perfectly matched the distinctive smell. Annoyingly, Nessa was right too – but then when wasn't she – the cider wasn't at all rough. In fact, it felt thick and full. And moreish.

And it was clear that Nessa could tell she thought so.

'You see what I mean about it now, don't you?'

Responding to Nessa's observation, May nodded. 'Happen I'll just have another little…' The mouthful she took this time was less of an accidental gulp and more considered, only swallowed after she'd let it linger a while on her tongue. 'Honey. Green grass. Not especially sweet. But none too sharp either.'

'That's quite the palate you've got there. You should try wine tasting. You'd be a natural.'

With no idea what Nessa was talking about, May took another mouthful. 'Apple sauce.'

'All right. Don't hog it.'

'Sorry,' she said, surprised by how each new mouthful made her want another. Who would have thought it would be so truly delicious?

'Another go, Bonn?'

Looking as though she'd thought the jar was never going to get back to her, Bonnie gave an eager nod. 'Pears?' she said after a rather greedy swig. 'Or maybe pear drops. And cheese.'

'*Cheese?*'

Finally, Nessa drank, her first sip modest, her second and third rather longer. 'With the exception of Bonnie's cheese, all of those things. And flowers, too.'

From there, the jar made two more rounds before, to her concern, May noticed that Bonnie appeared to be blurring around the edges. Unsettled, she blinked several times and then lowered herself to the grass. The feel of the ground pressing into her back surprisingly reassuring, she stared up at the sky. When it was as empty of clouds as it was tonight, the vastness of it made her feel small and insignificant, the otherworldliness of the dusk making her believe she might be almost be able to see heaven. Unexpectedly, she giggled. Unlike looking at Bonnie, at least the sky didn't keep going all smudgy.

Alongside her, Bonnie chose that moment to hiccup. 'Whoops.'

'So, when this war's over...' To May's ears, Nessa's voice seemed to drift across from a considerable distance. 'What's the first thing you'll do?'

'Is there still rationing?' Bonnie asked.

'Nope. Life is completely back to normal.'

'Then I'll draw out some of the money I've put in my National Savings account, take Mum and Gran into Weymouth... and buy us each a new frock. And then we'll go for ices at Rossi's. They will have opened up again by then, won't they?'

'Of course they will,' May heard Nessa reassure the girl.

'And then I'd see if my best friend, Ronnie – her real name's Veronica but we like being Bonnie and Ronnie – see if she wanted to go dancing down the... down the... pier. And we'll meet two handsome chaps with plenty of money... and sports cars... and...'

'You all right, Bonn?'

'Uh-huh. Just... ooh... everything's gone a bit... woozy...'

'It'll pass. Just lie still for a moment. What about you, May, what will you do?'

It was a good question. On the one hand, this war had taken so much from her – everything, in fact – and yet, even had it not, would she want to go back to her old way of living? Would she want to return to the daily grind of charring at the Sovereign Hotel just to scrape by in the squalor of Albert Terrace? Unlike Bonnie and Nessa, who presumably still had homes to return to, and for whom Fair Maids Farm was only ever a war posting, she didn't have anything to go back *to*. *This was* her new life, and she was hoping to cling on to it, war or not.

'Not sure I can answer that,' she said, wary of admitting to feeling that way; Nessa could be so quick to ridicule.

As it was, she seemed incredulous. 'Honestly? There's not something you're simply itching to do? Something you miss, or have been simply dying to try?'

'Well, course. I can't wait to have a decent meal.'

'All right, so if you could choose anything, what would it be?'

If she didn't feel so slow of thought, she would try to picture something more elaborate than the plain fare her mother had had no choice but to give them. Saying jam roly-poly and custard – even if it *was* a favourite – would only invite disbelief.

Stuck to come up with anything Nessa wouldn't mock, she tried to picture the fancy glass case that had housed the menu outside the King's Restaurant & Grill on the ground floor of the Sovereign Hotel. Imagining herself polishing away the fingerprints from where some eager diner had stabbed at his idea of heaven, she tried to recall which of the dishes had always struck her as something she might one day like to try.

'Roast beef with Yorkshire puddings and horseradish sauce.'

'Truly?'

'Well, when was the last time *you* had roast beef?'

'Fair point.'

'So, what would *you* choose then?' Waiting for Nessa to answer, May closed her eyes, grateful for the way it stopped everything from constantly shifting about in front of them.

'To start, I would have cheese soufflé. For the fish course, I would have lobster, and with it I would drink a Chenin blanc, nice and acidic to cut through all the butter I'd order the chef to use.' Unexpectedly, May yawned.

'Then I would have coq au vin, which would obviously require an exceedingly rich burgundy to accompany it.'

'Obviously.'

'For dessert—'

'Assuming you had the room for it,' May commented drily.

'Having been denied proper food for so long,' Nessa assured her, 'I'd have room for it. I'd *make* room for it.'

'Funny, though,' May said, noticing how the velvety shades of night had begun to envelop them. Out here in the countryside, dusk seemed even more magical than dawn. 'How one of the things all three of us apparently miss is food.'

'Perhaps,' Nessa said, 'because for young women like us, war has already brought a number of the things we might once have craved… much of what we previously dreamt of simply landing at our feet.'

Still staring up at the heavens, May frowned. 'Not sure what you mean.'

'Before I joined the Women's Land Army, I was sleep-walking into marriage. It wasn't a case of "if" but "when". As soon as Mummy had Pen – my sister, Penelope, that is, older than me by a year – safely chained to Spencer, then her thoughts would have turned to me. Actually, they already had. The moment Spencer, or *The Colonel*, as I call him just to annoy Pen, asked Daddy for permission to marry her, I overheard Mummy suggesting that if he ever had any *charming fellow officers at a loose end* – for which, read *unattached and eligible* – then he might like to bring them down one weekend.'

'But that's not what you wanted – an officer for a husband, I mean.'

'Certainly not one as old as Spencer. For heaven's sake, the man is *well* into his forties. Don't get me wrong, I'm not against *men*. Nor am I against officers. In fact, I rather like a man in uniform. And that's the problem.'

Struggling to follow, May raised herself up. 'What is?'

'How to choose just one. Especially when, if you're from a family like mine, it's not the done thing to try out a selection first. At least, not openly. And certainly not to get caught doing so – to bring about Mummy's worst nightmare of a *ruined reputation* and all that goes with it.'

'So...' Did she understand correctly, May wondered? Had Nessa joined the Land Army, ending up sleeping in a lean-to and working ankle-deep in mud and icy slush, just to escape getting married? 'Couldn't you just have said no?'

'Not indefinitely. There's only so many times I could have resisted on the grounds that the men she paraded before me were too old, too fat, too boring.'

*Too filthy. Too cruel. Too drunk.* Ironic, really, May thought, that while their start points in life differed so wildly, she and Nessa had both feared the same outcome – getting trapped in the sort of marriage they didn't want.

'So, what will you do once the war's over?' she asked. 'When you no longer have the excuse of war work for not getting wed?'

'That's the thing,' Nessa said, the new brightness to her tone drawing May to study her expression. 'Even were this war to end this very moment, I've escaped the clutches, haven't I? I've left home. After this, it will be jolly hard for Mummy – or anyone else for that matter – to stop me getting another job, or to stop me mixing in whatever circles I choose. Who knows, if this war drags on very much longer, perhaps Mummy won't even bother trying to marry me off at all. If I spend too long as a land girl, maybe she'll consider me so soiled as to be unmarriageable and instead, direct all her efforts to the next generation – to Pen and Spencer's offspring. Assuming the old boy's up to the task of giving her any.'

'So…' Given what May had pieced together about Nessa's family, she doubted it would be that simple. '…you really only joined the land army to annoy your mother?'

'Guilty as charged. You see, I'm not like Pen. Pen is the good daughter – terribly docile, only ever wants to please everyone. Whereas I don't give a hoot. There are far too many things I want to see and do to worry about offending a bunch of stuffy old relics. That said, standing up to Mummy requires considerable guts. She lives by an old-fashioned code and can't see beyond it, won't be deflected from her duties as wife and mother. She's even blunt with poor old Pen, who wouldn't say boo to a goose. "Darling," I overheard her saying one day, "all the while there's a war on, you don't have a great deal of choice. It's either marriage and children, or else nursing. And you know you're not good with blood. Besides, Spencer's a catch. A little older than I would have chosen, granted, but all the more settled for it. You won't want for a thing. Tell her I'm right, darling." And then Daddy piped up something along the lines of, "Penelope, dear girl, Spencer is an all-round good chap. Doubtless it will seem a bit odd at first, but you'll soon cleave to his ways." That was when I went straight out and signed up to be a land girl. It was the grubbiest thing I could think of doing. I mean, obviously, an armaments factory would have been good, too. But that might have meant being sent somewhere *really* grim, when all I wanted to do was make Mummy so appalled that she'd wash her hands of me.'

*Really* grim? Sometimes the girl had no idea. 'Hm.'

'What about you?' Nessa asked. 'What brought *you* here?'

'You know what brought me here,' May replied.

'You were bombed out.'

'Well then—'

'Only, you must admit, choosing a farm in the middle of nowhere does reek of a certain desperation, doesn't it? Begs the question of whether you, too, were running from something...'

She would mark Nessa's directness down to the cider. And she would certainly be careful not to give too much away. 'I wasn't running from anything. I just needed work.' There was no need to mention that her mother's experience at the hands of Charlie Warren had set her, too, completely against marriage.

'So, no jilted fiancé?'

'Don't be ridiculous.'

'Not even some chap in uniform penning passionate letters from a posting overseas?'

Wearying of Nessa's prying, May shook her head. 'None.'

'Well, good for you, May Huxford. Say,' Nessa suddenly remarked, sitting upright and reaching for the cider jar, 'we should have a toast. A toast to us for holding out. For refusing to bow to pressure. To having the guts to furrow our own paths.'

On that point, May couldn't take issue. And so, reaching across, she accepted the jar. Although she made considerable show of raising it to her mouth, she was careful to allow only the merest dribble pass her lips. She could already feel an almighty headache coming on. No sense risking making it worse – even if she had taken a liking to the stuff.

'To us,' she said.

'To us,' Nessa echoed as she took the jar. 'Bonn, what about…'

But when the two women turned in Bonnie's direction, it was to see her reclined on the grass, eyes closed, arms thrown wide. Together, they giggled.

'I did say, did I not,' May remarked, suddenly overcome by a longing for her bed, 'that *I'm* not carrying her back.'

'We'll manage her between us,' Nessa replied, hauling herself to her feet.

'I'd say we haven't much choice.'

'It's been fun, though,' Nessa said, reaching to touch Bonnie's arm and wake her up.

'Mm,' May agreed carefully. It might seem that way now but, tomorrow morning, at least one of them was going to wake up with a very thick and remorse-filled head indeed.

# Chapter 17

They hadn't spotted her. Yes, she'd felt mean sneaking away without inviting Nessa and Bonnie to come with her but, tonight, she was hoping to just enjoy the beauty of nature without anyone enquiring about either her past or the direction of her future. And she definitely didn't want any more of Mr Beer's cider! Lovely though it was, even the small amount she'd drunk last night had left her this morning with eyes that felt like squares in round holes, and a slowness to her thoughts that she had struggled all day to shake. It was all right for Nessa; she was clearly used to alcoholic drinks. In which case, she should have known better than to ply Bonnie with it quite so freely. Poor girl. It was a wonder *she* hadn't spent the night being sick. What terrible agony she'd been in at first light, though. Had Mr Beer noticed it was Nessa milking the cow instead of Bonnie, they had agreed to say the poor girl was bedridden with cramps. It took a brave man to challenge *that* excuse.

Arriving back at the river again, she spotted the patch of flattened grass where the three of them had last night lain to dry off. Somewhere here was the plant she'd come back to identify. It shouldn't be hard to find because the flowers were the sunniest of yellows. In fact, yes, there it was, beneath those trees. She suspected it would turn out to be nothing more than buttercups, but she would check anyway, it being some time since she'd ticked off a new flower in her book.

As she edged her way down the bank, she could see that the leaves were large and dark and fleshy. Reminding herself of the need to be careful, she bent to examine the flowers; golden and glossy, they certainly resembled buttercups, but not so the foliage. Opening her book, she flicked through the pages until, almost by chance, she spotted an illustration entitled *Marsh Marigold*, the smaller print underneath reading, *also King Cups*. The drawing matched perfectly, as did the description: *large mid-yellow flowers resembling cups, this plant most often colonises riverbanks, ditches, damp meadows, or the margins of ponds.* Rising to her feet, she smiled. She was getting good at this: another plant identified. Although, by the look of the browning petals, only just in time. *Flowers March to May/June*, her book observed.

Having edged her way back up the bank, May glanced to the sky. There were more clouds this evening than yesterday, and the breeze had more of a freshness. Not that she minded; a cooler night would be good for her head. Who would have thought just a few mouthfuls of Mr Beer's cider would have such a long-lasting effect?

Turning her attention to the water flowing languidly between the banks, she sighed. She should have thought to bring her towel; a quick dunk would probably have done her the power of good. She glanced over her shoulder. She supposed she could still risk it. Nessa said no one ever came down here, and in this warmth it wouldn't take her skin long to dry. But as she stood debating the wisdom of it, she heard the swish-swish of someone coming through the long grass.

She turned sharply. Dan? Again? Was he following her about?

'Oh,' she greeted him. 'Hello.' Good job she *hadn't* decided to risk a dip! She could easily have been stripped off and halfway down the bank by now. Then what would she have done? Jumped in and hoped for the best, she supposed.

'Sorry, you were minding your own business. I'll move on and leave you to it.'

'No, it's all right. I was just... here with my book.'

His expression brightened. 'Any new ones?'

What? Oh, he was referring to wildflowers. 'Yes. Marsh marigolds.'

'Yeah. Normally over by now. One of the first flowers of spring. Well, after celandines. And dandelions. But they don't really count. They never really go away.'

'No.'

'All right, well, I'll leave you to it. I only came across here to listen for the nightingale.' Gesturing with his hand to the far bank, he went on, 'They like that coppice because it's damp. By all accounts, it's pretty rare to see them this far west, but we seem to get at least one pair turn up every year.'

She supposed that explained why he was all this way across his uncle's land. 'Is it pretty?' she asked, hoping to sound friendly. 'The song, I mean?'

'Finest of all. Real hard bird to spot among the branches but impossible not to hear. They start singing around dusk and keep going well into the small hours. Course, by now they're likely finished for the season. Tend to stop singing by mid-June... and tonight's the summer solstice.' When she frowned, he went on, 'Longest day.

The night for spirits and fairies… if you believe in that sort of thing.'

'Ah.' In truth, she didn't know what he was talking about; she could only presume it to be some sort of folk-lore. There was a lot of that in the countryside.

'How are your cabbages, by the way? Are the deer keeping away?'

She gave in to a smile; when it came to conversing, he was as straight to the point as George. It had to be a family trait. 'Nessa seems to think so. But I was about to go home that way to look.'

'I'm going to Cooper's in the morning. On the way back, I'll bring you the Epsom salts.'

'Thank you.'

'And the extra pumps for you to borrow.'

'You're very kind.'

'Well then, since I don't hear no nightingale, I'll leave you to it.'

'All right.'

'See you tomorrow, then.'

'Tomorrow. Yes. Good night.'

So handy having a neighbour like him, May thought yet again as she watched him head back in the direction whence he'd just come, especially given George's determination to have nothing to do with the vegetable growing. In fact, if Fair Maids survived the next inspection by the War Ags – and, since it was her home, it had better – it would be as much down to Dan as to her and the two girls. It would certainly be no thanks to George Beer.

With a wide yawn, she turned to clamber back up the bank. For the first time in years, she would admit to feeling settled and happy. All she could do was hope nothing came along to change that.

With a sense this morning that all was still well with the world, May placed her pen on her notepad, raised her eyes to the sky and drew a long breath. Getting up before everyone else and making the most of the quiet was something she had come to enjoy. While no one else was about, it felt as though the morning belonged to her. She could order her thoughts, savour the fresh air, get ahead with the day. This morning, having awoken with the thought to write to Clemmie, she had taken one of the wooden stools from the scullery and gone to sit out the front. And now, with her news – such as it was – painstakingly put down on paper, she read it back.

*Dearest Clemmie,*

*Thank you for your letter. I am sorry it has taken me so long to reply. You know how it is. I was glad to learn that you are all right and was relieved no end to learn that you have somewhere proper to live. I hope all is still well there. I haven't heard from Pearl yet but that is no surprise.*

*I am going along well. A couple of days ago, someone asked me whether I was settled here now, which made me realise that I am. Hard though you will find this to believe, I have really taken to this way of going on. Not only do I keep the place up together indoors, but I have also taken to overseeing the land girls. Learning about the crops is turning me into something of a land girl myself, the proof of which can be seen from my nut-brown arms and sunburnt nose.*

*Not long after I wrote last, I came across a book about wildflowers, and since I often find myself knee-deep in them, I thought I should try to learn what some of them are called. Already I know quite a few.*

*Couple of weeks back I went to a WVS fayre in the church hall. It was quite good but the Easter one you and I went to was much better. Don't suppose there's anywhere left there to hold a fayre now. I also went to a dance in the church hall. Nessa and Bonnie talked me into it but I didn't stay long. Come suppertime, I'm too tired to go gallivanting. I must be getting old.*

*Anyway, I'd best finish here. It's early morning and the girls will be up soon and wanting their breakfast.*

*Take care and God bless. Your loving sister, May*

Staring down at what she had written, May sighed. She did miss Clemmie terribly. She missed Pearl, too. Although, if she was blunt, perhaps she no longer missed them *quite* as much as she had at first. Strange, really, but after just a few weeks, she felt a very different person to the May Warren who had slaved away, day in, day out, for a pittance of pay in that hoity-toity hotel, and all just to scrape by in Albert Terrace, with its vermin and its smells and its noise, and where the furthest she could see from the window was the back wall of the laundry. *Wolcott Professional Launderers & Pressers Established 1875* was the faded decree that had greeted her as she drew aside the curtain each morning. And while she had always maintained that housework was the same wherever you did it, since arriving here she had come to realise that wasn't strictly true. How much say you had over when and how you went about it made all the difference. Her fingers might still be red raw from boiling sheets in detergent, her nails permanently ragged and broken, and her back might still creak from scrubbing floors, but here, she slept like a log, could fill her lungs with fresh air, and could watch the sun rise above the horizon or sink below it. On top of that, she also had a certain freedom. And that, she realised now, was priceless. So, no matter the pull she felt when she thought of Clemmie and Pearl, and no matter that she'd never understand George Beer even if she lived to be a hundred, Fair Maids Farm had come to feel like home.

The place wasn't perfect; she was level-headed enough to recognise that. But then where would be? Wherever she was, there would still be a war on. That said, other than suffering the odd shortage – only last week she'd heard that, by order of the government, soap was to be restricted to three ounces per month and there was to be no more white bread! – out here, the ill effects were significantly fewer. And yes, she had been naïve to think that growing vegetables would be plain sailing. But, despite this latest round of bad luck with the deer, things *were* beginning to look up. And although the three of them wouldn't be able to keep going without Mr Beer contributing in some shape or form – even if that only amounted to him settling his account at Cooper's – she had a suspicion that once he saw them harvesting the first of the vegetables, and the War Ags got off his back, he might feel inclined to get stuck in, even take pride in producing food for folk to eat. It wasn't as though he'd been told to chop down his beloved trees and plough up the orchard to grow them. If he would but see it, there was space enough – and, with the girls now pulling their weight, sufficient labour – for him to do both.

With a wide yawn, she got up from her stool, put her notepad and pencil down on top of it and stretched her arms high above her head. There was Mr Beer now, left hand pressed to the trunk of one of his beloved apple trees as he stood staring up through its branches. Lord, he was a funny old soul. Should she go and tell him about the Epsom salts Dan was bringing today? No, probably best to wait until the job was done and then tell him.

Bending to pick up her stool and go indoors, she noticed that the fruits on the nearest tree, which just a few days ago had seemed minuscule, were now double the size. With a smile, she went to admire them more closely, only to stop dead: on the grass beneath the branches were dozens of them. Feeling a jolt of alarm, she went to the next tree. They were under this one as well. And the next tree, too. What was happening? Why were the apples falling from the trees? She bent to retrieve one and examine it. Although smaller than a florin, it was perfectly formed. *Please*, she willed, *don't let the apple crop be failing*. If there was no apple crop, there would be no cider, and if there was no cider, then heaven only knew what would happen.

Gathering a handful of the fallen fruit and ignoring that he'd warned her to keep out of the orchard, she hastened to George. If he didn't already know, he probably should.

'Mr Beer,' she said, approaching where he still had his hand pressed to the trunk of the tree.

Very slowly, he turned towards her. 'Ah?'

'The apples.' To show him what she'd found, she held out her hand. 'They're all on the ground.'

'Ah. 'Tis June drop.'

Irritated by the way he always stopped short of a proper explanation, she shook her head in despair. 'So, what do it mean? What's wrong with them? How do we stop it?'

'Can't stop it,' he said without even looking at her.

'You *can't*?'

''Tis the tree's way of shedding more than it can ripen. More than it can grow to a decent size.'

'So…' Not understanding what that meant, she racked her brain for a way to ask without looking stupid. 'They won't *all* fall off.'

'Best hope not.'

Honestly, sometimes his manner made her want to growl with frustration!

'So, they *won't* all fall off?'

'Three-quarters is what's usual to lose. But the time to gauge the harvest is St Swithin's. Them apples still on the tree for St Swithin's blessing will likely go on to ripen.'

'And those that get blessed,' she said, 'they're enough? For your cider, I mean.'

'For a tree like this, that's reckoned a full crop. If too many cling on, we'd have to thin 'em by hand.'

Feeling reassured and foolish in equal measure, May opened her palm and let the tiny apples tumble to the grass. 'Well, that's all right then.' Clearly, she still had a lot to learn.

'Of more concern should be this 'n here.'

About to walk away, she turned back. 'This one?' To her eyes, the tree in question seemed to have the same amount of fruit swelling as any of those around it. 'Not sure I understand.'

'Canker.'

'Canker?' Wasn't that a disease? Wasn't it a sore of some sort? It certainly didn't sound good. 'That's bad?'

'Bad on any apple tree,' George said, smoothing his hand over the tree's bark. 'But this one here's the king tree.'

*King tree.* Presumably, that made it valuable in some way. 'Oh.'

'Oldest and most important tree of the lot. 'Tis in this tree the spirit of the orchard resides.'

Despite having no time for superstition, she immediately understood. 'And the spirit in the king tree watches over all the others?'

'More 'n that. Sees to a good pollination. Wards off misfortune. Ensures a good harvest.'

'So, what do we do?' Behind her back, she crossed her fingers. They really didn't need any more misfortune.

'Only one thing for it.' When he paused, she held her breath. 'See this?'

Looking to where he was pointing, she saw how the bark appeared sunken, while in other places patches of it appeared to be flaking off. Sores. *Canker.* 'I see it.'

'If that were on a limb, it could be sawn off and burned.'

'It won't get better? What I mean is, you can't treat it with something – a remedy of some sort?'

Slowly, George shook his head. 'Only remedy for canker is to remove the whole limb. But this here's on the trunk, which leaves just the two choices.' Rather than ask what they were, May waited. 'Leave it to suffer a long and lingering demise and risk having it infect the others… or chop it down and burn it.'

And neither of those, May knew without needing to ask, were steps to be taken lightly – at least, not by anyone with more than a passing regard for folklore and superstition.

'Well,' she said, lost for even a single word of comfort. 'If anyone knows what to do, it has to be you.'

'Ah.'

'And in which case, since I've to go and get the breakfasts, I'll leave you to it.'

Wandering back to where she'd left her stool and her writing pad, May sighed. Silly, really, to pay heed to such old-fashioned beliefs, but she couldn't help it; in the pit of her stomach, a sense of foreboding had set in. First there was the deer eating the cabbage, and now this. Since bad luck usually came in threes, she had to wonder what lay in store for them next. What third misfortune was about to strike?

Going through to the kitchen, she told herself not to be ridiculous. There was no need to think like that. Bad luck coming in threes was just an old wives' tale. Just lately, things had started to look up. Today, for instance, Dan was bringing them the Epsom salts and the pumps to spray the crops, which would be another obstacle overcome.

Yes, one hurdle at a time; that was how she would choose to go on. Worries over which she had no control, most notably the prospect of George's beloved king tree facing a fiery end, she had little choice but to shut from her mind.

*VII. Canker*

# Chapter 18

The colour of the sky came as a disappointment. Having for so long drawn back the curtain each morning to an apricot sunrise, today May found herself staring out at a featureless expanse of pale grey cloud and a wind sufficiently blustery to sway the tops of the apple trees. For the first time, it didn't feel particularly warm, either.

With a sigh, she went to the chest of drawers, found a cardigan and pulled it over her dress. Were they in for some rain at last? She hoped so: Nessa had said that the cabbages and the kale were starting to need more water than was easy to carry all the way over there. She'd also said that in one of the barns she'd found a pump and that if, when she'd tried to start it, the motor hadn't been seized, they would have been able to draw water from the stream. Appreciating how that would make life easier, May had promised to speak to Mr Beer – although why Nessa couldn't do it, she didn't know. Deciding to go and find him now, she went downstairs and started towards the picket gate into the orchard.

Without the sunshine this morning, the yard had a very different feel, the dreary greys and browns of the outbuildings, together with the wind swirling the dust and flapping at the corrugated iron roofs, serving to highlight the general neglect. Still, she chided herself, there was no need to feel downhearted; there was plenty of the summer left yet. And as she'd reminded herself just now, while endless sunshine might do wonders for her spirits, if they were to have a successful harvest they needed rain.

Passing one of the barns, her attention was caught by a group of starlings picking about by the water tank, their dark and scruffy plumage reminding her of schoolboys kicking about in the gutter. In the same instant, something beneath her feet made a squelching noise. Exhaling in dismay, she looked down. Blast. Somehow she'd walked straight through a patch of mud. But wait – mud? Had there already been some rain? She cast about. No, everywhere else in the yard was bone dry. As the starlings took flight, she studied the expanse of waterlogged earth. It was so wet, and spread so widely, she could only imagine the galvanised tank that collected rainwater from the roof of the big barn had sprung a leak. With a frown, she picked her way closer and reached out a knuckle to tap the side of it. The tinny echo told her the tank was empty. Just what they didn't need; they relied on that water for everything from keeping down the dust to mixing up weedkiller; from cleaning boots and tools to filling the trough for the hens. As if the loss of all that water wasn't sufficient inconvenience, she now had *two* things to see Mr Beer about. And it wasn't going to be easy to get him to attend to either of them.

'Hundreds of gallons, all lost,' Bonnie lamented when, over breakfast, May explained what she'd found.

Nessa's reaction was rather more to the point. 'What's George doing about it?'

'He said…' Trying to remember his exact words when she'd told him, May frowned. '…he'll look at it. Something along the lines of, if the hole's not too big, he might be able to plug it.'

'Well, as long as he gets on with it. It'll take weeks of rain to replace that amount of water. What did he say about the pump?'

'To be honest, not much.' There was no need, May decided, to tell Nessa that all he'd actually done was shrug. 'But I'll make sure he looks at that, too.'

'Good. We could do with that thing working even more now we've lost all that water.'

As it turned out, less than five minutes later George came in from the yard and stood in the doorway to the scullery, from where he stared across at the three of them eating breakfast.

'Weren't no leak,' he said flatly. 'Some damn fool left the tap open.'

'*Left the tap open?*'

Unable to see how anyone would walk away and leave water running, May shared Nessa's incredulity. 'So… who was last to use it?'

It was Bonnie who replied. 'Me, I suppose. Last night, I topped up the water for the hens. But I turned it off after like I always do.'

'Any chance you didn't turn the lever all the way?' May enquired carefully.

'Well, I can't say for sure now, can I? But I do it every day well enough.'

'Even if she *had* left it dripping,' Nessa observed, 'it would take more than a trickle to drain the entire tank.'

'And it was definitely left open—' Turning to address her question to George, May was irritated to find he'd already left. 'Let's hope he's gone to fix the pump,' she grumbled. 'As for what happened with the water tank, I suppose we'll never know.'

'Probably not.'

More importantly, she thought but chose not to say, please let that be the third and final piece of bad luck because, as disasters went, it could have been worse.

As May was to discover the next morning, though, luck – bad or otherwise – seemed to have very little to do with it. Instead, a more malevolent force appeared to be at work. The previous evening, at Nessa's suggestion, the girls had ferried several jerrycans of water from the stream to the tank, the thought being that for the thing to have emptied completely, the leak must have been right at the bottom. Thus, if there *was* a hole, then overnight the same thing would happen again: beneath the tank this morning would be a freshly damp patch of soil. Except that as May went towards it, she could see straight away that the ground had continued to dry out, which could only mean that George had been right – someone had left the tap open. On the upside, at least she wouldn't have to goad him into fixing it; an ill wind, and all that.

When she turned back to the scullery, though, she stopped in her tracks.

'What the devil…?' Was that smashed eggs? As she hurried to take a closer look, the sight of broken shells on the ground confirmed her suspicion that someone had thrown half a dozen at the lavatory door. Hands on hips, she stared in disbelief.

'Is that… egg?' Appearing from the lean-to, Bonnie came to join her.

'Would seem to be.'

'But who on earth would throw eggs? And at the lav door, of all things.'

'I haven't the least idea,' May replied. 'No one in their right mind, that's for—'

'Oh my. The hens. I hope they're all right!'

When Bonnie darted away, May went after her, arriving at the chicken coop to find her latching the door behind her. All six hens were apparently safe and well.

'No eggs,' Bonnie groaned, closing the hinged roof of the nesting box.

'Bit early yet, isn't it?' From what she remembered Bonnie telling her, hens didn't usually lay until a couple of hours after sunrise.

'Yes, but…'

'But what?' Why, May wondered, was that feeling of foreboding back in her stomach?

'But I didn't come in to collect them yesterday.'

Trying to recall yesterday morning, May frowned. 'Are you sure?'

'Perfectly. With the kerfuffle about the water tank, I forgot. And though I realised later on, I never did get round to coming back for them.'

'So…'

'All I'm saying,' Bonnie went on, 'is that there's none here. Sometimes if you don't fetch them out, the hens might try an' incubate them. But all the birds are out here in the run, so it's not that. Other times, they might even try to eat them. But if they'd done that, I'd see the remains.'

'So, whoever threw them at the door,' May surmised, 'stole them from our coop.'

'Must have done.'

With that, Nessa strolled round the corner. 'It's got to be children,' she said when May explained what had happened. 'A prank. Lucky they chose a door to aim at and not a window.'

'Lucky?' Had Nessa really just said that?

'You know what I mean.'

'Maybe it's the same wrongdoers as emptied the water tank,' Bonnie suggested. 'Doubtless they'd think *that* a prank, too.'

'Well, I'm afraid *I'm* not seeing the funny side,' May replied tautly. 'Especially since not only is it a criminal waste of eggs, but now I have to clear up after them.'

Despite the two incidents being tedious, May told herself not to stew over them. No *real* harm had been done. With any luck, the perpetrators would now go on to find somewhere else to amuse themselves.

The following morning, though, in the kitchen kneading dough for a loaf, her thoughts were interrupted, not so much by the pounding of boots running across the yard but by the way they came to a stop at the scullery door. Hearing the panting of breath that followed, she wiped her hands and went to see who it was.

Doubled over, Bonnie was clutching her side. 'May... quick...'

'Good Lord, girl. Whatever's the matter?'

'The sheep... have got into... the kale.'

'Sheep?'

'Higher Cleave's... ewes. Nessa's... gone for Dan.'

Feeling her insides knotting, May reached to the doorframe. 'Is there much damage?'

Red faced from running, Bonnie nodded. 'They've eaten... most all of it. Trampled... the rest.'

'You go on back. I'll get my shoes and catch up.'

To have reached the kale, May realised as she rinsed her hands, cast aside her housecoat and slipped her feet into her outdoor shoes, the sheep must have got through the fence. While she didn't know Dan very well, she was certain he wouldn't have put sheep into a field from which they could so easily wander away. So either the fence had

216

become broken down, or else a gate must have been left open. And she didn't think Dan would be so careless. The only other possibility was that the pranksters were back. If they were, then by the sound of it, this time they'd gone too far. Interfering with fences and gates wasn't just mischief; they had endangered animals and destroyed a field of vegetables. For that recklessness, they should be made to pay.

Arriving at the kale field, she stumbled to a halt and stood panting for breath. The damage was worse than she'd thought. So much worse that flooding down her cheeks came hot angry tears. How *dare* someone show such disregard for another person's livelihood? Had they no idea what had gone into raising those plants? There were the seeds, there was the water, not to mention endless weeks of hard work. And all of it now for nothing. What an utterly senseless and criminal waste! And for little more than devilment – for the momentary thrill. If she ever got her hands on the people who did this...

Unable to see for her tears, she snatched her handkerchief from her sleeve and blew her nose. Over by the fence – and somewhat pointlessly, given the scale of the devastation – Bonnie was trying to shoo the sheep away from the remaining plants, while running across from Higher Cleave were Nessa and Dan, slinking low alongside them Flash. As they drew near and Dan whistled a command, the collie stole under the bottom wire of the fence. Alerted by her arrival, the sheep raised their heads and stood stock still. But as Flash came round behind the furthest ewe, the entire flock started for the lane, where Nessa and Dan were waiting to herd them through the open gate and back into their pasture.

'Someone...' Dan said, gasping for breath, as he came towards her a moment later, 'must have... opened... the gate.'

'But who would do such a thing?' As May gestured forlornly to what was left of the kale, the sight of it pulled at something in her chest. 'Who would be so mean?' Her eyes once again filling with tears, she sniffed. What were they going to do now? How on earth would they ever make up such a hefty loss? Even if there was still time to start over, how would they get the seeds? And who was going to pay for them? It was a disaster. A disaster made worse by the fact that someone had deliberately done this to them. 'Breaking a few eggs is mischief. But this...'

The look Dan shot her was one of puzzlement. 'Breaking eggs?'

'And the water tank was an inconvenience—'

'Water tank?'

'But this, this...'

'This,' Nessa said, coming to join them, 'is wanton damage.'

'Look,' Dan said, glancing to Flash. 'Let me see to the ewes and I'll come back over. By the look of it, they've had a right old feast.'

'They're not supposed to have too much kale, are they?'

In response to Nessa's observation, Dan shook his head. 'A little mixed in with the usual legumes is fine. They like it. But too much of it gives them bloat.'

'And is that serious?' May asked. So far, she'd only considered the plight of their crop.

'Left untreated, it's deadly. Which is why I need to get them penned up so I can keep a close eye on them. First signs of any distress and we have to act fast.'

'Do you have plenty of bicarbonate of soda?'

May had no idea what Nessa was talking about, but Dan nodded.

'Always make sure to have a barrel. You've treated bloat?'

'I know of it. If the worst happens and you need a hand, let me know.'

'All right.' Piquing May's curiosity was the way Dan seemed unsurprised that Nessa should offer. 'Thanks.' Turning back to May, he went on, 'I'll call by later and you can fill me in what's been happening. But I'm telling you now, as God is my witness, I did not leave that gate open.'

'I know you didn't,' May said softly. 'But we need to find out who did.'

–

'They're all right, then, your sheep?'

When Dan had arrived back and tapped at the scullery door, May had invited him in, and the two of them were now seated at the kitchen table with a pot of tea.

'So far. Helps that your plants were still young. Kale's only fibrous once it grows bigger, so not only was there very little for them to gorge on to start with, but the risk of bloat was lower.'

'Small mercy, I suppose.'

'For us, maybe. Not much comfort for you, though. How are you? You looked real upset earlier.'

With no intention of admitting she'd come back and had a good cry over the unfairness of it all, May shook her head. 'Oh, I'm all right, thank you.'

'Good.'

'What *I* don't understand,' she said, praying his kindly tone wouldn't trigger fresh tears, 'is why anyone would do this? I mean, where are they even coming from? There's not another house for miles.'

'Seems to me,' Dan said, 'that until today, the pranks have been little more than mischief-making. Though no doubt even letting sheep out of a field seems harmless when you're a lad.'

'You think it's children?' She recalled Nessa being of the same mind.

'Has to be.'

'But whose?'

Dan shrugged. 'We're only going to find that out if we catch them.'

Catch them? 'How do we do that when they don't come until after dark?'

'We lie in wait.'

*We?* Was he proposing they sit up and keep watch? 'But they might not come back again.'

'In which case,' he replied, 'the problem's gone away, and all we will have lost is a couple hours' sleep. But, since you tell me this was the third night in a row, I reckon they're getting a taste for it. Rather than give up now, I think they'll be back. I think they'll get bolder, keep pushing their luck, looking for bigger and bigger thrills.'

'So...' She still wasn't clear what he was suggesting. Was he proposing to sit up and keep watch alone? Or was he expecting the two of them to take turns? Truth be told, she didn't fancy spending even part of the night on the lookout for prowlers.

'So, how about tonight, we keep watch?'

'Together?'

'You might not know me very well, Mrs Huxford' – Mrs *Huxford?* Goodness, yes, she still hadn't explained the mistake. And perhaps she wouldn't – at least not if he was proposing they spend the night alone together! – 'but I'm not the sort of feller to let you watch for intruders by yourself. I might have been born and bred on the land, but I do know what's right and proper.'

For the first time in a while, May raised a smile. 'Wouldn't dream of suggesting you didn't.'

'Look, it strikes me that if this *is* children, they probably won't be out much past midnight. If nothing else, they'll be tired. So, if we keep watch until then and nothing's happened, we can call it a night and try again tomorrow.'

His suggestion did make sense. Not that she was in a position to take issue with him had it not; his offer to help was most generous. 'All right. Yes. Thank you.'

'I'll come over around ten.'

'All right.'

'I suggest we sit in the old haybarn. Leave the doors wide and we'll hear anyone moving about.'

'I'll make a flask of cocoa.'

'And if I make the odd patrol—'

'Then we should catch them.'

'That's what I'm thinking.'

When he got to his feet and went out through the scullery, she accompanied him a few paces across the yard. 'Ten o'clock, then.'

'Yeah. Thanks for the tea.'

Watching him head away, May sighed. While his idea was a good one, she didn't relish having to try to stay awake until gone midnight. Perhaps she should take a couple of blankets over there; knowing her luck, it would turn out to be the chilliest June night ever. Moreover, for the sake of her reputation, perhaps she would hold off telling the others. If nothing else, she could do without the ribbing.

Turning to go back indoors, she caught sight of George watching from the wicket.

'What did *he* want?'

No need to tell *him* what they were planning, either.

'Came to tell us his sheep are all right.'

'Huh.'

Feeling how her shoulders had suddenly tensed, she determined not to let his attitude get to her. 'And that he wouldn't need Nessa's help.'

'Told you growing ruddy vegetables would be trouble.'

Yes, she thought, standing there scoffing is all you're good for. But as she watched him shamble away, a thought occurred: what if Mr Beer was behind all of this? What if, aware that they were beginning to see the fruits of their labours, he'd got it into his head to sabotage their efforts? No, that would be ridiculous. He might be stubborn, and for certain he could be crabby, but he'd never come across as vindictive. What did he even stand to gain by such pettiness? Spoiling their hard work wouldn't get the War Ags off his back: setting out to prove that growing vegetables couldn't be done wouldn't save the farm – they'd just replace him with someone prepared to try harder. So, why go to the bother? Besides, while emptying the yard's water supply and smashing a few eggs made life tiresome, it was a far cry from risking the lives of an entire flock of sheep.

With a weary sigh, she went through to the kitchen, collected the cups and saucers from the table and carried them through to the scullery. Well, if Dan was right, then a few short hours from now the mystery of who *was* behind all of this would be solved, and the perpetrators would turn out to be someone other than George Beer...

## Chapter 19

'At least it's a warm night.'

'They don't come much warmer than June.'

'They don't.'

As good as his word, a little after ten that night Dan arrived back in the yard, the only change to his appearance from earlier being the heavy sweater thrown over his shoulders. 'Useful for all sorts of things, this,' he said when he saw her eyeing it. 'Makes a good cushion to sit on; good pillow if you need forty winks when you have to stay up all night.'

May grinned. 'Stay up all night often, do you?'

'During lambing we've no choice.'

'Yes, of course.' Lambing. Every day she came to appreciate a little more about life on a farm.

'Tell you what…' Looking about the barn, Dan appeared to spot something in the corner and went to retrieve it. Returning with a canvas tarpaulin, he shook it out and spread it on the floor. 'There. Save you dirtying your clothes.'

'Thanks,' she said, lowering herself onto the slightly cleaner of the corners.

'Honeysuckle smells nice tonight,' Dan went on, pulling off the sweater and tossing it aside before gesturing with his head out through the open doors.

So that was the sweet scent she'd noticed in the air these last few evenings – honeysuckle. She must remember to look for it in daylight and see if it was in her book. 'Very fragrant.'

'Smells strongest in the evening, to attract moths.'

'Oh.' For a while after that they sat in silence until eventually she said, 'I hope it *is* just children doing this mischief.' Several times during the afternoon, she'd pictured coming face to face with adult intruders and been left feeling distinctly uneasy. Who knew what a full-grown man might do when challenged? And if anything were to happen to Dan, she would never forgive herself.

'It'll be children right enough. You comfortable?'

In the darkness of the barn, May smiled. 'I've put up with worse.'

After a few minutes more, Dan said, 'Can I ask you something?'

Wondering what was coming, May paused before answering. 'You can *ask*.'

'What happened to Mr Huxford? Lose him recent, did you?'

She flushed hotly. Clearly, it was time to come clean. 'Oh, no, if you're referring to me being Mrs Huxford, that's a mistake.'

His laugh seemed to erupt from deep within his chest. 'A mistake, eh? I reckon there's many a woman as would say that of their union!'

'What I mean,' she said, joining in his mirth, 'is that somewhere along the line, Mr Beer supposed I was a Mrs. But I'm not. Never have been and never said so.'

'I see.'

That he appeared nonplussed by the revelation gave her the confidence to be honest. 'And since I was in terrible need of this job, I… well, let's just say I chose not to correct him.'

'Fair enough. When I heard you'd been bombed out, I came to thinking perhaps you were widowed… and happen that was why you'd come here, you know, to start over.'

That he should reach such a conclusion was less of a surprise than the discovery that he'd been considering her situation at all. 'Not widowed, no,' she said softly. 'Though I did come for a fresh start. Not that I had much choice. Not after we lost everything.'

Beside her on the tarpaulin, Dan shifted his weight. 'Can't imagine that. Must have been terrible.'

'I just thank the Lord we were spared – me an' my sisters, that is. Many was the moment when I didn't think we would be… when I thought the walls of that horrible little shelter might be the last we ever saw… when I couldn't help wondering whether, if the place took a direct hit, anyone would ever find our bodies – whether they would even bother to look or whether that would forever be our tomb.'

When Dan responded, it was softly. 'Christ, May. Shouldn't no one have to go through that.'

The memory of that night now vividly back in her mind, she could feel the same knot of terror twisting in her stomach, while to the back of her throat returned the foetid stench of fear, and into her head the eerie whistling of the HEs.

'Six seconds is all it takes, you know. Six seconds from the moment you hear the bomb start whistling until it hits its target and explodes.'

*Six, five, four…* She could feel herself back there, perspiring from terror, braced rigid in anticipation. *Three, two, one. Boom! Crash.* And then a rumbling through the earth so thunderous it had rattled her bones. Only when the tumult from each explosion had finally faded had she risked letting go of her breath and opening her eyes. *Another one had missed them. They were still alive.*

Dan's eventual reply was barely a whisper. 'Must have been the longest six seconds on Earth. I can't imagine it.'

'No one can. Not until you go through it. The worst part was feeling so helpless – was knowing there was nothing you could do to see to it you survived. That all you could do was sit and wait. And pray.'

'If your number's up, it's up.'

'Pretty much. You know, upstairs from us, we had a neighbour called Mrs Tuckett. Jolly old soul that she was, she took it upon herself to keep trying to make light. One time, there was this real close hit that brought down bits of the shelter's roof, and as we were all coughing and brushing ourselves off, she piped up, "My Harry says that if you can hear the bomb whistling, it ain't got your name on it." I remember thinking what utter phooey. I mean, if that was true, if you *didn't* hear the bomb whistling, then it *did* have your name on it. So, once it had hit, you'd be dead, and no longer around to tell the tale.'

'Happen the notion comforted her,' Dan observed.

'Happen so.'

'But eventually you all got out.'

'We did. Although not my stepfather.' *Bother. Why on earth had she told him that?*

'Good Lord, May, I'm sorry. I didn't know.'

'No matter,' she said plainly. 'Truth to tell, we're all three of us glad he's gone. Even his own daughter couldn't stand him. Anyway,' she picked up again, anxious to avoid talking about Charlie Warren, 'to go back to your original question, no, I'm not married, never have been, and don't intend to be.'

'No?'

'No. But I'd ask you not to say so to Mr Beer. I'd rather that if anyone told him, it was me.'

'None of *my* business,' Dan said. 'No reason for me to tell him anything. He might be my uncle, but in general we don't have anything to do with one another. But then since his wife died, he hasn't had much to do with anyone.'

A throwaway remark to Dan, to May it confirmed everything she'd suspected.

'Long ago was it, that he lost her?'

'More 'n twenty years. For certain *I* was too young to know her.'

'Oh.'

'According to Gran, it him real hard.'

'I suppose it would. He must have been quite young.'

In the murky light, May could just make out Dan's eyebrows knitting together as he paused to reckon George's age.

'Not much different to me now, I shouldn't think.'

'You got any siblings?' she asked, her question seeming innocuous.

'I was the only one to come along. Shame, really. Growing up out here there were times when I would have given my right arm for a brother. Or even a cousin.'

'You do look like your uncle.' It wasn't something she'd meant to say but, since she had, there could be no taking it back.

'So everyone tells me. But I look like my father, too. When you meet him, you'll see for yourself.'

*When* she met him? Why would she have reason to meet the other Mr Beer?

'I'll make a point of having a good look.'

'Reckon you'll see out the winter?' he changed direction to ask.

'Is winter out here bad, then?'

'Can be. We get a fair bit of snow. Though we're usually only cut off for a few days at a time. And then not every year.' Listening to Dan talking, May recalled something Bonnie had said about the previous housekeeper, Alma: *when the snow came, she said it was the final straw.* 'Comes from us being not that far from the top of the moors.'

That was something to look forward to then. She never had fared very well in the cold. Maybe next time she was in the village she should buy a copy of *Woman's Weekly* and see whether there were any of those advertisements for long johns and vests that she'd always found amusing. If there were, it might not be a bad idea to find out how to go about sending off for some – what with the matter of rationing coupons – and maybe a couple of pairs of bedsocks, too. She couldn't imagine her little attic room keeping very warm, even if it was currently stifling.

Largely to change the subject from talk of snow, she asked, 'Would you like some cocoa?'

She saw him glance to his wristwatch, its hands glowing green in the dark.

'All right. But first I'll make a quick check outside. If they're coming, you've got to think they won't be much longer.' Getting to his feet and slipping his hands into the pockets of his trousers, he went to the open doors and looked about. 'Back in a mo.'

She hoped he was right. She didn't like the idea of sitting around waiting on her own. After all, they still didn't know for sure that the miscreants *were* only children.

Barely a couple of minutes later, though, he was back. 'All quiet,' he whispered, settling back beside her on the tarpaulin.

Having poured some of the cocoa into a mug, she handed it across to him. 'I think the seal on this Thermos must have gone. It don't seem very warm.'

He took the mug from her. 'Worse where there's none.'

After another spell spent in silence, May got to her feet and went to stand by the open doors. With a cursory glance about the yard first, she emptied the dregs of her cocoa onto the ground. But as she stood back up, she shrieked.

Instantly, Dan was beside her. 'What?' he hissed. 'What's the matter?'

'Something flew past my face. Real close. I felt it against my cheek.'

'Bat, most likely. Come and sit back down. They won't bother you down here.'

Trembling from the shock of having something she couldn't see passing so close to her, she did as he said. 'Do… do they attack people?'

'Bats?' From his tone, she sensed he was trying not to laugh. It wouldn't be the first time she'd said something daft in front of him. 'No. Nor will they land on you nor bite you. *You* might not be able to see *them*, but they can see you all right. Though not in the sense that we see with our eyes. They come out after dark in search of food – insects, that is – and have a special way of sensing them in the air.'

'Oh.'

'No need to sound so doubtful. It's true. They'd avoid flying into you same as they'd avoid flying into the side of a building or you would avoid walking into a door. They probably roost up here in the rafters.'

'Oh.' She still didn't like the idea that they flew about in the dark, not if they were going to miss her that narrowly. 'Here,' she said in a bid to think about something else, 'I'll put your mug with the Thermos.'

'Thanks.'

A few moments later, she asked, 'Do you still think anyone's coming?'

'More likely they will than they won't. Like I said to you earlier, I reckon they've got a taste for the thrill. And since it's less than an hour until midnight, I can't think we'll have that much longer to wait.'

'Do you think you'll always be a farmer?' she asked as the thought went through her head.

'War permitting. Farming's one of those things that's in your blood. When you're the only son of a man who farms his own land, there's never much doubt where you're headed. Like it or not, the day I was born, the die was cast.'

She'd never thought about it like that. 'I suppose so.'

'Fortunately, I like it out here. Far rather be in the countryside than a town.'

'I like the fresh air,' she said. 'And the flowers and the trees. And the birdsong.'

'Must be very different to Exeter.'

'Very. Although—'

'Shush.' Feeling his hand come to rest on her arm, she stiffened. 'Listen.'

Above the pounding of her heart, she strained to hear. Was that...? Yes, boots scuffing across the yard, and apparently more than one pair of them.

'Should we—'

'Wait here.' Rising noiselessly to his feet, Dan crept towards the open door and secreted himself behind the frame.

'Hey, look,' a small voice said. 'Over here. C'mon. It's open. Let's go in an' see what's to be had.'

Watching as two hazy forms came in through the door, and wondering why Dan hadn't pounced on them, May held her breath.

With that, a beam of torchlight picked out two boys in vests and short trousers. Startled, they swung towards it and then made as though to run. But with Dan stood between them and the door, they were trapped, trying to dodge around him merely resulting in both being caught by the arm.

'Stop trying to fight me,' Dan warned. When neither of them took any notice, he hardened his tone. 'Do as I say. I shan't hurt you.' The two writhing forms fell still. 'May, come and take the torch, if you wouldn't mind.'

Her heart still thudding, May took the light. This close to, neither child appeared to be more than ten years old. With identically cropped sandy brown hair and matching snub noses, they had to be brothers.

'You were right,' she said to Dan.

'Yeah. Evacuees most likely.' Addressing the boys, he said, 'What's your names?'

It was the slightly taller one who replied. 'Not telling you.'

'Where do you live?'

Neither spoke.

'If you won't tell us where you live,' May said, directing the torch at each face in turn and noting that both looked in need of a good scrub, 'we can't take you home.'

'We lives in Ex'ter,' the smaller of the two replied. 'And we wants to go back there.'

'But we can't.'

'So, where are you staying round here then?' Dan asked. His grip on their wrists, May noticed, hadn't slackened. When neither of them replied, he looked across at her and shrugged. 'If they won't tell us where they're billeted, there's only one thing for it. We'll have to get the police.'

'Get off. This ain't fair.'

'We've not done nothing. Let us go!'

'After the damage you've caused round here these last nights?' Dan said. 'I don't think so. No, you're off to Sergeant Smale. You ever been in a police house?' The boys hung their heads. 'Then perhaps I'd best explain that for vandals and troublemakers, there's a special cell with bars on the door. I should probably also tell you that the sergeant won't be best pleased when we wake him up in the middle of the night with you two. Nor will he be happy tomorrow morning, when he has to take you back to the place you're billeted. And I don't suppose *they'll* be happy, either, when they have to tell your family.'

'The rectory,' one of the boys replied sullenly. 'We're at the rectory. We're from St Peter's School in Ex'ter.'

'But we was bombed out.'

'And we hate it here. We wants to go and stay with Mum.'

'But they won't let us.'

'She took our sisters to Aunty Glad's. But her said her couldn't have us two as well.'

'And Bully Collis makes him give us our food.'

'Bully Collis?' May and Dan repeated.

'We've tried fighting him but he's bigger than us.'

232

'And he punches real hard.'

'His dad's a boxer.'

'All right, all right,' Dan said wearily, finally slackening his grip. 'I'm taking you back to the rectory.'

'No!'

'Well you can't stay here. And since it's the middle of the night, I'm not just letting you go. It's the rectory or the police house. Really, since you've done damage to this lady's property and caused her a lot of work, it should be the police house.' In desultory fashion, one of the boys kicked at the ground. 'And you can stop that, too. Haven't you been taught to stand up straight and listen when a grown-up talks to you?'

Finally, May thought, the two of them had the sense to look contrite. Unexpectedly, rather than feel fury, she felt sorry for them. Being sent out here to live with strangers had to be tough. She knew well enough how it felt to be bombed out and lose everything you'd ever known. And now they were separated from their mother, too. And who knew where their father was – whether he was even still alive. Viewed in that light, it was no wonder they'd gone off the rails. But even so…

'Last night,' she said, forcing a sternness into her voice, 'when you opened the gate into that field and let those sheep out, they ate something they shouldn't have. And that made them so ill they might all have died. Think what would have happened to you then.'

'Sorry,' the elder of the two mumbled.

'We didn't mean for that.'

'And yet—'

'Come on,' Dan said to them. 'I'm taking you back to the rectory, and I'm going to speak to whoever's in charge. Say you're sorry to this lady, say you're sorry to me, and we'll go an' see what's to be done about Bully Collis. All right?' The boys regarded Dan doubtfully. 'Go on,' he said. 'There she is look, waiting to hear how sorry you are for what you've done.'

'Sorry, Missus. We didn't mean to cause trouble.'

'Yeah, sorry,' the younger one added.

'Right then, both of you. Come with me.'

'Thank you, Dan,' May said when he turned towards her. 'Let me know how you get on?'

'I'll drop by tomorrow. Afternoon, maybe. You go on in and get some sleep.'

'All right. And thanks again. Good night.'

'Night.'

Listening to three pairs of boots heading across the yard, May let out a weary sigh. Dan Beer was a good man. Shame it wasn't him in charge of Fair Maids instead of George; with gumption like Dan's, this place – and her own part in it – might look very different indeed.

# Chapter 20

'So, you see what you've got to do?'

The child May now knew as Robbie nodded. 'Use this 'ere 'oe thing to poke out them weeds.'

'That's right. But not the plants. You're clear on the difference.'

'That there,' he said, pointing with the hoe, 'is a spud. I'm to leave that be.'

'Funny-looking spuds,' his younger brother quipped.

'And you, Neville, you're all right watering them?'

'S'pose.'

'Good. Well, after a bit, you can swap over. But not till I say.'

'Yes, missus.'

'And in a while, I'll bring you over a drink.'

'Yes, missus. Thanks, missus.'

Wondering as to the wisdom of what she'd agreed to, May turned away to see Dan coming across the field towards her.

'They've turned up, then.'

She smiled. 'The rector brought them in his motor. Said he wanted to make sure they got here. But they're to walk home after.'

'To be honest,' Dan said, eyeing the two boys at work, 'even if they only come twice it should make them stop and think before getting up to mischief again.'

'I should like to think so. Oh, and the rector said to tell you Bully Collis is being sent to family up near Holsworthy. An uncle, I believe.'

'Right then,' Dan said and glanced about, 'since it looks as though you've got everything under control, I'll be getting back over yonder. But let me know if they play you up.'

'If they do,' May said with a grin, 'I'll bang their heads together. And I said as much to the rector.'

Watching Dan laugh as he walked away, May let out a sigh. But rather than one of despair – as seemed recently to have become the norm – it felt like one of relief. Perhaps now, life would go along quietly for a while. Perhaps two afternoons' penance would work wonders for young Robbie and Neville. If nothing else, it ought to put some colour in their cheeks.

Watching Robbie wrestling with the hoe, and then turning to see Neville struggling along the path with a jerrycan filled with water, she chuckled. Who knew, it might also leave them so exhausted they would sleep straight through the night, the stamina required to roam about in the small hours beyond them to summon.

–

Finally, a moment to catch her breath.

Sitting at the kitchen table the following afternoon, May folded back the cover of her notepad, placed the lined guide sheet beneath the uppermost page, unscrewed the lid of her pen, and thought for a moment before starting to write.

*Dearest Clemmie,*

Pausing to wipe fluff from her nib, she picked up again.

> *I hope this letter finds you well. I know it's not my*
> *turn to write but since I find myself with the ~~luck~~*
> *luxury of a moment or two to spare, I thought I*
> *would let you know how I am going along. After a*
> *bit of a bumpy patch, of which more later, I feel I*
> *can once again say that things are running smooth*
> *and that, for the most part, I am glad I came here.*
> *I do miss you, of course, and would love to see you*
> *before too much longer, but I do truly believe that*
> *in taking this job I did the right thing.*

Pausing to look up, she realised she was smiling. And why shouldn't she? It felt good to be able to write cheery news. She just had to hope that by doing so, she wasn't tempting fate.

She was about to lower her pen to continue when she caught sight of the clock. This afternoon was the second of the two that Robbie and Neville were to spend helping in the fields. Since she'd promised them a drink halfway through, she would take them each a mug of milk now. They looked like they could do with the goodness, poor little devils – their arms and legs were like spindles. She could finish writing her letter to Clemmie later.

The heartening thing, she realised as she drew close to where she'd put them to work on the cabbages, was that they'd been as good as their word. This afternoon, they'd walked from the rectory, they'd knocked on the door and greeted her politely, and they'd listened to her explaining all over again about only hoeing the weeds and not the plants. Judging by the number of rows they'd already done, they hadn't been bunking off, either.

'Drink, you two?' she called towards them.

Dropping the hoe, Robbie nudged his brother, who she'd set the task of weeding by hand around the base of each plant. 'Ta, missus,' he said. 'I haven't half worked up a thirst.' Grasping the mug in both hands, he drew a long slug. 'Blimey, this is thick milk.'

'Got our own cow,' May said, handing the second mug to his brother.

'What, here?'

'In the field up behind the byre. Bonnie milks her.'

'Cor. Reckon she could teach me to do it?'

'Perhaps one day. If you both behave. Here,' she said, reaching carefully into the pocket on the front of her housecoat. 'You like strawberries?' Extending her palm, she revealed a dozen glossy fruit. 'Bonnie grows them. These are some of the first to ripen.' Surprised by the wariness with which the two eyed them, she continued to hold out her hand.

'I'll try one, Nev,' Robbie said, picking one from her palm, 'and tell you if I think you'd like them.'

*They'd never had strawberries before?* Admittedly, they weren't something she'd had that often herself. But most children in the city had a grandparent or uncle with an allotment, or had otherwise swiped one or two from the greengrocer's barrow – before quickly being tanned for their trouble.

She offered her hand in Neville's direction. 'Go on, try one for yourself. Your brother seems to like his.'

Neville didn't wait to be told twice.

'Them other ones for us, too?' Robbie wanted to know.

May nodded. 'They are. But I'm only giving them to you on the understanding you don't spend the rest of the afternoon mucking about.'

'We won't,' Neville was quick to assure her as he handed back his empty mug.

'Because if you do, I shall wish I'd eaten them myself.'

As she went to leave, Robbie piped up, 'Oi, missus, wait. Afore you go, you might want to come an' see summat queer.'

With a frown, May turned back. 'What do you mean by queer?'

'Queer plants.'

With an impatient shake of her head, May followed Robbie around the edge of the field.

'Up here.'

She looked to where he was pointing. 'What is it?'

'Well, look,' he said. 'That side of the field, the plants is all green. Then this lot is all shrivelled and brown.'

'Like old Mr Rogers.'

'Old Mr who?'

'Mr Rogers. Him what digs the graves,' Neville explained. 'Got a face like a rotten apple.'

Ordinarily, May would have reprimanded the boy for being disrespectful, but her attention was taken by the cabbages. To the far left, the plants looked green and healthy. A third of the way across the field, they became paler and limp. This far over, they were brown. In fact, they looked dead.

She turned back to Robbie. 'You know the lady called Nessa?'

With his hands, Robbie mimed the curves of a large chest. 'What, her, you mean?'

Beside him, Neville burst out laughing. ''E's got a crush on her.'

'Oh, for goodness' sake, the pair of you,' May chided. 'Since you clearly know who she is, go and get her for me, would you? She said she'd be working in the beet field.'

'Where's that to?' the boy paused just long enough to ask.

'Over there,' May said, waving in its general direction.

'And anyway,' Robbie called over his shoulder as he scampered away, 'it's not a crush. I'm going to ask her out. Nev's the one with a crush. He's daft on your Bonnie.'

As quick as a flash, Neville ducked to the ground, scooped up a pebble and was just about to launch it at his brother's head when May shot out a hand and grabbed his wrist. 'Uh-uh. We don't never throw stones. Specially not at people.'

'But he—'

'No matter,' May said sharply. 'Tease him back if you must, but you throw a stone and I'll take you back and tell the rector. Don't think I won't.' *Daft on Bonnie?* The boy looked barely nine years old!

As was his habit when given a scolding, Neville hung his head. 'Sorry, missus.'

'Yes, well. Just stand here while we see what's to be done with these plants. Happen you'll be able to help.'

'You really got a cow?'

'We really have.'

In the distance, May could see Nessa striding along the field edge. Beside her, skipping every other step to keep up, Robbie was gesturing with his hands, clearly regaling her with some or other tale.

'What's the matter?' Nessa asked when she arrived. Angling her head to indicate Robbie, she raised her eyebrows.

Robbie, May noticed, seemed unable to take his eyes from Nessa's scarlet lips. 'What do you think's going on here?'

'I would say they look dead.'

'Clearly. But look, over the far side they seem all right.'

When Nessa bent down, Robbie crouched beside her. 'For the love of God, child,' she remonstrated. His face flushed, Robbie shot back up. Rising to step carefully across the next few of rows of plants, Nessa inspected some of the foliage that had begun to yellow. 'It's strange,' she said. 'See how they seem less badly affected as they go across?'

'I noticed that, too. So, what do you think it is?'

'I would say they've been sprayed with something.'

'Such as?'

'Well, I hate to say this, but my first thought would be weedkiller.'

'Weedkiller?'

Instinctively, May looked to Robbie and Neville. But the way they were stood, jostling each other in distracted fashion, told her this wasn't their doing.

'Look, tell you what,' she said to the boys. 'You go on back to the rectory. You've pretty much finished what we asked you to do anyway. So, thank you for your help and off you go.'

'Can we come back next week?' Robbie asked, reaching to retrieve the shirt he'd cast off and flung over a fence post.

'Tuesday,' she said.

Seeing Robbie turn and look longingly at Nessa, Neville pushed him in the back. 'C'mon, you soppy date. Let's go an' see if old Mr Rogers is digging any graves.'

'Yeah, all right.'

When the two boys shambled away, May sent Nessa a despairing look. 'Handful though the pair of them are, I wouldn't mind their energy.'

'Nor their front. That Robbie only asked me if I'd take him to the Bell.'

May laughed. 'Whatever did you say?'

'I said the minute he was old enough.'

'Hm. So you think this is weedkiller.'

'I can't think of anything else it could be. All I can suppose is that someone accidentally sprayed them with it.'

'So, there's no hope for them. That's it. They're lost.'

''Fraid so. These are already dead, and the yellow ones won't be far behind. It's as though they only suffered a weaker dose.'

'So, we've lost two-thirds of the field, that's what you're saying.' Feeling her throat tightening as though she might cry, May struggled to believe it. Deliberate damage was bad enough, but a careless accident? All that work to get the seedlings this far, only to lose them?

'If it's any consolation, the green ones look to be positively thriving. It's as though— Christ. Bonnie…'

'Bonnie *what*?'

'A few days back,' Nessa began, 'Bonnie asked whether the cabbages should have a second dose of Epsom salts, you know, against the deer and the rabbits. I said I thought it was a bit soon but that if she didn't have anything better to do…'

May's heart sank. If Bonnie had done this – inadvertently or otherwise – she would be distraught. 'But you think now she might have used weedkiller by mistake.'

As May feared, when they found Bonnie and told her what they suspected had happened, she was inconsolable.

Yes, she said when they asked; she had given the cabbages another spray with a solution of Epsom salts. And yes, she had found some already made up. And no, she didn't rinse out the hose or the cannister: she'd had no reason to. She hadn't for one moment thought it might be weedkiller.

'Couldn't you *smell* it?' Nessa demanded.

Tears now streaming down her cheeks, Bonnie shook her head. 'I had that cold, remember? Couldn't smell a thing for days, even when the drain was blocked and you all said it smelled evil. Don't you remember?'

In unison, May and Nessa sighed.

'Which side of the field did you start?' Nessa enquired.

'Nearest to.'

'And you just kept adding a new pail of solution each time.'

'Yes.'

'Explains the pattern,' Nessa remarked. 'By the time she reached the last plants, any traces of the weedkiller were gone, and those last few rows just had a nice feed.'

Having thought she'd seen the last of their bad luck, May felt as though she'd been punched in the stomach. There was no point shouting at Bonnie; her mistake was a genuine one. Yes, it might have been careless of her not to check what was in the sprayer. But it could have happened to any one of them.

'How long until the War Ags make their next visit?' Nessa asked. Beside her, Bonnie was now sobbing.

'Few more weeks yet.'

'Well, we've still got the beetroot.'

'And the taters,' May agreed.

'And we'll have *some* cabbages,' Nessa said. 'It would seem unreasonable of them to take us to task over a genuine accident.'

'But not *many* cabbages,' May pointed out. 'And thanks to Robbie and Neville and the sheep, no kale now either.'

'No.'

'Maybe it's not too late to plant something else,' May ventured.

But Nessa shook her head. 'This late in the year, there's not much that will do well. I suppose a late sowing of autumn carrots might be worth trying, if we could get some seed.'

'Perhaps I'll talk to Dan,' May said wearily. 'He might have an idea. He seems to have an answer for most things.'

Although that did rather assume, May thought as she wandered distractedly back towards the house, that he wasn't already heartily fed up with her and her constant requests for help…

–

'Not carrots.'

Watching Dan jump down from the tractor, May tried to hide her disappointment. 'No?'

'They won't do well this late on – never do round here. Even out the back, in Mum's kitchen garden, we don't get a decent late crop. Ought to, given the soil, but if it was me, I'd go for something else.'

Moments earlier, having spotted Dan driving across the sheep pasture and then stopping to fill one of the water troughs from a bowser on his trailer, she had hurried to the fence and, pulling a handkerchief from her pocket, had waved to attract his attention.

'What would you recommend then?' she asked him now.

'Well, I'm no expert—'

'Rather more of one than I am.'

'—but it's not too late to sow winter cabbages.'

Winter cabbages? Had he forgotten their track record with the things? With a light laugh, she shook her head. 'You seem to be overlooking what happens to cabbages over here.'

'Nah. Lightning can't strike twice. Besides, winter ones are different. You sow them in the summer for harvesting in the new year. Although, if it were me, rather than chance it with seeds, I'd go with young plants – if you can get them. What's more, by replacing the cabbages you lost with something similar, the War Ags will be hard pushed to complain. They'll still get what they wanted… just a bit later than they were expecting.'

'Mm.' While she could see the sense in what he was saying, the thought of relying on cabbages again left her with a feeling of doom.

'The only thing is you can't plant the new ones in the same place as the old. And not only will new ground require proper preparation, but it won't have had a manuring, so you'll have to rely on plenty of fertiliser later on. Apart from that…'

May sighed. Why couldn't there be something other than cabbages? But if they were what Dan would grow… 'Well, then I suppose we'd better—'

'Look, tell you what, I know a seed merchant who also raises his own plants. Cost you a bit more than seed, obviously. But, with proper protection, seedlings would give you a head start. Give you more certainty than starting from scratch.'

'All right, then.' There didn't seem to be much point asking for his advice and then ignoring it.

'Poor old Bonnie. Costly mistake.'

Again, May sighed. Just lately, sighing was something she was doing an awful lot. 'I haven't told Mr Beer. Mainly because it always seems as though he can't never wait for us to fail. And this latest disaster will be just another reason for him to say *I told you so.*'

Extending an arm, Dan leaned on the fence post. 'He's queer fish all right.'

'Hm.' *Queer fish* just about summed him up.

'Look, what are you doing right now?'

Guessing that Dan wasn't expecting her to say *talking to you*, she pictured the chores waiting for her back in the house. 'Nothing that can't wait. Why?'

'I was going to go to Cooper's tomorrow. But I could always go this afternoon. The nursery I told you about is just up the road from there. Why don't I take you to see what he's got?'

'You wouldn't mind? I mean, here I am, yet again, prevailing upon your good nature…'

Despite feeling thoroughly miserable, the abandon with which Dan threw back his head and laughed made her smile.

'Fifteen minutes. I'll drive round and pick you up.'

Picturing Mr Beer's reaction if he saw her going off with Dan, May shook her head. While it might be none of his business, she could do without having to explain herself, especially to him. 'I'll just tell the girls and then I'll walk down to the lane.'

'Sure?'

'Yes, thank you.'

'As you wish.'

—

The place to which Dan drove May was just outside of Crediton and looked to her like a smallholding.

'I'll help you out,' he said as they came to a stop in front of a small timber kiosk. 'Unless you want to stay here. On second thoughts, you probably should. The ground's rough and you're not wearing boots. In fact, yes, let me go an' see what he's got. Then if it's all for nothing, at least you won't have spoiled your shoes.'

'That's kind of you.' While May could see the wisdom of his suggestion, she disliked how it made her appear useless and unprepared – even though she was clearly both.

As it happened, barely three or four minutes later, Dan was back, opening her door to say, 'He's got spring cabbages. He sells them by the gross. How many plants did you lose to Bonnie and the weedkiller?'

She tried to picture the field. 'Nine, ten rows.'

'The length of that field's about… yeah, all right. You want them?'

'I do, but…' Fishing about in her handbag, May pulled out her purse and opened the clasp. Distraught at the sight of just a couple of coppers in the bottom, she felt tears welling. 'I haven't enough money. I never thought—'

'No matter. I'll buy them and George can pay me back. Stay there.'

George? *He* wouldn't buy the plants. Now what was she going to do? Why hadn't she stopped to think about the cost? She couldn't let Dan be out of pocket because Bonnie had made a mistake and his uncle was a mean so-and-so.

Carrying a wooden tray in which she could see greenery, Dan was quickly back. Twice more he returned carrying the same, and put them in the rear of the Austin.

'They look like good plants,' he remarked of them as he opened the driver's door and got back in.

'That's good. Thank you.'

'Right, back we go— Hey…'

May sniffed. Clearly, however well she thought she'd covered her tears, she'd failed. 'Sorry…'

'Look, nothing's worth getting upset over. Especially if it's George Beer.'

But it wasn't only George, May reflected. It was everything. 'Sorry,' she said again, glancing to his profile as he turned the vehicle out onto the main road. 'It's just that I seem jinxed. No matter how hard I try to keep things going in the right direction, something always comes along to knock us back. Most of the time, I haven't a clue what to do… and I wonder how I came to get involved in the first place. Slightest thing throws me off.'

'If it helps you to hear it,' Dan said, glancing between her and the road, 'I for one can't believe how well you're doing. I mean, you're just a housekeeper. And before you bite my head off—'

'I wouldn't ever—'

'I'm not making light. Keeping house is a job and a half by itself. I see what Mum does. On top of which, you keep an eye on those two girls. Your Nessa alone is a handful. Far too fast, that one.'

In the passenger seat, May tensed. 'Not sure how you mean.'

248

'Lost count of the number of times she's propositioned me—'

'*Propositioned* you?' By her sides, May's hands had formed into fists.

'*You should come over the barn some time.*'

His impression of Nessa's voice was so accurate May couldn't help but laugh. 'She *said* that to you?'

'So many times, I've lost count.'

'Oh, dear God, I'm sorry.'

'It's not for you to be sorry. You'll make me wish I hadn't told you. Anyway, if it's of any comfort, both Mum and Gran reckon you're the best thing to happen to Fair Maids in years.'

'Me?'

'They've both said they'd like to meet you but don't want to put you in a tricky position by just calling in.'

Tricky position? 'I… don't understand.'

'George,' he said. 'They know how he can be.'

'Oh. Oh, I see.'

'Shame, because I reckon the three of you'd get on like a house on fire.'

May sighed. She wouldn't mind getting to know his family. If they were as welcoming as he was, it would be nice. 'Happen our paths will cross one day.'

'Happen they will. Anyway, we're almost home now.'

'Tomorrow,' she said, 'I'll go to the post office and get you the money you paid for the plants.'

'No rush.'

Looking out through the window, she realised they were passing under the railway bridge by the church. 'Hey, you forgot to go to Cooper's.'

'I did, didn't I?'

Turning sharply, she saw his lips pressed together in a grin. 'You didn't have to go there at all!'

'I didn't.'

'So why say that you did?'

'Because if you'd thought we were making a special trip for your plants, you wouldn't have come. And then you wouldn't have them.'

'But now I can't trust you,' she said, her tone laced with despair.

Dan's shrug suggested he was unconcerned. 'Don't see why not.'

Through the window, May noticed they were turning in to Higher Cleave. Now what was happening? She'd rather supposed he would take her back to Fair Maids. How was she going to get three trays of plants back there now?

'Well, anyway,' she said. 'Thank you for your help. Again.'

'Happy to oblige.'

With no idea why they had pulled up alongside the back door to his house, she fastened the clasp on her handbag and made to get out. She supposed she would have to come over for the plants tomorrow – maybe with Bonnie and a wheelbarrow. Certainly not with Nessa – not after what Dan had just said about her. 'Well, then—'

'Cup of tea?'

With a frown, she turned towards him. 'What?'

'Come in and have a cup of tea. If the mountain can't come to Mohammed…'

'What?'

'You said happen one day your path will cross with Mum's and Gran's.'

'Well, yes… but not now, for heaven's sake. Look at the state of me.'

'Saints alive, May Huxford, it's a farmhouse. We've a late-born lamb being kept warm in front of the range, you won't hardly be able to get through the scullery for boots, nor anywhere close to the fire for the dogs. So, please come in. When I said my mum and gran want to meet you, I wasn't making it up. Besides, it would do you good to get to know some folk out here. Folk other than your Bonnie and Nessa. Folk you could rely on if you needed to.'

'Seems I rely on you.'

'Not what I mean. But you know that. Come on, for once, stop being so stubborn.'

'Stubborn?'

'Come and have a cup of tea and then I'll take you and your cabbages home. If you hate meeting them so badly, you need never come again.'

More than anything, May felt too exhausted to keep objecting. 'All right. A cup of tea. But if I don't go straight back after that, there won't be any supper.'

'I'll see to it they don't keep you too long.'

'Then apparently, I'm fresh out of excuses.'

## Chapter 21

'You like elderflower tea, love?'

'I do, yes. Though it's a good while since I've had any.'

'Come on in, then. Gran was about to brew some. Stretch it to three cups, can you, Gran?'

From somewhere unseen, an elderly voice responded. 'Course I can.'

'Then let's move that dog blanket off that chair and clear a space on the table. There you go, love, sit yourself down.'

To May it seemed peculiar to be within the walls of the house she'd spent the last month and a half looking across at from Fair Maids Farm. She could still remember how her spirits had lifted at the sight of it that first morning as she'd plodded along the lane from Pippinswell. Standing so white against the green of the hillside, she'd been buoyed by the prospect of having it as her new home. Now that she had finally come inside, she could see that she wouldn't have been disappointed. Still, she reminded herself, in terms of size the little old place at Fair Maids *was* more manageable, especially since, of the farm's four residents, she was the only one to occupy it.

'So, Dan tells us you're from Exeter.'

Lowering herself onto the ladderback chair, May returned Mrs Beer's warm smile. 'That's right.'

'Bit different out here.'

'Very.'

'He tells us you've really got stuck in, though.'

'To be honest, Mrs Beer—'

'Call me Lorna, love. Out here, don't nobody much call me Mrs Beer. Save maybe old Doctor Fry.' *Lorna*. She'd try. But she wasn't used to addressing her elders by their first names. 'Sorry, dear, you were saying.'

Returning to the dresser, Lorna picked up a couple of plates, on top of which she stacked some saucers. Having brought them to the table, she returned for cups and then, opening one of the drawers, selected some spoons and a knife.

'I was just going to say that sometimes, I'm minded I'm guilty of spreading myself a bit too thin.'

'Aren't all of us women guilty of that, love?'

Unexpectedly picturing the way her mother had been constantly on the go just to keep them all afloat, May recognised the truth in Lorna's observation. 'I suppose so.'

'Can't none of us sit down while there's work still to be done.'

'No.'

'Piece of carrot cake with your tea?'

Watching Lorna remove the lid from a dark-coloured tin and lift from it a square of golden cake, May suddenly felt ravenous. 'Yes, please.'

About to take the knife to it, Lorna paused. Then she went to the door and stepped outside. 'Dan? You hovering about for some cake or just to eavesdrop?'

In less than two seconds, Dan was on the doorstep. 'For the cake, obviously.' Shooting a smile in May's direction, and then raising his eyebrows at her, he went on, 'Though I'll take mine outside.'

'Yes you will.'

When Dan had left with his cake, the woman May assumed to be his gran came through from the pantry.

'So, you've made it through your first month then.'

'Gran, honestly,' Lorna implored the older woman.

'Hope you like it well steeped,' Granny Beer went on as she approached the table.

Shooting to her feet to assist, May moved a wooden trivet to where it might more easily be reached. 'My mum would have said it's the only way,' she replied with a smile as the woman set down the oversized teapot. In truth, she would have agreed however it came offered.

'And she'd have been right. Anyways, I'm Primrose. But most people call me Gran. Or as often as not, especially behind my back, Old Granny Beer.'

'May Huxford,' May said, reaching to shake Granny Beer's hand. Although the woman's fingers were long and bony, they were warm, and the skin covering them astonishingly smooth.

'So, you're the slip of a thing taking our George in hand.'

'Um…' What on earth had Dan said about her? 'Not sure about that. Much of the time I'm just flailing about, trying to keep on top of everything.'

'Don't do yourself down, girl. Dan says you've become the backbone of the place. Says you've got those land girls licked into shape. Says it's only down to you that George will be given a second chance by those fellows from the Ministry.'

Next time she saw Dan, May thought she might have to throttle him. 'It's not hard to bring a *bit* of order where there's none.'

'Those that went before you wouldn't agree. Come and gone like the seasons, they have.'

'So I'm led to believe.'

'Not giving you any trouble, is he, our George?'

'None.' Since it didn't feel right to talk about her employer behind his back, she would be careful what she said. One false move, and she could still be out on her ear. And then where would she go?

'Spoon of honey in it?'

May glanced to the pale liquid Granny Beer was pouring into her own cup. 'Please.'

'White clover,' Primrose said, sticking a wooden dipper into the honeypot. 'From my own hives.'

'Lovely.' Watching her, May was salivating so much she had to force a swallow. She'd been hoping to taste some honey.

'There you go, then. Take a sip and see if it's to your liking.'

Raising the china cup to her lips, May tried the tea. 'Delicious,' she said. 'Just right.' She'd forgotten how fond of it she'd once been, the taste and the fragrance conjuring a picture of her mother. *Here*, she used to say, handing over the wicker basket she used to take to market, *take Clemmie and go down the canal for some elderflowers. You know which ones to pick. But stay away from the water's edge. And come straight back.*

'If that's too much,' Lorna said, and with which May realised she now had a slice of cake in front of her, 'don't feel you got to finish it. Dan won't mind an extra mouthful or two.'

As the other women tucked into the cake, May glanced about. The room was long and wide but made to feel cosy by its low ceiling. At either end stood immense fireplaces, the one by the back door home to a range, the one at the other end blackened by soot and containing a sturdy grate.

Both chimney breasts were of the local brown stone, and both had a door to either side. Homely, May thought as she tucked into her cake.

'This is very nice,' she remarked when she'd swallowed a mouthful.

'For once, the greengrocer had carrots,' Lorna replied. 'And though it might only be marge instead of butter, at least we don't have to rely on powdered eggs. Hopeless stuff.'

Dare she ask for the recipe, May wondered? Or would that be a step too far? As yet, she didn't know either of these women – although Dan was right to say that she really should. Was it odd that she already felt comfortable here?

While they ate the moist cake and sipped the fragrant tea, the conversation flowed easily, the women's questions showing their curiosity without making her feel as though she was being subjected to an interrogation. In turn, she learned a little about them, too, including how, on his fourth birthday, Dan had been given his first sheepdog pup, on the strict understanding that he alone would have to care for it.

It was only when May noticed a clock on the dresser and saw to her disbelief the time, that she realised how long she'd been out.

'Regrettably,' she said when there was a lull in the conversation, 'I think I had better be getting back. If nothing else, I've suppers to see to.'

'Why not take some soup back with you? It's spring vegetable. A meal in itself.' Such an unexpected and generous offer left May uncertain how to respond. Was she, in these days of shortages and rationing, being offered a ready-made meal?

'Well, that's real kind,' she said, fearing that inadvertently giving the wrong answer might offend, 'but I have to feed all four of us.'

'That's all right.' With a smile, Lorna got to her feet. 'We've plenty, and you're more than welcome to some of it.'

'Oh. Well…'

'I'll put some in a saucepan and secure the lid. You can bring me back the pan in a day or two.'

'Then thank you,' May said, floored by the kindness she was being shown.

'And while she's seeing to that for you,' Granny Beer started to say. Noticing that she was struggling to get up from her chair, May rose and offered her arm. 'You come with me. I've a feeling you could do with a tonic.'

*A tonic?* What was this place? And did they treat everyone who just dropped in with such warmth? 'Well…'

'You'll have to bear with me. Takes me a while to get up the stairs these days.' Having trailed behind Primrose up the steep and narrow staircase, May found herself in a passageway beneath the eaves. Looking along its length, she counted four doors, which she guessed were bedrooms. 'In here,' Primrose said, when they reached the far end.

Having ducked under the low doorframe and followed Primrose in, May stood, wide-eyed. What an astonishing room. In the centre was a table of scrubbed timber – or perhaps more correctly a bench – upon which stood an assortment of objects, among them, jars, jugs, bowls, and an oversized mortar seemingly fashioned from a lump of granite, by its side the matching pestle. Next to it was a spirit stove upon which rested a tin kettle. Arranged along the gable wall, crammed cheek-by-jowl beneath the roofline, was a series of cupboards and cabinets, some with drawers, some with glass fronts. Behind the latter were rows of identical stone jars: meadowsweet, lady's mantle, feverfew, she read from the labels on those nearest to – all names, she supposed, of plants. And under the dormer window away to her left, where muslins were rippling in the breeze, stood an old-fashioned bedstead with a striped blanket, the faded colours of which must once have been eye-catchingly vibrant.

'Golly,' she breathed, her eyes continuing to flit from one discovery to the next.

Taking a step closer to the bench, she looked up. Suspended from the ceiling by leather straps was a wooden frame, hanging from which were a dozen or more bunches of leaves, twigs and seed heads. Combined with the tang from the spirit stove, they were, she supposed, what gave the room its distinctive smell: the dusty aroma of dried foliage mixed with the warm tones of herbs and spices. Feeling as though she had stepped back in time, she recalled the apothecary down in Saltings Street, where her mother had once taken the three of them for something to put an end to hacking winter coughs that had persisted well beyond Easter. That little place had been filled with jars just like these. They had fascinated her even then.

'You forever feeling tired?'

'Somewhat,' May replied. Apart from always being on the go, she still hadn't really recovered from sitting up late that night with Dan.

'Your monthlies heavy?'

May shrugged. 'Sometimes.'

'Eating much meat?'

'As much as anyone.'

'Any liver?'

'Not in a long time.'

'Ruddy war,' Primrose grumbled, going to stand in front of one of the cupboards and then reaching to lift out first one jar and then another. 'Poor food's the root of many an ailment, anaemia among them.'

'Anaemia?' May frowned. 'I'm not sure I know what that is.'

'Lack of iron. Iron you'd normally get from meat and dark vegetables.'

'Oh.'

'And made worse by heavy bleeding.'

'I see.'

Rounding the end of the bench, Primrose came towards her. 'For someone who's outdoors so much, you're too pale.'

'I think I've *always* been pale,' May replied. 'My mother was the same.'

'I'm sure. Here.' From the top of a chest of drawers, Primrose picked up a small hand mirror and held it so that May could see her reflection. 'Do this.' With the fore-finger of her other hand, Primrose pulled down her lower eyelid. 'See,' she said when May did the same. 'Inside, that should be red. But's it pale. You need iron.'

Letting go of her eyelid, May watched Primrose replace the mirror. 'Ask the butcher for some liver. If he tries to tell you he can't get it, tell him Primrose Beer said you need it and that if he tries to fob you off, he'll have me to answer to. And those two land girls – get extra rations, don't they?'

'They do.'

'Then make sure they get what's due to them or they'll go the same way.'

'I do try—'

259

'Now,' Primrose said, going back to her bench. 'I'm giving you something to make a tea. One cup a day.'

Watching the old lady's fingers, and hoping it wasn't going to taste vile, May nodded. 'Thank you.'

Having removed the stopper from the first jar, Primrose picked up a set of measuring spoons threaded onto a leather thong and searched for the one she wanted. Into a stone bowl, she then measured four quantities of what looked like dried leaves. From the second jar, she added a similar amount. To May's eyes, the contents of both looked identical. Once stirred together, Granny Beer tipped them out on to a square of paper, folded the corners together and then twisted the top tightly closed.

'Equal parts nettle and dandelion. Enough for a week. Nettles are rich in iron. Better than that, they contain all the vitamins needed to get it into your blood.'

May conveyed her understanding with a nod. 'All right.'

'Nettle by itself is prone to being somewhat potent, which is why I've made it up with dandelion leaf, which will also help with getting it into your body.'

'I see.'

'Two teaspoons into a pot. You got a little teapot over yonder?'

'Um, actually…' May pictured the contents of the dresser. There was really only the Brown Betty.

'Here,' Primrose went on, opening the door to another of her cupboards and bending to look inside. 'Take this 'n.' Into May's hand, she pressed a small pot painted blue and white. 'Two teaspoons in there, boiling water to fill it up, steep for five minutes with a stir halfway through. Strain it into a cup, let it cool a moment. No sense scalding your tongue. And then sip it. Once every day, mind.'

'Once a day. Yes. Thank you.'

'Enough there for a week to see how you go. Might be all that's needed to perk you up.'

'Thank you,' May said again. 'Thank you for your kindness.'

'Bah. 'Tis nothing.'

Moments later, out in the yard, May found Dan leaning against the side of his pickup.

'Got all sorts here for you,' he greeted her. Accepting his help to get in, she frowned. 'Saucepan of soup, hunk of cheese, best part of half a carrot cake—'

'Cake?'

With Dan climbing into the driver's seat and starting the engine, May looked hastily through the window towards the house. 'But I didn't know… and I haven't said thank you to Mrs B— to Lorn— to your mother.'

'She won't notice. No doubt you already thanked her for the soup and the tea and whatnot anyway.'

'Well, yes, but even so…'

'You know your trouble, May Huxford?'

Unable to hold back a wry smile, she treated him to a dismayed shake of her head. 'What, apart from the fact I'm apparently anaemic and in need of nettle tea and some liver?'

'You worry too much. About nonsense.'

May scoffed. 'It's just who I am.'

'We've all got worries. There's the war. There's shortages. There's the price fetched for lambs and the cost of the vet. Or, in your case, the pitfalls of growing vegetables…'

'Hm. I'll ask you not to remind me.'

'So, some things, you just got to let go. You just got to accept it happened – or didn't – and spare your time and energy for something that truly needs it.'

'If only it were that easy.'

'Try it now and again. You'll be surprised. Anyway, here we are then.'

Looking out to see that Dan had just pulled up at the front of Fair Maids farmhouse, May withheld a sigh. Despite everyone having been so nice to her this afternoon, she wished now that they hadn't – that she hadn't been invited in for tea or been given cake and soup and cheese – because here she was now, about to come back to earth with a thud. Here she was with a sullen and untalkative employer, two overwhelmed land girls, a lost field of kale and only half the number of cabbages worthy of the name. Oh, and the imminent return of those two War Ags. And all of that *before* considering the heap of wild and unruly feelings she suddenly had about Dan.

'Thank you,' she said. But then, remembering all he'd done for her this afternoon, she turned towards him and smiled. 'Truly, I'm real grateful. I don't know where I'd be without you.'

Cocking his head, he got out, walked around the bonnet and arrived to open her door. 'We're neighbours. And out here, neighbours look out for one another. Not only that, but they usually count one another as good friends.'

*Good friends.* Yes, May thought, watching Dan carry the soup pot and set it down on the doorstep, she'd like that. In fact, she'd like it a lot.

262

## Chapter 22

'Mrs Beer?'

Startled to see a woman in tweed jacket and slacks peering into the scullery, May wiped her hands on the corner of her apron and tried to think who she might be. Despite having the air of a minor official, her immaculate fair hair made it seem unlikely she was from the War Ags.

'Mrs Huxford,' she corrected the visitor. 'Mr Beer's housekeeper. There is no Mrs Beer. But happen I can help you all the same.'

'Sorry, Mrs Huxford. I did knock at the front door, but no one answered. Am I in the right place? This *is* Fair Maids Farm?'

It was a couple of mornings later that week and, although May had been gainfully employed at the sink, trying to persuade a scorch mark – of her own making – from a pillowslip, she'd been miles away in her thoughts, which had to be why she hadn't heard anyone arrive.

'It is. What can I do for you?'

'My name's Susan Thorn. I'm here to see your two land girls… Miss… um…' May watched as the woman withdrew from her capacious handbag a notepad through which she proceeded to flick. '…Miss Hutchison-Croft and Miss Hawkins.'

'In connection with?' Although she tried not to let it show, May felt a prickle of unease rise from her stomach and settle in her throat. In a bid to make it go away, she swallowed hard.

'Goodness, yes, what a silly! I haven't said, have I? I'm District Rep for the Women's Land Army. I pop out from time to time to ensure the girls' welfare and whatnot.'

District Rep? Neither Bonnie nor Nessa had ever mentioned one of those. Was it possible even *they* didn't know they had one?

Momentarily flummoxed, May nevertheless nodded. 'You'll be wanting to see them, then.'

'Would you mind? I shan't keep them long. And perhaps you could show me their quarters.'

'Quarters?'

'Where they sleep.'

May hesitated. It didn't seem right to let a stranger just go poking about among the girls' belongings. 'Well, since I don't go in there myself without asking aforehand, maybe you could check with them about that. Only—'

'Of course. Absolutely. Could you point me at them?'

May glanced to the clock. It was a while yet until they would stop for their dinner. Or lunch or whatever. 'Far side,' she said pointing towards Higher Cleave. 'They're hanging nets of hair to deter the deer, bloomin' things.'

'Golly.'

With a quick look down to the woman's sensible brogues, worn even more sensibly with thick woollen socks, May said, 'Happen it would be for the best if I were to show you.'

'Would you? That's terribly kind.' As May gestured across the yard, the woman continued, 'So, you've had them about six months now.'

May frowned. Six months? Oh, she had to mean Nessa and Bonnie, not the deer.

'Since I've not been here long myself, I couldn't say exactly, but yes, I suppose about that long.'

'Any problems with them, that you know of?'

Pausing briefly to remind herself of what was at stake here, May shook her head. A single word of complaint might see either or both removed from the farm. 'None to speak of. When I first turned up, the place were terrible disorganised. But just lately we've been going along a lot better.'

'Yes, I read a note on the file from County to say that the need here was urgent.'

*Best not to be drawn on that*, May thought. 'Couldn't rightly say.'

'The request came from the local War Ags. Bumped this place right to the top of the list.'

'If you say so.'

'And Mr Beer. Would *he* be about for a quick chat?'

'I doubt you'd find him right now, no. Not with you turning up out of the blue.'

'No, of course not. But there's no… uh… no problems there.'

Beneath her housecoat, May felt herself growing hotter and hotter; there were just so many ways that this could all go awry. If this woman asked Nessa about George, there was no way of knowing how she would answer. Bonnie would be all right – assuming Nessa didn't manipulate her into supporting one of her multitude of gripes.

'No. No problems.' Anxious to allay her fears, she asked, 'So, you have a chat to each of them on their own?'

'Wherever possible. That way, each girl has the chance to speak more freely. You'd be surprised how many girls we place together don't hit it off.'

There was a *glimmer* of hope, then. Besides, it was rare for Bonnie and Nessa to be truly at odds.

'Well, there they are,' May said, pointing to where Bonnie was stood steadying a fence post and Nessa was brandishing a lump hammer.

'Jolly good. I'll pop back for a word when I'm done… if that's all right.'

'Fine by me.'

It was to be a full thirty minutes before May finally heard footsteps in the yard; an agonising half-hour in which she imagined every conceivable outcome, from Bonnie and Nessa being taken away, to the recommendation that she herself be dismissed on the grounds of her general unsuitability to oversee them.

'Well, that's all good,' Susan Thorn remarked in a cheery tone as she arrived at the back door. 'They seem happy enough, don't they?'

Barely in time, May prevented herself expressing surprise, managing instead a simple, 'They do.'

'Tell me, how many hours a week would you say they work?'

Recalling Bonnie once mentioning what was expected of them, she said, 'No more than forty-eight at most. When the weather's hot, a bit less because I make them take a few more breaks.'

'Very sensible. And what about weekends?'

'Just Saturday morning, a little longer if needs warrant.'

Susan Thorn scribbled something in her notebook. 'Good. And they haven't raised any complaints about conditions here?'

'None that they've shared with me.'

'Well then, they both said they didn't mind me taking a look at their room but, to be honest with you, I can see from even just standing here that your standards are well up to the mark, so there's really no need for me to take up any more of your time. It was nice to meet you, Mrs…'

'Huxford,' May said, accepting the woman's hand and giving it a firm shake.

'I'll be back at some point, although I can't say when. I don't get out to the more remote places as often as I'd like. People see me turn up in a motorcar and assume I must have access to limitless gallons of petrol. If only! But having to account for every last drop of the stuff does rather restrict me to visiting just the neediest of cases.'

'For certain it must do,' May agreed.

Only when May had heard the door of a motor slam, followed by the rattle of an engine starting up, did she allow herself to relax. All was well – at least, assuming Miss Thorn didn't consider them one of her *neediest cases*, it was.

Turning to head back indoors, she saw Bonnie and Nessa ambling towards her. Yanking off her hat and rolling her head in circles as though to relieve a stiff neck, Nessa met her look. 'Stuck-up little madam.'

May had to fight the urge not to laugh; talk about the pot calling the kettle black.

'Did she go in and look around the lean-to?' Bonnie asked. 'Seemed like she wanted to.'

May shook her head. 'Told me you'd said it was fine then didn't bother.'

When Nessa headed to the lavatory, May waited to hear the bolt being drawn across the door before beckoning Bonnie further away. 'Everything all right?' she asked, her voice lowered against being overheard. 'Nessa didn't put you in a difficult position at all?'

Bonnie looked puzzled. 'No?'

'That's all right then.'

'I think Nessa was more worried what *you* would have to say about *her*.'

'Me? Why would I—' With that, they heard Nessa pulling the chain. 'No matter.'

With a look towards the lavatory, Bonnie smothered a giggle. 'Well, she's hardly the easiest of people to get along with some days, is she?'

May grinned back. 'The two of you fancy a drink while you're here?'

'Yes please.'

'Thought you'd never ask,' Nessa concurred.

Yes, May thought as she went indoors to see to some refreshments, Dan had been right to say there was only so much room in a person's head for worries. In future when she was fretting, she would try to remember that. In the meantime, she would notch up this morning's favourable inspection as an achievement. She might even allow herself to believe that *finally*, their run of bad luck was behind them.

In fact, later that same week she became even more convinced it was the case. Hanging smalls from the washing line, she heard an engine, and turned to see a little black motorcar coming up the track. Going to investigate, she was taken aback to see that getting out of it were Messrs Robinson and Stone.

'Mrs Huxford, good morning.'

Less concerned by the fact that she couldn't remember which was which than by the fact that they should be there at all, her greeting was a wary one. ''Morning, gentlemen. I thought you weren't due to make your inspection for several weeks yet.'

'It's true. We're not,' the taller of the two said.

'But we were due at a neighbour of yours and so we thought we'd drop in.'

'Not for your formal inspection—'

'Just to see how you're going along.'

'Whether you've been able to make a start on the remedial action we noted on our report.'

'Whether we might be able to offer advice...'

Frantically, May tried to work out her best approach. Since she probably couldn't stop them from doing so anyway, she might as well suggest they look around. Having them witness progress might even prevent them coming back again before their proper inspection was due.

'Please,' she said, gesturing beyond the yard. 'So long as you're not intending to write your report on us yet, you're welcome to look around. The girls are out there somewhere. They'll show you what we've been about.'

'Then we won't delay you, Mrs Huxford.'

Tipping their caps, the two men strolled away.

*No need to panic*, May whispered fiercely as she spun about. *Disasters or not, there's plenty over there for them to see we've taken heed. And George has gone out, so he's not here to lay into them, either.* The fact that he couldn't abide what they represented might still, to his eyes at least, constitute reason to pick a fight. And were they not in the middle of a war she might take his side, even though, in the overall scheme of things, the war barely touched him. But no one was exempt from making sacrifices for the greater good, and no one was above the law.

Despite checking the yard every couple of minutes, to May, it seemed ages before the two officials returned. Even when she did finally see them coming towards the scullery, she couldn't bring herself to go out to them, instead fiddling about in the pantry and forcing them to come to her.

'We've had a good look around—'

'And I have to say we're impressed.'

In contrast to when Susan Thorn had come back to see her, May didn't even attempt to hide her relief. 'Thank goodness for that.'

'Keep on as you're going, and we'll be able to report back that the place shows signs of turning round—'

'Is on the way to meeting the basic standards and requirements.'

'Tell Mr Beer he's not quite there yet,' the shorter of the two cautioned, 'but not far off.'

*Tell Mr Beer?* What, and give him the satisfaction of no longer having to worry? Oh no. No, that little nugget she was going to keep firmly to herself. Let him know *that*, and he'd show even less concern.

'Well, thank you,' she eventually said.

'We'll be back to make our formal inspection as scheduled.'

'Of course.'

'Good day to you, then, Mrs Huxford.'

In that moment, May felt so light-headed she had to pull out a chair and sit down. *Keep on as you're going, and we'll be able to report back that the place shows signs of turning round.* Oh, the relief! Nessa and Bonnie would be thrilled. She should go straight over and tell them.

But what she realised, as she trotted off to find them, was that the person she most wanted to rush and tell was Dan. After all, without his endless support, things this morning could have turned out very differently indeed.

# VIII. The Canker Spreads

## Chapter 23

May smiled. Not only had she just drawn back her curtain to find another bright dawn but, for once, she had woken up with her mind free from worries. For a change, everything felt to be going in the right direction: the vegetable crops were coming along nicely – helped in recent days by the odd shower of rain – and Nessa and Bonnie were finally keeping on top of things. The icing on the cake was that yesterday, the post had brought a newsy letter from Clemmie, who also seemed happy and settled. Delighted and relieved by the discovery, May had written straight back to say so, deciding at the bottom of the page that it wouldn't be tempting fate to add, *finally, we seem to be a match for the struggles involved with this farming lark.*

At the post office later that afternoon, though, having cycled to the village to post her letter and buy some more stamps, she became party to news that was to spoil her day.

'Ah, Mrs Huxford,' she was greeted by Joyce Haldon the moment she stepped through the door. 'I was just telling Nan about the land club.'

Hoping that Mrs Haldon wouldn't want to stand and gossip for too long, May expressed only the slightest interest.

'Oh yes? Being kept busy, is it?'

'Well, that's just the thing. Poor old Peggy – you'll remember she had to go an' help out at her mother's? – well, the old soul's gone right downhill, so Peggy's had to move in up there to look after her.'

Just as May had feared: a long story. 'Oh dear.'

'And now, I've got my Clive under the doctor, too.'

May swallowed her impatience. What this had to do with the land club she couldn't imagine. 'I'm sorry to hear that.'

'So, as I was just telling Nan, I can't see my way to carrying on.'

Suddenly, May spotted the connection. 'With the land club?'

Joyce Haldon nodded gravely. ''Fraid so. It's not like me to let folk down—'

'I'm sure it isn't.'

'—but there it is. One of those things. Can't be helped.'

As the implications sank in, May exhaled heavily. No more land club. What a loss that would be. Fair Maids might be on more of an even keel these days, but she knew just how quickly the situation could change. Being able to call upon volunteers might still one day be vital. Only yesterday, Nessa had hinted that when it came to actually getting the crops out of the ground, the three of them would struggle to manage by themselves.

'Isn't there anyone to take over from you?' she asked. Behind her back, she crossed her fingers.

'That's the problem. Though I've asked around, there's no one. Nan will tell you. Folk have their hands full with all sorts these days. Home Guard, ARP, fire-watching, WVS. Everyone I've spoken to says they're already spread too thin as it is.'

To May, it seemed hard to believe; all the way out here, so far from the effects of the war, she struggled to see how most people filled their days. More likely they didn't want the headache. And in a way she couldn't blame them. Which made what she went on to say surprise even herself. 'I suppose *I* might be able to help...'

Behind the counter, Nan Parker nodded approvingly. 'There you go, Joyce. There's your answer.'

Was it too late, May wondered, to point out that she'd merely been thinking aloud?

But the speed with which Joyce Haldon pounced made even that question moot.

'Mrs Huxford, you're a lifesaver. A godsend, no less.'

'Not sure about *that*,' May replied. 'I mean, I don't even know what's involved.' It was then she spotted her way out. Taking care to sound casual, she went on, 'Fair Maids hasn't even got a telephone.'

'No, but Higher Cleave has.' Trust Nan Parker to spot that!

'Ooh, yes. And you *are* neighbours with them. And Mrs Beer's real organised. You know, it was such a shame she gave up running our branch of the WVS. Though Mrs Brown do try real hard, it's never been quite the same as when Mrs Beer was in charge.'

No longer really listening, May stood in a fog of dismay. On the one hand, the demise of the land club would mean the loss of their safety net. Even so, what on earth possessed her to think *she* would be any good at running it? She'd never run a thing in her life!

'I'd have to talk to Mrs Beer first,' she said, spotting how she might still get out of it. 'So, I'll have to let you know.'

But Joyce Haldon had the bit between her teeth. 'Do that this week, could you? There's no jobs in the book for this weekend but the week after could be a different story. And like I said, I do so hate to let people down, not when there's a war on and we all got to pitch in…'

'I'll do my best to let you know on Friday,' May replied. 'I assume you're still doing the church?'

'I am indeed.'

'Well, all right then. But now I really must see to what I came in for and be getting back.'

'Course, dear. Just don't forget to let me know.'

'I won't.'

Walking home afterwards, May had to question her sanity. Not content to lumber herself with a task that could turn out to be a hideous burden on her time, she'd also somehow roped in Mrs Beer. She supposed she could always tell Joyce Haldon that Lorna had declined to help. Or would that be too deceitful? For all she knew, the two were firm friends, meaning she would quickly be caught out in a lie.

Plodding under the railway bridge, May caved to a despairing groan. Would she never learn not to be such a soft touch?

–

'So, what do you think? Would she help me? Or at least allow me to use her telephone to try and do it myself?'

It was the day after May's encounter with Joyce Haldon and, having seen Dan working in the neighbouring pasture and managed to attract his attention, she had just been explaining about the fate of the land club.

From the other side of the barbed-wire fence, Dan had listened patiently. 'Only way to know is to ask her.'

'I realise that,' she said. 'But afore I do, I was hoping you might offer an opinion as to how she might reply.'

With a shake of his head, Dan grinned. 'Wouldn't dare be so bold.'

'Couldn't you just… oh, I don't know, mention that you'd seen me and that I said—'

'You want me to sound her out?'

'Would you?'

'I *could*…'

'I mean, I wouldn't need her to do anything other than maybe point me in the right direction if I felt adrift. I heard the other day she used to run the local WVS.'

'She did.'

'So…'

'When are you taking over?'

May tried to remember what Joyce had said. 'Next week – assuming there's a farmer in need of help.'

'All right. I'll sound her out. But that's all. After that, it's down to you to come over and ask proper.'

'Course. That's only manners.'

'You do know I wouldn't do this for just anyone.' Despite sensing that he was teasing her, May blushed. 'Serious. This is a debt I shall one day call in. So you'd best state, here an' now, that you're happy with my terms.'

Given how long he held her look, her reply was as casual as she could make it. 'That don't seem fair. How can I agree when I've no idea what you might ask?'

With a good-natured shrug, he went to turn away. 'Up to you. You accept at your peril.'

'Oh, for goodness' sake,' she said hotly. 'Very well. I'll owe you a favour.'

'See. Wasn't so hard, was it?'

'Hm.'

'I'll let you know what she says.'

'Thank you,' she called after his departing back. 'I don't know what I'd do without you.'

His response, as he ambled away, was almost too faint for May to hear. But she was reasonably certain he said *That's what I'm counting on*.

–

'Bonnie? You fit?'

From within the lean-to, Bonnie called back. 'Just a mo.'

It was now Friday evening, and last night Dan had arrived to suggest that May go over and talk to his mother about the land club.

By way of preparation – but mainly to demonstrate that when it came to organising things, she wasn't entirely a lost cause – this morning May had cycled to the church, where Joyce Haldon had passed her two notebooks. In the one with the green cardboard cover, someone had ruled the pages to resemble an address book, the front half containing telephone numbers, addresses, and general details of the local farms, the latter section filled with the names of the volunteers and a note of the gang with whom they usually worked. The second book was more of a diary, within which were recorded details of the farmers' requests for help and the teams sent to fulfil them. Studying the pages while she'd walked home, May felt a modicum of relief; it looked straightforward – even if the number of crossings-out did suggest there was plenty of scope for even the simplest of arrangements to go awry.

It was only when she'd been about to set off for Higher Cleave, though, that she'd had the idea to take Bonnie,

278

thinking that way it might appear to Mrs Beer as though the quantity of help she was bringing with her outweighed what she was hoping to gain. Bonnie had been happy enough to accept, saying that since Nessa was going out, popping over to Higher Cleave was preferable to being left on her own.

'So,' May said, her voice lowered as the two of them set off, 'where's Nessa going to?'

'Bonham Arms.'

'The pub?'

'Uh-huh.'

'Not on her own, I hope.' There was a name for women who went into a public house on their own; in fact, more than one, and none of them were complimentary.

'No. Someone from Bonham Hall is coming to pick her up from the lane.'

'She kept that quiet.' Probably because she knew I'd disapprove, May thought as she said it.

Beside her, Bonnie shrugged. 'Only found out myself because she was putting on more lipstick. I think secretly she was desperate for me to ask what she was up to.'

'Mm.' May didn't doubt it. Nessa Croft was one of those girls who couldn't bear to be out of the limelight, which just made it all the more peculiar that, over these last few days, she'd seemed quieter and more secretive, even a bit snappy on occasion. Perhaps it was just her monthlies. She did wonder how the girl had met someone from Bonham Hall in the first place, though; the two lots of land might share a boundary but, by all accounts, the house itself was almost two miles away across the fields. She could only suppose she'd met someone at that dance.

'All she said,' Bonnie picked up again, 'was that he's not a pilot. She says she doesn't want a pilot.'

'I thought she didn't want *anyone* in the services, full stop.'

Again, Bonnie shrugged. 'She's what my gran would call a Contrary Mary.'

'Well, there's no rule as says she can't go out with a fellow if he asks her to. Just as long as she doesn't get into trouble and bring it here.'

'Mm.'

When the two of them arrived at Higher Cleave, Lorna Beer was at the sink, filling the kettle.

'Tea?' she asked as she beckoned them in.

'If you can spare it,' May replied.

'Same,' Bonnie added.

'Well, come on in and sit down, both of you. I'll just see to the pot and then you can tell me what this is all about.'

'Course. Thank you.'

After a minute or two of excruciating small talk as May tried not to dive straight in, and then several clumsy attempts to explain the land club, May found herself telling Lorna how, to avoid seeing it fold, she seemed to have unwittingly become saddled with the running of it.

Nodding or shaking her head as May's explanation seemed to warrant, Lorna heard her out. While doing so, she leafed through the two notebooks, pausing now and again to examine more closely anything that caught her eye.

'And how is it you think I can help, dear?' she eventually asked.

Wary of being too quick to mention the telephone and yet, at the same time, desperate not to be seen as underhand, May did her best to explain.

'On my own, I'm not sure I'll manage. I don't know any of the farms, nor how far out they are. But with the benefit of a second opinion – you know, as to whether something is reasonable, or how many volunteers would be needed for a particular job – then I might make a fair stab at it. Having agreed to take it on, I should hate to make a mess or let people down. The land club folk were such a help when we had all those taters to plant. So, if I can somehow keep it going for the benefit of others in the same sort of a fix, then I should like to do so.'

'Very noble-hearted of you.'

'We all got to do our bit,' Bonnie piped up in May's support.

'We have indeed,' Lorna acknowledged. 'So, what was it you were wanting – to come over here of a Thursday evening?'

Sensing that Mrs Beer was close to agreeing, May tried to rein in her excitement. 'Could we? The last thing I'd want is for us to be a nuisance.' Waiting while Mrs Beer thought for a moment, May held her breath.

'No, that would be all right. Put it this way, I'm prepared to see how it goes.'

Exhaling with relief, May smiled. 'Thank you.'

'You'd better write down our telephone number and work out how you're going to tell everyone where to call if they want you.'

It was at this point May was grateful for having given the matter so much thought beforehand. 'I thought a card on the church noticeboard, another in the box outside the village hall—'

'Maybe one in the Bell and another in the Duke's,' Lorna suggested. 'Farmers do like a drink.'

Mrs Beer's suggestion was a good one. 'Yes. And I thought I could ask Nan Parker to tell people. I mean, folk are in the post office almost as much as they're in the pub.'

Lorna Beer smiled. 'Nan Parker is certainly one way to get the word out.'

'That's what I thought.'

'You know, I'm not sure you need my help at all.'

'Oh, please, no,' May said. 'Believe me, I do.'

At the earnestness of May's plea, Lorna laughed. 'It's all right, dear. I shan't go back on my word. I happen to think it's a good thing you're doing. You can have as much of my help as you need.'

On the way back to Fair Maids, May couldn't stop grinning. Mrs Beer was right: it *was* a good thing she was doing. Admittedly, it wasn't without risk. Once word was out that she was the person in charge, she would have to give it her all: do whatever it took to make a go of it.

Thought about like that, the responsibility hit home. But since it was too late now to back out, all she could do was hope she really was up to it.

–

'Pippinswell 253. Yes, this is the land club. Mrs Beer speaking, how may I help you?'

Throughout that Thursday, May allowed herself to become so nervous that, as she was clearing away the supper things, she genuinely thought she might be sick. But once the three of them were seated in the kitchen at Higher Cleave, and Lorna had answered the first telephone call, nerves were replaced by a determination to do a good job.

'Who is it?' she asked when Lorna put her hand over the mouthpiece of the receiver.

'Mr Collins out at Elm Tree Farm. He's got strawberries need picking. He thinks six boys and girls for a morning, but he'd like an early start.'

'Girl Guides,' May replied. 'There's twelve names on their list. We ought to be able to get six for strawberry picking. If not, we can make up the number from the Scout group.'

'It's little more than a mile from the church,' Lorna said, 'so I think we could agree to an eight o'clock start.'

'Finish at midday,' May observed. 'Before the worst of the heat.'

Lorna nodded. 'That's right.' Into the telephone she said, 'Yes, Mr Collins. We'll have six Girl Guides with you at eight o'clock, for four hours.'

When Lorna replaced the receiver, May couldn't help grinning. 'Who do we ring for the Girl Guides?' she turned to Bonnie to ask.

'It says here to call Mrs Doris Nunn.'

'There you go, then,' Lorna said, lifting the telephone and setting it down in front of May. 'You'd better dial her number.'

In the hour that followed, the land club received two further requests from farmers, which, with assistance from Lorna, May agreed they could fulfil.

'I think that went well,' she remarked to Bonnie when, later, the two of them were strolling back across the fields to Fair Maids. 'Dare I risk saying I even enjoyed it?'

Bonnie grinned. 'Me too. Made me feel important. Like a sort of secretary in an office. I kept expecting you to say, *Hold the line, caller, while I check for you.*'

'I wish I had a telephone voice.'

'Like Mrs Beer?'

'She did sound different when she answered it, didn't she?' May said. 'Not posh or anything—'

'But like she was in charge. *Pippinswell 253. Yes, this is the land club. How may I help you?*'

Listening to Bonnie's attempt to mimic Lorna Beer's voice, May giggled. 'Perhaps I should practise sounding efficient.'

'Just don't end up like Nessa. She can *really* put it on when she wants to.'

'I have an inkling,' May said, 'that in Nessa's case, *that's* not her put-on voice.'

Bonnie's look was a quizzical one. 'You think that's how she speaks at home? That she just… tones it down for *our* benefit?'

'Wouldn't surprise me. Was she going out again tonight?'

'Tomorrow.'

'Do you know where?'

Bonnie gave a decisive shake of her head. 'Uh-uh. But I'm minded it's the same chap as last time. By the way, did she tell you there's to be a dance?'

'In the village?'

'No, over at Bonham. Apparently, young ladies go in for free. And they don't have to pay for their drinks, neither. Nessa said I can go with her if I like. She said it'll be a good do, with a proper band and a decent bar.'

'Are you going to?' May asked. Although not surprised Nessa hadn't mentioned it to her, she still felt miffed. Just lately, Nessa was being very guarded. She was still working hard enough; it was just that she seemed much less inclined to be friendly.

'I'll go if you will,' Bonnie replied.

May shook her head. 'Haven't been invited.'

'I'm sure she'll ask you eventually. Oh, do come, May. If I just go with Nessa, then the minute we get there, she'll abandon me. I just know she will. And it won't be any fun left on my own.'

'I doubt you'll be on your own for long – not if it's packed with young pilots.'

'Even more reason not to go on my own. *Please* say you'll come.'

Despite having no intention of agreeing to go, May made as though to consider it. 'I'll think about it,' she said. 'But to be honest, these days, I'm mostly too worn out to feel like bothering with the effort. Come eight o'clock, all I want to do is fall into bed.'

'I'll get Nessa to ask you anyway,' Bonnie picked up again regardless.

'As you wish. But that don't mean I'll go. Anyway, thanks for your help tonight.'

'Thanks for asking me. It made a real change.'

'Now we've just got to hope that come Saturday, all the volunteers turn up where they're supposed to and do a good job. What we don't need first time out is farmers complaining. You know what funny folk they are.'

Bonnie grinned. 'Not *all* of them are funny. Dan Beer seems rather nice.'

Knowing it was beyond her to respond without blushing, May stared straight ahead. Dan *was* nice. And so, it turned out, were his mum and his gran. They were a nice family with kind hearts and time for everyone. That was why, where Dan was concerned, she had to be on her guard against getting carried away. He was so nice and so friendly that it would be easy to let things slip out of control. And in her shoes, a good and long-lasting friendship was more important than a brief and dewy-eyed romance that ended badly and ruined everything. But now, by the sound of it, she was going to have to make sure that Bonnie didn't go after him either. And no, that wasn't spite or jealousy talking: it was just plain common sense.

–

The earlier brief but thundery July shower had left everything feeling refreshed: the dust had been damped down; the leaves on the trees had been rinsed clean; the mugginess of the morning had been replaced by air that felt restorative rather than suffocating. And as she set out to take an after-supper stroll, May realised it was the first time in ages she had done so purely for the sake of it. She certainly hadn't been out with her wildflower book in a while, and wondered whether she would spot anything new.

Drawing long slow breaths, she cast her eyes out across the fields. All around were signs that the growing season was in full swing: in the copse, the emerald shades of spring had already given way to the deeper forest-green shades of high summer. In the orchards, the grasses were now tall enough to ripple in the breeze like water on a lake. And at first light, the cacophony of the dawn chorus had fallen still. Its fizzling out had caught her unawares, requiring Dan to explain that when the mating season was over and the birds started to moult, they no longer sang in defence of their territory.

That she was coming to appreciate so much about nature pleased her – things that in Exeter she'd never even noticed, out here quickly coming to seem the norm. Creatures like bees, she thought, watching the stem of a cornflower bend under the weight of one settling on the cobalt-blue head. And butterflies: who knew there were so many different kinds? There was one now, flitting between those tall spikes of pink. Recognising the plant as one she'd seen many times but never stopped to look up, she opened her book, turning the pages almost to the end before finding it: Rosebay Willowherb. *Spires of pink flowers borne above lance-shaped leaves spiralling up the stem. A favourite plant with elephant hawk moths.* Another new name to try to remember.

Succumbing to a long yawn, she stood for a moment and looked around. For some reason, this evening her heart wasn't really in it, but rather than just retrace her steps, she would follow the longer path back.

Some minutes later, coming upon the yard from this different direction, she paused to take in the ramshackle collection of sheds. To her mind, it always seemed as though every time more space was called for, another little building was thrown up from whatever materials lay to hand: a small timber store here; an open-sided bay to house the tractor there; a larger corrugated-iron lean-to, the doors flung permanently wide to display the hotch-potch inside. How anyone ever found what they wanted she would never know.

Studying the whole untidy mass, her eyes came to rest upon one addition in particular: fashioned from roughly hewn planks and standing in the lee of the old haybarn, it was small – no more than eight feet square under a low roof – its door secured with a padlock. Intrigued, she went towards it. What, on this farm, could possibly warrant locking away? There being no window through which to peer, she rattled the door. The padlock and chain securing it were weighty, the shininess of the metal suggesting they were new. Unable to satisfy her curiosity as to what was within, she sighed. Nessa would probably know; there wasn't much about this place she hadn't found out.

As she went to turn away, though, a whiff of something pungent and almost sweet brought her to a halt. Was that petrol fumes? Perhaps, then, this was the store where Mr Beer kept fuel for the tractor and his little van. It would explain why it was locked. Even so, she was pretty sure she wasn't supposed to be able to smell it – certainly not so strongly.

Noting in her mind to tell Mr Beer, she turned away. But fewer than a dozen steps further on, something else brought her to a stop: was that *laughter* she could hear? Tucking her book under her arm, she angled her head to listen. Yes, it was the sound of someone giggling – and it seemed to be coming from the barn: children mucking about? She doubted it was Robbie and Neville; they came good as gold each week to do their two afternoons and then went straight back to the rectory when they were done. But just because it wasn't them didn't mean it couldn't be others. As Dan had pointed out, farmyards presented children with all manner of adventures.

Although the laughter appeared to have stopped, she decided to check anyway, arriving at the open doors to the barn and staring in. If children *were* in there, no doubt they were up in the tallet; climbing the ladder was an exciting prospect in itself. And once up there, they would consider themselves hidden from view.

Convinced she was onto something, she looked about the barn and, spotting a sawing horse, put her book on top of it. Crossing to the foot of the ladder, and with one hand grasping her skirt, she edged her way up the first few rungs until, with her head just short of the platform, she held her breath to listen: scuffling – and far too noisy to be mice. About to call out, she stopped: better that she caught them red-handed.

Steeling herself for what she might find, she edged up another couple of rungs. But what she saw as she peered over the ledge made her gasp: reclined in the straw, in nothing but her underwear, was Nessa; alongside her, some RAF chap with his shirt unbuttoned.

'Hello, May.' When Nessa turned languidly over her shoulder, her smile was more akin to a sneer. And when the airman's only response was to sit up and grin, May began to think the two of them had been expecting her – to suspect that she'd walked into a trap.

'Say, honey,' the airman drawled, finally tossing his jacket in Nessa's direction, 'you might want to cover up.'

Spotting braid on the garment's sleeve, May realised the man was an officer, and by the sound of it an American one.

'No need,' Nessa said, making as though to unhook her bra, her expression suggesting she was enjoying May's discomfort. 'She's seen it all before. Haven't you, May?'

'Yeah? Then would she like to come on up and join us?'

'What do you think, May?' Nessa purred and leaned towards her. 'Hank's just given me a pair of nylons, so it seemed only fair he should see them on.' Shooting her companion a sly grin, she continued, 'If you come on up he might get you a pair, too.'

*Hank?* What sort of ludicrous name was that? *Really,* a different corner of May's brain remonstrated: *that's* the thing concerning you? *Nessa's stripped off in the barn with a foreign airman and all you're bothered about is his ridiculous name?*

Despite the number of reprimands flooding her head, May faltered; choose her next words poorly and she risked being humiliated by one of Nessa's cutting retorts. But what should she do? Slink away and pretend she'd never come through the door? Leave with as much dignity as she could muster and wait to speak to Nessa later? Or did she demand, here and now, that the wanton harlot got dressed and came down? And what about her airman chappie? Did she take him to task as well, or simply tell him to leave? One thing was certain: she was *not* going any further up the ladder.

'Nessa,' she eventually settled for saying, her voice carrying rather less force than she would have liked, 'for God's sake, get dressed and come down.'

When Nessa started to laugh, May felt her palm itching to slap her.

'Ooh, *get dressed and come down*. So *stern*, May.'

'Nessa, for heaven's sake. Tomorrow morning you're going to look back on this and regret it—'

'Regret having fun? Hardly! Come on, admit it. You're jealous. You're just a jealous old spinster with no—'

'Hey, honey,' the airman said, his voice bringing to May's mind an actor in a film, 'no need to be unkind.'

'And you, sir.' Feeling her jaw clenching, May determined not to back down. 'I must ask you to leave. What Nessa does when she's off this farm is her own business. But here, it's mine. So, Nessa, for the last time, get dressed, come down, and escort this... your... gentleman from the farm. Do as I say, and this need go no further. I'll let the matter drop.'

With no intention of remaining there a moment longer, May forced her trembling legs back down the ladder. When her feet touched the ground, she turned smartly, retrieved her book from where she'd left it, and went out through the doors into the yard. God, she was livid! But if anyone had lost their dignity, at least it wasn't her. And to ensure it stayed that way, she would wait until morning to put that shameless hussy in her place; the girl might be invaluable about the farm, but that didn't give her licence to carry on like a harlot. Nor did it give her the right to humiliate her in front of strangers.

No, though Nessa might not recognise it for herself, the cocky little madam was skating on very thin ice indeed.

## Chapter 24

'Why on earth would I care what *you* think? I don't work for you. I work for George.'

The morning after she'd found Nessa in the barn with the airman, May had awoken with the determination to be firm but fair; no sense causing an irreparable rift between them, not when things had been going along so nicely.

'It's *Mr Beer* to you,' she responded as calmly as she could to Nessa's tirade. 'And while you're employed on his farm, you work for whomever he says. And that happens to be me. So, it's *my business* because Mr Beer *made* it my business.'

'Huh.'

Ignoring Nessa's derisory scoff, May pressed on. 'Look, my only concerns here are to do my job and to get this place up together, and with most of our problems stemming from Mr Beer himself, the only way I can see us doing that is by the three of us working together despite him. That being the case, I think I'm being both fair and reasonable. For certain there's worse people you could have, telling you what to do dawn till dusk.'

'If you're so reasonable,' Nessa said shortly, 'you'd respect how and with whom I spend my time off, instead of carrying on like the head girl who, discovering her friend smoking behind the potting shed with the groundsman's labourer, feels put out.'

'What?'

'Face it, May, you're jealous.'

'Jealous?' The girl couldn't possibly be more wrong! 'Look, Nessa,' May responded stiffly, her barely concealed rage curling her fingers into the palms of her hands, 'all the while you do your courting beyond Fair Maids, it's none of my business. But you can't bring a man – a man I suspect you hardly know – onto this farm and then cavort with him up in the hayloft and expect me to turn a blind eye. And as for jealousy, nothing could be further from the truth. I mean, do you *want* to get yourself a name? You know as well as I do fellers like him are here today, gone tomorrow. And even if your reputation is of no concern to you now, what about your future?'

'What about it?'

'Want to end up an unmarried mother, do you, with all that entails?'

'Christ, May. I know how to avoid getting pregnant. There are ways other than just keeping your legs crossed, you know.'

'Well anyway,' May said, mortified to even be discussing such things. 'No more men on the farm.'

'And if I choose to ignore you?' Nessa asked. The look she flashed at May was a steely one.

'Then,' May said, equally coolly, 'you'll find out, won't you?'

–

Try though she might, May couldn't shake the feeling that Nessa had let her down. Throughout the following day she kept catching herself standing, shoulders hunched, fists curled, snatches of her argument with the woman still replaying in her head.

That they'd fallen out wasn't the surprise; she'd been expecting the girl to make trouble at some point. The moment she'd set eyes on her, she'd marked her down as defiant — a fact she'd had confirmed when Nessa had talked about her parents and her reason for joining the Women's Land Army in the first place. That said, just lately she'd thought they'd settled to a good way of carrying on: when it came to planting and nurturing the crops, she'd bowed to the woman's superior knowledge — given her free rein over how and when things should be done. As result, they'd been going along nicely: Bonnie had remarked as much; that Susan Thorn woman had seen it, too. Even those two from the War Ags recognised what they'd achieved, none of which would have come about without Nessa playing her part. But now the air had a distinctly brittle feel; despite being convinced she was entitled to reprimand the girl, *she* was the one left tiptoeing about on eggshells, afraid of rocking an already rickety boat and being the cause of its capsize. Indeed, the atmosphere today reminded her of the times in Albert Terrace when she and her sisters had crept about, wary of upsetting Charlie Warren and ruining the precarious peace for days to come. Yes, it felt as though all it would take was one wrong word or look, and Nessa would walk out. And since land girls were only supposed to do that if they feared for their safety, Nessa would see to it Susan Thorn thought that the case.

Giving a weary shake of her head, May sighed. The trouble was, without Nessa Fair Maids would fall apart; their hard-won progress thus far would count for nothing if the vegetables withered in the fields for want of someone who knew what they were doing.

'You all right there?'

Swivelling about, May saw Bonnie peering at her from the doorway. 'Fine, thanks. And you?'

'Just finished earthing up the taters again.'

'Nessa helping you?'

'Grudgingly. She's still ever so cross, though. Her face is like thunder.'

'Doesn't surprise me. No doubt my name is mud.'

Bonnie sighed. 'She does keep cursing you. Though I probably shouldn't say this, I do fear she's plotting some sort of revenge.'

'I don't doubt that for one minute. Anyway, did you come in for something in particular?' It wasn't fair, May decided, to draw poor Bonnie any further into the mire.

'Only to pop to the lav.'

'All right. Well, just mind how you go with Nessa then.'

'Always do.'

Yes, May thought, looking around the kitchen and trying to remember what she'd been going to do next, she doubted she'd heard the last of this; if anyone was the vengeful sort, it was Vanessa Hutchison-Croft.

–

Why was this proving so hard? Why, May wondered, given that she'd already written to Clemmie several times, was she finding that today, she could come up with nothing to tell her? Could it be because, with each week that passed, the distance between the two of them seemed to widen, the feeling most noticeable when she tried to think of something to tell her sister that didn't stem solely from events on the farm? Similarly, as much as she looked forward to receiving her sister's replies, Clemmie's life in Exeter was becoming ever more difficult to relate to. Not only did the city and its daily routines seem changed beyond all recognition but, from her letters, Clemmie sounded to be turning into a properly independent young woman, who wrote with enthusiasm and passion about the increasing number of good causes with which she was now involved.

Not aiding May's struggle on this particular Saturday morning was the way that her own thoughts kept drifting back to Nessa. She did wish the woman would either apologise – something she had to concede felt increasingly unlikely – or else get on with whatever it was she was plotting by way of revenge. Waiting on tenterhooks, suspicious of the woman's every move, was becoming thoroughly wearying.

Staring down at what she had written to Clemmie so far, she reread the last few lines.

*Of late, the weather here has been more unpredictable but, on the good side, the rain has helped the vegetables put on a real growth spurt. The deterrents we put in place to keep deer and rabbits away seem to be working and I suppose it won't be long before we start to harvest. The beetroot are getting to a decent size now, though I can't help thinking housewives would far rather farmers grew onions, as they seem the one thing continually in short supply.*

How dull she must sound, May thought as she put down her pen and racked her brain for something – anything – more interesting to write.

In the end, unable to come up with anything, she signed her name, addressed an envelope and affixed a stamp. Then she went to see whether Bonnie might fancy a stroll to the postbox.

'Got quite the different feel to the air now,' Bonnie remarked when, a while later, they were wandering along the lane. In her hand she was clutching letters addressed to her brothers.

'It has,' May agreed. 'You only got to see the grasses turning to straw to know summer's on the wane.'

'True.'

'You know, until I came here, I never realised you could see the seasons changing. Living in Albert Terrace, I never gave them a thought.'

'Nature's clock, the seasons are.'

'To me, it was either warm or cold. Cardigan or mac.'

'It's different in a town.'

'Mm.'

'Talking of cardigans,' Bonnie said, 'in Mum's last letter she wrote that there's new rules about clothes now.'

May frowned. 'Clothes?'

'Apparently, to save material, dresses and skirts can't have neither pleats nor pockets no more. And can't nobody have long socks. We're all to wear short.'

'Really? Strikes me, rules like that will just make folk even more browned off.'

'Oh, and she also said there's to be no more petrol allowances for private motoring.'

At the mention of petrol, May realised she hadn't told Mr Beer about the fumes coming from that funny little shed. She must try to remember when they got back. 'Mm,' she agreed absently.

'I suppose you know Nessa's gone out again this afternoon.'

May sighed. She'd seen the girl go trotting up the track about an hour back. 'Did she say where she was going?'

Bonnie shook her head. 'Not as such. When I saw her getting all dolled up, I asked if she was seeing that airman again.'

'And...?'

'She just said no.'

Well, that was something to be thankful for. With any luck, the fellow in the hayloft had decided she wasn't worth the trouble. On the other hand, Nessa hadn't got all dressed up for nothing; she had to be going to see someone.

By the time they'd dropped their letters into the postbox and were returning up the track to the farmhouse, May felt in need of cheering up.

'Nice cup of tea?' she suggested when the two of them were crossing the grass towards the front door.

'Don't mind if I do.'

'Then how about, since the sun's come out, we put the rug out the front here and treat ourselves to a sit-down. The cake should be cool enough to cut by now, too.'

'Won't say no to that.'

'You know, I'm pleased with the way this one's turned out. I soaked the dried fruit overnight in apple juice. Plumped up nicely. Might help it stay moist a bit longer.'

'With the way we wolf it down, I can't see it needs to. Anyway, I'll just pop to the lav and then I'll see to the rug.'

With a smile to Bonnie, and humming a little tune, May went in through the door and along the passage to the parlour. But as she stood unbuttoning her cardigan, the sound of cutlery clinking made her frown.

'That you, Mr Beer?' she called ahead.

As she ducked through into the kitchen, though, she stopped dead. Cutting a wedge from her newly baked fruit cake was a man, stripped to the waist, his air-force blue trousers the only clue to his identity. Watching him from the doorway to the scullery was Nessa, the airman's shirt the only thing protecting her modesty, the look in her eyes as she stood licking something from her fingers clearly intended to provoke. *Now what are you going to do*, it taunted.

Apparently unbothered by her arrival, the man at the table grinned. 'Hi there. Want some cake?'

Slowly, May uncurled her fists. 'Leave it alone. I spent all morning making that.'

'Whoa.' Hastily setting down the knife, the stranger backed away. 'Forgive me, ma'am. Nessa here said I should help myself.'

'I don't doubt it,' May responded tartly. Nessa, she determined not to look at. 'She says that to all the men she brings here. But if you thought her offer included a piece of my cake, you were wrong. Now, take yourself out of my kitchen and get off this farm. You've had what you came for – same as that feller the other night – and so now you can go. And unless you want me making a complaint to your superiors, I suggest you don't come back. If you're desperate to see her another time, take her somewhere else to do your business.'

At least this one, May thought as she watched him turning awkwardly for the door, had the grace to look embarrassed. They would see no more of *him*.

Feeling how tightly she was clamping her jaw, she moved to inspect the damage to her cake, noting from the corner of her eye Nessa turning to follow the man out. Moments later, from the yard came raised voices. With a bit of luck, incensed at being humiliated, this latest chap was putting Nessa in her place – better still, would want nothing more to do with her. Who knew, perhaps being torn off a strip would teach the girl a lesson. She could only hope so, because, where that girl's behaviour was concerned, her only other recourse was to report her to Susan Thorn, and who knew what hares that might set running? They really could do without Women's Land Army officials poking around – with a few well-chosen words, Nessa could see to it that Fair Maids had no land girls at all. And although May longed to see her get her comeuppance, she didn't want it at any cost; there was just too much at stake. No, better to let Nessa Croft stew for a bit – force her to wait to see what might happen next.

'What the devil was all that about?'

When May spun round, she saw Bonnie, her eyes wide and her cheeks flushed. 'Nothing,' she replied evenly. 'Nothing whatsoever.'

'So, we're still having tea and cake?'

'You still want some?'

'Course.'

'Then get that rug spread out on the grass and I'll bring the tray.'

As the afternoon wore on, though, May's belief that she had handled the situation to her advantage quickly became submerged by an indignant rage. How dare Nessa behave with so little regard for the rest of them? How dare she act so brazenly and so… so provocatively?

By the time George trudged in for supper, her anger had taken such a hold over her that she could bear it no longer. 'You need to speak to Nessa,' she confronted him the moment he came through the door.

George's response was to glance about as though he'd missed something. 'Why must I?'

'Because she's taking liberties.' When all he did was look to the stove as though fearing for his supper, she went on, 'She's started bringing men here. And… and doing things with them. This afternoon, I've caught her with the second chap in a week.'

'What you expect *me* to do about that?'

'Talk to her. Tell her it's not on.'

'Ain't that for you to do?'

'Me?'

'You seem to be the one getting upset about it.'

'I *am* upset about it. And so should you be. It's not even as though she's being discreet. She's… she's flaunting it, standing about half-naked. Not content with frolicking in the barn, she brought this latest one in here. I found him helping himself to your cake—'

'Cake?'

No surprise *that* should grab his attention. 'You're lucky there's any left.'

'What sort of cake?'

'For God's sake, Mr Beer, are you going to talk to the girl or not?'

'Woman, I got bigger problems than some strumpet dropping her knickers for soldiers.'

Bringing her hands to rest on the table, May examined George's expression. *Bigger problems?* Now what had happened? 'Such as?'

'As if canker ain't enough to be going on with, now I've got bitter pit.'

Bitter pit? That didn't sound good.

'I… don't know what that is.'

'All that dry weather, that's what's caused it. When the soil's so parched, trees can't draw up no goodness. On top of that, the ruddy canker's spreading like wildfire.'

'So—'

'So, like I said, I don't have time for no girl. In any event, since she's here to work them blasted vegetables, she's your problem.'

'But I—'

'Though afore you go charging in, you might want to stop and think about how you getting all uppity paints *you*. She's young. She's a looker—'

'Looker my foot. She's a floozie.'

'—and doing no more than letting off a bit o' steam. Happen you might want to think about doing the same.'

'Mr Beer—'

'My advice? Leave her be.'

'*Leave her be?*'

'Now, since you've had my five penn'orth,' George continued calmly, looking up as Bonnie came through from the scullery, 'are we eating that supper before it spoils or not?'

–

Standing at the sink the following morning, her thoughts still on Nessa, May let out a weary sigh. The problem she faced was that apart from cavorting with servicemen, the woman gave little other cause for complaint. By virtue of being bigger and stronger, her efforts out in the fields –

when she put her mind to it – exceeded Bonnie's almost twice over. In addition to which, she knew what she was doing: the vegetables were weeded, watered and, as far as was within anyone's power to achieve, kept free from pests. In fact, it felt as though, knowing her value to the place, Nessa was deliberately testing her. But why? What had *she* ever done to upset the girl? After a bumpy patch back at the beginning, the three of them had been getting along nicely.

Reaching to dry her hands, she gave a despairing shake of her head. What could have happened to set Nessa against her? It wasn't as though the two of them were competing for men, nor, for that matter, the attentions of the same one. So, what did Nessa have to gain from provoking her? Moreover, why carry on like a harlot? Didn't she care what these men would think of her – didn't she care how she would be talked about behind her back? Pippinswell was a small place, and people liked nothing more than a good old gossip.

And then there was Mr Beer. Why was he so reluctant to take Nessa in hand? Granted, he had problems in the orchards, what with the canker spreading and this new thing… this bitter pit. But could he not set that aside for just one moment and take charge? Could he not see she had good reason to be cross?

The washing up from supper dried and put away, May glanced about the kitchen. If the matter had related more directly to farming, she could have discussed it with Dan. But this was more delicate – more the sort of subject for his mother. In fact, yes. When she went over there on Thursday for land club, what if she was to mention being in need of some advice? But advice about what? What *was* the root of her problem? That Nessa was seeing men?

That she was bringing them onto the farm? That it turned out she had the morals of a tomcat? Or was it because, as Mr Beer had alluded, the girl was having a good time? Looked at like that, she could see how she might come across as jealous; worse than that, as an old maid. *Was* she an old maid? By being wary of marriage on the grounds that it might turn out like her mother's experience with Charlie Warren, was she in danger of becoming a sour and disapproving old spinster? She didn't think so. Even if she was, that was a separate matter from Nessa and *her* behaviour.

In her quandary, May went to the door and stood looking out into the yard. No, the fault wasn't with her; this was Nessa's doing, fair and square. The woman was baiting her. And while she might not know why, she wasn't going to let her win. Unlike Nessa, she, May, knew right from wrong. She knew what was and was not acceptable behaviour from a young woman employee, because that's all Nessa was – an employee. So, no, she would wait, and she would watch. Whatever the girl's game, she was not going to be beaten by her. The day George had handed her control of everything apart from the orchard, it was on the understanding that she was free to run things however she chose. Where Nessa and Bonnie were concerned, that would be in a right and proper manner, with due regard to decency. And woe betide either of them if they chose to ignore that.

–

May's resolve was to be tested sooner than she'd expected. Wandering back into the yard after an hour spent with Bonnie at Higher Cleave, where they had received just two requests for help from the land club, May was confronted by the sight of a man in uniform coming out of the lavatory and turning immediately towards the back door.

'Oh, hi there,' he greeted them, pausing uncertainly when he saw them heading in the same direction. 'After you, ladies.'

To May's mind, he looked too young to be in service, certainly too young for Nessa. Although perhaps that was part of his appeal. Perhaps she was becoming lazy, and someone so young was more easily seduced.

'May I help you?' she asked. Poor lad: she actually felt sorry for him. 'Are you lost?'

'Um, no ma'am. I'm…'

With that, through the scullery door slunk Nessa, her look sultry and defiant, the unbuttoned neckline of her blouse leaving no doubt what she was up to. 'He's with me.'

'Is that right?' May directed her question to the young man.

'Uh, yes, ma'am.'

'Well, I'm sorry to disappoint you, but despite what your fellow servicemen have probably led you to believe, this isn't a knocking shop. She does not conduct her business from here. Besides, what a wholesome fellow like you would want with a…' On the tip of May's tongue was the word 'trollop', but at the last moment she thought better of saying it. '…with someone like her, I can't imagine. Plenty of nice young ladies around without getting mixed up with this one. Anyway, since you're on private property, I must ask you to leave.'

As she'd known they would, her words had the desired effect. Too young to want trouble, the fellow blushed.

'Yes, ma'am. My apologies, ma'am. Good night.'

By contrast, showing no concern whatsoever, Nessa continued towards the lean-to, the sight of her doing so making May stiffen.

'Oh, no you don't, young lady. I'm not finished with you. You go back inside.'

Nessa continued walking. 'On whose authority?'

'On mine.'

Turning to regard her, Nessa scoffed. 'Yours.'

'That's right.'

'And what if I choose to disregard your supposed authority? What if I just keep on…' In ridiculously exaggerated fashion, Nessa continued walking.

'Then I'll say my piece to you here. Left to me, I'd choose somewhere private, but since you clearly conduct yourself unhampered by the small matter of decency, I don't suppose hearing what I have to say in public will bother you.'

'Why would I worry what *you've* got to say?'

Determined not to snap, May forced herself to draw a breath; but her mind was made up. She'd had enough.

'Nessa Croft, your services here are no longer required. I will not have you bringing this farm into disrepute. Your wanton behaviour will be tolerated no more—'

'*You* can't dismiss me.'

Neither Nessa's expression, May noticed, nor her demeanour displayed an ounce of contrition. In fact, she looked smug. Well, the woman underestimated her at her peril.

'I've already warned you twice on this same matter. First thing tomorrow morning, you are to pack your things and leave.'

'You can't dismiss me.'

May held firm. 'I can. I've checked. Since you are in breach of your terms of service, I am perfectly within my rights. You signed a pledge to the Women's Land Army to uphold their good name, and you've done anything but. I've been more than fair with you – with both of you. I've asked only that you conduct yourselves decently and do your work as directed. I have never imposed a curfew upon you, nor have I prevented you from going out and about as you please. I assumed you knew right from wrong. While you clearly do, you have nevertheless chosen to behave wantonly. So, tomorrow morning, you will leave. When you are gone, I shall telephone Susan Thorn. If you go without a fuss, I shall tell her only that we have had a disagreement that can't be mended. However, if you choose to be difficult, I shall regale her with every gory detail. It's down to you. You can have a black mark against your name for wanton conduct – about which word could so easily reach your folks – or you can simply leave here and not come back.'

Waiting for Nessa to respond, May held herself rigidly. Golly, she felt light-headed. The other evening Lorna Beer had been right to say she didn't have to put up with this. The expectations of a land girl were clear. No employer had to tolerate such transgressions. If nothing else, May had Bonnie to protect. And yes, with Nessa gone, they would be a full worker down. She knew that. But it couldn't be helped. Susan Thorn would have to send them someone else. And that's all there was to it.

In the event, after having appeared to consider her choices, Nessa stormed into the lean-to and slammed the door.

'Do you think she'll just go?' Bonnie asked.

'If she's got any sense, she will. For all her bluster, and for all she professes not to care about her folks, she wouldn't want word getting back to them.'

'I suppose not.'

'You be all right in there with her tonight?'

'I'll manage.'

'You can come in and share with me if you'd prefer.'

Slowly, Bonnie shook her head. 'No, it's fine. I'll just ignore her.'

'All right then. Well, I'll see you in the morning.'

'Yes. Night, May.'

But despite feeling more exhausted than she could ever remember, May knew she stood no chance of falling asleep. Tomorrow, though, would be different. Tomorrow, Nessa Croft would be gone, and with her all the tension and the woe. In fact, from tomorrow, life would be better all round.

# Chapter 25

'You did *what*?'

Startled by the sharpness of George's tone, May backed away. 'I… told her to leave. I told her last night… and this morning she went for the first bus—'

'Without so much as a word to me beforehand?' Unsettled to see George's nostrils flaring, May backed away further still. 'You didn't so much as *think* to check with me?'

Feeling the wall pressing into her back, May came over hot. George's reaction to the news that she had dismissed Nessa wasn't what she'd been expecting. Given his opinion on land girls generally, she'd assumed he would merely grunt; at best, comment to the effect that she'd better be double-quick finding a replacement. Instead, here he was, flying off the handle at her.

'I didn't think you'd—'

'You and your *blasted* meddling. Do you have any idea of the trouble— Do you have *any idea* what you've done?'

What *she'd* done? What on earth had got into the man? He hadn't been *this* livid when he'd threatened to aim his shotgun at the War Ags.

Despite mounting panic, May determined not to apologise. 'What I've done,' she said, 'is what *you* should have done but wouldn't. Nessa Croft's behaviour was intolerable. Nothing short of shameful. I tried speaking to her. I tried reasoning with her. I warned her. And on more than one occasion. But all my warnings seemed to do was make her even more brazen, even bolder and more defiant, as though she was… as though she was taunting me to see what I'd do. Finding her cavorting with men she didn't know from Adam was bad enough. But having to watch her going about the place half-naked… well, that I could not allow. She never showed so much as a shred of regard for neither me nor Bonnie. Nor for you. On top of which, she was soiling the reputation of the Women's Land Army. And no, before you say it, I couldn't just have looked the other way.'

'It still weren't… *your* place… to get rid of her.'

He might be her employer, and such was his rage that he might be spitting at her, but May was determined not to back down; *she* wasn't the one in the wrong here. 'I had no choice.'

'You had *no right*.'

'I don't agree. You made it abundantly clear you wanted nothing more to do with either of them—'

'You got any idea what will happen now?'

May withheld a groan. Of course she knew! 'I admit we'll be left short-handed. I'm aware of that—'

'*Short-handed?* You think this is about your ruddy vegetables?'

'I'm perfectly aware that—' Wait? What? This *wasn't* about the War Ags? Then what *was* it about?

'I wish now I'd never taken you on, constantly poking your nose in where it isn't wanted. You've turned out to be nothing but a curse.'

'Mr Beer!' From where she had been stood in the corner, watching, Bonnie leapt to May's defence. 'Don't say that. May's quite right. Nessa were up to all sorts—'

'Meddling, that's all you women are good for. From day one, you've done nothing but interfere.'

Aware that she was close to saying something she might regret, May held her hands firmly by her sides. 'That's not true and you know it.' The man's lack of interest in what the three of them had achieved these last weeks was bad enough, but to be told now that she was a curse? Still, she thought, eyeing the man with distaste, just lately he'd drunk so much cider she doubted he even knew what day of the week it was. And yes, she knew full well this was *his* farm, upon which he was free to live howsoever he chose, but she didn't expect to be cursed for looking out for him, for only doing what had to be done. 'My only concern, ever,' she said, her voice taking on a tremble, 'has been to try and stop you losing this farm. I came here expecting to do nothing more than keep house but ended up seeing to everything *you* wanted no part of. I worked out what to plant. I oversaw the work. When our own labour wasn't enough, I got help from the land club. I worked out what to do about deer and rabbit and just about every other pest or problem known to mankind. And *why* did I do all of that?' He couldn't, she noticed, even bring himself to look at her. 'I did it because you refused to. I did it to keep the War Ags off *your* back.'

'*Those* bloody buffoons.'

'I'm not looking for thanks,' she pressed on. 'That's not why I did it. I did it because, for whatever reason, you wouldn't. And on the matter of Nessa Croft, I should have thought you'd be grateful to be shot of her. Since the day I turned up here, you haven't had a single good word to say about her. Nor, for that matter, about Bonnie. Do you

311

have *any* idea of the hours she puts in on your account? Do you?'

'She's paid for 'em.'

'Hardly the point.'

Slamming his fist down onto the table, George shook his head. 'Why in God's name couldn't you just let things be? I told you, didn't I? I told you to take no notice of her, but no, you had to go and—'

'Then sack me.' From the corner of her eye, May saw Bonnie flinch. 'Go on. If, as you claim, I've made a high old mess of things, then give me my marching orders. But if you do, know that I'll take Bonnie with me. And know also that the minute we're gone, my first telephone call will be to the War Ags. It'll be to tell them how, in a fit of drunken stupidity, you've got rid of all the help and have no intention whatsoever of harvesting a single crop from the ground. So, when they turn up with a notice to evict you, you'll have no one but yourself to blame.'

Despite the glassiness of his stare, when George jabbed a finger at her, his tone contained real venom. '*They* can't evict *me*. This is *my* land. *Mine*. If they so much as set foot past that gate, so help me God it'll be the last thing they ever do.'

At her wits' end, May hung her head. Why was she even bothering? Didn't she remember how trying to reason with a drunk was only ever a waste of breath? Besides, with Nessa already gone, it wasn't as though he could change the situation.

Edging a step closer to Bonnie, she put a hand on the girl's arm and, in a brittle tone, said, 'Well come on, Bonnie. Can't stand around here all day – not when there's work to be done. How about you an' me go over the fields and take stock?' Lowering her voice, she went on,

'And when we come back, perhaps someone here will have slept it off… will see things in a different light.'

Despite visible uncertainty, Bonnie turned to accompany her out. 'All right.'

Once in the fresh air of the yard, May growled with frustration. What right had the man to speak to her like that? Yes, this was his farm and the final say on matters should rest with him. But until this precise moment, he'd never had a single good word to say about Nessa Croft. So, what had suddenly changed? Why, now that she was gone, was he carrying on as though the sky was about to fall in? Accusing her of being a curse she could put down to drink. Charlie Warren had been the same; whenever he staggered in, too drunk to even negotiate the door without walking into the frame, he would curse any woman he set eyes on. But with George, the situation felt different. With George, there seemed more to his anger than could be explained by an excess of cider alone.

'*You* got any idea what's brought this on?' she turned to Bonnie to ask.

Her face drained of colour, Bonnie shook her head. 'I've never known him have a good word to say about either of us, but 'specially not about Nessa.'

'Quite.'

'You know,' Bonnie went on quietly, 'I feel a bit sorry for Nessa.'

As the two of them started to amble without direction across the yard, May turned to study the girl's expression. 'Sorry for her?'

'She was dreadful unhappy, you know.'

'Unhappy? What, here, do you mean?' Waiting for Bonnie to answer, May found herself wondering yet again whether she had missed something.

'No, I meant with her folks.'

'All *I* recall her saying was that she didn't want to get married.'

'Yes, but I'm minded that was merely the final straw. From the bits and pieces she let slip over the months, her parents did sound terrible overbearing. And while she didn't much like being *here*, I know for a fact she was determined never to go home. I recall her once saying her father knew plenty of people who could have got her out of war work completely, but that she would never give him the satisfaction of asking him to help. What was it she said? *Clearing out a flooded ditch in the depths of winter is better than being indebted to that man.*'

'If that were true,' May said, reminded of their cider-fuelled confessions that night down by the river, 'then perhaps she should have thought more about how she'd taken to behaving. If this place truly was her salvation, happen she should have gone out of her way to stay clear of trouble. It's not as though anyone would have objected to her seeing some chap now and again – not if she was discreet about it. But no, she had to go and overdo it.'

'My gran always says,' Bonnie replied, 'that girls like Nessa – girls who put themselves about, I mean – just want attention, and that they have no pride.'

'My mum would have said the same,' May observed. Nessa always did strike her as someone who craved attention, certainly men's attention. 'She was forever propositioning Dan, you know. She couldn't even talk to *George* without flirting. It was like she couldn't help herself.'

'I always thought the freedom of being away from her family went to her head and that she just sort of… went off the rails.'

'You might well be right,' May said. 'Either way, she brought the outcome on herself.'

'She did.'

'It's not as though I didn't give her plenty of chances.'

'Plenty.'

'But here we are anyway.'

'Here we are anyway.'

Yes, Nessa Croft's downfall was no one's fault but her own. Eventually, Mr Beer would surely see that for himself.

'So,' she said, treating Bonnie to her best attempt at a smile, 'later on, I'll go over Higher Cleave and ask Mrs Beer if she wouldn't mind me telephoning Susan Thorn. If I can get through, I'll explain what's happened and see if we can go on the list for a new girl.'

'All right.'

'In the meantime, the two of us will carry on as usual. In fact, why don't you go on over the fields, let me know what jobs seem most pressing, and I'll put us down for some help from the land club?'

'And Mr Beer?' Bonnie asked, evidently still uneasy.

'Mr Beer, we'll leave to stew in his own juices and trust that once he eventually sobers up, he'll see sense.'

'Do you think he will?'

With a shake of her head, May sighed. 'Can't say as I've the least idea. All I can think to do is put him to the back of my mind.'

'Then I'll try an' do that too.'

'Good. Because we've plenty more important things to think about.'

'We have.'

Watching distractedly as Bonnie wandered away, May heaved an exhausted sigh. Sentiments like those were all

315

well and good but if George *didn't* see sense when he sobered up, then she and Bonnie were going to have to be very careful indeed…

–

It wasn't just that the room was stuffy, although that clearly wasn't helping. No, keeping May from getting to sleep was the fact that the entire day had passed and yet, although he must surely have sobered up, at no stage had George returned to the house. When, at midday, he hadn't come in to eat, still fuming from their earlier altercation she'd thought no more of it; as she had said to Bonnie at the time, he was probably sleeping it off somewhere. But when he didn't arrive for supper either, genuine concern set in. A check of the orchards and the barns failed to find him. And his continued absence had to be why, at gone midnight, she was hot and restless, and stood so little chance of getting to sleep that she might as well get up and do something useful. But do that, and tomorrow she would pay for it by being even more grouchy.

Hauling herself up from her mattress, she swiped at her pillow and pummelled it with her fists. Then she folded back the sheet and sat staring into the darkness. Even with the curtain left wide and no blackout at the window, the air felt sultry and humid, as though a storm was brewing.

In despair at her continued wakefulness, she swung her legs down to the floor and padded across to the window, where she knelt to look out. Away to her right was the faintest of orangey glows. She fumbled about for her torch. She knew she had lain awake for hours, but surely that couldn't be the dawn? In the beam of light, she angled her wristwatch. No – ten past one, still the middle of the night.

Mystified, she went back to the window. The glow had become brighter, casting flickering patterns on the ceiling. Through the stillness, she could hear crackling. If a building nearby had been hit by incendiaries, she would have heard the aircraft overhead. So, it had to be a bonfire. But who on earth would light a fire at this time of night – especially in defiance of blackout regulations? Deciding that perhaps she ought to go and check, she looked about the room and, spotting her housecoat, pulled it over her nightdress. Then, for good measure, she wrapped her dressing gown over the top; who knew what she might find once she got out there?

Her sense of foreboding deepening, she went downstairs, pushed her feet into her shoes and, spotting the rolling pin where she'd left it on the drainer, grasped it in her hand.

Out in the yard, the crackling grew louder, greeting her nostrils the smell of woodsmoke. Clearly, she was heading in the right direction. But, as she rounded the corner of the lean-to, she stopped dead. Among the trees, the flames from a bonfire were leaping high into the night sky. A picture of a defiant-looking Nessa flashed through her mind: was it possible the woman had come back to take her revenge? Had she decided to teach them all a lesson? It wouldn't be beyond her. However, as she stood, thoughts racing, she realised it wasn't a bonfire *among* the trees, it *was* the trees. Against the blinding glow from the flames, she could just make out a silhouette. Dear God. This wasn't Nessa's doing – it was Mr Beer's. Mr Beer had set fire to the king tree!

With no idea what to do for the best, she cast about. Did healthy apple trees catch fire, or just dead ones? Would the flames engulf the whole orchard? Spread to the house?

While none of the buildings seemed in immediate danger, she had better wake Bonnie anyway – and fill some pails with water just in case. But as she went to turn away, a tremendous *crack* was followed by a roar, and a tongue of flame shot high into the darkness. In that same instant, she felt a ripple of breeze lift her hair: the wind had risen – and was snatching up embers and carrying them towards the outbuildings! She yelled in the direction of the fire. 'Mr Beer!' Apparently spellbound, the figure didn't move. 'George! The barns! George!'

*It's no use. He can't hear you. Fetch water. Pails of it! Damp down the barns.*

With that, Bonnie arrived. Her face illuminated a pale apricot colour from the blaze, she was wrestling her dungarees up over her nightdress.

'What's going on—'

'Go for Dan! Get the fire brigade.'

Without stopping to fasten the bib of her overalls, Bonnie took off. 'Just you be careful!' she yelled over her shoulder.

Plunging into the scullery, May grabbed two laundry pails and sped across to the water tank. Thrusting one of them under the spigot, she threw open the lever. But with the tank all but empty, she was left staring at a miserly dribble. Not wanting to waste time, she shot back up. Overhead, glowing specks were drifting down through the darkness. Having fanned the flames and whipped up embers, the breeze had subsided, abandoning the burning debris to fall onto the barns.

She tried calling out again: 'Mr Beer! Mr Beer! The barns!'

This time, as though roused from a trance, the silhouette turned. Then it darted through the trees and disappeared behind the outbuildings.

Hurtling back to the tank, May dragged the half-full pail of water from under the tap and replaced it with the empty one. But in the same instant, an intense yellow-white light illuminated the yard, and a tremendous boom rattled her ribs.

Her first thought after that was that she could taste wet soil. And in her ears was a high-pitched ringing. Gasping for air, she opened her eyes. What in the name of…? Why was her face pressed against the ground? *Petrol. She'd forgotten to tell Mr Beer about the smell of petrol.*

Unable to hear anything but the roar of flames, she raised her head and staggered to her feet. Through the surrounding smoke and haze she caught movement; turning into the yard was a tractor and trailer; jumping down from it, Bonnie; gesturing to her from the driver's seat, Dan.

'May! May!'

'Mr Beer…' she struggled to yell to Dan as Bonnie came running towards her. 'He went… round the back…'

Her recollection of events after that was patchy. She remembered a second tractor arriving and people filling buckets from the bowser on its trailer. She remembered a cacophony of shouted instructions; the hiss of Tilly lamps; the intense heat from the inferno and the sizzle of water meeting flame. But most powerful in her memory were the smells: hot tar; scorched timber; earth turned to mud by all the water.

Later still, she would recall stumbling over to help, only to have someone drag her from the path of the firemen. She would also go on to recall how, with the

319

fire eventually doused, they had all had stood, stiff with shock, united in a disbelieving silence as the pale light of dawn gradually exposed the scale of the destruction. With Bonnie sobbing beside her, she remembered thinking for a moment that she was back on the night of the Exeter blitz, staring in horror at the ruins of Albert Terrace. But most deeply etched into her memory would be the jolt she'd felt when Lorna Beer had come to explain that the fireman had found a body – and that it was George.

## Chapter 26

'I was wondering, should I go over the fields and check everything's all right?'

From where she had been sitting in the parlour, lost to a sort of daze, May looked up. 'Sorry,' she said. 'I was miles away. What did you say?'

'I was just wondering,' Bonnie repeated, 'whether I should go over the fields and see that everything's all right.'

Weighed by exhaustion, May shook her head. What did it matter now about the fields? George was dead. He could hardly be thrown off his land by the War Ags now, could he?

'Maybe leave it for today,' she replied. 'Happen we should try and get cleaned up here first.'

'I suppose.'

'There's smitches and soot everywhere.'

'There is.'

'And mud walked in all over the place.'

'That too.'

'The chappie from the fire brigade said we can clear up as long as we don't touch the barns. He said the police might want to take another look.'

'Do you think the police will want to speak to either of us?'

Noticing how the prospect seemed to make Bonnie uneasy, May frowned. 'Couldn't rightly say. But since neither of us saw George actually start the fire, or could know what was going through his mind when he did, what can either of us say now that isn't already obvious? Like Dan said, what fool sets light to a tree without first felling it and carting it away somewhere safe? I simply can't fathom what came over the man.'

'Too much cider again?'

May sighed. 'Must have been. I know the business with the canker really got to him. Add to that the drink, and perhaps he just… took leave of his senses. If the police do ask me anything, I shall say only that he'd been distraught of late and taken to having a bit too much cider.'

'Thing is,' Bonnie began.

Something about her tone made May look up. 'What's that?'

'I know what was going on…'

Having been slumped in her chair, May pulled herself upright. Back in her stomach was the prickling sensation she got when something was wrong. 'Going on with what?'

'Nessa… and the petrol. And Mr Beer.'

Feeling as though every sinew in her body had just been wound taut, May forced a swallow. 'The petrol?' *That* had something to do with *Nessa*?

'But maybe,' Bonnie said, her tone doubtful, 'I shouldn't say anything. I mean, I only know that because I heard them arguing. And even then I couldn't hear all that clearly.'

With no clue what Bonnie was talking about, May sighed. 'Well, I shan't force you to tell – not if you think it would be wrong to. But if what you know has any bearing on what happened, then you need to think long and hard about keeping quiet.' From a selfish standpoint, she hoped Bonnie *would* keep her counsel; once the girl had divulged what she knew, she, May, could no longer claim ignorance. On the other hand, they did say that forewarned was forearmed.

'Nessa knew this airman fellow.'

The decision apparently taken out of her hands, May scoffed. 'More than just the one, I think you'll find.'

'No, what I mean is, there was this one in particular. Not one she went out with, nor any of the ones she brought here. This was one she used to go and meet in the lane.'

'In the lane.' Yes, she remembered Nessa trotting down there often enough.

'And then of a night, he used to come up through the fields in one of those funny little trucks all the Americans drive about in.'

To May, this was genuine news. 'Did he come here, into the yard?'

'Though I never saw him myself, he must have done, for how else would Mr Beer have found out what was going on?'

George had *known*? She was the only one who had been in the dark? 'So, what *was* going on?'

'Well, from what I could gather, this chap would bring petrol – jerrycans of it – to put in one of the little sheds, you know, all the way round the back of the old barn.'

May's already taut sinews pulled tighter: the shed with the padlocked door – the one where she'd smelled fumes and had meant to tell George. Oh, dear God. If only she'd done so! Then all of this…

'Go on.'

'Apparently, Nessa was letting him keep it there ready to sell – on the black market, I suppose.'

'No doubt in return for a share of the money.'

Bonnie shook her head. 'I think it was more likely in return for lipsticks and scent, and soap and the like.'

How pitiful. How tawdry. 'Amounts to much the same,' May said dismissively. 'Anyway, go on. You said Mr Beer found out.'

'Must have done, because I overheard him demand to know what Nessa thought she was playing at. She was terrible short with him – said all he had to do was turn a blind eye for a while longer and the petrol would be gone. She also told him it would pay him to keep his mouth shut because, if anyone came asking questions, she would say she'd seen *him* putting it there… and that he'd told her it would make him a nice little profit. She said he'd be done for black-marketeering and go to prison.'

May's fingers curled around the edge of her chair. 'Then what happened?'

'I heard Mr Beer laugh. And Nessa get cross. "Think about it," she said to him. "Which one of us are they going to believe? Me, with my family background, or some hard-up yokel farmer threatened with eviction by the local War Ags?" I remember thinking if it came down to it, Mr Beer wouldn't stand a chance.'

Struggling to contain her anger, May shook her head. 'No.' Oh, how she wished she'd known all of this before! Together, she and Bonnie and Mr Beer could have gone to the police and told them the whole story.

Slumping low in her chair, May exhaled in despair. Now that it was too late, so much made sense. Now she understood why Mr Beer had refused to take the girl to task – could see why he'd declined to speak to her about her behaviour and why he'd dismissed her antics as just a bit of fun. Nessa had him over a barrel. Who *would* the police have been more likely to believe? Who *would* there have been to vouch for Mr Beer's character? Certainly no one from the War Ags. It also explained why he'd taken so heavily to the cider. He'd always seemed fond of a tipple; she'd smelled it on his breath from day one. But it was only more recently that he'd started partaking to excess; coming together with the canker and the bitter pit, Nessa's threats must have felt like the final straw. The irony was that Nessa had probably only got involved in the first place for the thrill of it. She certainly hadn't needed the odd bar of soap, nor had she been short of male attention.

From that recognition, a thought occurred: believing she had a hold over Mr Beer must have been what had allowed Nessa to grow so brazen. In the belief that she held all the cards, and with George unable to risk reprimanding her for fear of the consequences, she'd felt able to do as she'd pleased. She'd probably also decided that without Mr Beer's support, she, May, would be powerless to bring an end to her shenanigans. Believing she had the upper hand, the evil little madam had taunted her without fear of recrimination, the woman's only mistake being her failure to consider that anyone might use the same approach on her. Threatened with having her own reputation sullied – with having the Hutchison-Croft name dragged through the mud and incurring her parents' wrath – she'd had to back down; sticking to her guns not worth the risk.

Rather than seethe with anger at the recognition, though, what May felt most was an overwhelming sadness and regret. If only she'd known what was going on. If only Mr Beer had been minded to confide in her, had thought to enlist her help. Had he not been so infuriatingly stubborn, together they might have put an end to Nessa's games before anyone got hurt. But, for reasons she would never understand, he'd chosen to keep quiet. Embarrassment on his part? Possibly. Too late now to know.

'So, what do I do? If the police ask me, I mean?'

Having forgotten Bonnie was there, May looked up. 'Well,' she said, battling to gather her thoughts. 'In all honesty, how does what you tell them now make any difference? Nessa might have been responsible for the petrol being there, but she didn't start the fire. Mr Beer did that. Despite knowing there were jerrycans of petrol in his shed, he set fire to a tree anyway. So, I suppose most people would think as we do – that he brought the misfortune upon himself. Even without the petrol, setting fire to a dead tree was a damn fool thing to do. Anyone would think he *wanted* the whole lot to go up in flames.'

'Perhaps then,' Bonnie said, 'I won't mention it. But if the police ask me straight, I'll have to tell them.'

Slowly, May nodded. 'Fair enough.'

'Otherwise, like you say, how does it help?'

'Can't see that it does,' May said dully. 'Can't see how it's of the least help to anyone now. For certain it won't bring Mr Beer back. Nor will it help either of us two.'

No, May thought, the truth of their situation hitting home: with Mr Beer gone, and a fair portion of the farm buildings destroyed, what *would* happen now? Susan Thorn would find Bonnie another farm. But when it came to her own future, the situation looked rather less certain – frighteningly less so.

Ironic, really, she reflected with yet another sigh, how just as she had begun to put down some roots, her new life had done precisely the same as her old one in Albert Terrace had done – gone up in flames.

# Chapter 27

She'd never liked being idle. She never had understood how women could sit around, *taking a little break*, when there were still jobs to be done. Do the work, sit down afterwards; that was her way of going about things.

One week on from the fire, though, for May, even just the thought of trying to get back to her former routine felt not only beyond her, but also disloyal to Mr Beer. Waking each morning to the smell of charred timber, she would stare up at the ceiling and wonder whether today would bring news of what was to happen to her. Over the last week, she and Bonnie had tried to keep busy: they had scrubbed all traces of soot from the inside of the house and the lean-to; they had swept up cinders from the yard and taken them to the heap; they had scraped away the worst of the mud left by the water from the firemen's hoses. And yesterday, for only the second time, they had gone to the fields, where they had made desultory efforts to hoe weeds from between the rows of potatoes and earth up the haulms. But despite being busy all day, to May it felt as though all they were really doing was filling time.

'Did you know we're out of marge?' Drawn from her reflections, she looked up to see Bonnie staring into the pantry. 'And there's not much tea left, either.'

That was another thing. Mrs Beer had said that they were to go to Higher Cleave for their meals but, enormously kind though her offer was, neither of them felt inclined to impose. However, without George, they had no means to buy food; they had eggs from the hens and milk from the cow, but there were only so many times she could make them omelettes.

'I'll go over and see Mrs Beer,' she said in answer to Bonnie's observation. 'See if there's any word.' What sort of news she was expecting there to be, she didn't know, but at least by asking she would feel as though she was doing something.

—

'Come on in, love,' Lorna Beer welcomed her when she tramped over there a while later. 'You on your own?'

Checking the soles of her shoes, May stepped inside. 'I am. Bonnie's darning her shirt.'

'How are the two of you going on?'

Unable to pretend otherwise, May shrugged. 'We try an' stay on top of everything. But though there's sufficient weeding to keep us busy dawn 'til dusk, our hearts don't seem in it.'

'Course they're not, love. It's the shock. We're the same here.'

Christ, yes. How had she not remembered? This was George's family. And though, to her mind, the two sides had always seemed estranged, they had to be feeling the loss far more deeply than she and Bonnie.

'Yes. I'm sorry.'

'Look, dear,' Lorna said, placing a cup of tea on the table and gesturing her towards it. 'I know I've offered before, but the two of you are more than welcome to come and stop here. We've a spare room upstairs. You'd be a bit cramped, but mightn't that be better than waking up to the sight of them blackened ruins every morning?'

It was a generous offer, May knew that. And she felt ungrateful declining. But it still didn't seem right to impose, especially when they didn't know how long it might be for – how long it might take for things to be sorted out.

Waiting until Lorna Beer had pulled out a chair and sat down, May thanked her. 'Please don't think we're ungrateful. It's real kind of you to offer. But we'd prefer to stay where we are.'

Lorna nodded. 'I understand.'

'I don't suppose there's been any news?'

With a sympathetic smile, Lorna shook her head. 'It's too soon, love. You know how it is with solicitors. Just yesterday John went into Crediton to see Mr Browning. You do know, I suppose, that John and George were brothers?' When May nodded, Laura went on, 'It always used to be old Mr Browning who took care of the papers and deeds and whatnot. But now he's retired, his son's taken over.'

May nodded. 'I see.'

'Anyway, some long years back, George was persuaded to make a will. And that's what young Mr Browning is sorting out.' While May could only suppose a will would make Mr Beer's affairs more straightforward to deal with, she couldn't see that it helped her own situation; with him having had no heirs, the farm would surely be sold just the same. Unless he'd left it to his brother. It wasn't something she could really ask. 'George's situation,' Lorna continued, 'was… well, let's just say it was unusual, which means it's likely to be a while before anything happens. According to John, there's papers got to be lodged here, there, and everywhere.'

Despite 'a while' being the last thing May had been hoping to hear, she managed a smile. 'I suppose so.'

'But in the meantime, you're not to worry. No one's going to turn you out. Neither of you. In fact, I'd been going to come over later… see if we can't sort out a few arrangements.'

At the mention of arrangements, May tensed. 'What sort of—'

'At the very least, you have to eat. If you won't come here for your meals – and don't fret, I fully understand why you might not want to do that – then John and I have decided you're to get what you need, *whatever* you need, and charge it to Higher Cleave's accounts. By rights, you should continue to be paid. For the moment, no one can get to George's money, and getting the ministry to pay Bonnie's wage into another account, where John can get at it, won't be quick, either. So in the meantime, least we can do is feed you – clothe you, if needs be, too. Both of you. Besides which, John is keen for the two of you to stay on. Keeping Fair Maids tended is more than he and Dan can manage, what with this place as well. So, what do you think? How do you feel about going along same as you have been? Soon as John can make up your wages, he will. In the meantime, we'll see to your needs. We've accounts in the usual places – Newcombe's for your groceries, Wilford's for your meat rations. Next time they come up here, or I'm in the village, I'll tell them what's to happen.'

To May, it felt as though Lorna had lifted a ton weight from her shoulders; at least they wouldn't go hungry. For the moment at least, it seemed they were saved.

'That's real kind of you,' she said. 'Me and Bonnie were wondering only this morning how we would keep going.'

'Then that's settled. But remember, you're not to struggle. When you need help, you're to come and ask for it.'

'We will.'

'Well, don't let your tea go cold. And while you drink it, I'll wrap up some bits to tide you over. It'll be mostly cold cuts, but there's also some lamb hotpot and some fruit cobbler. How do that sound?'

'Like a lifesaver,' May said, her worries lifting further still. 'But I was wondering if I might use your telephone?'

'Course, love.'

'Only, I'd better speak to that Land Army woman and let her know what's happened.'

'You go right ahead.'

Raising her cup to her lips and taking a sip of the strong tea, May finally felt the stiffness in her neck starting to soften; for now, at least, everything was going to be all right. And given their circumstances, 'for now' was about as good as they had any right to expect.

–

'Golly. How awful. When did it happen?'

The speed of Susan Thorn's arrival at Fair Maids Farm had taken May by surprise. Was such prompt attention a good sign or a bad one, she wondered? From the woman's manner, it was hard to tell. As for Bonnie, when May glanced across the kitchen table at her, the poor girl's expression was close to panic.

'Last week,' she replied to Susan Thorn's question. 'The night I called to speak to you about Nessa.'

'How truly dreadful for you. So fortunate the house was saved. And that no one else was lost.'

'Fortunate, yes,' May agreed, watching as the woman turned her attention to Bonnie.

'So, dear, it seems we must work out what to do. Uncharted territory for me, this one. Nothing in the handbook for *this* sort of eventuality.'

To May, the woman's manner seemed a little too glib. 'We've been told it could take ages to sort out what's to happen.'

'I should imagine it will.'

'But in the meantime, we've arranged with Mrs—'

'I want to stay.' When both women turned to look at her, Bonnie hastened on, 'I want to stay for as long as I'm needed. There's so much to do.'

Susan Thorn's expression was one of incredulity. 'You want to stay? Here?'

Blushing vividly, Bonnie nodded. 'It would be a crime to waste all them vegetables… but without me an' May, that's what'll happen. I don't mind if I don't get paid. I been saving up all my wages anyway.'

'The Beers – the other Beers over at Higher Cleave, that is,' May took it upon herself to explain, 'are making sure we have food. And anything else we need.'

'Well.' Susan Thorn frowned. 'Leaving you here would be somewhat irregular. But you're certain, Bonnie? You wouldn't rather I place you somewhere else?'

The prospect clearly filling Bonnie with dread, she gave a vigorous shake of her head. 'No. I want to stay. I couldn't have it on my conscience to leave. Not now. Not after all we've done.'

'And you can manage? I mean, Mrs…' Susan Thorn's eyes flicked to her notepad. '…Mrs Huxford is only the housekeeper. As I understand it, she has no farming background.'

*Only* the housekeeper?

'As Bonnie will tell you,' May rose carefully to her own defence, 'I've learned a good deal. Besides which, our biggest trials are behind us now.'

'Very well. If you're sure that's what you want, both of you. I shall report to County that for now, arrangements should be left as they are. Although, I do think I should hold off placing another girl with you. No sense getting someone new settled here, only to have to move them after a couple of weeks.'

Able to see the wisdom in that, May nodded. 'Fair enough.'

When Susan Thorn set off back to her car, Bonnie gave May a hug. 'Thank you.'

'If only everything were that easy,' May replied as the pair stood watching the whirl of dust being thrown up by Miss Thorn's little motor.

'Just got to hope now I don't live to regret it,' Bonnie added with a sly grin.

After Susan Thorn's visit, May felt more settled. She supposed it had to do with certainty: they weren't about to be turfed out; they weren't going to starve; they had control over their own labours.

Lorna Beer was as good as her word, too. When May bought groceries from Mr Newcombe, he didn't bat an eyelid at charging them to Higher Cleave's account. He even started bringing his van all the way up to Fair Maids' back door to make life easier for them. And Lorna continued to send food parcels too: a chunk of rabbit pie; half a sponge cake; a steamed pudding and a jug of custard. And although it was always Dan she sent over with them,

May couldn't help noticing that he seemed different. His mood was distant and preoccupied, as though he'd had all the stuffing knocked out of him. But then, he had just lost a member of his family.

'Everything all right?' she risked asking when he arrived one evening with half a sack of oats for their porridge.

'Fine. You?'

A couple of days later, she noticed the difference even more keenly. 'Don't suppose I could prevail upon you to take a look at that blasted pump again?' she asked as he dropped off a link of sausages wrapped in butcher's paper.

'I'll ask Dad to come over.'

'Oh, I'm sure there's no need to go troubling your dad,' she said, noticing how he seemed barely able to look at her. 'For certain it'll be the same problem you sorted out for us last time.'

'Happen it will,' he replied, already turning away. 'I'll ask him to pop over.'

His manner was so chilly it left May to wonder whether she'd done something to upset him. Until the fire, he'd been so friendly – quick to see the funny side, not to mention endlessly patient with her shortcomings. So, what had happened?

'You notice anything different about Dan?' she asked Bonnie when the two of them were clearing away after supper.

Bonnie didn't even look up. 'Nope.'

Perhaps it was delayed shock, May thought. After all, Dan *had* been the first to go in search of George among the burning barns; seeing his arm still in a bandage was a daily reminder of that. While uncle and nephew hadn't been close, she knew from experience how losing a family member brought pain like no other.

Lost for a better explanation, she sighed. Maybe he just needed time to come to terms with it all. She could only hope so, because already she was surprised by just how sorely she missed him.

–

The jolt May felt stemmed from guilt. Staring at Clemmie's handwriting on the envelope just delivered by the postman, she realised it was a long time since she'd even thought about her sister, let alone written to her. Yes, she had been rather preoccupied of late, but it was still inexcusable.

Remorse twisting at her insides, she wandered back indoors, pulled out the thin sheet of notepaper, and started to read.

> Dearest May,
>     I hope this letter finds you well. I am mainly going along well, too.

Why only *mainly* well, May wondered. Was her sister's new job not what she'd hoped for? Was something amiss with her lodgings? In her last letter, she'd seemed so content.

Anxious to allay her fears, she read on.

> I don't know about you, but I find it hard to believe we are on the verge of autumn now and do wonder where the summer has gone.
>     I am getting along so-so at the shop. I enjoy seeing so many people every day and having a chat.

*Some of them I have got to know quite well. The owner is an odd fellow, though, and at times makes me wonder what he is up to.*

*Although I miss you often, at this very moment I wish more than ever that you were close by as I am in a quandary over something. It is nothing that need alarm you for, as I say, I am quite well otherwise. But I do wish you were here to lend me your thoughts. Apart from you, there is no one else I trust to be neither so honest nor so fair. Anyway, since you are not here, I shall have to rely on my own judgement in the matter. I suppose it hasn't served me too badly thus far.*

*Please take every care, dearest May,*
*Your loving sister Clemmie*

With an uneasy sigh, May reread the line that bothered her most. *I am in a quandary over something.* Since her sister had chosen not to elucidate, all manner of worries were now running amok in her mind.

Poking the letter back into its envelope, she went on through to the yard, where her eyes fell upon Bonnie staring at the ruins of the barn.

'Ooh, lucky you,' she greeted May. 'A letter. Don't suppose there was one for me?'

May gave an apologetic smile. 'Sorry, no.'

'Bit greedy to expect one so soon. Both Mum and Gran only wrote last week.'

'This is from Clemmie,' she said. 'And if you don't mind, I should like to pop in and write straight back.'

'Course. Everything all right?'

In a bid to play down her concerns, May shrugged her shoulders. 'Not altogether sure. She says she's in a quandary and wishes we could talk.'

'So, why don't you go and see her?'

'And leave you on your own? That wouldn't be right. Not with everything here as it is.'

Bonnie tilted her head. 'I suppose you could always invite her here. I know everything's a bit upside down, but at least you'd get to see one another. If she's in a fret over something, you never know, she might jump at the chance to get away – to put some distance between her and whatever's bothering her.'

Why hadn't *she* thought of that, May wondered? It was obvious. 'Yes,' she said brightly. 'You're right. Thanks. I'll do that.'

'Besides, if we're thinking of getting them apples off the trees in a week or two, she'd be another pair of hands…'

'Miss Hawkins,' May said with a laugh, 'though no one would imagine it to look at you, behind that innocent expression of yours there lurks a real sly fox.'

'Just saying. Only, it's going to be something of a big task for just the two of us.'

'Mm.' And gathering up the apples was only the start of it. What they were going to do with them after that, she hadn't a clue; all she knew was that she owed it to George not to let them go to waste. Thinking of George reminded her of something. 'You seen anything of Dan?'

Bonnie shook her head. 'Not since the other day. Why?'

'I was hoping he might point us in the right direction – with what to do about the apples. I mean, *I* don't even know how to tell whether the bloomin' things are ripe.'

'I don't know the first thing about them either. I just supposed that when they're ready, they drop off.'

'For all I know, they do.'

337

'Then there's the problem of the big press needing mending. Sorry old state it looks now, all scorched and blackened.'

'Well, anyway,' May went on, 'if you do see Dan, sound him out for me, would you – about when to pick the apples. But for heaven's sake try an' do it without making it seem like we're angling for help.'

'You forget,' Bonnie replied with a cheeky grin, 'underneath this innocent appearance there lies a sly old fox!'

–

Having reread the letter she'd just written to Clemmie, May sighed. Since her sister might not be able to just drop everything and get on the bus to Pippinswell, she had resolved not to write too much about what had happened, mentioning only in passing that a fire had destroyed one of the barns. Explaining about Mr Beer was something she didn't feel right putting down on paper; not only would she make herself upset, but she didn't want her sister agreeing to visit solely because she thought she ought to. No matter how badly she wanted to see Clemmie, she only wanted her sister to come all this way if she genuinely believed doing so would benefit her.

Her eyes falling upon the paragraph in question, she reread what she had written.

> *I, too, often wish we could talk. But if you like, and if you could find a way to do so, would you care to come for a visit? If you were here for a couple of days, the distance might help you see your quandary in a different light. If nothing else, we could certainly have a good old chat!*

Yes, looking at the way she'd worded it, she didn't think she'd pressed her sister either way. But oh, how she hoped she would come! Being able to talk to Clemmie might help her face up to her own dilemma. After all, sooner or later she was going to have to decide what to do. Once Mr Beer's affairs were sorted out, it seemed increasingly likely the farm would be sold, Lorna having just the other day hinted that Dan and his father would be unable to manage any more land even if they wanted to. And yes, finding a new owner might indeed take months. But it might only take weeks. Moreover, the Beer family couldn't go on supporting her and Bonnie indefinitely; they were only doing so now out of kindness.

No, she had to face facts: once Fair Maids' crops had been dug up and carted away, there would be no further need for either her or Bonnie. And that was where she was hoping Clemmie might be able to help; presumably, in her role with the WVS, she was well placed to know first-hand what sort of jobs women like her were being sent to do. Last year, when single young women had been required to register for war work, she'd of course gone to do so, her responsibility for Clemmie and Pearl being the only thing exempting her from immediate call-up. By virtue of then coming to work on a farm, she had continued to remain exempt. However, were she to return to Exeter then, with both her sisters now living by their own means, she would be left facing conscription either into one of the services or else into a factory. It wasn't that she objected to doing her bit, it was more that she didn't relish having no say in where she ended up – worse still, in what she would be made to do when she got there.

With a slow shake of her head, she gave a wry smile. She supposed she could always become a land girl. She was as good as one already. And working outdoors was far and away preferable to filling shifts in a factory, or getting married and becoming exempt on that basis, only to find herself quickly bound to several offspring.

The envelope containing her letter to Clemmie sealed and addressed, she let out yet another lengthy sigh. In truth, she was unlikely to have much choice: one way or another, she was probably going back to Exeter. She supposed it might not be *too* bad. After all, current *quandary* aside, life there seemed to suit Clemmie well enough. And by all accounts, Pearl had settled down, too. Who knew, there might even be a young man back there, with whom she would find herself acceptably happy.

*Acceptably happy?* Realising where her thoughts had taken her, she gave an ironic laugh. Was that really the best she could hope for? After all she'd achieved here, settling for *acceptably happy* amounted to giving up. And while it might be true that she had more faults than talents, giving up wasn't one of them!

*IX. Harvest*

## Chapter 28

'Oh, my goodness, May! It's so lovely to see you.'

Releasing Clemmie from their hug, May wiped away tears of happiness and returned her sister's delighted grin. 'Lovely to see *you*, too. Look at you, all… different.'

With a puzzled frown, Clemmie took a step backwards. 'Different? I can't think how.'

It was now early September, and this morning May had walked into Pippinswell to await the arrival of the bus bringing Clemmie from Exeter. But when her sister had alighted onto the pavement, May had found herself withholding a gasp of surprise. Clemmie had changed – not in the sense of having gained or lost weight; nor did she have a new hairstyle. It was more that in her neat low-heeled shoes, smart blouse and skirt, and with a proper coat over her arm, she had gone from being the girlish slip of a thing in May's memory to someone with… well, with a womanly bloom about her.

'I suppose you just look real grown up,' May replied to her sister's remark. It was unsettling to think of her sister turning into a young woman without her, to see her looking so *finished*. She was glad to see her looking so well, though; relieved to discover that someone was obviously looking out for her and caring how she went along. That it ought to have been *her* doing so, she tried to push from her mind.

'About time I looked grown up! I'm not *so* far off nineteen now.'

'I suppose that's what I forget,' May said, eyeing Clemmie's smart little bag. Presumably, someone had loaned it to her. 'I hope you remembered to bring some old clothes to work in.'

When Clemmie gave a hapless shrug, she looked more like the girl May remembered. Perhaps she hadn't changed *all* that much then.

'Haven't really got any. But I did bring my old lace-ups. Though were it not for Miss Evercott, I doubt I would have thought to.'

'Never mind. I'll lend you a housecoat or something.'

'Thanks.'

'Come on, then, it's this way to Fair Maids.'

'Lead on.'

As they started across the green, May asked, 'So, how was your journey?'

'Can't complain.'

'The bus looked full.'

'Pretty much, yes.'

Faced immediately after that by a lull in the conversation, May tried to think what to say. 'I'm afraid it's a bit of a walk.'

'You said in your letter.' Beside her, Clemmie glanced to the sky. 'At least it's fine.'

'And it'll give us the chance to catch up.'

'Yes.'

But with seemingly *so much* catching up to do, neither of them seemed to know where to start.

'While I was waiting for you to arrive,' May took it upon herself to say, 'I found myself struggling to believe it's not even four months since I left. It feels so very much longer.'

'Waking up this morning, I thought the same. And though I don't know why, I worried how we'd pick up again, you know, after so long apart.'

May smiled. So it wasn't just her. 'Same here.'

'I was sorry to hear about Mr Beer,' Clemmie went on. 'Must have been dreadful hard for you.'

May's reply was little more than a whisper. 'It was. Still is, truth to tell.' She was glad now that when her sister had accepted the invitation to stay, she had written back to explain more about the fire, it seeming only fair to let her sister know what she was coming to.

'Still no word what's to happen to the farm?'

Aware that her sister was regarding her, May shook her head. 'Not yet. Though I can't imagine it'll be too much longer. The solicitor has finally sorted out Mr Beer's money… and all his accounts, so at least me an' Bonnie are being paid proper again.'

Clemmie nodded. 'That's something.'

'And the other day, a couple of fellows from the War Ags came to check on the crops. You see, by now, we should have dug the maincrop taters. But since they were late going in, it was agreed we should leave them another month. We're going to need a lot of hands from the land club for *that* job, I can tell you. Back-breaking work, that'll be.'

'I've a feeling you'll manage.'

'If I'm still here.'

When Clemmie once again turned to look at her, May fixed her gaze along the lane.

'You think the new owner won't want to keep you on?'

'Can't see why he'd go to neither the expense nor the bother. At most the place only needs a man and wife – maybe along with a son or a hand. No, I reckon once the last of the crops are dug and carted away, Bonnie will be sent off to another farm, meaning there'll be no need for me here at all.'

'Seems a shame,' Clemmie remarked. 'From your letters you sounded settled.'

Noticing Clemmie shifting her bag to her other hand, May reached down to relieve her of it. 'Here,' she said, 'let me take a turn with that.'

'Thanks.'

'I *was* settled. And trust me, there's no one more surprised about that than me.'

'So,' Clemmie said as they eventually started up the track, and the roof of the farmhouse came into view, 'what will you do if you can't stay on?'

Wandering across the grass to the porch, May shrugged. 'Sadly,' she said as she reached to unlatch the lower half of the door, 'I haven't the faintest idea.'

–

'Come on, then. You'd better show me what to do.'

Dressed in overalls and a pair of wellingtons May had borrowed from Lorna, Clemmie stood at the edge of the field, gazing along the rows of ragged green leaves.

'Well, as you can most likely make out,' May replied, 'these are beetroot. Some time back, we thinned every other plant to allow space for the rest to get bigger. Some of the thinnings we ate fresh. Some we pickled. Some I gave to Mrs Beer to do the same.'

'Waste not, want not.'

'That's right. But now's the time to get the rest of them out.'

'*All* of them? Just the three of us?'

'All of them,' May said. 'And yes, I do see the irony. A bit like the cobbler's children having no shoes – once I'd taken care of land club requests from two farmers digging taters this weekend, there weren't no volunteers left to help us with this.'

Clemmie grinned. 'You always were a soft touch.'

'It's not the worst crop we could be harvesting,' Bonnie said, coming to join them. Earlier, she had carried the dozens of wooden crates and stacked them at intervals around the borders of the field. 'By the time the beet get to this size, they're sort of sitting on top of the soil and don't need much of an effort to get them out.'

'But there's still only one way they get into those crates,' May said. The scale of the task ahead of them was something she preferred not to dwell on.

'In which case,' Clemmie replied with a grin, 'hadn't we best get stuck in?'

With the three women working along the rows at roughly the same speed, they found they were able to keep up the bones of a conversation.

'What time did you say… that chap's coming with the lorry to collect the crates?'

'Around six. Him and his lad. We got to remember… to count how many he takes.'

'Uh-huh.'

'I'm jolly glad it's not cold.'

'Or wet.'

'Me too.'

And after a while, their thoughts turned to refreshments.

'I'm gasping. Shall we take a break in a bit?'

'Course. Let's just get to the end of another row first.'

'Slave driver.'

Eventually, they stretched themselves upright and perched for a rest on some of the upturned crates.

'Tea all right?' May enquired of her sister.

'As Mum would have said, *it's hot and it's wet.*'

'Tell me, what's it like in town now?'

Clemmie shrugged. 'Not so very different really. The main streets have been cleared of rubble, and so some of the buses are back and running on their old routes again. But to be honest, I don't go in all that often and so I don't really know. The WVS centres have all been moved further out, and we're not supposed to travel unless we have to. *Is your journey really necessary?* and all that.'

'Mm.'

'But when I do go in,' Clemmie picked up again as they wandered back towards the beetroot, 'it still seems strange, even now, not to be living there any more – not to be in the thick of all that bustle and commotion… not to be among all those people we knew like family.'

'Strange for all of us,' May remarked. 'Maybe more so for you, though, what with you still being close by.'

'I heard the other day that Mrs Tuckett ended up going to her son's down near Topsham. She didn't want to – kicked up a right fuss, apparently – and her son and his wife didn't want to have her. But there was nowhere else for her to go.'

'Suppose not.'

'You know, sometimes, in my mind I still see pictures of what happened that night. They come without least warning. I dream about it now and again, too.'

'So do I,' May said.

'Wake up in a real panic sometimes. But then I suppose it would be odd if we didn't – dream about it, I mean. All that noise. All that trembling with fear.'

'I shouldn't think we're ever likely to forget it.'

Each withdrawing into their private recollections of that night, the women worked on, stopping a while later for a stretch and another drink. Around midday, they paused again to eat chunks of bread with cheese and pickles, helped down with barley water brought for them by Lorna Beer. Later still, when the sun began sliding down the westerly sky, they stopped again, this time for longer, devouring pieces of Lorna's carrot cake and draining the second Thermos of tea.

'You know what?' Clemmie said once they were back at work. Reaching the end of her row, she eased herself upright and stood, hands on hips, to roll her head in circles. 'I'm enjoying this. And yes, I know,' she went on when the other two looked at her askance, 'I'm sure I *am* only saying that because it's something of a novelty. I'm also sure that tomorrow morning, I won't be able to move an inch. Even so, it's good to be here. It's fun.'

'Relieved to hear you say so,' May replied with a grin as she, too, straightened herself up, 'because out here, you got to earn your keep.' When Clemmie laughed, May smiled. Her sister's habit of giggling like a schoolgirl was one of the things about her that hadn't changed.

'Fair enough. Oh, say, look, some feller's coming across that field. Is he coming here?'

Looking to where Clemmie was indicating, May saw Dan tramping across the pasture.

'It's Dan,' Bonnie replied. 'I'll go an' see what he wants.'

Unsure where she stood with Dan these days, May nodded. 'All right. Then if we're to get finished on time, we need one last push.'

All the while Bonnie was stood at the fence talking to Dan, May kept finding herself glancing across. When she heard Bonnie laugh, in her chest she felt a stab of what felt a lot like betrayal. How were those two getting along so easily, when she couldn't even remember the last time Dan had done so much as pass the time of day with *her*?

'He wonders if he can have a word with you,' Bonnie eventually returned to say.

With a begrudging grunt, May stood up and went towards him. He left it, she noticed, until she was almost at the fence before he spoke.

'Afternoon.'

'My sister,' she said, gesturing over her shoulder. 'Clemmie. Come to stay for a few days.'

Dan nodded. 'Handy.'

'Yes.'

'How are you getting on?'

To what, she wondered, was he referring: to the beet harvest or to things more generally? It was so long since they'd spoken that she had no idea.

'Need to be done by six,' she said, deciding he had no reason to enquire about anything other than the beets.

'Better not detain you then.'

Clearly, May reasoned, he hadn't come all the way across here just to exchange pleasantries. Unless, of course, it wasn't her he'd come to see at all; unless he'd only ever been coming to see Bonnie and this, now, was an afterthought. A politeness.

'It's all right,' she said. 'We've just been having a sit-down. Daft, really, since none of us wanted to get back up again.'

'Aye. A sit-down will do that to you.'

Frustrated by his hesitancy, she said, 'Any news about the farm?'

'Some.'

There was news about Fair Maids – news he had to know she would be dying to hear – and yet the first person he'd told was Bonnie? What was going on here? What didn't she know?

'Anything you can tell me?' This was harder than pulling teeth.

'Not just yet.' Finally, some of the conviction was back in his voice. 'It's not fully settled, and I've been warned not to jump the gun. But I *can* tell you about the inquest.'

*The inquest.* Heavens, yes, she'd completely forgotten about that. 'Right.'

'The coroner ruled George's death accidental.'

'I see.' *Accidental.* Presumably that meant there need be no further poking about in the poor man's business, nor any besmirching of his character. It was a proper shame Nessa and her chap had got away with their part in it but, since what was done was done, this outcome was probably for the best.

'The coroner did say that obviously, there's still a good many unanswered questions, you know, about what George was doing setting light to a tree in the first place – whether he'd been sober, or even in his right mind.'

Yes, quite what had come over him that night, they would never know. 'Well, thanks for telling me,' she said. 'Must be a relief having that over and done with.'

'It is. Look, May... I came over to talk to you. But I should have seen how you'd want to get finished. So, I'll come back another time.'

'If there's news,' she said shortly, 'I'd rather know now.'

Staring back at him, she wondered what on earth could have happened to make him so uncertain. Where was the plain-spoken Dan she had come to know? Why did he seem so shifty, so uneasy around her?

'I do want to tell you. But it's a long story...'

In her experience, when somebody billed something as a long story, it was usually to excuse what they were about to tell you; to absolve themselves of the fact that you weren't going to like what they had to say – that, in some way, they were going to let you down. 'And you don't want to detain me. Yes, you said.'

'Right. Well, then, I'll let you get on. We'll speak another time. Don't go overdoing it.'

Now not only was she puzzled but she was also unsettled. Turning away from the fence, she glanced to Bonnie. But with the girl doubled over her row of beet-root, she couldn't even see her expression, let alone read anything from it. Would it be fantastical of her to think there was something going on between those two?

'*He* looks nice.'

Looking up to see Clemmie gesturing towards the fence, May nodded absently. 'He is nice.'

'So, what did he want?'

'I have no idea.' *Could* he be seeing Bonnie? While she herself had been distracted with the business of Nessa and the aftermath of the fire, could the two of them have been spending time together? Or was she adding two and two to make five? If she was, then what else could have happened to change Dan so profoundly? Seemingly overnight, he had gone from straight-talking and jolly to preoccupied and withdrawn. Obviously, there was George's death, the very manner of which had shocked them all so deeply. But there had to be more to it than just that. Perhaps, being privy to information about the fate of the farm – knowing how it was going to affect her but being unable to say anything – was the cause of his unease.

Looking up and realising that while she had been lost to her thoughts, Bonnie and Clemmie had continued tossing beets into crates, she picked her way across to where she had left off. Well, when – *if* – Dan came to talk to her as he'd said, she supposed everything would become clear. But if, as she now suspected, the news wasn't going to be to her liking, then before Clemmie left, she could do worse than sound her out; explain what was going through her mind and see what she thought of it. After all, if there was no longer going to be a position for her at Fair Maids, returning to Exeter and hoping for the best was beginning to seem more and more like her only choice.

–

'Heavens above. I ache even just sitting here.'

Catching sight of her sister wincing as she shifted her weight, May grinned. 'It's my fault. It was mean of me to put you to work like you were from the land club.'

The gesture Clemmie made was a dismissive one. 'Don't be daft. It was fun.'

For both girls, their two days together had passed far too quickly, which was why, last night, sat in the parlour with the light fading around them, they had spoken plainly to each other about their respective concerns, Clemmie sharing her unease about dubious goings-on she had uncovered at her place of work, May urging her sister not to turn a blind eye, wartime or not. Her advice appeared to coincide with Clemmie's own thoughts on the matter, so she had expected her sister to seem more relieved. That she'd instead seemed fidgety and ill at ease had left her wondering whether her sister had something else on her mind – something she felt less able to confess. She *had* mentioned in passing about a friend 'having to get married', but Clemmie wouldn't get herself into that sort of fix. What else might be bothering her? She had no idea. Either way, since her sister didn't seem to be in any sort of danger, she had resolved not to press her.

When it came to disclosing her own problems, May had previously determined to make no mention of Dan but to confine herself to the more practical matters of her home and her work. Admitting to Clemmie about Dan would only muddy the waters and distract from the problem bothering her most. 'It's the only thing I can see to do,' she had said of her situation. 'If there's no place for me here, I don't see as I have any choice but to go back to Exeter.' And this morning she saw things no differently. Any day now, Dan would arrive with word of Fair Maids' new owners. When he did, she wanted to be braced and ready for disappointment. Looking across now to where Clemmie was reclining against the trunk of an ash tree, she did her best to raise a smile. 'Don't get too comfortable there,' she warned. 'No good you claiming in a minute that you're too stiff to walk back for the bus.'

By way of response, Clemmie sighed. 'I was just thinking about what you said last night, and what a shame it would be if you did have to leave. It's so peaceful here. The air is so lovely and clean. Mind you,' she went on, hauling herself more upright, 'it's a lot cleaner in Exeter recent times, too, what with so many factories being bombed out.'

'It is nice here,' May agreed. In fact, the fresh air and the quiet was one of the things she would miss most. And who would have thought *that* when she'd first got here? Not her, that was for sure.

It went without saying that the other thing she was going to miss was Dan – although Dan as he had been until recently, not Dan as he was now. With the power of hindsight – and yes, she knew hindsight showed no mercy – it was apparent that she'd been a bit quick to shoot herself in the foot. It wouldn't have needed much: she could have held his look a moment longer than was normal; let her hand come to rest on his arm; ask him to teach her about trees or birds... or about anything, really. Show some interest, pay him some attention. But she hadn't. Instead, she'd done the opposite: she'd kept her distance; deliberately prevented herself from falling for him. So consumed had she been by memories of Charlie Warren, and the endless instances of cruelty to which he'd subjected her poor mother, that she'd thrown one too many obstacles into Dan's path so that, by the time it had become obvious he was nothing like Charlie Warren, she'd made it emphatically clear that she wanted nothing to do with either husbands or marriage.

Well, it was too late to do anything about that now. All she could do was wish him well and hope that he and Bonnie would be very happy together.

'In fact, it's *so* nice here that I think you need to be careful of making a mistake.'

Having completely forgotten Clemmie was still there, May looked across at her and frowned. 'I'm sorry. What?'

355

'I *said*, I think you need to be careful of making a mistake – of deciding in haste and doing the wrong thing.'

'I don't doubt it. But I don't see as I have a choice.'

'And eventually that might turn out be true,' Clemmie replied levelly. 'But for all you know, the new owner might want you to stay on. You might not have to leave at all. If you come back to Exeter without even waiting around to find out, you'll never know, will you? You might give all this up only to find out later on that you needn't have.'

She supposed her sister had a point. 'Perhaps.'

'All I'm saying,' Clemmie continued, 'is why not wait just a little bit longer before you make up your mind? If it turns out they *don't* want you, then by all means come back. As I promised you last night, I'll do all I can to help you get settled. But at least by waiting, if returning to Exeter does become your only choice you won't be left looking back and wondering whether you were too hasty.'

'Mm.' Her sister always had been one for letting things take their course; for waiting and seeing what happened. In contrast she, May, preferred to act quickly to lance the boil; to take matters into her own hands and move forward, least said, soonest mended.

More warily, Clemmie continued. 'I shan't ever tell you what to do—'

'I know that.'

'But maybe think on it.'

'I will.'

'I mean, what's another week or two?'

Another week or two, May thought, merely prolonged the agony: was more time for uncertainty to set in; more time for regret to fester and ferment; more time spent ruing missing her chance with Dan. Not that there was any way of knowing whether it would have come to anything had she not; they *might* have turned out to be as different as chalk and cheese, the two of them constantly rubbing each other up the wrong way. Not that it mattered now. With Dan appearing to have taken up with Bonnie, it was something she would never know.

Beneath the weight of her regret generally, she heaved a sigh. At least she hadn't made a fool of herself. Nor had she had her heart broken – had it filled with regret, possibly, but at least it was still intact. And going forward from here, that's how she would endeavour to keep it.

Even later that afternoon, though, while she was waiting with Clemmie at the bus stop in Pippinswell, her decision to wait and see didn't sit comfortably; the greater part of her was more convinced than ever that catching the bus back to the city would have been the better course. Still, she reminded herself, at least this way she wouldn't be letting anyone down. Bonnie wouldn't be on her own. Not that Mrs Beer would have let that happen; no, Bonnie would be welcomed into the Higher Cleave fold with warm and open arms.

'You know, Clemmie,' she began, making a point of meeting her sister's look, 'Mum would be real proud of the way you've turned out.'

Tears welling, Clemmie reached to give her sister a hug. 'Do you mean that?'

'I do.'

'*I* think she'd be proud of *you*. Unable to believe her eyes, happen, but jolly proud all the same.'

'Mm. Well, anyway, look, here comes your bus.'

Having bent to pick up her bags, Clemmie grinned. 'Thanks for the apples. And the beetroot!'

'When you eat it, you'll be able to picture pulling it out of the dirt.'

'I will. Though if there was a way to keep one as a trophy, I'd do that too.' With the bus pulling up alongside them, Clemmie hurried to add, 'Promise me you'll write soon. The moment there's news I want to know.'

'You make sure an' write too,' May replied. Kissing Clemmie's cheek, she attempted a smile. 'And just be careful.'

'I will. You, too.'

The sight of the bus pulling away left May in tears. And on the long walk home, it became apparent that saying goodbye to her sister wasn't the only reason for them. It did make sense to stay and see out these next couple of weeks, she knew that. So, why did she still wish she'd gone with her first thought and just left? Save for the quietness and the fresh air her sister had found so welcome, she had no reason to remain out here, in the middle of nowhere, keeping an old house that no one lived in while trying to do farm work for which she was completely unskilled. In fact, put like that, the evidence was plain: she should pack her belongings and be on the next bus. However, since she couldn't abide people who let others down, nor who felt sorry for themselves and wallowed in pity for their plight, she would go back to Fair Maids and get on with whatever there was to do. When news about the farm finally came, she would take it on the chin. It was what she did. She knew no other way.

Back in the kitchen at Fair Maids, though, she was dismayed to find herself unable to settle. Were it not for the need to cobble together a supper for her and Bonnie, she might even be tempted to go to bed, so miserable was her mood.

Rousing herself nonetheless, she went to the pantry and stared at the shelves. What could she bother to make?

She didn't really fancy anything – certainly nothing that was within her power to cook.

Turning back into the kitchen, she paused to listen. The voices in the yard belonged to Bonnie and Dan: it was impossible to mistake either of those two when they laughed. Despite a deep-seated dislike of eavesdroppers, she strained to hear: Dan's voice was a low mumble, Bonnie's reply indistinct. Moving a fraction, she peered through the doorway. On Bonnie's sleeve was Dan's hand, on her lips a smile. And on her cheeks was a pink flush. *You're just jealous*, May chided herself. *Your face right this moment is probably as green as Higher Cleave's hillside.*

Forcing herself away from the door, she went to the pantry, reached to the shelf for the jug of dripping and carried it through to the kitchen. Behind her, she heard Bonnie kicking off her boots.

'May? You back?'

'In here.'

'Bother. Hang on.'

'What's the matter?' she called to where the girl sounded to be putting her boots back on again.

'Dan… came to see you. But since I hadn't… heard you… return… I told him you weren't in.'

Feeling the dagger of jealousy at work again, May exhaled in despair. 'I doubt it's important.'

'Happen not. But I'd best go after him anyway.'

Hearing Bonnie canter away over the cobbles, May gave another sigh. This was it, then. Dan was coming to break the news. Fair Maids had been sold and Bonnie would be going to live at Higher Cleave. *That's lovely*, she fixed a smile and imagined saying out loud. *Good for you. I'm so pleased.* At least it meant that tonight, she could pack her bag. And tomorrow morning she could walk into the village and get on the bus. It had been nice here while it lasted, but it was plain now that she had been – what was it she'd once heard the headmaster say of a girl who'd been had up for stealing? – that she had been the architect of her own downfall. Yes. When it came to her own situation, it was the perfect description. All that was left for her to do now was reflect upon where she had gone wrong, learn from her mistake and, with Clemmie's help, search for somewhere new to make yet another fresh start. Oh, and try not to let Dan see how upset she was when he explained to her about him and Bonnie.

# Chapter 29

'I don't understand.' Stood in the doorway to the scullery, May frowned.

'Can't say as I blame you. I did sort of dive straight in…'

'You did.'

'…when, to be fair, there's a whole story you really ought to know.'

With a despairing shake of her head, May glanced to the sky. 'In which case, I suppose you'd better come in.'

In turn, Dan also glanced to the heavens. 'You don't mind? You're not busy?'

'I'm always busy,' she said. 'But for God's sake, it's starting to drizzle. Come on, we'll go through to the parlour.'

Pausing long enough to remove his boots, Dan followed her through. 'Were you making your supper?' he asked, looking about the kitchen.

'Only for want of something better to do.' In the parlour, she gestured to one of the armchairs. 'Why don't you sit down?'

'Thanks. I think I will.' Wiping a hand across the seat of his trousers, Dan lowered himself to perch on the edge of the cushion and then waited until May was seated in the adjacent chair.

'How about I start over?'

Largely to give her hands the chance to do something other than tremble, May smoothed her housecoat over her lap. Christ, she felt sick. She'd been dreading the moment there was news. 'Might not be a bad idea.'

'Yes. Well. As I said on the doorstep just now, Fair Maids has a new owner.'

In her chest, May felt her heart speeding up again. 'Yes.'

'But since he doesn't have a family, he'll want a house-keeper.'

'You said that, too.'

'I did.'

What hadn't been plain when he'd said it just now, though, was where all of this left *her*. Was she to be kept on or not? Did the news signal her salvation or the end? If there *was* to be an offer to stay, she must make sure not to jump at it. Grasping it solely because there was no ready alternative would be foolhardy; she must wait to learn the facts. All of them, this time.

To that end, she asked, 'So, what do you know of this new feller?'

'Plain-spoken chap. Simple needs.'

So far, so good. But then anyone who didn't know George all that well might have said the same of him. 'No family, you say?'

'Not as would be living with him, no.'

The problem with that, she realised, was that a man on his own would expect to live in the house, which would require *her* to move into the lean-to. Hardly an appealing prospect. But she was a housekeeper, so what did she expect? With Mr Beer's preference for the barn, she had been spoiled.

'Old, is he, this chap?'

'Young.'

*Young?* Nan Parker and her cronies would have a field day.

'I see.' Already, she felt less hopeful. Keeping house for a younger man would create any number of pitfalls. On the other hand, when she'd replied to Mr Beer's advertisement, she'd had no clue as to *his* age – hadn't even stopped to wonder. In fact, she'd known nothing of the set-up here at all. And yet she'd gone ahead anyway. Looked at like that, how was this any different?

'Do you know him?' she asked. 'What I mean is, can you vouch for his character?'

'Not… personally, no. But you could ask Mum. Or if it's the warts-and-all truth you're after, you could do worse than talk to Gran.'

Noticing he had started to grin, May frowned. 'I'd prefer it if you took this seriously,' she said, her tone short. 'As I am obliged to do.'

Dan's expression straightened. 'Yes. I know. Forgive me. But see, this is tricky… least, for me it is.'

Before her eyes, his manner had gone from schoolboyish to uncomfortable.

'Dan, please. I don't ask much. I know I'm only a domestic in an empty farmhouse, but this is my livelihood. So, if I'm to decide what to do, I need to hear these things from you straight.'

'Did you know,' he said, his demeanour changing yet again as he brought his hands to rest in his lap and looked straight at her, 'that George was once wed?'

Despite nodding, she hadn't known for certain. 'I always assumed as much.'

'Her name was Jenny. By all accounting, George was besotted with her.'

George besotted by anything other than cider was hard to imagine. 'Go on.'

'Scarcely twelve months after they were wed, they had a baby. I'm told it was a hard birthing and that within days…' Guessing what was coming, May's hand shot to her mouth. '…Jenny was gone.'

'Oh, dear Lord.' It explained so much: the locked room; the general melancholy of George's manner; the way he managed to be both protective of women and at the same time seem to loathe them. Unexpectedly, so much now made sense. But why had George never said anything? Steeling herself to hear the answer, she asked, 'What happened to the baby?'

'Since George could see no way to raise a child on his own, he begged John and Lorna to take him in.'

*Him?* 'And… did they?'

'May, I'm telling you this because that baby was me. George was my father and Jenny my mother. But I swear to you, first I heard of it was a couple of days after the fire. Mum and Dad – more properly now my Uncle John and Aunt Lorna – saw no choice but to tell me.'

That he was telling the truth about not knowing she didn't doubt. She also understood now why he'd been so withdrawn these last weeks; what a thing to learn – and in such dreadful circumstances, too. 'So…'

'In truth, it doesn't make that much difference. Not now, anyway. I never knew my mother, and George always kept his distance. So, in many respects, nothing's changed.'

Surprised to find her immediate thoughts with George rather than Dan, May wasn't sure what to say. 'I can't begin to imagine how hard it must have been for him,' she said, her voice little more than a whisper. 'Seeing you growing up and knowing…'

'First thing *I* thought, too,' Dan admitted. 'Course, I wish now it wasn't too late to talk to him — to let him know I understood why he did it.'

'That he was just doing the best for you.'

'He couldn't have cared for me. Not from a week old.'

'Course not. And your aunt and uncle — they never had children of their own?'

'None. Gran once let slip that Mum never seemed able to carry them all the way. Sometimes you get ewes like that.'

'That's so sad. It's *all* so sad.'

'Anyway, George never did get over Jenny. For certain he never so much as looked at another woman.'

While all of this explained so much, May had to wonder why Dan was telling *her*? And why specifically now? 'So… the farm…'

'In many ways, straightforward. John and Lorna agreed to raise me as long as George wrote a will, setting out that when the time came, Fair Maids was to pass to me.'

'Right…'

'So, in the space of a few weeks, not only have I gained new parents, but this place as well.'

'I don't know what to say. Truly, I don't.' Setting aside that he seemed to want her to stay on as housekeeper — albeit, presumably, until he got the place sorted out — there was just so much to take in.

'Believe it or not,' Dan picked up again, 'even before the fire, I'd been trying to work out how to come and talk to you about… well, anyway, the moment I found out George was my father, everything turned upside down. So much had changed and yet so much hadn't. I had to let it sink in. I had to be sure what I wanted to do.'

'I see that.' Now she understood why he'd been so quiet. Overnight, his world had changed beyond all recognition – had shaken his very idea of who he even was.

'But having to stand back and take stock helped me to get things clear in my head. You see, May, I want to make a go of this place. I want to live long enough to see Fair Maids and Higher Cleave joined back together like—' Seeing her frown, he changed tack. 'You do know, I suppose, that these two farms were originally one – Cleave Farm – orchards and sheep? And that when Grandad Beer died, it was split in two, half for each son?'

May nodded. Somewhere along the line, she recalled hearing as much. 'Yes.'

'Well, John's half was to be called Higher Cleave, and George's Lower Cleave. But from the off, George was furious, thought he'd got the lesser deal. So, in what Dad says now was a fit of spite, George refused his half the sheep, cut himself off from his brother, and changed the name of this place to Fair Maids, saying he wasn't going to have no property of his called *Lower* anything. Cocking a snook, I suppose he thought he was.'

'I see.' Clearly, the chip on George's shoulder had been there a long time.

'Anyway, since at some point in the future I shall also inherit the other half, it's my wish to one day see the whole lot back together as one farm – Cleave Farm – rearing sheep, grazing them through the orchards as well as up on the hillsides and down in the pastures. But I also want to understand apples and cider, and how to make a proper business of it. Cider might have been George's whole life, but he was still going about it the same way as his father and his grandfather – and no doubt the folk even before them. But come the end of this war, seems to me that after everything folk have been through, they won't want the old ways of carrying on. And unlike George, I want this place to keep up with the times. Fair Maid's cider is proper stuff, and I want it to be known and drunk beyond this little corner of Devon. Done right, I reckon there's real money to be made – a proper living.'

In Dan's eyes, May could see passion and fire. 'And that's where Bonnie comes in?' She could see now that it would be a sensible match; the girl was young enough to learn and robust enough to weather the knocks.

'Bonnie?'

'You want her to help you. Once the war's over.'

'What? *No.* Christ, May. Whatever gave you that idea?'

Feeling how fiercely she was suddenly blushing, May stared into her lap. 'I thought… well, I seen the two of you together. I seen you with your hand on her arm.'

'Good God, no, you daft woman.' To her alarm, he shot up from his chair and came to crouch in front of her. 'It's *you* I want to help me. Since that first time I clapped eyes on you, I've done nothing but admire your get-up-and-go… admire how you get stuck in. Half the time, you've not the least clue what's needed, but you never let that stop you. The word *defeat* don't seem to enter your head. You can't *know* the ribbing I've had off Mum and Gran for going on about you. Teased me no end, those two have.'

Her thoughts in turmoil, May fumbled for a response. 'But…'

'Look,' Dan said. 'I know this is sudden. I also know I've done exactly what Mum warned me not to. But please, tell me you'll stay on here and help me make this a place to be proud of.'

'I—'

'No need to answer me right this minute. I'm not so dumb as to think you'd agree, spur of the moment, to something as almighty as this. But please, at least promise me you'll think about it.'

'Well...' To May's mind, there was still something Dan hadn't explained. 'What, exactly, is it you want me to agree *to*?' No sense consenting to something without knowing precisely what it was, even if it did sound like the most incredible chance to do something that would bring her both purpose and reward.

'Well, since I happen to be crouched down here, I *could*, like the hot-headed fool that I am, do the expected thing.' Having thought she'd calmed down a little, May's heart started racing again. 'But, not so long back, you made quite plain you're not looking for a husband. So I see no point setting myself up for a disappointment on that score.'

Did she stop him right there? Did she tell him that was no longer strictly true? Or did she heed the corner of her brain urging her not to get lost in a fog of elation?

Aware of the need to tread carefully, she said, 'If you *were* daft enough to propose, my answer wouldn't be an out-and-out "no". I think it important I say that here an' now.'

Immediately, she could tell her admission had thrown him.

'All right. Well... that's good news.'

'But I won't do anything in haste. And nor should you. Shouldn't neither of us one day regret we didn't take a little more time to think this through.'

'See,' he said, waving a hand. 'That's what I mean. You're sensible.'

It wasn't the most flowery of compliments, but she would take it. 'Thank you.'

'So, if it's not a "no", then what are you suggesting?'

To May, he seemed to be regaining confidence. 'That we try it?' she said, her heart pounding so heavily she could barely utter the words. 'That you move in here… and we see how we get on – as a couple, I mean?'

The way his expression softened suggested he was both relieved and amused.

'May Huxford, you can't know how many times that very idea's gone through my own head – that we give it a go, on the quiet. But seeing as how you always seemed so proper – and rightly so, too – I hadn't the gall to suggest it.'

She chuckled. Proper? Her? Not any more, apparently.

'Not sure I can believe *I* just did,' she said, astounded by how this was turning out. 'But if we choose to say nothing of it to no one, then who is there to be any the wiser? Folk already know I keep house here. Beyond that, who's to say what goes on behind Fair Maids' broken-down fence… what happens beyond that faded old sign rotting on the gatepost—'

'All right, all right—'

'Let alone behind these four crumbling walls—'

'—for Christ's sake, woman, don't do the old place down *too* much. Her well-being's as much in your hands now as it is in mine.'

'Sorry.'

'So, we're in this together, then?' he asked.

'Together.'

When he stood up and extended a hand to help her to her feet, she rose smartly and gave it a firm shake. But as she did so, the fog of her shock lifted: marriage to this man would be nothing like her mother's to Charlie Warren. Dan Beer hadn't tried to sweet-talk her; he had been straightforward and honest about what he wanted. And for her part, she wasn't a widow with two small girls and no means to support them. No, this was about as different to her mother's situation as it was possible to imagine. And folk did say that your greatest regrets in life were the chances you didn't take…

Still grasping his hand, she looked straight at him. 'And on the other matter…'

'Other matter?'

'The one that if done proper requires a ring.'

At the corners of Dan's eyes, tiny creases betrayed his amusement. 'What of it?'

'Well… how about you an' I agree that, if I haven't already upped sticks, and you haven't already sent me packing, and if you still feel so inclined and think I do too, then when you spot the right moment, you seize the chance and ask me proper.'

'You mean that?'

'I do.'

'Then I'm going to hold you to that, May Huxford.'

'And I'm going to hold *you* to that, Dan Beer.'

## Chapter 30

For October, the weather was surprisingly benign. And with the mound of ripe apples outside the old barn rising ever higher, May felt a sense of pride. For the first time, she felt as though she'd been afforded a glimpse of why George had lived and breathed for these trees; the apple harvest had a feel to it that struck her as almost spiritual. In its own quiet way, she supposed the orchard had begun to exert the same sort of pull on her as it had on George, its circle of nurturing, growing and harvesting slowly reeling her in. Out here among the trees, she felt bound to the seasons, tethered to the earth, a servant of Mother Nature. The old lady was a real fickle mistress, though, forever testing their mettle with pests and blight, or challenging them with either flood or drought. Odd that the spirit of the earth should make their lives such a trial when all either of them wanted was a bountiful harvest!

Returning her eyes to the activity going on all around her, May gave a contented sigh. If George could see them all working so industriously, she suspected he would be impressed – even if it was grudgingly. He might even go so far as to concede that the half-dozen land club volunteers, whose labours she had been so fortunate to secure, had proved worth their weight in gold. The presence of Robbie and Neville she imagined he would comprehend rather less. But the pair of them had proved impossible to keep away; the moment they'd got wind that the harvest entailed knocking apples from trees, they had pleaded, begged and cajoled to be allowed to join in. For a while she'd refused, on the grounds that it would mean them playing truant from school. But their unrelenting eagerness had worn her down. As it turned out, she didn't regret giving in to them; sparing her not an ounce of their energy, they'd quickly commandeered a couple of the hooked poles used to shake the fruit from the branches and had gone at the task with the fervour only a small boy could keep up: *thwock, thwock-wock*, the apples had soon started falling to the soft turf.

To May's even greater delight, Clemmie had seized upon the invitation to pay another visit, the two women picking up this time round as though having scarcely been apart. And a little over an hour previously, the Beers from Higher Cleave had arrived, John carrying on his shoulder a flagon of cider for Primrose to spice and mull with pokers made red-hot in the fire, Lorna bringing potatoes that she pushed into the embers to bake. With so many helpers, and the end of their toils in sight, the atmosphere among the trees had all the gaiety of a celebration.

The smile on her lips not fading, May broadened her gaze: at the far end of the orchard, a coil of pale grey smoke was curling languidly up from the bonfire, filling the late-afternoon air with the sweet scent of applewood; through the branches drifted snatches of laughter, the warbled lament of a robin and, from further away, the low grumble of the tractor making its way back from the barn, its trailer relieved of yet another full load.

Her contemplations broken by the sound of someone approaching, she turned to see Dan coming through the trees.

'I still say that outfit suits you,' he remarked drily, as he drew alongside and gestured more generally. 'Makes you look like you were born to all this.'

The shake of her head to which she treated him was a despairing one. 'Anyone ever tell you you're daft?'

Earlier in the week, he had returned from the agricultural merchants with a parcel wrapped in brown paper, on his lips a broad grin. 'Here,' he'd said, handing her the string-tied package, 'don't say I never give you nothing.'

Opening it to find a pair of dungarees and an all-weather hat like the one Bonnie wore, she had burst into laughter. 'My mistake, clearly, but I was under the impression it's customary to give a sweetheart jewellery.'

Her remark ran like water off a duck's back. 'If the overalls are too big when you put 'em on, next time I go I'll fetch you a belt.'

Recalling now the look on his face as he'd said it, she broke into a fresh grin. Sometimes, she had to pinch herself. Sometimes, it was almost beyond her to believe that things had turned out so well. Who would have thought that barely five months on from losing her home and her livelihood, she'd be stood here, in farmer's overalls and wellington boots, drawing satisfaction from the sight of trailers being filled with ripe apples? Who would have thought she would even notice, let alone draw pleasure from, the way the low autumn sunshine was painting the orchard in a hazy golden glow, and casting long indigo shadows across the ankle-deep grass? More surprising still, who would have thought she'd be doing all of that alongside a man who not only apparently adored her, but who respected her opinions and treated her as an equal? Not her, that was for sure.

Spotting Clemmie bent low among the trees, May allowed herself a sigh. More than once lately, her sister had remarked that Mum would be proud of her. And she liked to think it was true. She liked to think her mother would look beyond the fact that, by most people's reckoning, her eldest daughter was living in sin, and see instead that she was happy, maybe even applaud her for having the courage of her convictions – for not wanting to be rushed, for wanting to make sure. In that same vein, she hoped her mother would also have understood the path Clemmie was about to take, and be glad she hadn't hurtled into *that* headlong, either, carefully weighing instead the consequences of taking such a momentous step. That her sister's path would be rich with all manner of opportunities, she had no doubt. That it was unlikely to be plain sailing was also painfully clear. Still, it could only be a sign of Clemmie's maturity that she saw the pitfalls and was going in with her eyes open. Given how firmly her sister's heart seemed set, what more could she ask?

The thought of her mother unexpectedly triggering tears, she hastened to blink them away. 'Look at those two,' she remarked by way of distraction. Motioning with her head, she indicated where Clemmie and Bonnie were struggling with a wooden pail, their cheeks as flushed as the apples they were trying to tip into the trailer. 'Getting on like…' The expression *a house on fire* wholly inappropriate, she checked herself. '…like they've been doing this all their lives.'

'Fair maids of Devon gathering Fair Maids of Devon.'

She turned to him askance. 'You been at the cider? Only, for a fellow who don't never use two words where one will do, that's awful flowery.'

Her look of mirth met with one of surprise.

'You don't know?'

'Don't know what?'

'The apples.' Bending down, Dan plucked a lone faller from the grass and rolled it around on his palm. 'This here's a variety called Fair Maid of Devon.'

She flicked a glance to the nearest tree. Was he having her on? She wouldn't put it past him. 'Truthfully?'

'God's honest. It's after these apples George named the farm. If you don't believe me, ask Dad.'

That she'd never known this struck her as astonishing; other than thinking the name pretty, she'd never given it a moment's thought.

'Then come the day you join the two farms back together, you should keep it – the name, I mean. In fact, you'd be daft not to.'

With a glint of mischief in his eyes, Dan slid an arm about her waist. 'Reckon I'd be daft, do you?'

'Well, think about it,' she went on. 'Fair Maids Cider. What better name to stick in folks' minds? Besides, since you're the one always going on about moving with the times, why go back to a name from the past? Why hark back when right under your nose is something that suits so well?'

Tightening his grip about her waist, Dan grinned. 'Just yesterday I said to Mum that without your common-sense way of seeing things, I reckon I'd have been sunk here before I'd even got going. Fair Maids Cider. It's perfect.'

'Course it is. And while we're on the matter of moving forward, I've been thinking… if you're serious about this cider business, then shouldn't the orchard have a new king tree?'

'You're right. Let's go and choose one.'

'What, just like that?'

'No time like the present.'

He had a point. As *she* was forever telling *him*, *why put off until tomorrow* and all that.

'Fair enough. But how will you know which one to pick? How did George know to choose the one *he* did?'

Dan shrugged. 'I haven't the foggiest idea. But we could do worse than pick one that's tall and sturdy, with branches that look as though they've just borne us a good weight of fruit.'

While it was hard to argue with his reasoning, she'd been hoping to learn of a more mystical means of going about it – to be told of some centuries-old and jealously guarded method of divining the spirit – a way steeped in folklore and handed down with great pride to the next generation. But never mind; at least his way was practical. 'All right. Though I still don't see how you're going to narrow it down to just the one.'

'I doubt *I* will,' he said plainly. 'That's where I'm banking on *you*. Come on.'

When he caught hold of her hand and started into the heart of the orchard, she couldn't help but feel his faith in her was misplaced. While it might be true that Fair Maids Farm had got under her skin, she lacked his eye for these things; to her, each tree simply looked identical to the next.

After a while spent strolling between them, though, she slowed, came to a halt and reached to touch the nearest trunk. When her fingertips connected with the bark she felt a jolt, and through her mind flashed an image of flames leaping high into a pitch-black sky. 'Here,' she whispered, unsettled by the vividness of it. 'This is it. This is the one.'

Beside her, Dan ran a rather more critical eye up through the tree's crown. 'This one.'

She nodded. 'Call me fanciful, but I've a feeling that on the night of the fire, this is where the spirit of the old king tree came to take shelter.'

'See,' he said lightly. 'I told you you'd know it. This one it is, then.'

With the sounds from the harvest muffled by the mantle of russet and gold leaves, and her head filled with the syrupy scent of fermenting apples, May was suddenly certain about something else, too.

'Dan…'

From where he was appraising her chosen tree, he turned to regard her. 'Aye?'

'You remember some time back me saying… to ask me again one day?'

The frown that flickered across his face turned to a look of recognition. 'I might recall some hare-brained bargain along those lines…'

'Then ask me. Ask me now.'

'You're sure…'

She smiled warmly. 'I'm sure. See, when I stop to think about all the plans you've got for this place, I'm minded we're going to need a son.'

'*A son…?*'

His astonishment made her laugh. 'Or a daughter.'

'All right, then.' Reaching for her hand and clearing his throat, Dan dropped to one knee. 'May Huxford, impoverished farmer and hopeless dreamer that I am, if I promise to cherish you warmly, share with you all that I have, and love you through thick and through thin, will you please marry me?'

Making no effort to hide her tears, May lowered herself to the damp grass. 'Dan Beer, you've given me purpose and hope, shown me love and respect. And I can't think of anything that would make me happier.'

Moments later, her hand grasped tightly in his, and breathless from running to tell everyone their news, May found herself reflecting yet again upon the surprising way her life had turned out. When those German bombs had destroyed Albert Terrace, she had felt angry and lost, her future in ruins. But, apparently, just as her mother always claimed, when one door closed, another one really did open – you just had to watch for it to do so and then grasp the courage to march smartly through it and see where it led…

# Acknowledgements

With grateful thanks to Kiran Kataria for her ongoing support, and to Emily Bedford for her continued guidance and all round enthusiasm for my writing.